JUSTICE
IS SERVED

JUSTICE
IS SERVED

VERL D. WHEELER

To order additional copies of this book, contact:
Xlibris Corporation
1-888-795-4274
www.Xlibris.com
Orders@Xlibris.com
44982

This is dedicated to my mother, Alta Lila Wheeler,
who passed away just before the effort was completed.

ACKNOWLEDGMENTS

There are so many people to thank for their assistance in completing my first novel: close friends who for three years endured hearing about its progress; my lifelong friend, United States Magistrate Judge Kelley for his assistance in the legal portions [name withheld on purpose]; my lovely niece Angie Chandler, who did major detail editing along with substance suggestions; my bud Ed, who served in Vietnam and subliminally educated me on Vietnam. My soul mate Deanna, who endured hours and days of my frustration; my supercomputer whiz Scott Baker; Jamie and Renie, my two office assistants; and especially the manuscript coach, David Bischoff, for his supreme assistance in plot development and editing.

The sword of justice has no scabbard.
　　　　　　　　　　　—Antione DeRiveral

PROLOGUE

"Get ready, they're coming across the field now. Goddamn it, Dennis, do like I told you, both of you, put the damn ski masks on," said the shorter of the two men to his other two accomplices as he returned from the edge of the greenbelt where he was keeping watch for Justin and Robbie. "It looks like they have a goddamn mutt with them. You never said anything about a friggin' dog." He directed this comment at Lois, the female accomplice. She responded, "The old broad never said anything about the dog, just her two grandsons, the tree house and the money." Fred whispered, "It's too goddamn late to worry about it now, just watch out for the friggin' mutt. Lois, you grab the little one and hold him while Dennis and I grab the big one. Make sure you get your hand over his mouth so he can't yell."

Justin and Robbie didn't have a chance. Just as they approached the base of the tree house, the trio sprung on them. "I got the big one!" Dennis said in a loud voice. "Run, Justin, run!" yelled Robbie as he kicked and struggled with Dennis just before a big clammy hand clamped over his mouth and a blindfold was put over his eyes. Then Fred yelled at Dennis, "Look out, the fucking dogs after me. Get him, Dennis. He's got my goddamn foot. GET HIM!" Dennis let go of Robbie with one hand and smacked the dog on the head with a sap he had in his pocket, just as Fred slashed at him with a knife. The kid's dog, Bailey, dropped like a sack of spuds.

"I got him," Dennis said. "Goddamn it, where's my friggin' shoe? What the hell . . . ah shit . . . forget it we gotta get going. Let's get these brats tied up real good and in the motor home. Good job, Lois," Fred said as Lois was covering Justin's eyes and he and Dennis were doing the same to Robbie. "We need to get our ass moving and fast. Dennis, take that note I tied to the rock and put it on the front steps over at the house. And keep those latex gloves on so you won't leave any fingerprints. Be careful and don't let anybody see you. Now, get going so we can hit the road with these brats." Within thirty minutes, they were on their way—Dennis in the pickup, Fred and Lois in the motor home. Fred said to

Lois just as he turned on Highway 405 headed north toward Everett. "Not bad except for that fucking mutt. He almost took my foot off, and I never did find my shoe. Dennis must have killed him when he whacked him with that sap." In the back bedroom of the motor home, darkness settled on Justin and Robbie. All consuming darkness and fear permeated their little bodies.

CHAPTER 1

This is the story of life, death, and rain.
This is a story of a kidnapping.
This is the story of a trial.
This is the story of grandchildren, Jim's precious grandchildren.
Me?
Call me Narrator.

#

"Dad! Dad," exclaimed Jim's son on that that terrible day. "Dad! Oh my god." His voice broke. "They're gone!"

"What? Who's gone?"

"The kids! Dad . . ." The silence of a midnight fog on Puget Sound claimed the phone line.

"Mark," Jim said calmly as possible into the receiver. "Mark, I'm here."

Mark said, "There's a note. They want money."

#

Call my city "Seattle."

My name is Arnott.

Bob Arnott—byline Robert Arnott.

I cover the waterfront—hell, I've covered the whole damn city for my newspaper—the *Times*. So it was natural that I would cover a kidnapping story, all the way from the crime and through the trial—with all the punishment in between—and after. The fact that Jim was one of my two best friends was incidental. My other best friend is this city.

Seattle.

Seattle, Washington.

Before this sordid and sad tale of life and death, let me talk a little bit about rain.

#

It was late November when the trial began, the start of the rainy season in Seattle.

The time of year that brings out the London Fog raincoats and umbrellas bloom like mushrooms.

Yes, it rains in Seattle, and in November, it really rains. Combine that with the winds, big winds, and you have gloom and depression. Not a fun month, unless you're a Cougar or a Husky, depending on which team wins the Apple Cup, the annual rival college football game that gives half of the population bragging rights for twelve months. These are the two universities in our state in the Pacific Coast Conference, the Pac Ten as it is known on the street.

Pardon my digression, but football cheers me up too.

Washington State University, home of the Cougars, is located eastward in Pullman, a small agriculture town with a population of about fourteen thousand not counting the fifteen thousand full-time students attending school at WAZZU. It doesn't rain much in Pullman or Eastern Washington. It is cold and snowy in the winter, yes, but not much rain.

Seattle, though, gets lots of rain.

The University of Washington, UDub, home of the Huskies, is located in Seattle. The month of November, some Seattle people think, prepares you for December and January when it continuously drizzles, almost daily. And frequently, like I mentioned before, along with heavy rains the winds blows like a banshee.

Jim Malone, the protagonist of this tale I'm telling, had grown up in Bellevue, one of the many suburban towns surrounding Seattle. When Jim was in grade school, Bellevue's population was just slightly over twelve thousand, and there were only three streetlights in town. This was in the late '50s and early '60s. Little bitty Bellevue was just a town on the eastside of Lake Washington away from Seattle and its big city problems. There was very little crime other than helping a local overly inebriated Bellevuite get home safely and making sure everyone stopped at all of the three stoplights in town. There were no street gangs, no graffiti-adorned walls, few minorities, and more churches than bars or restaurants.

You need to know a little background about the entire Eastside, where Jim grew up.

Many of the areas wealthiest and most influential families—Boeing, Clapp/Weyerhaeuser, Freeman, John L. Scott, McCaw, Ballinger, Nordstrom, Bell and Valdez, Smith just to mention a few—lived in Medina or had summer homes there, right by Jim's Bellevue. In the '50s and even now, the difference between Bellevue and Medina was major and can be explained in one word *money*.

The greater portion of Medina is waterfront property located right on the shores of Lake Washington, looking west at the Seattle skyline. In the late '40s and '50s, many of these Seattle bluenose families only had summer homes in Medina. They were multiacre estate type settings with such amenities as tennis courts and swimming pools. Almost all had boat docks on Lake Washington where their families could swim, boat, water ski, and frolic in fresh, breezy summer fun. The rich still live there, but now it's their main residence; and many of the estates have been subdivided into smaller areas with large permanent houses, not summer homes.

Unlike his martini-sipping, water-skiing neighbors in Medina, Jim was solidly middle-class as were most Bellevue kids. He grew up in Bellevue, attended Bellevue schools—grade, junior high, and Bellevue High. His family was comfortable, but he didn't have a silver spoon poking out of his mouth; like Medina kids, he was a Bellevue brat.

That's what Seattle kids, who lived in the lesser affluent areas, frequently called all the Eastside kids because they thought everybody on the Eastside was rich.

Let me take a minor digression from life and death and rain. I'd like to talk about computers and a thing called Microsoft. Microsoft would be the final major driving force that would thrust the Eastside into the new century of high tech, causing unbelievable population increases and gigantic economic growth. Prior to that, Boeing's huge plant on the south end of Lake Washington in Renton had started the population migration from Seattle eastward. And, with population increasing so rapidly, it was accompanied by its partner—crime. It seems to always be a fact that the larger the city, the more criminals you have. It's probably logical.

Jim grew up in Bellevue way before Microsoft.

Way before Bill Gates built his eighty-million-dollar house in Medina. But those with the capacity to plan for the future knew all the seeds had been sown on the Eastside, and it was just a matter of time before they bloomed. Fortunately for the entire Seattle area, the Gates family had a seed named Bill. The Gates' family probably had a summer place on the Eastside where son Bill spent many fun days. Nostalgia and loyalty may be two of the primary reasons, Gates chose to build Microsoft's main office complex on the Eastside. Not in Bellevue, but in adjacent Redmond. His partner, Paul Allen, was also from the state of Washington and was well aware of the Eastside area and probably agreed that's where they should locate Microsoft after their high-tech nerd time in New Mexico and California.

Gates and Allen combined their high-tech talents and formed Microsoft and changed the face of Jim Malone's hometown.

The entire Eastside is comprised of Bellevue, Kirkland, Redmond, Issaquah, Woodinville, Mercer Island, even as far out as Monroe, Snohomish, Carnation, Duval and North Bend. All small towns and are located east of Lake Washington near the Cascade Mountains. These towns were destined to become cities, not only because of Microsoft, but also due to eastern migration to the Northwest and the demand for affordable housing expansion away from the congestion of downtown Seattle. The affordable part would change in time.

The skyline of Bellevue was to become almost as large as Portland's, thanks to a man with far-reaching vision, Kemper Freeman. Freeman built a premiere shopping center known as the Bellevue Square. At the time it was built, Bellevue and the entire Eastside population did not warrant having a shopping center of the magnitude of the Bellevue Square. But Kemper Freeman convinced major Seattle retailers, such as Fredrick and Nelson and Nordstrom's along with many established old merchandisers like Sears and J.C. Penney's that the future was on the Eastside of Lake Washington. Time would prove his visions were correct. Then later and even more awesome, Kemper Freeman Jr., who had even greater aspirations than his legendary father, constructed skyscrapers, hotels, and luxury condos, not to mention quadrupling the size of the Bellevue Square shopping center. And by adding retailers, such as Armani, Victoria Secret, Tiffany's, Macy's and many more nationally known retailers, not to mention 90 percent of the parking was covered out of the rain, and an abundance of new theme restaurants were located everywhere in the square. Northwest shopping centers in the future would emulate the Bellevue Square.

The Eastside was destined to become one of the most affluent areas, west of the Cascades. Property values in these areas would explode beyond anyone's imaginings.

Jim Malone would become part of all this growth.

He didn't have a clue when he was in high school this would be his destiny. He was just a Bellevue brat, and his father was a carpenter. All he'd planned to do after high school was to go to Washington State University, become a true Cougar, and study architecture.

This was not to be.

Later, however, his son, Mark would go to WAZZU and become an architect. The war was just beginning in Vietnam, and it would change Jim's life and his parents' lives forever. It did the same thing to thousands of other families and especially to the young men and women of the '60s.

Everything changed.

But still, in Seattle, there was life and death and rain.

#

"Dad . . . Dad . . . the kids . . . they've got my kids!"

\#

The look on Big Jim Malone's face, as he sat there in the courtroom in front of twelve of his peers, was totally void of any emotion. No anger, repugnance and certainly no happiness, just void.

A wooden chair scraped. There was the smell of floor wax and the lingering odor of starch they put in judges' robes. Outside was rainy and cold, but inside it felt close and hot. The bitter taste of Starbucks coffee lingered in my mouth.

I was concentrating on Jim's face, attempting to ascertain what he had to be feeling.

Hatred?

No, it wasn't hate. As long as I have known him, he was never capable of hating anyone or anything.

Anger?

That's entirely different. But even if you were a close friend you would never detect this emotion. I always thought maybe his experiences in Vietnam, even though he had never talked about them to me in any great detail, contributed to how he chose to deal with situations, emotions, and people.

Yet there was something lingering below the surface of his face as he sat in the courtroom, even I, as well as I knew him, no matter how hard I concentrated and knowing more about kidnapping and its consequences, found it impossible to detect any obvious emotion.

However, I knew he had to feel something. I thought that once more it had to be some form of anger. Then, looking at his face as he sat there next to his defense attorney, I again questioned this thought.

No! If he had been angry, it might show, and there was no detectable sign of such an emotion.

Satisfaction?

Absolutely not, I knew him well enough to know it just wouldn't be natural for him to enjoy any part of what he's accused of committing.

But there definitely was a look on his face I had never seen before, and I've known Jim Malone for over three decades.

I wondered as I sat in the court, reporter's pad in lap, number 2 pencil gripped in my left paw. "What could be going through his mind?"

Maybe that's why we have trials. Not only to seek the truth as to guilt or innocence of people accused of committing crimes, but also to let society find out the "why" of the crime.

Might there even be legal justification that would excuse a person from prosecution and punishment?

Hopefully, I thought this trial would assist us all in finding out why two people are dead, why two young boys are psychologically damaged, and why society is now calling upon twelve citizens to facilitate the death of another.

#

I told you my name is Bob Arnott.

I told you I was a reporter.

I didn't tell you that I'm currently a national freelance columnist in semiretirement.

For over thirty years, I was an investigative reporter for Seattle's main newspaper the *Times*.

I covered many criminal trials.

However, this is the first time I ever had to cover a story involving a friend as close as Jim Malone.

And, to add to the drama, this is one of those trials that will captivate the entire country.

CNN, Fox News, CNBC, all three networks; *USA Today*, Associated Press, all the major newspapers in Washington, Oregon, and most majors from around the country, they're all here. The media knows what the public desires—decadence and smut—and they'll deliver it to them. The public wants to hear the real story, all the gory details. It has become obvious to the media that the masses in our country thrive on other people's miseries. The news people will give them all they want and then some, embellishing every sordid detail. It'll give the public relief from news about our president or Congress or another asinine sports figure screw up.

The media will relate how this man, Jim Malone, not only rescued his grandchildren, but how he also caught and allegedly eliminated those responsible for such a heinous crime.

The general public is mesmerized by trials such as this. TV viewers have become almost voyeuristic as they watch a court system go through the legal process of prosecuting people like Jim Malone.

In this case, news polls have even shown many of them think they would also have done the same thing if placed in an identical situation. They seem to empathize totally with his dilemma. More specifically, the general opinion is, the kidnappers got what was coming to them. At least that's what the majority of our citizens were saying everywhere the topic was brought up for discussion. And believe me, it was being discussed everywhere people congregated and especially in the Seattle area. National and local polls even indicated the public, by over 80 percent, felt Jim should be exonerated.

And I, too, am obligated, as a reporter, to give them exactly what they crave. As I said, they thrive on trials such as this one. Better than any soap opera Hollywood and television networks could fabricate. The news will feature information and details about the participants. It will dig to the bottom for anything personal about the defendant, victims, witnesses, information the jury will not have the opportunity to see or hear during the trial. Things people feel should somehow be factored into the jury's decision of guilt or innocence. The news reporters will feed the public daily with exaggerated details about trial participants and their personal involvement with either Jim or the victims. As I said, most of the information contained in these so-called news stories cannot be presented in court by either the prosecution or the defense; and in actuality, the news will be much more colorful than the trial itself. The public will read and hear how the kidnappers lived their lives prior to committing this heinous act of kidnapping and physically abusing two young boys. The news stories will be very graphic and many times embellished beyond reality. The stories will try to depict stories about Jim when he was involved in the Vietnam conflict, most of them huge fabrications. Good reading, but they'll describe things that didn't really happen. The news of today . . . makes something happen.

Let me reiterate, unfortunately, most of what is contained in these so-called news stories cannot be presented in court by either the prosecution or the defense.

Only the public gets to enjoy them.

Initially, it appeared without question, even to me, Jim Malone without doubt would be found guilty of killing the two men who kidnapped and physically damaged his grandchildren. Complicating my involvement, when Jim asked me whom I thought he should get for an attorney, I instantly recommended J. Edgar Ewing.

Over the years, when I was covering such sordid crimes and trials, I witnessed many attorneys in the state of Washington, who defended people being tried for crimes similar to what Jim is accused of committing.

Of these, in my judgment, J. Edgar Ewing was the absolute best defense attorney around. Very expensive, but when you want the best, it'll cost you; and besides, Jim Malone could afford the best.

Ewing's past records for achieving success were legendary. He was so adept in the courtroom law schools would require their students attend his trials.

However, J. Edgar was now seventy years old. For Jim's sake I prayed he was not over the hill. If he failed to succeed in defending Jim, I would forever regret my recommendation.

#

As I sat there in that grim, tense courtroom, I thought back to where this all really began for Jim Malone.

An important portion of the real story began with a letter to Jim's mother in April 1964 from the president of the United States.

I'll spare you the flowery bureaucratic bull crap. In essence it said, "I'm sorry to inform you that your husband, Matthew R. Malone died while serving his country in Vietnam."

I was not acquainted with Jim or his family at the time. Jim and I met on the Bellevue municipal golf course six or seven years later and developed a close friendship. This was just a couple years after he returned to Bellevue and had fully recovered from being seriously wounded when he was serving his country in Vietnam. It took months before he shared the story why he had ended up fighting in that stupid war.

When I met him, he and his wife Deanna had only been married for a few years. Jim's construction company was still in its embryonic stages. Like his father, he was more of a carpenter in the beginning; and due to the quality of his work and the demand for new houses, he developed a full-size construction company, whose specialty was building personal custom residences. His lovely wife, Deanna, was his nurse after the terrible firefight he encountered in Vietnam. Once he completely recovered from these wounds and received his honorable discharge, he convinced her to marry him and move back to Bellevue where he planned to start his construction company.

As our golf friendship blossomed, Jim relayed to me how his family's participation in the Nam conflict changed his life forever.

Jim was barely eighteen, soon to graduate from high school, when his mother received that fateful letter about his father. At the time, even with the Vietnam War going on, everything in Bellevue, seemed so, well . . . normal.

No, better than normal.

He'd already been accepted to attend college at Washington State University. He and his father were as close as a child and a parent can ever be. His father was a carpenter, and from the day Jim could walk, he taught him how to build things. They also spent time together hunting, camping, and fishing.

Matthew Malone had taught him a love for the outdoors. During those times they spent together hunting, fishing, and camping, his father would tell him war stories he and his father, Jim's grandfather, had endured when they were serving the country during World War II and in Korea. He always stressed, "The Malone families were patriots from way back." His father, had he known what was coming, would never have told Jim those stories.

When John Fitzgerald Kennedy called up the reserves of a few specialist groups to serve as military advisors in Vietnam, Mathew Malone was one of those to be selected.

He was only to be an advisor, of course.

Who would guess our president would lie to you, especially Pres. John F. Kennedy!

Jim's father was one of those men trained by our military for very secret special action, often covert operations the public and the press were never aware was happening.

Advisor? Sure!

Sometimes even many members of Congress had no information concerning the activities by these Special Forces, these remarkable, highly capable, extremely well-trained soldiers such as the Seals, Rangers, Green Berets, Special Forces, our country's absolute best fighting machines.

Jim's father spent four years in the Special Forces and participated in several covert military operations prior to Vietnam. Operations so secret no one, not even our ever-vigilant press, ever heard or wrote about any of them. Only the highest level CIA personnel, senators, and advisors close to the president would know about such actions. He was frequently sent on missions without even knowing really what the cause was about or where he was going. Jim's grandfather had been involved in similar action in World War II and in Korea for Roosevelt and Harry S. Truman, our presidents during those conflicts. Jim was only a sophomore in high school when his father was called to serve his country again. So it was inevitable when Jim's mother received that very polite letter from our president, Lyndon B. Johnson, this was shortly after the assassination of President Kennedy, informing her that her husband had been killed in Vietnam serving his country. Jim decided, over the strenuous objections of his mother, it was his duty to replace his father. His duty, as his grandfather and father had done, to serve his county in time of need.

Jim had to do his duty, and college could wait.

Duty and his sense of justice had started Jim down his fateful road, first with the duty he felt impelled to perform for his state, his country, and then the duty he felt for the personal protection of his family; and our government trained him for both obligations.

And now, ironically, here in this Seattle courtroom his beloved state of Washington seemed to be trying very hard to end his life.

#

CHAPTER 2

JIM MALONE

There was a blue jay squawking on the veranda and steaming coffee dribbling out of an espresso machine when the call came.

"Dad, can you come over right away?" Over the phone, Marks's voice quavered with fear.

Fear was not something I associated with my son Mark.

No, it was not like him at all.

I knew immediately something had to be very wrong. "What's going on, Mark?" I couldn't conceal the concern in my voice.

"Please just come over right away, Dad, get here soon, please. We need you, and I can't talk on the phone!" Mark said, his voice was still quivering.

Mark, his wife Joan, and my two grandsons Justin and Robbie live only ten minutes away from me. Their house was located in one of our premiere residential developments just on the outskirts of Bellevue. That's what we do, my son and I.

We build houses.

And we build good houses.

Fortunately, we started the company in the Bellevue area, the Eastside, before Microsoft became such a powerhouse. When those computer whizzes arrived with all their money, they wanted the best, and they were willing to pay top dollar for it. My son, Mark, had finished getting his architect degree from Washington State University and was a newly wed when he decided to join my company, Malone Construction.

And it became "Malone and Son Inc."

We're that, the best around.

Mark is the architect, and I am the contractor. We probably built a thousand houses for Microsoft employees alone. Not to mention Boeing executives who were not a great deal different.

In addition to, they all but forced us to buy that stupid stock in the early years, which turned out to be not so stupid after all.

We made a lot of money.

This call though, was the crisis, the beginning of the watershed moment in my life when I realized a million dollars wouldn't buy what I wanted most—safety and happiness for my grandsons.

Like I said, Mark only lived ten minutes away.

That day I made it in almost five.

When I pulled into the sprawling driveway, I could sense something was very wrong.

Later, I would find out it was worse than even I could ever imagine.

This was early Saturday morning, the last day of August, Labor Day weekend and, in my opinion, the best time of the year in Seattle.

The smell of late summer flowers hung in the air, alongside fresh-mown grass. Wind sloughed through the cedar and fir trees in the front yard.

Usually when I drove up Bailey, the family German shepherd and my grandsons would tumble out the front door to greet me.

They weren't there.

I could feel problems in the air.

You know what I mean . . . it kind of hangs there . . . a feeling of dread that permeates everything around you. It seeps into your body. You know instantly something is wrong. It was similar to the kind of feeling I frequently had when I was on patrol in the jungles in Vietnam.

It had been years since I had such an ill-omened sensation, and I had forgotten how it consumed your entire being.

Mark was at the front door just as soon as I stopped the car.

"Dad, hurry," he shouted from the front door just as I opened the car door to get out.

He started babbling almost incoherently. As I stepped into the house, I saw that Joan, my daughter-in-law, was worse, all but hysterical. In spite of this, I was able to ascertain what the problem was, and it made their reaction understandable.

Mark recovered long enough to blurt out the problem. "Dad, it's Justin and Robbie . . . the boys. They're gone, they're gone. There's a note."

What would become my worst nightmare since Nam started that instant.

My grandsons, Justin and Robbie!

My precious grandchildren.

They'd been kidnapped.

I saw the ragged piece of paper now, clutched in my son's hand.

Mark showed me the kidnappers' note and then stood almost frozen waiting for my reaction.

I tried to stay calm. My special training took hold.

The rules—keep calm in a crisis, evaluate the situation, and then react.

"Calm down both of you and tell me what happened," I said.

Mark yelled, "Dad, Justin and Robbie are gone, kidnapped. Here, read the damned note!" His hand was trembling as he held out the note to me.

It was brief and to the point.

The note consisted of cutout words, pasted on a sheet of white paper. I read it slowly.

We have your sons. Get a million dollars together in old twenties, fifties, and hundreds; and we'll call you with instructions in twenty-four hours. Don't call the cops or we'll kill the kids.

"Okay, Mark and Joan." I breathed deep. "Calm down. We'll get Robbie and Justin back. Don't worry!"

I said this without a clue at the time how this could be accomplished. I did think no matter what, we had to call the police.

I told them it's what we should do.

Joan shrieked, "No, Dad, they'll kill Justin and Robbie." She was now more out of control than before. Hysteria was totally engulfing her mind and body. I knew Mark and I must bring her back to reality.

"Joan, please, try to calm down and listen to Dad, he'll know what to do," Mark said and put his arms around her.

He then turned to me waiting for my response and, at the same time, held Joan in a comforting embrace.

She was sobbing almost uncontrollably. "Joan, we won't let them do anything without making sure Justin and Robbie are safe," I said with as much confidence and compassion as I could conjure up, considering I had no idea how to accomplish what I was promising.

They listened and stood there holding on to one another.

"I'm going to call John."

They knew instantly who I was referring to and before Joan could react further. I proceeded to call the Bellevue chief of police, John Hammond. I called his home because I thought he probably wouldn't be in his office on Saturday morning, especially on a Labor Day weekend. John lived just about twenty minutes away and had been a family friend for years, so I had his private number on my cell phone.

"Hello?" Chief Hammond answered the phone after five rings. Thank god he was there.

"John, it's Jim Malone," I said. John asked with a degree of professional concern to his voice. "What's happening that's important enough for you to call me on a Labor Day weekend, on my private line nonetheless?" My response was quick and to the point. "John, my friend, it's too difficult to explain on the phone;

but I'm at my son's house, you know Mark. Well, we have a major crisis, and I'm positive we need your expertise. I know it's Labor Day weekend, but this is a horrible thing or you know I wouldn't bother you. I really need your help."

Without waiting for him to respond, I ask if he could possibly come over to Mark's house right away. I stressed again it was too difficult to explain on the phone, and that it would be better to do it in person. His reaction was just what I anticipated.

"I'll be right there," John said.

He seemed to know instantly I wouldn't make such a request unless it was true we were in need of immediate help. He agreed to come over and said he would be there within thirty minutes. While we waited for Chief Hammond to arrive, I called my wife, Deanna.

"Sweetie, I'm at Mark's, and we've got a big problem."

I had left so fast I didn't have a chance to say one word to her. I told her where I was again and emphasized we had a terrible situation and needed her to get here as fast as possible. I further emphasized it was a true emergency, and I would explain more when she got here.

Deanna was a nurse when I met her.

As a matter of fact, she was my nurse when things went wrong for me in Nam. I'll always remember the vision of her standing by my bed when I came to after they had operated for six hours to remove shrapnel from my body.

The shrapnel was a result from a night patrol that had gone bad in Nam. My squad walked right into an ambush by the Cong. It was a fierce firefight that ended up in hand-to-hand combat. When we were finally able to retreat, we were showered with mortar shells, and all of us sustained serious shrapnel wounds. Fortunately, we suffered no loss of life. My wounds were serious, and I had lost a great deal of blood before we were able to return to camp and receive medical attention.

They airlifted those of us who had sustained life-threatening wounds to a MASH (Mobile Army Surgical Hospital) unit located far from the war zones. When I came to, it was like seeing an angel standing vigilantly at my bedside.

Deanna.

I decided right then I wasn't ever going to let my angel leave me. It took a lot of persuading before she finally agreed to become Mrs. Malone and then only if I promised to leave the service when my tour was complete or as soon as I could get an honorary discharge due to my physical condition. She was quite aware of the type of duty I participated in during my time in Vietnam, and she expressed her viewpoint, there was no chance in hell she could live a lifetime with someone like me. But I was obsessed with my goal to marry this angel I knew God had sent and agreed to everything she wanted in return for her becoming my lifetime companion.

Deanna had been one of the volunteer RNs who went to Vietnam when the conflict escalated into a major war. She chose to leave when I was released from the hospital and received my honorable discharge. For years, after we moved to Bellevue and started our construction company, she continued to do volunteer work at the hospital, kept books for my small company, and raised our son, Mark.

"Oh, and bring some kind of sedatives. Valium or whatever you have. We could use something to calm things down over here," I asked her in the calmest tone I could conjure up.

"Yes, of course I think I have something, Jim. I'll grab it and get there as fast as I can." She was always like that, nothing seemed to rattle her.

#

Deanna and Chief Hammond arrived almost simultaneously.

I opened the front door and ushered them both into the house to the great room where Mark and Joan were standing, still holding on to each other. Deanna instantly went to Joan, who was still crying, and put her arms around her without even knowing what was wrong. Mark moved away and turned his attention to John and me.

After taking a deep, aching breath, I explained everything to the new arrivals.

Moments later, the chief looked up from the note I'd handed him. Hammond was a beefy guy with short steel-gray hair. His metallic eyes were grim now set deep in his ruddy face. We filled him in with what we knew, and after thinking about the problem for a few minutes, he made a recommendation.

"Jim, Mark, we need to call the FBI."

Mark's face turned dark. You could see it. He usually had such a bright sunny disposition, beaming out of that face that looked so like his mother's. But he had a dark side too, the Irish side, I guess. I could see it welling up in him instantly. He was going to object to this idea. So I responded before he or Joan could say anything.

"I agree totally." Then I turned to face my family. "Mark, I truly feel John is correct, it's the right thing to do," I said with as much full conviction as I could muster considering the circumstances. "I've known this fine, experienced man for years. I have complete confidence in Chief Hammond. It's his job, and we have to depend on his experience."

The chief then assured Mark the safe return of the boys would be his first and highest priority. He continued to explain we needed to get the FBI'S manpower, equipment, and expertise; and he emphasized the sooner the better.

And as Chief Hammond explained, "The FBI has a special unit trained just for handling kidnappings."

"I don't know, Dad, you read the note, maybe we shouldn't have even called John," Mark said.

"Mark, listen, let's do what the chief says. I know he wouldn't do anything to jeopardize Justin or Robbie. Right, John?"

Chief Hammond nodded yes.

"Besides as John said, we need all the expertise and manpower the FBI has available."

The chief nodded in agreement and added, "That's correct, Mark, and I assure you even with the FBI, the children's safe return will absolutely come first. I can't stress enough, the sooner we move on this, the better."

Mark and Joan both finally acquiesced to our suggestion.

Without a second of hesitation and before anyone changed their mind, Chief Hammond called FBI special agent Jack Watkins, the FBI director for our region. Chief Hammond and he go way back. Fortunately the chief had his private, direct number and was able to reach him at his home. The chief didn't waste any words; he immediately indicated to Watkins a kidnapping was involved and stressed the urgency of the situation and asked agent Watkins if it was at all possible for him to come over right away, and he would then explain more. We were in luck. He agreed! The chief gave him the address to Mark's house and explained how to get there.

While we were waiting for the FBI, I asked Mark where Bailey, their German Sheppard, was. Bailey and the kids were almost inseparable, and I was sure he would have been with them at the tree house when they were abducted.

"I haven't seen him since this morning. I'm positive he went with the kids. He always does," Mark said. I noticed every time he talked his speech was still shaky, and his face was showing a great amount of stress, not a good sign in a crisis.

I said I would go outside and look around for him while we were waiting for the FBI.

Just as I started to go outside, Chief Hammond stopped me and recommended I stay in the house until he and the FBI had an opportunity to search the area for clues.

I have to say now as I look back on the whole horrible business, this turned out to be one of his more intelligent directions.

My life would have been so different if I'd followed all his directions.

#

CHAPTER 3

BOB ARNOTT

How did I get involved?

When did Jim call me?

I have to say, as an investigative reporter, I have found the most difficult problem with writing about traumatic events is to get the participants to tell you not only the truth, but to also open up to let you know their true inner feelings.

But with this story, because of who I was and my close relationship with all those involved, I got straight into just what the story needed.

Not only did I get the scoops that would be used when the time was right . . .

I also got the viewpoints of the people involved, including the authorities.

I understood the Malone kidnappings better than any other reporter or news media. To me it was more than just a story, it was personal.

Investigative reporters must accomplish several things. After we have the full confidence of the person or persons involved, we must then do a factual description of the actual events being described.

With this story, I had both.

I've known Jim Malone for years. I watched him grow from a basic carpenter to one of the most respected builder of houses in the total Seattle area.

Jim and I drank together . . . played golf together . . . . Our families socialized frequently when my wife was alive . . . . We even spent many New Years together.

Needless to say, Jim Malone, the subject of this story, and I were very close, almost like brothers. Also, like brothers, I guess there were unspoken resentments.

The fact he had so much money was part of it. But Jim? Jim Malone, hale and hearty back-slapping building genius . . . He was everything I'd always wanted to be and wasn't . . . He stood for something about the American spirit I'd always yearned to find in myself . . . He had so many loyal friends, wonderful money . . . He was John Wayne without the gut. A healthy John Wayne, who lived his principles and looked out at his country and life through his steel blue eyes that never wavered from anyone or anything, always focused.

Me? I was a conservative reporter with values, smacked down in life by the system, but too damned stubborn to give in. I had the talent to be a top reporter or a columnist for the *Washington Post* or the *New York Times*. Jim's political values had served him well. Mine had not.

As I said, Jim was tall and handsome with steel blue eyes. The women wanted him, but the best one got him. His close cropped hair gave him a kind of sincere Clint Eastwood look.

Me? If I were in broadcast journalism, mine would have been a face meant for radio. People used to say I reminded them of Edward G. Robinson, when people remembered who Edward G. Robinson was. Women did not hammer on my door.

Jim was tall and handsome, and I was homely and short. Jim had made it—a successful company, a wife to kill for, an intelligent son, a beautiful daughter-in-law, and two wonderful grandsons.

I hadn't. Not really.

#

So here I was in Seattle, trying hard to hang onto my values while newspapers seemed to sinking into twenty-first century political sludge. And even though I sometimes resented Jim, it was his spirit that helped me often to maintain my own resolve. He constantly reminded me there are two sides to all stories.

When did I get involved with this kidnapping story?

I entered the picture shortly after the event.

Jim had called, and we met privately, away from the FBI's knowledge so he could to tell me the entire story in person.

Jim Malone asked me, if things turned bad, could I coordinate a campaign that would be directed to the public via mass media that would request their assistance in finding his grandsons.

He emphasized this course of action would only be taken if and when it became apparent the kidnappers took the money and did not return the kids. Jim wanted me to make sure I would also document everything he chose to share in the event the legal authorities' efforts failed or time became a factor and circumstances forced him to take an alternative course of action.

Jim didn't elaborate or offer any information what this alterative course of action would be, but I knew his background and his resolve in tense situations, so I could only imagine what he meant by an alternative course of action.

Naturally I agreed.

What a *story*!

What an opportunity to not only assist a close friend in his time of need, but to also be an involved observer and at the same time have an "exclusive" to a story I knew would become national news, if and when the time came and I got the opportunity to write it.

It could very well be, I realized, this story would bring me back to the news reporting prominence I once had. Give me standing in this crazy media.

Hell, maybe I'd even get a book deal out of it.

Enough.

I'm getting ahead of myself.

After the meeting where I first heard from Jim of the unfolding events, there wasn't anything for me to do, but wait until he requested my active participation.

The only thing Jim wanted at that moment was my assurance I would keep silent until he gave me a go-ahead or told me what he needed.

He felt it was of utmost importance at this time to keep his contact with me private, away from the local authorities and especially from Director Watkins and the FBI. I was the only press he wanted involved. He did say he would mention to his family my potential involvement if it became necessary and would make sure they kept this information totally confidential. He said their knowing I was there if needed would maybe comfort them.

Needless to say, this arrangement suited me just fine other than having to wait.

So there I was in the midst of a fantastic story in the making, and I would have just to sit on it.

What else could I do?

If I broke the story I'd lose a friend.

Maybe I could even cause the death of my best friend's grandchildren. I certainly didn't want that to happen. I loved those kids myself. They called me Uncle Bob.

Who knows, I remember thinking at the time. Maybe I'll be of some help when the time was right and then maybe I'd still have a great story.

But I knew I would always have a great friend, and Jim knew his confidential request would be honored.

There was no choice.

I would have to wait.

I would have to wait for something to happen.

And something did happen.

#

CHAPTER 4

JIM MALONE

I remember the moment well.

It was the day of the kidnapping.

Panic and adrenaline had turned to confusion with a drop of despair.

I was gazing out the front window at Mark's house at their rhododendron bushes, reflecting on the events of the last few hours.

I felt so helpless.

Then my moment of solitude was interrupted.

Bailey, the German shepherd who usually greets my arrival but had been gone that morning, staggered into view. It caught me totally off guard. I had to look again to make sure my eyes weren't deceiving me.

Yes, it was Bailey, but there was something wrong with him. He staggered, wobbling from side to side. Each step he took looked like it would be his last as he labored his way down the driveway toward the front of the house. He looked like he had been hit by a truck or been in one hell of a fight. It was obvious he was in trouble and needed assistance.

"Hey, look! There's Bailey," I yelled as I rapidly headed for the front door.

Chief Hammond, Mark, and the FBI agent named Watkins who had arrived at the house a bit earlier and had been filled in on the situation turned and looked out the front window to see Bailey just as he reached the front of the house. He, along with Chief Hammond and Mark, immediately followed me out the front door.

Something about Watkins had bothered me the moment I saw him. I guess I always thought of FBI people as efficient, button-down Efram Zimbalist Jr. types. Trustworthy and dedicated servants of democracy. This guy though . . . His blond hair was kind of long for an FBI guy, and he looked a bit like that lawyer on the TV show *Boston Legal*, kind of chubby and smug and ambitious. When he saw Bailey, he didn't look alarmed at the blood. The bastard seemed to kind of smile. A clue! That's what he appeared to be thinking, and maybe he was right. Not a detectible degree of empathy for Bailey.

By the time I swung the door open, Bailey had reached the front porch. He totally collapsed and was just lying there, not moving, eyes open; and he seemed to be looking right at me.

"Bailey!" cried Mark.

We went to him.

As I'd guessed the moment I saw him, Bailey indeed looked like he had been in one hell of a fight. There was blood and dirt all over his body. When he fell, he dropped a bloody tennis shoe he had been carrying in his mouth. Later after searching the tree house area, we concluded he must have attacked one or more of the assailants who now was minus one tennis shoe. It appeared he had put up a pretty good fight and at least had inflicted physical damage to someone. At this point we had no idea how many people were involved.

"Look at this," said Director Watkins as he picked the tennis shoe up by one shoe string. "The dog has at least brought us some clues." My reaction was immediate but silent. "Is this an attempt at humor, or is this his bedside manner? The man isn't wrapped right."

We'll never know Bailey's total involvement, but yes, he did supply us with what turned out to be our first set of clues. In his jaws he had clutched a size 11 ½ Nike tennis shoe. Bailey also provided human blood samples and hair follicles when tested later would prove to be that of a male. This in itself wasn't much use in identifying a kidnapper. The FBI had already presumed it was from a male because of the size and design of the Nike shoe. However the blood type and the DNA could be important if and when they were able to apprehend any or all of the kidnappers.

"Don't touch anything on the dog," said agent Watkins in that cold voice he possessed. I was only too happy to let him take command of the situation. "Let me bag everything."

Oh yes, I thought. Obviously Watkins sees this as an opportunity. He wants to solve this case, put it on his CV, and then boast about it over cognac and cigars at the squash club. I knew it was really stupid of me to have those thoughts when I didn't really know Watkins at all. He just looked and acted like one of those guys you would never play golf with.

I noticed a gun peeking out of a shoulder holster as he got a satchel out of his car. This person carrying a gun looked totally out of place. He donned some latex gloves and put the shoe in a plastic bag. Then he proceeded to extract and bag samples of blood, dirt, and hair from Bailey's matted coat. He then instructed one of his assistants to get these to the lab for tests. He told the assistant to stress the importance of processing them as rapidly as possible. I was starting to feel better about him at this point. He was professional, cold, but professional.

All the while, Bailey just lay there with his big brown eyes watching every move anyone made. He appeared to be oblivious to any pain he was feeling from his wounds.

Mark and I then knelt down to see to what extent Bailey was injured and what we needed to do.

"He's been cut bad, Dad, look here." Mark showed me two deep cuts around his shoulder area and a wound to the head. All the blood around the wounds had coagulated and was mixed with dirt and grass.

"Better take him to the vet," said Chief Hammond after conferring with Watkins. He recommended we not offer any explanation other than Bailey had showed up at home in this condition.

"Joan and I will take him," said Deanna. She was obviously desperate to be of assistance in any way possible.

By now, they both seemed to have called up that inner strength people seem to posses when faced with a crisis. Even Joan was now somewhat calmer. We placed Bailey in the back of Deanna's SUV, and while we were loading him, Mark was already on the phone with the veterinarian clinic explaining we had an emergency and needed to bring our dog in right away. Then Deanna and Joan headed for the vet.

Now, the waiting began.

The waiting for the kidnappers to contact us.

We felt confident they, in all probability, did not know whether or not we had contacted the police. Mark's house is in a somewhat private, protected area off the main road, and that's why it was difficult for the authorities to comprehend how they could pull off the kidnapping without being detected.

We didn't know the kidnappers had been planning this for weeks. They even knew about the boys' tree house.

This tree house is located on the edge of Mark's land inside a large protected greenbelt that surrounds the entire housing development.

It was still undeveloped, covered with trees, dense overgrowth, and difficult to get to.

But the kidnappers had!

Because we had called Chief Hammond and the FBI Director Watkins on their private phones, we had circumvented the normal channels the media so vigilantly monitors in hopes of being first with a news scoop like this. So at this time no one but the authorities and the immediate family knew what was going on. The police and the FBI promptly put a blanket on the situation so only a limited, necessary number of people would be involved.

Agent Watkins had been busy organizing the FBI's plan of action. He set up manned phone recording and tracking equipment, assigned his people their various areas of responsibilities.

Then, when he was satisfied with his preparations, he came over to where Mark and I were standing. We both had been closely scrutinizing all that was transpiring. We purposely stayed out of his way, and even though we hadn't said a word to each other, it was obvious we were both somewhat impressed by the precision the FBI and Watkins had proceeded to get the entire operation in place. Just watching the speed and professionalism the FBI was applying to the situation made Mark and me feel we had done the right thing by calling John and allowed the FBI to enter the picture. In other words, I was feeling better about Watkins.

"Mark," he asked, "where were the boys and about what time was it when you last saw them?" He had a Bic pen and a small notebook to jot down information.

"About nine this morning, they said they were going to play in their tree house over in the greenbelt," answered Mark.

"Where is this greenbelt tree house?"

Mark told him and then escorted him out front to point out exactly where it was located. Watkins motioned to two of the people he called and had now arrived to assist in the investigation. He instructed them to go to this area and secure it until they could totally search what he perceived could be where the abduction had most likely taken place.

You can bet I made sure I was never too far from Watkins.

I felt I needed to be in close proximity of Agent Watkins's every step of the way.

Watkins moves, I move.

He looks at something. I look at it.

They were my grandsons.

I was going to make sure he got them back, or ...

Well, never mind the "or."

About thirty minutes later, after Director Watkins made arrangements for more FBI people to come and man the listening, recording, and tracking devices, he suggested the chief, Mark, and I should accompany him to the tree house. He explained we might be able to assist his people in searching the area he had perceived would have been where the abduction possibly occurred.

After searching the entire area, they came up with a couple of different-size footprints, the FBI thought at the time, may or may not have been made by the perpetrators. The footprints did appear to have been freshly made. In consideration of the fact they had been unable to find any other discernable signs of activity in the area, the FBI investigators were pretty confident the perpetrators had left them. They proceeded to take pictures and make plaster casts of the prints. They also deduced it would have taken at least two and more than likely, probably three or more individuals to coordinate everything that was necessary in committing the abduction and delivering the ransom note.

Later this assumption would prove to be correct.

Along with the footprints, they found minute traces of sand in the tree house and around the base of the tree. Because there was no sand in the area, they assumed the kidnappers might have brought it in on their shoes. They also concluded the kidnappers must have been waiting in the tree house area for the boys to show for an extended period of time because they retrieved three cigarette butts that had been discarded not too far from the tree house. Several traces of blood and what appeared to be hair from Bailey were also discovered close to the base of the tree.

Because the brush was trampled down in this area, the authorities figured it was where the struggle with Bailey might have taken place. Maybe even the boys had put up some resistance.

During this portion of the investigation, they found traces of activity in the brush that led to an old logging road in the greenbelt area. It appeared to be where the perpetrators parked one or two vehicles while waiting for the children. It was far enough from the tree house, so it would be almost impossible to detect a vehicle or vehicles from either Mark's house or by the children as they approached the tree house.

Until it was too late!

After further investigation in this area, the investigators discovered some unique tire prints left by two different vehicles. They surmised because of the size difference in the prints that one set was left by a large pickup or van and the other set by a smaller vehicle. They presumed both vehicles were used in the kidnapping.

Once again this indicated two or more individuals had to be involved.

Unfortunately the vehicles tires were the size of many types, makes, or models of cars or pickups like Fords, Chevys, and Dodges; so their discovery turned out to be a minimum of help. As they did with the footprints, the FBI agents made casts and took pictures of these too.

I was there with director Watkins and the investigating team every step of the way.

As they were returning to the house, Director Watkins said, surmising out loud, "If the boys went directly from the main house to the tree house at 9:00 a.m., they probably would have arrived there by nine fifteen or nine thirty at the very latest. The perpetrators then with some resistance from the boys and obviously your dog left the tree house area. I estimate it probably took them an hour to an hour and a half to accomplish everything necessary to complete the kidnapping, and leave the area. When did you discover the note?" He directed this question to Mark. Mark nervously ran his fingers through his nicely barbered brown hair as he replied, "Just before noon, I had been working in my den on a new housing development. Joan told me to yell at the boys to come for lunch. I walked out onto the porch and started to yell when I noticed the note right there on the first step. It was wrapped around a rock with a rubber band. I picked it up and you know the rest." Jim noted Mark's speech pattern was getting more normal, and his face was showing less stress, which gave him some comfort.

Director Watkins asked what he had done with the rock.

Mark said he dropped it by the walkway after removing the note.

Unfortunately after locating the rock, they only found Mark's fingerprints on it.

"There had to be more than two people involved," said Watkins in an almost-academic tone of voice as he rubbed his chin like they used to in old Sherlock Holmes movies. He seemed to be talking out loud to himself as he continued, "Someone had to place the note on the steps after the boys had been abducted and removed from the tree house area. It's logical, therefore, that one or more persons would be left to guard the boys." He paused and then turned to Mark and Joan and asked, "Think back for a minute. Are you sure neither one of you heard anything unusual this morning?"

They both said they hadn't heard a sound.

Joan and Deanna had just returned from the vet about thirty minutes before the investigation of the tree house area was completed and everyone had returned to the main house. They were waiting for them in the great room where all the FBI equipment was being put in place, and it's also where everyone involved congregated.

Deanna explained they left Bailey at the clinic, and the vet said they would keep him for a few days to make sure there was no infection. The vet didn't question their explanation about how Bailey had been hurt. He said Bailey should fully recover in a week or two.

Watkins then asked Joan what she had been doing from nine o'clock on. She explained she was working on the other side of the house in the kitchen cleaning and preparing lunch.

She added, without Watkins inquiring, she knew Mark, as usual was engrossed in his home office located in the den working on a new housing project. Watkins very politely said Mark had already explained to him what he had been doing.

"If only I hadn't let them leave," Mark said, shaking his head. "Mark, we can't dwell on what-ifs. Don't worry we'll get them back and make the kidnappers pay dearly for what they have done," I said emphatically, using a tone of voice that Mark had come to know meant business.

Later, I would regret saying this in front of Hammond and Watkins, but at the time I had no idea what would transpire as everything unfolded.

Agent Watkins then asked Mark, "Mr. Malone, perhaps we should deal with a practical matter now. Can you get the money together?"

Mark nodded wearily, as though accepting the fact he thought we could and then turned to look directly at me, obviously wanting me to supply the answer. I responded instantly, "The money's not the problem, the difficulty is it's Saturday and Labor Day weekend to boot. That almost certainly creates a problem. I don't really know if it can be done. We have the money, but getting it together this fast might be difficult. The bank president is Don Collier, a very good friend. I'm confident he'll do what he's legally capable of doing once we explain the circumstances."

Jim stroked his strong handsome chin thoughtfully, and then added, "I'm positive he'll cooperate if at all possible, like I said, the money's not the problem. Getting it today, together in old twenties, fifties, and one hundreds, now that's another story, I'm sure. I have no idea how he could accomplish such an undertaking."

"Call him, now, explain the situation, and emphasize the necessity for his total silence; and then John and I will speak with him," Watkins said.

I then did exactly what Watkins had instructed me to do.

Don, the bank president, fortunately was at home when I called.

After much conversation, including talking to Chief Hammond and Director Watkins for an extended period of time, Don finally confirmed he would cooperate in every way possible and would get the process in motion as rapidly as possible.

I thanked him, again stressing the importance of secrecy. He asked to speak to Watkins once more in order to coordinate everything.

Watkins took the phone from me and was obviously listening to Don explaining the bank's problems with a transaction like this. After a couple minutes, he responded. He told Collier he would have a couple of FBI agents meet him at the bank within an hour so he would have security and perhaps lend some assistance if they were needed.

Collier liked this idea and said he thought the FBI's presence at the bank during this unorthodox process would be enough to cause the bank employees he would have to call in to work, not to question or inquire what was transpiring.

They concluded their conversation after Collier gave Watkins the bank's location and said he would call back when the task was completed. He added it would be necessary to have the agents sign a release for the money, and they then could bring it directly to Watkins.

Watkins hung up the phone and then turned to address everyone present.

"Okay, everybody, pay attention," said Agent Watkins as he put the phone back in its cradle. His lake blue eyes were steadfast and calm. "We're getting everything in place. It appears that we are almost set to go. Phone taps, recording equipment, tracking devices, all in place; and the money is being put together."

He turned those blue eyes, that professional gaze onto my son.

"Mark, you and Joan know what to say when we get a call. Let me go over it one more time. Just listen to what they say. Agree to anything the kidnapper's request and assure him or her, the caller, the money is being put together. Explain it's difficult to accomplish getting that much money together on a weekend, let alone on a Labor Day weekend. Reassure them you are working on it, and then ask to speak with the boys so you can be positive they're okay. Remember to try and stall the caller as long as possible. But let me emphasize, don't overdo it. The fewer suspicions they have you are cooperating with the police the better. At all times assure them the money is not important, but getting it all together today is difficult. Emphasize it takes time. Tell them all you want is to get the boys back with no harm done to them, that's your only concern. Are there any questions?"

No one responded.

"Good, now it's a waiting game."

I was actually very impressed at the speed the FBI and Chief Hammond had coordinated all these people and put everything in motion.

At the same time, I was also amazed at how quickly they were able to evaluate clues from the crime scene. For instance, the preliminary DNA tests on the cigarette butts indicated they'd been smoked by a man and a woman.

I thought the process would take days.

The FBI said the final reports will take several days, but they had succeeded in getting the preliminary results back before the end of the day on Saturday. Agent Watkins reflected he felt a woman being involved would be good for the boys. It was his feeling she might be less likely to harm them. The lab tests on the one shoe Bailey had brought back after the altercation we assumed he had with at least one of the kidnappers in the tree house area, revealed traces of sand and diesel oil similar to what the FBI found in and around the tree house. This in itself confirmed the earlier thought that these were real clues left by the kidnappers, and the FBI reflected they could be helpful in locating where the kidnappers were hiding the boys. In the end, they turned out to not really be much help because there was sand and diesel oil all around Puget Sound. It could have come from a hundred locations.

Furthermore, the blood was determined to have come from a person with A positive type blood, just like fifty million or so other people.

This evidence, along with the DNA on the cigarette butts and logically deducing to be able to handle the note delivery, the kids, two vehicles, when added together, all but confirmed their earlier suspicions were correct in assuming two maybe three men and one woman were the perpetrators.

Now it was a waiting game.

At least the FBI said it was.

But me?

No, it has always been too damned hard for me to wait.

#

CHAPTER 5

BOB ARNOTT

"Uncle Bob! Uncle Bob!" cried Robbie with unalloyed glee at my arrival.

Justin was more reserved, but I could tell from the light of his smile and the glow of his brown eyes that he was happy to see me too.

Maybe even happier.

After all Justin was my guy.

"Hey, Uncle Bob," he said casually, trying to stay cool, but obviously wondering, like his big brother probably was, if I'd brought anything for them.

"Howdy, fellows!" I said. "How about a hug?"

Robbie scurried over. I swept him up and twirled him around, as well as these middle-aged muscles and back would allow.

Justin stepped forward, patiently waiting his turn. I remember thinking how tan he'd gotten. The summer had been a warm and sunny one. He must have played outside by the lake a lot. Then I remember both Jim and Mark commenting on what a water lover he'd become. A really good swimmer, Jim had commented with no amount of pride in his booming bass voice.

"Here's you go, cowboy!" I said, gathering his lithe and strong little body up in my arms.

They were two little wonders, I'd always thought, two little dynamos of health and vitality. It was great to watch them growing up strong and proud and American.

My two little Patriots, I would call them, which always made the Malone elders laugh.

"Okay, kids. Let Uncle Bob relax for a bit," Mark said. He'd been behind the bar, building me a drink. And now he came out, holding a crystal glass filled high with scotch. It tinkled and glittered with its generous freight of ice cubes.

"He looks like he could use a break."

"What do I have I here?" I asked, accepting the glass with a grin,

"Always the best from the Malone's liquor cabinet." as I offered a salute in Mark's direction and took a sip. "Dewars, just what I needed!" I smiled to double show my appreciation.

Mark added, "I've got some single malt here if you prefer to have that instead."

"Oh no, no," I said. "You know what I like."

"I guess I should after all these years, and all your visits."

I sipped deep of the stuff. Cold became warmth. I could feel myself relaxing already.

Mark looked on, approvingly. He could see that I'd been wound up. Mark was more like his mother in his ability to perceive people's feelings and empathize with them. Looked more like his mom than his old man too—and shorter. Not as short as me, but I didn't have to peer up anywhere near as much as when I'm with his father.

Mark had a lithe, runner's body topped with a head of reddish brown hair. He should have been damned proud of it, but the way he always looked at Jim made me realize he'd always felt inadequate.

How could I tell?

Hell, I know from inadequate.

"So?" he said.

"So . . . what?"

"Okay."

I grinned, went over, and patted him on the back. "I don't know what it is about you, Mark. But you just read my mind or something. It's exactly what I needed, and even I didn't really know it . . . No other drink, no other booze would have hit the spot. You're the best!"

His pupils opened wide. I could feel him suck it all up: the approval. There was no doubt that his father loved him. But Big Jim Malone was pretty damned tight with his approval of his son; and the way he always acted, he seemed to disapprove of him. As though, somehow being a mere architect was . . . well, kind of sissy, you know. Not quite square with some unspoken Malone tradition. Jim apparently had long ago forgotten that's what he had wanted to be if Vietnam hadn't interfered, and maybe that was the real reason, his own regret or resentment of not going to college.

"Thanks." Then he looked at me a little deeper; and as usual, he detected I had a problem and then asked kind of jokingly, "So what's eating you? Something a juicy red barbecued New York steak and a big Idaho smothered with butter, sour cream, and chives won't cure?"

I took a gulp of the scotch.

"No. Looks like there's a damned good chance by next year they're going to pull my column from what syndication it has left."

"What?" Joan came out of the kitchen, wiping her hands on a red-checkered apron. Her beautiful green eyes above a button nose were flashing with alarm. "They're pulling your column! But it's so good!"

"Damned straight," said Mark. "I've been reading it forever. Hasn't ever been a boring one!"

I took another sip of my drink and contemplated the near-empty state of the glass.

It was like my soul.

"Seems as though the conservatives are looking for hipper younger pundits, or I have to become more like a liberal, god forbid." I shrugged. "Oh well. I always figured I'd be munching on pasture grass eventually in this business."

Mark's eyes narrowed with concern. "Are you sure of this, or is it just your own paranoia speaking?"

I shook my head. "It sincerely doesn't look good, Mark." Mark and Joan invited me over regularly. Sometimes I invited myself. This was one of the latter times.

Mark and I had been close since he was a kid bout the same age Justin and Robbie were now. Like Justin and Robbie, I had brought him books to read—old beloved books like the many Oz books and Freddy the Pig books and Uncle Wiggly books—wonderful story books with pictures . . . almost forgotten these days, it seemed. I had early noted Mark's penchant for reading for the more intellectual side of things. Sometimes Jim would laughingly accuse me of making him an egghead as though I'd robbed him of a famous sport-star son.

So Mark had encouraged me to bring books for his kids, and like I had read to him when his father was too busy, so I read to Justin and Robbie.

And oh, how they sucked the stories in. How wide-eyed they got when I read to them from the Howard Pyle books about pirates and Robin Hood. I could see that they both had good artistic taste since they would note how much better the old classic American illustrators were. They were both great kids. Justin, the youngest was a bit shy and nearsighted. Although Mark, and certainly "I want perfect grandkids" Jim, wanted him to get that simple laser operation to correct the vision problem, Justin would have nothing of it.

"I want to look like Harry Potter," he'd say, insisting on great big horn-rims.

Jim was baffled of course that he had an introvert for a grandson, and it frustrated him that Justin wasn't particularly interested in sports. But I'll give this to the old extrovert—it didn't take a jot of love away from his feeling for the boy.

It was obvious, though, that it was Robbie who was truly the apple of Jim's eye. Robbie was fascinated with anything involving a ball. Soccer, baseball, football, golf—you name it. When he was four, he'd decided that he was a superhero named Superball because everyone said he bounced off walls so well.

I used to like to take the kids down to a local arcade. Justin often as not just brought along some comic books and read, but Robbie and I were made for skeet-ball—that old-fashioned wood ball and wood hoops I used to play in my childhood on boardwalk arcades in New Jersey.

Mark would take them camping in some of the great parks we have here in the Pacific Northwest, and sometimes Jim would come. Mostly though he'd invite me since I was the one with the great campfire stories.

In addition to, I got along better with Justin and Robbie—and with Mark for that matter. Jim was most of the time too serious except when we were playing golf or cruising in the San Juan Islands.

"Your journalism career really doesn't look good?" Mark inquired in a quiet, concerned voice.

"I was put out to pasture, like they used to do with broadcast journalists. It's just like they did to David Brinkley, when Chet Huntley died. They made him a "commentator." I take journalism seriously, always have and always will. I do my research . . . I tell the truth as I see it . . .

I looked from Mark to his pretty brunette wife Joan who I knew read the damned things because she would e-mail me when there was a typo—and then back to Mark.

"Out to pasture. And now they want to shoot me and feed me to the chickens."

"Don't let them shoot Uncle Bob!" cried Justin.

"Stupid!" said Robbie. "It's just a figure of speech." "Is that like a figure eight in skating?" Justin wanted to know.

"Kids, Uncle Bob is talking to us," chided Joan gently. "Let him talk."

"Let me have another one of these first, please." I held out my glass, and it was replenished.

I took a healthy—or unhealthy rather—come to think of it, swallow, and then continued in a very sarcastic manner.

"My good friends . . . I'm a reporter . . . I'm a reporter in the classic sense . . . I have a civic duty . . . My duty is to get the news, get the story to the people. I'm after the truth . . . because the truth is what keeps this country free. Not agendas. Not marketing. Not even politics, though I know about politics. The truth . . . the facts. Because with the truth and with the facts . . . justice is served. Justice is always served. And I am all about justice." I stopped, realizing that this was not the time or place for me to feel sorry for myself. Besides, nobody likes a whiner.

"So it's pretty ironic that justice isn't serving you," said Mark.

I shrugged. "I guess I saw it coming. The whole field of journalism has changed. Journalism isn't about factual news reporting anymore. The who, what, when, and where news that I know how to write, this approach to reporting is disappearing. It's become a media for selling the public on the political positions of the editors and owners of the various newspapers. The powers that be are in control of what people read and how it is slanted. And I've been so stubborn that I haven't kept up with the times even if I adamantly disagreed with this approach." Then I silently thought to myself, *Guess Jim Malone's values have served him well. Wish mine had.* And again I mentally admonished myself. *Damn, stop this whining attitude it's stupid and a waste of time.*

"You ought to write a book or something," said Joan deliberately, interrupting my moment of obvious melancholy. "You're a great writer."

"Oh, I'm working on books. Believe you me, but I'm losing my 'platform.'"

"Platform . . . you've got a political platform! That's for sure," said Joan in a supportive tone of voice.

"Not the kind the book biz yaps about all the time. Yeah, yeah, I'm working on a book of collected columns and that series of mine about the difference between politics on the East and West Coast is still a possibility." I shook my head. I realized I'd better slow down before the alcohol took over completely.

"No, I'm a reporter. I want to get back into the thick of it. I want to do crime reporting again for a few more good years. I love the stuff! And then use that to get into . . . I don't know, true crime books"

"Why can't you?" asked Mark.

"I got distracted . . . and forgot about the ambitious competition. And let me tell you, folks, there's some serious competition for bylines out there!"

"Well, whatever you decide to do I know you'll do well," said Joan with obvious concern in her voice and no patronization at all.

"Thanks" was about all the response I could summon up. Mark then jumped in with his own pearly words of wisdom.

"And take it from me, a guy who knows about opportunity and competition, Bob. Life's a damned funny business. You never know . . . maybe just the story you need may drop into your lap, and then you'll show 'em, won't you?"

I saluted them all again with my drink. "You're damned right I'll show them." I winked. "Now, what about those steaks?"

#

CHAPTER 6

JIM MALONE

The time you spend when you're waiting for an important phone call always seems to stretch on forever.

That's the way it felt, after the kidnapping. The clock hands hardly seemed to move.

A minute felt like an hour. Time does not fly by. You have no option except to sit and stare at the stupid phone.

Even if you try to concentrate on something else, your eyes eventually return to focus on the phone or the clock.

Stupid phone, RING!

That was everybody's private thought.

It certainly was my thought as I waited on that awful Saturday.

There was a Seattle Mariner baseball game on television we were halfheartedly trying to watch with no sound so we would be sure to catch the phone, if it ever rings. After pacing a while, Mark tried lying on the couch. No good. Nothing worked.

So like all of us, he had just sipped coffee all day—very black coffee.

Then finally, just before 11:00 p.m. Saturday night, the phone rang.

"Oh my god," gasped Joan. She leapt up to grab it.

"No. Wait," said Mark quickly before she could touch the phone. "It might be the kidnappers. The FBI said to let it ring four times."

It was sooner than the kidnappers said they would call. As instructed, Mark and Joan let it ring four times, giving the FBI time to turn their recording equipment on and hopefully enabling them to identify the caller and to trace the call location. They sprung into action the moment the phone completed its first ring. Before it completed the second ring, they were all in place, prepared to operate the equipment, just waiting for Mark to pick up the phone and answer.

After the fourth ring, Mark picked up the phone and answered. "Hello, Malone residence."

We could hear the conversation in the next room through a speaker they had installed.

The male voice was brusque and muted over the receiver.

"Listen closely. I'll call tomorrow with instructions. Be by your phone. Have the money ready. No cops or the boys die!"

The line then went dead. Mark stood there with the phone in his hand. He had no idea what to do. He hadn't even had a chance to say anything.

Agent Watkins responded first after getting a no headshake from the phone operator, shaking his head grimly. "I'm sure it was too brief to put a trace on it. The voice was not particularly identifiable other than I'm sure it was male. It was so short it could have even been a recording. We'll need a lot longer if we expect to get a trace. It wasn't your fault, Mark. The caller didn't give you a chance to do anything. We do know the call was made from a cell phone."

"Will that be traceable?" Jim asked.

"Yes and no," replied Agent Watkins. "There are so many variables with cell phones, and it'll take time to sort them out; besides, they're probably using a stolen phone. This probably is as much as we can expect to happen tonight. With your permission, Mark, I'm going to leave security at the entrance to your driveway plus at the front door, and we'll have the phones manned twenty-four hours a day just in case the kidnappers surprise us with another call. If any of our people have to answer the phone, they'll pretend they are you or Joan. I doubt this will become necessary, but we want to cover all possibilities. I hope this is all right with you and won't create too much of an inconvenience. Does this sound acceptable to you and Jim?"

Mark and I both agreed.

"Deanna and I are going to our house to pack some clothes. We'll be back as soon as possible and spend the night," I suggested.

Mark and Joan had already discussed this with Deanna, so for once they were way ahead of me.

Everything was arranged.

Deanna and I left their house.

When we got to our place, we quickly put everything together we would need for a few days.

Chief Hammond, Watkins, and his unneeded personnel departed, promising they would all return no later than eight Sunday morning. They stressed before their departure, if something unexpected happened, they both were to be contacted immediately, no matter what time of day.

They assured us that they would respond immediately.

Joan and Mark proceeded to make sure the remaining personnel had everything they would need to be comfortable during their long night. They set out coffee, water, soft drinks, snacks, and sandwiches. They then retired to their bedroom to wait up for our return. The guest bedroom was already prepared, so they just waited for us to return.

In about an hour we showed up, and all four of us sat in their bedroom and discussed the day's events for about an hour; and finally, exhausted, we all gave up and went to bed.

I wish I could say that I had pleasant dreams.

I did not.

#

CHAPTER 7

BOB ARNOTT

It was the second day of the trial.

I sat uneasily in my chair, wishing I'd eaten some breakfast to settle my stomach instead of drinking two large cups of heavily caffeinated Seattle coffee.

Jim Malone was dressed in a dark blue suit, white shirt, and dark maroon tie. He even looked big and vital sitting there, all six feet two inches, 230 pounds with no middle-age spread. It was evident he stayed in shape by working out.

I thought to myself, *Not bad for a man in his fifties.*

As Judge Arnold entered the courtroom from his chambers, the clerk announced to all those present. "All rise."

Up arose the obedient soldiers of society.

"Be seated," instructed Judge Arnold.

Dispassionately, the judge surveyed the assembly.

In my crime-reporting days, I had encountered Judge Arnold plenty of times. He accumulated a few more years of dust and grit since I'd viewed the old buzzard last, but it was the same old gristly bird.

Buzzard did I say?

More like an owl, what with those ancient black glasses, a beaky nose, and those round clear eyes that seemed not only to miss a thing, but to be seeking out some juicy mouse that might be scurrying about his courtroom. Judge Arnold was one of the finest judges in the country, and we were lucky to have him in the state of Washington. He looked a bit like Spencer Tracy at an older age, only with less hair.

He adjusted those specs of his as though there were focusing controls on them as he peered out into his domain—the court of law.

"I see both the prosecution and defense are present. I presume you both are prepared. So we'll proceed." He didn't wait for a response from either Ewing or

Shoemaker. The attorneys both understood what was expected of them. In its simplest Judge Arnold form, be ready for trial and they were.

He adjusted his glasses again and turned.

"Will the prosecution please call their first witness?"

The courtroom gallery was packed with news people, family, and a limited number of private citizens that waited in line outside the King County courthouse almost all night in the November Seattle rain to get a seat.

Robert Shoemaker, the district attorney, rose, walked from behind the prosecutors table, turned slowly around, and looked at the defendant—Jim Malone—and then redirected to face Judge Arnold. He was a tall stern dark young man with that lean and hungry look.

I'd seen him when he was a defense attorney, on the other side. He looked a bit like Sean Penn. Intense, ambitious, and maybe he appeared to be a little nuts in an academic way. He'd been a bit of a liberal radical in his college days. He claimed his work defending rich people prior to becoming a prosecutor made him realize justice tended to favor those with a lot of money. Hence, or so he claimed, his interest in prosecution enabled him to serve all of society. There, he said, he could help to keep the balance right on that blind woman's scales.

He turned back toward the twelve jurors, four men and eight women, two of whom were Afro-Americans and one who looked Hispanic.

I could tell he was probably thinking to himself, *Not a perfect jury from the prosecution's point of view.*

No doubt it was obvious to Shoemaker that Ewing had done a hell of a job in the jury selection. Then again he knew private citizens like Jim could afford better preparation for a trial of this magnitude. At least much more than the state could afford.

Jim, of course, had more to lose. His freedom, his family—maybe even his life.

Besides, Ewing only had one case on which to concentrate. Shoemaker's office had ten times that many. He was aware that none of the other pending cases were as important to his career as this one. Certainly once the kidnapping story broke and had attracted such total national attention by the media and the public in general, it took on a life of its own.

Shoemaker, if the truth were known, probably had mixed feelings about this trial because of what he knew the two victims had done to Robbie and Justin. Maybe his heart wasn't truly into prosecuting the individual accused of this crime. And to add to his concerns, for some unknown reason, there was somewhat of an ominous aura pervading the entire courtroom. A feeling kind of like a football game where all the fans were rooting for only one team, and it wasn't his. To Shoemaker, this was a strange sensation, one he had never encountered in previous trials. Maybe it was all the publicity. The stories in the media certainly were not favoring the prosecution. He didn't retain this line of thinking long because he was also aware of the trial's magnitude and importance it could have on his political future.

Whatever the situation, I could see him quickly shrugging off these negative rationalizations now as he stood, poised for the trial of his career. He was a pro. He knew his job is to prosecute criminals for their actions against society. And Jim Malone was one of those accused of criminal actions.

He'd killed two people, hadn't he?

However there was a perplexing problem still lingering—the legal authorities had not located the female perpetrator alive or dead. This was one of those loose ends that would not go away as the trial progressed and would continue to haunt Shoemaker and the rest of us.

The FBI was continuing a nationwide search for her. The FBI told Shoemaker they believed there was a strong probability she would be taken into custody before the trial was completed.

It was also somewhat curious to me that Ewing appeared unconcerned about this missing part of the crime.

At the same time, I could almost feel Shoemaker putting the Lois thing out of his mind for the time being and turning his focus on the task he was facing in presenting the case for the state of Washington.

Shoemaker had always been a person dedicated to his job, which to him was to uphold the law; and that's exactly what he was going to do. This combined with the attention this trial was receiving from the press, not only locally but also nationally kept him very focused. No doubt all of these things made him even more aware he had better be at his best.

And then if he nailed a rich, conservative bastard, so much the better.

"We call FBI Director Jack Watkins," said Shoemaker.

Director Watkins strode briskly to the front of the courtroom. After being sworn in, he took his seat in the witness chair.

I'd done my homework on all the people in this case.

Watkins had graduated from Yale with a law degree. Rather than practicing law in the courtroom or on a corporate level, he chose to join the FBI immediately after his graduation from law school. He'd been with the federal government for over thirty years. For the most part, his career had been quite successful; and now after over thirty years of service, he was approaching retirement. Solving this case, had he been successful, would have been an excellent conclusion to a great ride. He was like Shoemaker in that he had liberal roots, and he'd proven that a liberal could kick ass as well as Clint Eastwood's *Dirty Harry*.

However, this case had not gone well.

I could sense Watkins was hiding a deep anger with Jim Malone and the press. I'm sure he felt if Jim had stayed out of the way, he would have eventually found the children, captured the kidnappers, and prosecuted them. At least that's the attitude he expressed to the media. And the story Jim had concocted about the revelation he had revealing the location of his grandchildren was beyond anyone's comprehension. The news media ate it up, and the public bought the whole ball of wax because they wanted to believe in miracles. But Watkins knew it was all malarkey, made up by Jim for some reason known only to him. He knew revelations like that just don't happen.

However, Jim was unshakeable in his story, and the FBI had exhausted every avenue available in their attempt to discover how Jim succeeded when they had failed.

So Watkins had no alternative except to accept it at the time, and he moved ahead in his investigation. He'd known from the very beginning that this was a high-profile case. And if he had been successful in saving the kids and capturing the perpetrators, that success would have added a monumental star to his legacy.

However, such had not been the case.

Watkins gave up the one-million-dollars ransom. He didn't get the boys back. He'd let the kidnappers escape. Then to make matters even worse, an amateur apprehended and apparently killed them.

All of this happened right under his nose.

By then the press was on the story, and they did a number on the FBI and more specifically, on Jack Watkins, the area's FBI director.

Once the story broke, the media, as usual, made it into a soap opera. The TV, talk radio, and the newspapers had portrayed Jim Malone as somewhat of a folk hero. And they'd made Director Watkins look like an incompetent government buffoon.

I confess. I hadn't made him look too great either.

Oh yes, this is the kind of story that sells newspapers and attracts viewers to television and listeners to talk radio. They talked about and printed Jim's total background, including his tour in Vietnam. And they tried to get information about his activities when he was in the Special Forces, but most of this information was still highly classified. But since Jim's citations for bravery was public information, the press made up stories about his involvement in Nam. Jim hated these stories and expressed this to me frequently. However, at no time while the press was having a field day reporting the incompetent activities of the various participating government agencies, did Jim ever malign the FBI or Chief Hammond's Bellevue force? As a matter of fact, after his arrest and during the investigation, he was the epitome of cooperation.

Besides, it wasn't his nature to look backward; he had achieved what was his only real goal, and that was to rescue Justin and Robbie. His second desire was to make sure this would not happen again to some other family, at least not by these people.

Jim had known from the beginning, if the FBI failed, he wouldn't. From the very first day he knew he would need to know everything possible the FBI's investigation would uncover concerning the kidnappers in order to assist him in his own pursuit. He had to stay close to their investigation and be cooperative. They had no idea that in reality, Jim Malone, once the children were safe, was probably as qualified to go after these kidnappers as anyone involved. Certainly he was more dedicated.

Plus, he was able to utilize much of his construction team to assist in the search for the location of his grandsons. That combined with some information his son had privately imparted to him, gave him a distinct advantage over the investigation by the authorities.

This team coupled with his family, friends, the media, and a certain reporter, I—Bob Arnott—gave Jim a running head start over the professionals.

When the time came, I would break the story and keep it on the front page of the newspaper to the very end.

Like I said, all of this gave him more assistance than all the force the legal authorities could put on the case.

Factor in his crew almost to the man were Vietnam veterans who served as Jim had in Special Forces and had been hired by Jim in many cases for that specific reason. He knew they were dedicated in assisting him in any way he requested.

All of this should have worked, all this training, all this backup. But Jim had one flaw in his plan. Jim Malone had been trained to take no prisoners—and the prosecution knew it.

\#

CHAPTER 8

BOB ARNOTT

I well know, as a longtime crime reporter, one of the toughest parts of a kidnapping is the hours of waiting.

You wait.

Your mind continues to work, but it comes up empty. There's nothing on which to focus. You're helpless, and finally, your thinking comes to a complete standstill so you can't think about the kidnappers' threats.

That's what it must have been like for Jim Malone. He knew time was limited for Justin and Robbie and may be running out.

Every day, hour, minute, and second may mean life or death to the most precious beings in his life.

With these thoughts in his mind, Jim quietly went about his business of organizing eight of his construction crew into a search-and-find detail.

I presume Director Watkins and Chief Hammond obviously thought during this time he was just taking care of his construction business.

Jim made it clear to his crew that their specific mission was to find the location of his grandsons and report back to him and only to him. Not his son, the police, or the FBI—only to him. He also stressed the importance of keeping everything absolutely private. No talking to spouses, friends; and especially, he stressed they were to have zero communication with media people. Their only involvement, if it became apparent they were needed, would be to assist in finding the location of his grandchildren. The discovery and capture of the kidnappers would just be a bonus.

He wanted to be prepared to act whenever it became obvious that the authorities' investigation was failing or in his estimation moving too slow.

During these private meetings, he and Ed organized this team into a covert search-and-find group. This was what they had been trained to do when they were in the service of our country in Vietnam.

Now, maybe that training can now be put to good use.

I can just imagine Ed's hazel eyes lighting up. He was a squat, intensely well-built guy who worked with weights. He looked like Jack LaLanne, if LaLanne had been in Special Forces. Not calm though. Always looking for action, Ed was. He would clearly be thrilled to be of any help to Jim Malone, whom he idolized.

Certainly, the conditions and terrain were not the same, but the objectives would be similar and a lot more personal. Jim knew these men. He knew, if asked, they would even kill for him. This he absolutely would not ask them to do. Their involvement would be limited only to assisting in locating his grandchildren.

But that was then . . . and this was now.

The trial continued.

I watched and took notes, finding that my courtroom habits were starting to take hold of me again. I'm a smoker, and I sure as hell could never smoke in a courtroom, even in those wonderfully politically correct days when smokers could poison anyone they damned well pleased.

So I chewed gum. Juicy Fruit was the choice today. So far, my two sticks I was chomping on still had some flavor.

District Attorney Shoemaker proceeded to have FBI Director Watkins narrate all the events leading up to the money drop, their investigation of the kidnappers, search for the grandchildren, and what transpired after they went to Yakima and found the two kidnappers dead in the motor home.

Defense Attorney Ewing allowed the narration to completion without any objections and offered no cross-examination.

I could see Watkins left the witness stand with a total feeling of defeat. The somewhat cocky, confident air he usually maintained was gone. Still I knew there was an ace left up his sleeve, his nationwide search for the female kidnapper—Lois Griffin.

I could almost feel what was in his mind. He was thinking, if he could capture her before the trial was over, he was sure it would exonerate him and assist Shoemaker in his prosecution of Jim Malone. Then he would see what the reaction from the press and the public would be toward him. He thought it couldn't be anything other than favorable. In his mind it wasn't a personal vendetta; after all, it was his job to capture criminals and assist in their prosecution. Murderers and criminals like Jim Malone.

#

CHAPTER 9

BOB ARNOTT

During the dull stretches of the trial, I looked over the notes from my investigations.

THE KIDNAPPERS

In my mind's eye, I can see the scene.

In a nameless, tree-covered RV Park in a somewhat sordid area an hour and a half away from the deed, the people who had kidnapped the Malone children reconnoitered.

"Okay, we got the kids secured? Are you sure they can't get loose or see out at all?" asked the smaller of the two men, Fred.

Fred was blondish, slender, and slight with a small nose with a little fuzz under it and a knife slash for a mouth. His dark eyes seemed constantly darting around as though looking for something. He was a nervous man with nervous fidgets, and his shoulders were hunched over as though from the weight of his worry or from the drug-riddled life he had always led.

"Yeah, yeah, they can't move, and I really sealed it up and locked all the windows. Plus, they both have blindfolds on. Even Houdini couldn't get loose," bragged the other kidnapper, Dennis, Den for short.

Dennis was the antithesis of his partner. Big and hulking, he has a calm, stoic demeanor on his dark face. His movements were slow and considered, and his dark eyes were dull. His tattoos were amateurish with no obvious rhyme or reason to them and more than likely had been done when he was doing hard time.

"Besides, Lowee double-checked the ropes and everything. Didn't you, Lowee?"

Dennis always called her Lowee instead of Lois, which she intensely disliked. She thought, "Why does that asshole continue calling her this when she told him several times how much she hated it?"

Lois was a slender attractive woman in her early thirties, with dyed blond hair and faded discouraged blue eyes. Her perfectly formed face was marred by a touch of acne scars, which could be hidden by makeup, but weren't now. She had a nice figure with breasts and hips in perfect proportion. Tight clothes were her friends. Dolled up, Lois looked like a babe from one of those old fifties and sixties mystery paperbacks. She wasn't dolled up now, though, in loose jeans and a sweatshirt; she was still attractive, but obviously overworn by life.

"Fred, it's okay," she said. "The kids can't see a thing, and I'm sure they can't untie themselves."

"Just be sure to keep those blindfolds on even when they go to the can or eat," Fred said. "If they ever see us, we'll have to finish them off," he continued.

"Don't talk like that, you promised no one would get hurt," Lois said.

"Yeah, Fred, if we kill them, we would get the death penalty for sure," replied Dennis.

"Listen, shit-face, we're not getting caught," Fred said, exasperated. "I've got this down to a science, and besides, you can get the death penalty for kidnapping anyhow."

"What if they call the cops?" Dennis asked.

"It won't make any difference. They'll never trace us to these cell phones we bought from that guy in Portland." A smug grin split Fred's s pudgy face. "The guy assured me we could use them at least twice each without being traced, to be really safe we're supposed to destroy each one after using it a couple of times. What was even neater about him was he didn't ask and didn't care why we wanted them. The only thing he cared about was the money, a thousand bucks it cost me, cash in advance. But remember, we have to get this all done in a couple days or they won't be useful. Besides, after we get the money, before they figure out anything about the phones, we'll be long gone, down the road to life of luxury."

They were all in a thirty-six-foot RV motor home with the children secured in the back bedroom. They were drinking cold Budweiser beer from long-neck bottles. Lois's was almost gone. She knew she would need another.

A burnt smell wafted throuogh the gingham curtains on a warm early fall breeze. The air-conditioning wasn't working in this room, but was going full blast in the back room—and not just for the cooling effect.

Fred smiled as he continued, "I've got a foolproof plan for getting the money delivered. I know it can't fail; and once we get the money, we're off to a life of luxury. Just stick with me, and you'll both have more money than you ever dreamed of." He added, "Lois, why don't you take a look-see at those brats and make sure they're tied really securely and their mouths are taped."

"Fred, for god's sake stop worrying about whether they're tied up good, they are. And even if they got loose, they can't see out; and besides, the doors are locked so they can't go anywhere." Lois put the emphases on the word good. She knew it wasn't the correct word to use, but Fred didn't react. Instead, he continued his harangue, "Don't be so fucking stupid. If they were to get loose, think about what could happen, like what if they yelled and someone heard them and called the cops. Good-bye reward, hello jail. You guys are fucking lucky that I'm the brains of this outfit or we'd probably be in the slammer already." He finished off his beer, lobbed the bottle into the garbage can by the front door, and continued, "We probably should move our asses to a new location tomorrow." Maybe we can do a state park by the sound or something. Better yet we'll go to that tribal casino over by Marysville. I'm getting tired of the diesel smell down here in this hole you call an RV park. While we're waiting, I'm going to check it out; and since it's just off Interstate 5 coming down from Canada, we should blend in pretty good."

"Hey! Don't knock it, you said to find a cheap one and one that would put us way down on the end away from the others and leave room for the pickup," Dennis said, in a feeble attempt at standing up to Fred.

"Yeah . . . yeah . . . but what a hole. How long did you pay for our stay, and what did you tell them?" Fred asked.

"I told them we were heading south to Texas and we're just stopping to visit friends for a few days just like you told me to do," replied Dennis. "I paid them for four days just as you told me to do. I'm sure they bought it." Fred turned away from Dennis on the second just like you told me to do; and all he could think of was, "what am I going to do with this stupid bastard for a week or two or until this whole deal is over."

"The kids are fine," Lois said as she came out of the back bedroom. "The little one finally stopped crying and the big one seems to be struggling less. I put some salve on his arm where you cut him, Dennis."

"Hey, it was just a nick, he put up a real fight for such a little runt," said Dennis smugly and added, "How are we going to get rid of them anyhow?"

"If everything goes without a hitch, we're going to leave them in a packing crate that was left in an abandoned old boat warehouse I found down by Scott Paper Company in Everett. Talk about luck. It's perfect, no one around. And, Dennis, you can fix one side with a door and a lock; you'll find everything you need to do the job in that box in the pickup bed. Screws, hinges, locks, tools, the works, just make sure you're not seen by anyone when you're fixing it. Do the job right and make sure the door is reinforced so they won't be able to kick their way out. It'll work just fine. Besides, right now, I've got to get going; I've got to call and get the money drop worked out. We need to get this all wrapped up by

Sunday night. If everything goes right, we can get on the road Monday, Labor Day or Tuesday at the very latest. We want to be moving in the Labor Day traffic. It all has to be timed perfectly, and we'll be rich," Fred said and then continued, "Just have everything ready, and do exactly what I laid out for you both so we can get out of here just as soon as we get the money. Don't screw up. And, Dennis, don't try to think. That's when you get in trouble."

He continued talking in a braggadocio manner, gesturing animatedly and didn't take notice of the hateful look on Dennis's pock-riddled face.

"This will go down as one of the slickest kidnapping ever. We really lucked out when Lois worked at the hospital where that Malone broad did her public service work. I mean she told Lois everything. Where the grandkids lived, their tree house where they played, how rich and successful they were. Boy was she a talker. I mean she laid the plan out for us, perfectly. The mutt was the only thing she left out. He damned near took my foot off. I mean he can really bite. Damn mutt got my whole shoe and a little skin, before I got a couple good shots at him with my knife and you rapped him on the noggin. He sure went out like a light. I was afraid, the way he was going at me he was going to screw the whole thing up. What a vicious bastard!"

"Yeah, I whacked him pretty good. You think he's dead?" said Dennis with a faint dull smile.

"Who cares, dogs can't talk," replied Fred, smiling for saying something so clever. "I think I'll call them tonight before eleven and get 'em moving. Then if the cops are around, maybe they won't be on their toes. I hate to keep saying it, but these cell phones we got from that guy really are great. You can make calls on them from anywhere even while you're moving. We just have to be sure we destroy them after a day or two, and I'll make the calls from places that will lead them offtrack just in case they do trace the tower location from where the call originates or however these damn things work. But even if they do happen to trace them, they'll probably find them under some dumb jerk's name in Portland or Spokane or wherever they came from. Then when I rotate phones before each call, it'll really confuse them and should make it even tougher to trace."

#

BOB ARNOTT

In my mind's eye, I can see the kidnappers' self-satisfied smiles. What a clever, clever plan! I'll give them that.

#

CHAPTER 10

BOB ARNOTT

The buzz of conversation died as Judge Arnold slammed his gavel. "The court will come to order!" His steely gaze swept out over the courtroom. It had a calming effect, no one dared to utter a peep; it was obvious who was in control and then he asked, "Is the prosecution ready to call its next witness?"

I swiveled my head a bit and stretched. I'd learned some isometric exercises to help me stay in one place for a long time. The exercises were now a relief to my strained muscles. In truth, I was looking forward to this part. I knew he was going to call Chief Hammond next. Police were always interesting to watch testify; normally they are very careful and precise. I'd known Chief Hammond for years, and in my estimation, he was an excellent cop.

"We are ready, Your Honor. We call the Bellevue chief of police, John Hammond said the district attorney.

"Will Police Chief John Hammond please come forward and take the stand?" said the court clerk.

John Hammond rose and strolled forward. He was dressed in his official blue uniform and looked every inch the professional. The court clerk swore him in, and he was seated in the docket.

DA Shoemaker began his questioning, "Chief Hammond, would you state for the record what is your current position and what responsibilities does this entail."

Hammond raised his dark eyebrows. "I am chief of the Bellevue police department and oversee a staff comprised of over two hundred people that includes traffic enforcement, detectives for crime investigation, narcotics, and support people."

Shoemaker then asked, "How many years have you been a police officer?"

Hammond responded, "Thirty-one years."

J. Edgar Ewing rose and interrupted Shoemaker, "Judge, the defense will stipulate; Chief Hammond is an experienced and extremely qualified police officer with impeccable credentials."

During my career as a crime reporter, there have been hundreds of hours just sitting and watching court cases. During this time, needless to say, there was plenty of time to doodle or to be just plain bored. However, any case I watched involving J. Edgar Ewing was never boring. I always like to think of J. Edgar as kind of a Clarence Darrow for our age.

At seventy, he was gray and clearly not as spry as he'd once been. However, the clear gray eyes still sparkled when he took off wire-rimmed spectacles from his Roman nose and his long face if anything seemed wiser than ever. The bald spot on the back of his head seemed larger, and he was clearly older; but otherwise, he appeared to be very much the J. Edgar Ewing of yore. Shoemaker, well, he's a different breed of cat.

"So noted," said the Judge. "Mr. Shoemaker, please move on with your witness."

DA Shoemaker liked this response. He smiled a half smile and continued, "Chief Hammond, would you relate to the court what took place in your office on September 9 this year?"

Hammond thought for a moment, checked his notebook he had brought, and then began, "At around nine o'clock that morning, Jim Malone came into my office and reported we might find the two kidnappers of his grandchildren, tied up in a motor home just outside Yakima, Washington, in the RV parking lot at the Yakima Indian Casino." He paused for an instant, saw no reaction from Shoemaker, so he continued, "I asked him how he knew this, and he commented that was where he had left them."

Hammond then stopped and looked back at his notebook. "Did he say anything about their condition?" Shoemaker asked.

Chief Hammond referred to his notebook again before replying. "Yes, after I questioned him about what happened and how he was able to find them, he briefly said he had tracked them to that location, subdued them, and had left them tied up for me and Director Watkins. He said he would leave their arrest up to us, and I could take it from there. He also told me his participation was completed."

"Those were his exact words, nothing about their condition?"

Chief Hammond nodded and then answered, "Yes, those were his exact words, but he did say we ought to hurry while they were still breathing and said they had sustained some minor injuries."

Is this Jim Malone in the courtroom today?" Shoemaker moved to his right, enabling Chief Hammond to have an unimpeded view of Jim.

"Yes, he is. He is sitting right there!" Hammond pointed at Jim Malone, the defendant.

"Let the record show," Shoemaker said, "the witness has identified James Malone, as the person who, on the morning of September 9, reported the whereabouts of a motor home containing two bodies."

Ewing rose to his feet and said loudly, "Objection, Your Honor. The defendant did not at any time say that's where two bodies were. The prosecutor and Chief Hammond both know the defendant said that's where two kidnappers could be found alive, and they might have incurred some minor injuries!"

The judge sustained the objection.

Shoemaker rephrased his point with another question, implying that Jim had confessed to doing damage to the kidnappers. Ewing again objected even more emphatically that at no time did Jim confess to doing any harm to the so-called victims. He said they had sustained some minor injuries and did not confess to causing these minor injuries. He only admitted to subduing them and left them alive for the authorities. Judge Arnold confirmed the objection and sternly directed Shoemaker to abandon this line of questioning and to move on. Shoemaker appeared somewhat annoyed by Judge Arnold's decision, but with no other recourse, continued his examination of Chief Hammond.

"After you went to the location of the motor home, as directed by the defendant, would you tell the court what you found?"

"We entered the motor home and found two bodies in the living room," replied Hammond somewhat solemnly.

Shoemaker probed further, "Could you describe the condition of the bodies?"

"As I said, we found two bodies, both had gunshot wounds to the right side of their heads, and they were missing the thumbs on their right hands."

Shoemaker then asked Hammond to describe the condition of the inside of the motor home. Chief Hammond said there was a considerable amount of blood around the bodies from the gunshot wounds and maybe because their thumbs had been amputated. And other than that, the inside was intact.

Shoemaker then turned directly to the twelve people in the jury box and said, "Chief Hammond, let's make it very clear to the jury. On September 9 at about 9:00 AM, according to your testimony, James Malone, the accused, entered your office and reported to you the whereabouts of two people, who the authorities were looking for, and indicated that they may have suffered some injuries. Is that correct?"

Chief Hammond responded with one word yes.

J. Edgar started to object then decided even though this statement was not totally accurate there was no way it could cause problems to the defense or later during his cross-examination, so he sat back down. "Was there anything else unusual about the two bodies other than they were missing their thumbs?"

"No," Hammond said. He paused, drawing in a breath and continued, "Like I said, just that they had been shot in the head, and it was obvious their thumbs had been recently amputated."

There were a few gasps in the courtroom.

I knew this fact. Many people did not.

Shoemaker let this sink in on the jury. I could tell it had made an impression on members of the jury.

"Did the missing thumbs cause you to make a connection to the defendant?"

Hammond responded in a monotone, noncommittal voice, "Both his grandchildren had their little fingers cut off by the kidnappers."

Shoemaker continued, "Is it your belief that the defendant cut off their thumbs in retaliation, revenge, for what they had done to his grandchildren; and after chopping off their thumbs, he then shot them?"

"Objection!" Ewing quickly yelled as he rose out of his chair obviously irritated at Shoemaker for such a bush move.

"The prosecutor is leading the witness. Furthermore, I object to the use of the prosecution's words *retaliation*, *revenge*, and *chop*. They are neither admissible nor relevant, and whether Chief Hammond thinks the defendant killed them or not is definitely not acceptable. He can only testify to what the evidence shows or proves." Judge Arnold responded, "I agree. The defense's entire objection is sustained."

Then he looked directly at the jury and said, "The jury will totally disregard the last question." He swiveled to face Shoemaker. "Does the prosecutor wish to rephrase this question or move on?"

"I'll withdraw the question, Your Honor," said Shoemaker. He turned back to the witness. "Were you able to find the weapon that was used to murder these two individuals?"

"Yes, we did," Hammond answered in his official police chief voice.

Shoemaker followed with another question, "Would you tell the court how and where the weapon was found?"

Hammond sighed and closed his eyes as though he had to think for a second before he could call up the memory how they had retrieved the weapon. "In our search of the premises, we located it in the bottom of one of the dumpsters at the Yakima Tribal Casino."

"And how did you ascertain that this was the weapon used in the murders?"

"We test fired it, and the bullets we retrieved were a perfect match to the bullets we removed from the victims when they were tested by the FBI's ballistic experts."

"Were there any fingerprints on the weapon?" pressed Shoemaker. Hammond answered, "No, it had been wiped clean."

The DA then turned and walked slowly back to the prosecutor's table and picked up a plastic bag containing a revolver. He carried the gun back toward Hammond and asked, "Would you examine this gun and tell us if you can verify this was the murder weapon you found in the dumpster at the Yakima Casino." Shoemaker handed the weapon to Hammond.

Hammond examined the revolver carefully.

"Yes, this is the same weapon we retrieved from the dumpster. It's a .38-caliber Smith and Wesson revolver."

"And you're positive it's the weapon that was tested by the FBI, and these tests verified it was the one used to commit these two murders?"

Hammond, "That's correct."

Shoemaker, "How can you be sure?"

"It has my ID mark on it right there." Chief Hammond pointed to an ID mark on the weapon. Shoemaker showed it to the judge, jury, and the defense council. J. Edgar barely acknowledged that Shoemaker showed it to him.

Shoemaker continued, "I would like this marked as exhibit A please."

Judge Arnold turned to J. Edgar and asked, "Has the defense examined the exhibit?"

Ewing stood and responded, "Yes, we have, Your Honor; and we have no objections."

"Will the clerk please mark this as exhibit A," instructed Judge Arnold.

Shoemaker continued, "Chief Hammond, did you discover anything else at the crime scene?"

"Yes, we found a surgical scalpel along with other items we believe were used in the crime."

"And what significance did the scalpel have to the crime?" Shoemaker asked.

"We surmised it was used for the removal of the victims' thumbs."

"Objection!" cried Ewing and elaborated. "The prosecution has not laid any foundation for or how the kidnappers' thumbs were removed, and that this was the instrument used."

"That's true. Objection sustained," said the judge.

"Let me redirect, Judge," said Shoemaker. "Chief Hammond, what made you arrive at the conclusion that this scalpel was used to remove the thumbs of the victims?"

Hammond answered, "The FBI labs ran blood tests and DNA tests, and both were perfect matches to both victims." Shoemaker continued, "Were you able to locate the victim's thumbs?" Hammond, "No, we were unable to find them." For some reason some of the court spectators found a little humor to the last statement and laughed out loud. Judge Arnold rapped his gavel, glared at the gallery until they settled down, and then instructed Shoemaker to continue.

Shoemaker stopped for a minute, pondering whether he should inquire more on this subject waited for just a second more and quickly moved to his next question. "Let me now ask you, Chief, is it your professional opinion that these murders were committed by the defendant, Jim Malone?"

J. Edgar was anticipating Shoemaker would at sometime try to slip something like this into the trial, and he quickly rose to object. "Objection! Your Honor, there is no proof that Mr. Malone had anything at all to do with these murders, and Chief Hammond's opinion is definitely not admissible as evidence." He thought to himself, who in the hell does Shoemaker think he's up against, some rank amateur.

"Objection sustained," the judge ruled. "The jury is instructed to disregard any reference to Chief Hammond's opinion and to the question asked by the prosecutor."

"I have no further questions for this witness, Your Honor." Shoemaker then returned to his seat, looking smug and happy with his own performance.

Judge Arnold peered over the rims of his glasses at J. Edgar Ewing.

"Does the defense counsel wish to cross-examine the witness?"

"Yes, we do, Your Honor. We certainly do have some questions of this witness," J. Edgar Ewing said as he rose slowly from behind his table, glanced at Jim Malone, walked toward the witness docket, and directed his attention very deliberately and with a somewhat concerned look toward Chief Hammond. Ewing had a focused and earnest aspect to his face. It was the look of a man who seemed determined that Justice would not go awry.

"Let's see if we heard you correctly, Chief Hammond. You said Mr. Malone, the defendant, came into your office and informed you as to the exact location of what he thought were two of the kidnappers. Is that correct?"

Chief Hammond affirmed this was what Jim had said. "Yes, sir, that is correct."

"Were these people of interest to you?" asked Ewing.

Hammond, "Yes, they were."

Ewing, "In what way were they of interest to you?"

"Objection!" said Shoemaker. "The question is purely irrelevant."

"Your Honor," said Ewing, "the defense thinks it's important to specifically identify the two people Chief Hammond referred to in his earlier testimony and why the authorities were trying to locate them."

"Identify, yes," said Shoemaker. "Discuss or allude to other action, no."

"Your Honor, it's our contention that Chief Hammond, the FBI, and several other legal organizations were pursuing these people in conjunction with the kidnapping of Mr. Malone's grandsons." J. Edgar loved this discourse in front of the jury. Shoemaker was allowing him to control the flow. Great!

"Objection!" cried Shoemaker. "It has not been proven in any court of law that these two people were involved in the kidnapping of Mr. Malone's grandsons."

Judge Arnold said, "I'm going to sustain the objection, please move on, Mr. Ewing."

"Then let me rephrase the question. Chief Hammond, after you discovered the bodies of these two people, did you later identify them as suspects in any continuing criminal investigation from your office?"

Shoemaker stood and loudly said, "Objection, on the same grounds, Your Honor!"

"Overruled, I'll allow the question," declared Judge Arnold. "Please be seated, Mr. Shoemaker. You may answer the question, Chief Hammond."

Shoemaker sat back down, obviously irritated by the judge's ruling.

"Yes," Chief Hammond continued. "We were able to ascertain later, after discovering the bodies and some of the ransom money we found in the motor home and with information we obtained from casino employees, that these people were the suspects we were pursuing in our investigation of the said kidnapping."

J. Edgar thought again to himself, *Thank you very much, Mr. Shoemaker, you're making my job much easier*. He continued, "I ask you now, so it can be perfectly clear to the jury ... did Mr. Malone tell you precisely where you could locate these kidnappers?" Chief Hammond responded with a simple yes. Shoemaker objected on the grounds that Chief Hammond had already answered that question in previous testimony.

For some reason, Judge Arnold overruled the objection. J. Edgar continued with his cross, "Isn't it a fact that the defendant specifically told you where the live kidnappers were, not where you would find the bodies?"

Hammond said, "That's correct." J. Edgar then asked, "In your opinion, does that sound like something a man who just committed murder might do?" Before Hammond could even begin to answer the question, Shoemaker objected on grounds that the chief's opinion was inadmissible. J. Edgar started to raise an argument but knew it was a waste of time, and as he suspected, Judge Arnold sustained the objection and instructed the jury to disregard the question. "Was it your department that discovered the bodies?" asked J. Edgar.

Hammond responded, "Not entirely."

Ewing pondered this answer and asked, "Then who did discover them, and what was your involvement?"

Chief Hammond looked at his notebook and then responded, "Actually, when Mr. Malone reported to us their location, we notified Director Watkins of the FBI and accompanied him and the FBI agent in the Yakima area, along with the sheriff of Yakima County and some Yakima Tribal Police to the motor home where Mr. Malone indicated they would be found."

"You mean the kidnappers weren't actually found in your jurisdiction?" asked Ewing.

"That's correct," said Hammond; and Ewing then asked, "Tell us again, at what exact location you actually found the bodies?"

Hammond's answer was with a tone in his voice, I'm getting tired of this, "In a motor home that was in the parking area for RVs at the Yakima Tribal Casino, just outside Yakima, Washington." Shoemaker objected that the question was redundant and that the defense attorney was wasting Chief Hammond's and the court's time by repeating question after question. This time Judge Arnold sustained the objection and instructed Ewing to move into new territory.

Ewing continued, totally ignoring Shoemaker's objection, "Was there anything else at the scene?"

Hammond answered, "Yes, we found a metal suitcase containing money."

"How much money?" asked Ewing.

"A little more than two hundred thousand dollars," answered Hammond.

Ewing followed, "Were you able to verify where this money came from?"

Hammond, "Yes, we had recorded many of the serial numbers of the money Mr. Malone paid the kidnappers, and much of the money we recovered in the motor home corresponded with those numbers."

Ewing then asked, "I thought that he paid a million dollars. What happened to the missing amount?"

"Apparently, they stopped at various casinos and proceeded to gamble with a lot of it. Then we surmised that the third perpetrator, a woman we later were able to identify as Lois Griffin skipped with at least her share." He added, "We are currently pursuing the woman."

"Objection!" said Shoemaker. "Your Honor, it has not been substantiated that these victims had even been in the casino or that the woman had received any of the ransom money, or even if there was a woman involved!"

This objection caused Judge Arnold to have a sidebar out of hearing distance from the jury so he could quietly admonish both counsels to cease nit-picking and unnecessarily delaying the proceedings.

The sidebar was completed, and the trial continued.

Judge Arnold said, "I'll sustain the objection. Will the defense proceed with his examination of this witness?"

Ewing said, "Let me rephrase the question, Judge." He turned back to Hammond. "How were you able to verify that the suspects had been in the casino?"

"After we discovered the bodies, the FBI, the Yakima County Sheriff, and I proceeded to the casino; and after questioning the casino manager and various employees, we were able to reconstruct the fact that the two men, the ones murdered, were in the company of a female and had been gambling almost all day and into the evening at the casino. We also traced them to the Colville Tribal Casino known as the Mill Bay Casino in Manson and the Spokane Tribal Casino located on the Columbia River called the Two Rivers Casino. They apparently had wagered fairly large sums of money at the crap tables and playing blackjack at all those locations, according to our interviews with casino employees. We also recovered some money from these casinos that corresponded with serial numbers from the ransom money."

Ewing started to pursue the ransom part but instead asked, "Didn't the woman gamble?"

"According to the casino employees, she just watched, played nickel slot machines; and if she did any other gambling, it was sparingly and went unnoticed," Hammond answered.

Ewing, "Why do you think Mr. Malone didn't remove the remaining money after he allegedly found it with the kidnappers?"

Hammond said, "I don't know. You'd have to ask him."

Ewing, "Didn't you ask him during your investigation?"

Hammond, "Yes."

Ewing, "And what was his response?"

"His only comment was it wasn't about money."

"Chief Hammond, could you more specifically describe where exactly were the bodies located in the motor home when you found them?"

"The bodies were in the main living room."

"Was there anything else unusual about the bodies?"

"Not really."

"How were they killed?"

"Objection, Your honor," declared Shoemaker. "Mr. Ewing is again covering ground uselessly. The witness has already answered those questions in prior testimony."

"Objection sustained," said the judge. "The prosecutor is correct, please move on, Mr. Ewing."

Ewing somewhat ignored the judge and continued, "Was there any sign of a struggle?"

Hammond responded in a tone that showed he was getting annoyed at Ewing, "None to speak of."

Ewing shook his head in disbelief. "How was that possible, one man against three?"

Chief Hammond immediately answered, "I believe that whoever killed them had some kind of special training and was able to subdue the two men without any apparent difficulty." "Uh-oh!" J. Edgar thought, *I trapped myself, I didn't want that response.* Ewing immediately turned to the judge and requested that Hammond's response be stricken from the record and also asked the jury be instructed to disregard Hammond's opinion as to who killed them and what training may have been involved. Shoemaker then objected, and Judge Arnold reacted rapidly by sustaining Shoemaker's objection and at the same time partially complied with J. Edgar's request and instructed the jury to disregard Hammond's comment about special training and then instructed Hammond not to editorialize.

And of course, I thought grimly, Jim was in Special Forces; and once again, it was imbedded in the jury's subconscious. One more bit of evidence against him. And so far there was a lot of evidence to that effect. J. Edgar doesn't screw up often, but I thought he did this time.

J. Edgar took a moment to walk back to the defense table and perused a notepad for a brief moment. He was aware he had messed up but hoped he could fix the problem. He then turned around to face Chief Hammond and then asked, "Chief Hammond, after you discovered the gun in the dumpster and later your tests confirmed it was the one used in killing the two kidnappers, were you able to ascertain whether or not Mr. Malone even had access to this weapon?" Hammond looked a little befuddled and squirmed in his chair before he answered J. Edgar's question. He finally answered, "We surmised it had been in the possession of the kidnappers and was more than likely already in the motor home when Mr. Malone entered it on the evening of the murders." J. Edgar responded rapidly, "You surmised! Let me remind you, Chief Hammond. This is a murder trial. There is no place for surmising." Shoemaker stood up immediately and objected to J. Edgar's comments as irrelevant and asked the judge to instruct him to refrain from badgering the witness. Judge Arnold agreed and so instructed J. Edgar to comply. J. Edgar looked a little dismayed; this was on purpose and then he continued, "About the gun—" Before he could continue, he was interrupted by Judge Arnold, "Mr. Ewing, let me interrupt you for a minute. It's past 4:00 PM, do you anticipate the remainder of your cross-examination of this witness to last much longer?

J. Edgar answered immediately, "Yes, Your Honor. There's a lot more items this witness needs to clarify, especially those concerning the gun."

Judge Arnold started talking and was glancing at his watch at the same time. "In that case, due to the lateness of the day, I'm going to terminate today's proceedings; we'll excuse the jury, and you can continue tomorrow morning promptly at 9:00 AM. Court is adjourned." It seemed a little odd to me that the judge cut today's session a little short, but no one seemed to object. The room cleared in minutes. I guess maybe everyone wanted to beat the traffic.

#

CHAPTER 11

JIM MALONE

During Ewing's extensive cross-examination of Hammond, I began mentally reviewing the trail I'd followed in the pursuit of the scumbags responsible for the kidnapping.

After it had become obvious to me the FBI's investigation was consuming too much time, at least in my way of thinking, I came to the conclusion the authorities were not succeeding, and time for Robbie and Justin was becoming a major factor.

Even if they were successful, my grandchildren probably wouldn't last that long. Time was running out.

Frankly, I didn't even know for sure if they were still alive.

I couldn't deal with that particular thought, so it was quickly eliminated. I refused even to consider that possibility.

The methods of the authorities, as usual, were too bureaucratic and much too ponderous, so I had no other option. I had to put my team in full pursuit and maybe get Bob Arnott more involved.

The drop had been completed. No grandsons had been produced.

I thought from the outset that this could possibly happen.

I wanted to be ready before too much time elapsed.

I remember the evening well.

The final call came early—Sunday night. The kidnappers gave Mark instructions on how he was to make the delivery.

What they didn't know was that I would be the one making the drop.

I'd insisted on this.

And after much heated argument with Mark, Hammond, and Watkins, they all finally agreed I was much more qualified to handle the situation in case something went wrong.

It was their feeling since Mark and I looked very similar, even if the kidnappers were watching or had lookouts at the drop location, they wouldn't be able to tell the difference and, in all probability, wouldn't really even care as long as they got their money. Especially since they presumed the drop time would probably be at night. Plus, we factored in an assumption since their contact with us had always been via the phone, therefore they may never have actually ever seen either one of us in person.

And, as it turned out, these assumptions proved to be correct.

Ah yes, the call!

It was Sunday, September 1, Labor Day weekend.

A night when the highways would be jammed with people because of the long weekend, that made it even more difficult for any planned or coordinated surveillance.

The phone rang at 8:30 p.m.

Again, Mark answered after four rings.

The authorities went through their usual tracking procedure.

A kidnapper instructed us to put all the money in the metal suitcase the cabdriver had delivered with their other gift and take it to the corner of Lake Hills Boulevard and 156th NE. He said we had only forty-three minutes from right then. We were fully prepared to act when we received this phone call; the money was already in the suitcase, and I had listening and tracking devices on my body and my SUV. When the call came, it was brief and to the point. We were told to be at a specific location in forty-five minutes. I left immediately. I arrived at the prescribed location in Lake Hills about eight minutes early. I parked and got out of the SUV and waited. Other than the usual traffic, there didn't appear to be anyone around, so I just stood outside my vehicle and waited for something to happen. I had no idea what that would be. The moment was unbearable, but my only option was to stand there and see what would take place.

Watkins and Hammond said they would have officers undercover nearby watching every move I made. I must admit, I couldn't even spot them, and I knew they were there.

Then the phone rang at the nearby minimart outside phone booth. As I looked around, there was nobody but me in the immediate area, so I answered it. The voice said I was being stupid by having the cops there. This I denied as instructed by Director Watkins and then the voice on the other end of the line said for me to ditch the cops and head for the restaurant at the Bellevue Inn on 112th, and that I had thirty minutes to get there. The voice also told me to leave the police wire he knew I had and my cell phone in the phone booth or the kids would die. My immediate thought was this guy knows his stuff, and I couldn't comprehend how he could see me. I thought he must be well hidden because the police apparently couldn't locate where he was hiding either. It didn't even occur to me that he wasn't even there and was only guessing. I knew the cops would be upset, but I did as I was instructed—tore off the wire, the listening device, and left them with my cell phone in the booth.

Then I quickly jumped in my SUV and headed for the Bellevue Inn.

I was sure Hammond and Watkins heard my part of the conversation and would already be putting people in place at the Bellevue Inn. Besides, the tracking device they installed on my SUV was still intact, so I knew they could track me while I was driving.

Just as I walked into the lobby of the restaurant, I spotted a pay phone right by the entrance. Because of the other call and minus my cell phone, I anticipated the kidnapper would repeat what he had done at Lake Hills.

Sure enough, no sooner had I walked into the lobby area and headed for the pay phone, it started to ring.

I picked it up and a voice said immediately, "You had better be clean now . . . no more cops . . . look under the phone . . . there's a cell phone taped underneath . . . take it with you and head for the Hyatt on NE Eighth . . . be in the men's downstairs bathroom off the lobby in twenty minutes with the money . . . no cops and don't use the cell phone . . . if I call you on it and it's busy, the kids die!"

I again did exactly as instructed, grabbed the cell phone they had left, jumped in my SUV once more, and headed for the Bellevue Hyatt. Perspiration was starting to get in my eyes as I drove as fast as traffic would allow in downtown Bellevue. I could only hope the police were still tracking me and could be in position to observe what may be happening.

I drove directly in front of the Hyatt and parked in the passenger unload zone, grabbed the suitcase of money and cell phone, and walked through the front entrance and directly to the bathroom just off the lobby as instructed. I told the doorman I would just be a minute and handed him a ten. Just as I walked into the bathroom, I checked my watch . . . exactly twenty minutes had passed.

At that precise moment, the cell phone rang. The kidnappers' luck was running true to form, the bathroom was empty. I immediately answered the cell phone.

The voice then said, "You're doing good so far . . . now listen carefully and you'll have your kids back soon . . . . go to the last stall on the end and you'll find another identical suitcase . . . set the money one down and leave it in the stall and take the new one . . . then drive to Hector's Restaurant in Kirkland . . . . take the cell phone with you . . . wait in the bar at Hector's, and I'll call you in forty-five minutes and confirm I have the money . . . don't stop anywhere, and make sure you keep out of contact with the cops . . . If everything goes right, I'll tell you where the kids are . . . don't do anything dumb if you want them alive . . . and remember don't use the cell phone to tip the cops . . . you have forty-five minutes."

Again, I did exactly as instructed. My thoughts at the moment were positive. Maybe we were going to get Robbie and Justin back.

I exchanged suitcases and left the Hyatt immediately. There wasn't any way I could communicate with Watkins or Hammond about where I had left the money; and besides, I didn't care about it, I only wanted to have Robbie and Justin returned as soon as possible. This appeared to be a possibility at the time. I was now perspiring profusely, so I rolled all the windows down and let the damp Seattle air cool me down. I preferred the fresh air rather than the air-conditioning. The adrenaline was pumping, and undoubtedly, my blood pressure was rising.

I got to Hector's in Kirkland, parked, and went into the cocktail lounge. As usual, it was pretty crowded; but I found a bar stool at the very end, ordered a beer so hopefully I wouldn't be too conspicuous and waited . . . praying the kidnappers would keep their promise and call and tell me where we would find Robbie and Justin. Forty-five minutes passed . . . then an hour. And I still waited. My thoughts were becoming negative. I knew it; the kidnappers were lying and escaping without keeping their word. I couldn't think of anything else to do but sit there, sip on my Bud, and wait . . . Another thirty minutes passed and then the cell phone they had left me rang. I quickly got up and walked out the back entrance to a patio area as I was answering it.

The voice on the other end said, "You did good . . . except you had the cops with you all the way . . . DUMB . . . For that stupid mistake, you'll have to wait till tomorrow . . . We got the money and the kids are still alive . . . but don't do anything foolish again tonight, like trying to find me. You've already fucked up enough. That's if you ever want to see your kids again. I'll call you in the morning on your home phone and tell you where to find your brats."

With that final statement, the line went dead.

I knew it . . .

I knew they wouldn't keep their part of the bargain!

How was I ever going to face Mark and Joan, not to mention Deanna?

There now was no option. If I didn't do something, and do it soon, everything I cared about could be gone.

I realized now there was no choice left. The authorities had their way, now I needed to move more aggressively personally. The decision was made for me. The kidnappers had left no other options.

I called Chief Hammond on his cell phone from the pay phone at Hector's. He answered in one ring. Before he could utter a word, I blurted out what had happened.

"John, they got the money!"

"When? How?" He fired both questions simultaneously, so they sounded like one word; and without waiting for an answer, he continued, "We didn't see anyone. We knew you were solo when we lost wire contact; then our surveillance team found your cell phone and the wire at the Lake Hills site, but you were never out of someone's sight, and we tracked your SUV all the way to Hector's . . . what went wrong?"

I then explained the scenario at the Hyatt and the last phone call.

Hammond responded dejectedly, "We all screwed up, Jim. Our men saw you jump back in your rig at the Hyatt with the suitcase when you headed for Kirkland on Lake Washington Boulevard and ended up at Hector's. We didn't bother searching the Hyatt when you left with the suitcase. It never dawned on us that there were two suitcases. We thought it was just another location manipulation." He then said, "Meet Watkins and me down at the Kirkland Police Department; it's just two blocks away from Hector's. We're both already there. We need to get everyone together right now and coordinate where we go from here."

We did this.

At this meeting, we discussed all our possibilities.

They decided it was too late to set up roadblocks at possible escape routes out of Bellevue. Besides, it had been more than two hours since I left the money at the Hyatt; and by now, we knew the kidnappers would more than likely be miles away. There were just too many possible routes for us to cover with the available manpower, and too much time had already elapsed after the snafu at the Hyatt. All of us knew they had at least a two—to three-hour head start; combined with how precisely they had manipulated the drop, illustrated they were not sloppy, it all seemed to indicate our chances of catching them tonight were slim to none.

Our real hope now is they keep their word and call tomorrow with the location of my grandchildren. I didn't express my feelings as to the odds of the kidnappers keeping their promise this time but privately thought, FAT CHANCE.

The only other option we had left was to start reviewing what few leads we currently have and try to come to some conclusions what the kidnappers might do.

I then left Hammond and Watkins at the Kirkland police station and went back to Mark and Joan's to break the bad news. This would be one of the toughest jobs I've ever had to do in my entire life, and believe me, there were some really difficult tasks in Nam.

As bad as the situation looked, I convinced them there was still hope the kidnappers would call tomorrow and tell us where we could find Justin and Robbie.

Never give up hope.

Once again, it was a waiting game.

I considered taking them into my confidence and tell them about my total game plan with my crew and Bob Arnott. Maybe that would have a calming effect on them. However, I decided against this in case something went drastically wrong. There wasn't any way I would allow them to be involved in this part of the operation. It would be tragic enough if for some reason I had to use force and maybe be required to operate outside the legal system. I knew that was a possibility; and if it came about, I wanted to be the only person the authorities would find accountable. The only person they could arrest.

I understood with any aggressive actions on my part there was a risk, and the potential consequences were too great even to think about. So I concluded the less my family knew, the better it would be for everyone concerned.

Of one thing, though, I was absolutely certain.

Justin and Robbie were going to be rescued alive and be returned to their parents, my son and daughter-in law, safe and sound. I would do whatever I had to do no matter how far I had to go.

#

Chapter 12

THE KIDNAPPERS

The night seemed to move in with him as Fred entered the door of the motor home, smelling of mist and dead leaves. Fall was in the air.

"So how did it go?" asked Dennis.

Lois looked up from her crossword puzzle. She did not get up. Apprehension and strain pressed down on her shoulders. When she wasn't on drugs, and she was feeling stress, crossword puzzles sometimes helped. Not the *New York Times* puzzle, the easy ones you buy for a couple bucks from Wal-Mart.

She knew what might be coming next if this last call frustrated Fred. Before, in the distance of their planning, it hadn't seemed as important. But now . . . now.

She shuddered inwardly as she finally realized the reality of their acts and knew it could only get worse.

Fred oozed an egregious self-confidence. "Just like grease on a pole . . . really slick." He snapped his fingers like Fonzie in *Happy Days* . . . But as usual, he didn't get much sound out of the effort. "I'm positive they're getting the money together."

"How about the cops?" asked Dennis. His big eyes bugged ludicrously, his mouth open. Lois recognized the look of naked greed.

Both Fred and Dennis were odd birds. She had always thought that about them when she was thinking fairly straight. They were both in their late thirties and looked like they could be hippies of the sixties or seventies with their long hair and their love for pot and acid rock. (Fred was a huge Jimi Hendrix fan while Dennis preferred Black Sabbath and anything heavy metalish or rap.)

They seemed like characters from a much blacker version of *My Name Is Earl*.

But while their lifestyles seemed to reflect the social looseness of that time, they were both simple, timeless, criminal opportunists, living in a fogged and violent moment, while dreaming of riches and an easier life ahead. They were an odd pair, a warped set of brains and muscle, but they shared a common loathing of anything smacking of hard work. Both had contempt for suckers chained to a nine-to-five lifestyle.

"Cops? Oh yeah," Fred said, "I'm sure they called them. The phone rang four times, and then I think I heard two clicks when they answered. It coulda been my imagination, but I don't think so."

"What do we do now?" asked Lois, apprehensively.

"Since they brought the cops in, plan B," Fred said.

Lois cringed. He had already filled them in on plan B.

She took one more drag off her Lucky Strike and then jabbed it out.

"God, I hate that idea, Fred." She let out a long stream of bluish smoke. Her face reflected the stress that was seeping into her entire being. "Do we have to cut off their fingers?"

Fred stole a cigarette from her pack, lit up, and shrugged his shoulders dismissively.

"Just one each, part of their little fingers, at the last joint, they won't even miss them; and besides, it'll show the Malones we mean business," Fred said, sort of chuckling to himself. "The Malones will get the message. The sooner we get this done and get the fingers delivered, the sooner they'll get us the money. Believe me. It'll make them move. You know I'm right, so let's get it done." He leaned forward toward her. "I hope you got everything we need to do the job."

Lois closed her eyes and shuddered.

Her work in the hospital gave her a lot of training in this sort of stuff. When she was doing it for health reasons, she felt good about it. Now, though, it was a different story.

"I've got it all in that bag with a satchel of things," she answered, pointing at a bag in the corner. The emotional strain was really showing on her face, and her voice was about two octaves higher than normal. "Everything I need—scalpel, sutures, antibiotics, even Sodium Pentothal—so I can put them out during the surgery."

"Hell, just cut off the fingers, and let's get them delivered," added Dennis impatiently, "and let's get going."

He tried to snap his fingers, but got even less percussion than Fred.

"You're so friggin' stupid," said Lois, her anger invigorating her. "You wouldn't want them to have a heart attack and die. Believe me, it's best to put them out, a lot safer, and it'll make it easier to do the surgery. Plus, there'll be a lot less chance of them going into shock."

Her hatred for this stupid jerk was intensifying every time he opened his fat mouth.

"Okay, okay, knock it off, both of you," Fred interjected before the situation got out of hand between her and Dennis. "Do it your way. Just get it done, and don't mess up the motor home. We still have to live in it when we head for Mexico. Dennis, you go help her, and do it her way. Don't argue. Just do it."

"Hey, this might be fun," said Dennis.

"You, sadistic bastard!" said Lois.

This really got a reaction out of Dennis.

Long greasy hair flapping over his jean jacket, he jumped up and started to smack Lois.

Fred intervened and got between them before Dennis got close enough to hit her.

"Cool it, you two!" said Fred.

He shoved Dennis back to his chair.

Then he turned back to Lois, jabbing a finger at her. "Just get in there and do the job. Put the fingers in this metal container, and I'll get a cab to deliver them with one of those suitcases we got for the money. Get going! Get it done, NOW! Dennis, go help her and don't cause any problems or you'll have me all over your ass. Understand?"

Lois grabbed up the bag containing all the items she would need to do the surgery and headed toward the back of the motor home where Robbie and Justin were. Dennis jumped up and followed. He could see that Fred was getting pretty angry, and he knew he had better not fuck with Lois anymore. They reached the door, unlocked it, and Lois turned the light on.

Justin and Robbie Malone were laid out on the bed all tied up, gagged, and blindfolded.

They were conscious, but were very still.

Lois could tell they had been crying, but now it was almost as though they'd run out of tears. They were both just lying there now like a stunned deer struck by a car and lying on the side of the road.

She'd carried her bag of tricks in with her and now took the bottle of Sodium Pentothal out of the satchel along with the scalpel, syringes, antiseptic, bandages, alcohol, tape, and a bottle of antibiotic pills.

"Okay, guys," Lois said, talking to Justin and Robbie. "We're going to take the tape off your mouths if you promise not to yell, okay?"

They did not respond.

She sat down and stroked both of the boys on their arms in a comforting way.

"It's going to be okay, guys," she said softly and reassuringly. "You can't yell, though. Now nod if you understand."

Both boys nodded.

Obviously, they were both scared beyond belief. Lois continued, keeping the tone of her voice soft and soothing. She hoped this would have a calming effect.

"This is just like when we let you eat. Except now you have to swallow some pills so you won't get sick, understand?"

They both nodded.

"Get a glass of milk, Dennis, so they can swallow these."

She was giving them some antibiotics to avoid infection.

Dennis went out the door, and Lois continued talking to the boys.

"Now we're going to do something to you both. I promise you, it won't hurt, and it'll help you get home to your mom and dad sooner. Understand?"

Both nodded.

Dennis came back with the milk.

Lois then removed the tape from the littlest guy's mouth.

Justin.

He was shaking all over.

"Calm down, Justin. Just swallow this pill." She placed a pill in his mouth and held the glass of milk so he could take a drink and swallow the pill. He did as Lois told him, and then she wiped his chin off and replaced the gag covering his mouth.

When she'd heard about Justin and Robbie from their grandmother, they'd been just names to her. Brats. All her life, kids seemed to be selfish, churlish, loud, and obnoxious brats. She'd expected these kids, especially since they were rich kids . . . to be just that.

Brats.

But now that she had spent some time with them, they didn't seem like brats at all. Not *Little Lord Fauntleroy*'s . . . or even like that kid in the story "The Ransom of Red Chief." (Not that they'd given them the chance for that, the way they'd trussed them and gagged them.) No, they seemed . . .

They seemed like particularly fine examples of human beings.

In her life, Lois seldom ever encountered good examples of humanity that was for sure. All of her life she'd felt like a victim. Many people in her life were definitely better than Fred and Dennis, but not by much.

Robbie and Justin though.

They seemed so alive and so . . . well . . . personable and innocent, beneath those neat mops of brown hair. Even though they were frightened, their little souls seemed to peek out of their brownish eyes. She'd been touched, despite herself.

"Good boy, and now, Robbie, you need to take a pill too," she repeated the ritual with Robbie and then sat down beside them on the bed.

"Okay, guys, now I'm going to give you both a little shot that will help you sleep. It won't hurt, and it'll help you both rest. Nod if you understand. Okay?"

They both nodded again.

"Dennis, hold the big one up on the edge of the bed while I get the syringe ready." She then reached in the satchel and pulled out two syringes and proceeded to fill them with the Sodium Pentothal she had stolen from the hospital. She then took one, washed off a place on Robbie's arm with cotton and alcohol, and injected him.

In about twenty seconds, he was out.

They then did the same to Justin. Lois took out a flat square thing from the bag. It looked like a bread cutting board. She had wrapped it in plastic so the blood could be wiped off.

"Okay, Dennis, hold on to the big one and turn him around so I can put his left hand on the board."

Lois presumed they were right-handed so she had decided to remove the boys' left pinkies. In her mind, she thought this was an act of kindness. Dennis did as instructed. She then took a couple towels and laid them nearby.

"Okay, Dennis, he probably won't move but hold on to him just in case he does."

Lois then took the scalpel poured some alcohol on it over one of the towels and took Robbie's left hand and laid it on the cutting board.

"Now I'm going to cut his little finger off at the first joint; then I'll sew the end up after we clean off the blood, and I'll pour some disinfectant over the wound so it won't get infected. You just hold him still so I don't slip and then I can get it stitched together. Got it?"

"Hell, just cut the fucking thing off and let's get going!"

"Okay, okay, this is not as easy as it looks."

Lois then took the heavy scalpel and quickly cut Robbie's little finger off at the first joint and placed it in the metal container while continuing to hold on to Robbie's little finger, minus the last joint. Kind of like a tourniquet.

It wasn't bleeding too much.

She held a small pan under it while she poured some disinfectant over the wound. Then she proceeded to pull the skin over the end and took the suture needle out and stitched the skin together. Then she took a roll of gauze out and cut enough off to cover the finger. She sprinkled some sulfa powder on it and then bandaged it up.

"That'll hold him. He probably won't even have much pain when he comes to," she said.

Thank god she'd learned to do this kind of thing at the hospital by detaching herself from emotions. She probably would have made a good nurse if she had stuck with it.

"What the hell do we care about pain?" said Dennis. "He's not your fucking kid!"

Lois ignored his comment and said, "Just hold on. Now get the other one."

They then cut the end of Justin's little finger off and bandaged it up the same way.

"Let's get these to Fred so he can get their attention faster," said Lois.

"Yeah! Let's deliver them so we can get the money and get the fuck out of here." Dennis thought he was reinforcing Lois's comment. She ignored him.

They laid both boys down and locked the door on their way out.

"They'll start coming around in about two hours. I'll check later to make sure they're okay," said Lois.

"Sure, Nurse!" Dennis taunted sarcastically.

"Stick it!" said Lois, glaring hatefully at Dennis "Let me cut your pinky off and see how you like it, asshole!"

She put the satchel and bag in a closet, and Dennis took the metal box to Fred.

"Here's your insurance package. How are you going to get it delivered?" Dennis said to Fred as he handed him the metal box containing Robbie and Justin's little fingertips.

"No problem. I'll have a cab in downtown Bellevue deliver it along with the suitcase we got for the Malones to put our money in; all I have to do is give the cabbie the address, pay the cab fare with a big tip, give him the suitcase with this box containing the fingers inside, and it'll get delivered. Not to worry. Give me that dark-haired wig and that long black coat from the back closet," he instructed Lois.

She went and got them and handed them to Fred.

He put on the wig and the black raincoat, looked at his reflection in the mirror, and added a false mustache and dark glasses.

Then he turned to pose for Lois and asked, "See! How does that look?"

"Different, definitely different, I couldn't recognize you," Lois said. She was starting to feel a little calmer now that the surgery was completed.

Fred then added in a confident tone, "Don't tell me I don't know what I'm doing. It's all about taking care of the details."

Dennis just sat there.

He had pulled out a bottle of Bud from the refrigerator and was obviously enjoying it more than the conversation between Fred and Lois. He had that kind of thoughtless aspect about him. He seemed governed more by appetites than any kind of consciousness. Dennis definitely had more or less decided what kind of life he was going to lead, and it was not going to involve much hard labor. He had already done that when he was in prison; and now, with all this money, he was going to get he would never have to work again. That's how his simple mind worked. Lois had the feeling, though, that Fred might have been okay if he'd been brought up right. Even though she now disliked him, she found that quality to be much like her own story. However, with Dennis she couldn't conjure up a single sympathetic note for him. He was always worthless and always would be, a total jerk.

Fred continued, "I'm out the door, you two keep those brats on ice. When I get back, I think we ought to move locations. Let's go up to that Indian casino in Marysville. Dennis, why don't you put those other Canadian plates on while I'm gone just in case the manager of this place keeps any kind of records, you never know. They're on the top shelf above the stove. Then fix that packing crate. And make sure nobody sees what you're doing."

Dennis took a big swig from his bottle of Bud, belched, and nodded his head, so Fred knew he understood.

"Okay, I'm out the door."

#

Fred got in the pickup, slamming the door behind him with great authority.

He drove out the woods entrance of the RV Park, heading on for Interstate 5 and then 405 to downtown Bellevue.

It's time to do the cab thing. he thought to himself.

The early September air was warmer than normal; and although he had the air-conditioner on, he cranked down the window of the cab and shoved his arm outside into the slipstream. It felt good with the wind moving his hand around in different directions. He remembered doing that when he was a kid.

The highway was full of cars and bad drivers, as usual; but instead of being annoyed today, he found comfort in anonymity.

When he reached the Bellevue area, Fred drove around until he saw a line of cabs at the Bellevue Square Shopping Mall across from the Hyatt Hotel in the center of town. He found a parking place in a strip mall about a block away. Took out the piece of paper on which he had previously written the delivery address. At all times he was wearing driving gloves so he wouldn't leave any prints on anything.

The gloves were black and made of leather.

From the strip mall, he legged it to the cab line. He walked to the cab at the very end of the line. The chubby guy inside wore a Mariner's baseball cap and was smoking a cheap cigar. Fred could smell its fumes even through the fresh breeze that gently blew a wing of newspaper across the sidewalk in front of him as he approached the cab.

"Hey, Buddy, want to make a quick hundred-dollar tip?" said Fred through the open window on the drivers side of the cab.

"Sure, who wouldn't . . . as long as it's legal," he responded with much skepticism in his voice. There was a suspicious look on his thick face, but it was bright with the possibility of extra money. He kind of stared at Fred, trying to figure out what was wrong with his appearance but shrugged it off without giving it a second thought.

"Oh, it's legal all right. Just deliver this suitcase to the address on that slip of paper. It's a birthday surprise. Here's a hundred. Take out the cost of the fare and keep the rest. But you have to get it done right now or no deal. Don't bother looking inside cause there's nothing of value. It's just a birthday trick." He thought if this dumb shit cabbie looked in the suitcase, the jig would be up. He was willing to chance it because of the time element, and besides, it was locked.

"Let me see the address." The cabbie took the slip of paper from Fred, read it, and then said somewhat sarcastically, "I can get it handled in thirty minutes, is that fast enough for you?"

Fred didn't even detect the sarcasm in the cabby's voice.

"Just don't forget to deliver it, or it'll ruin the surprise," he said emphatically. "I'm going to call to make sure it gets there, and I've got your number. Get it?"

That was a lie, of course. But how would the cabbie know?

"You can count on me," said the cabbie, grinning. A hundred bucks, now that's a real tip!

Fred then handed him the suitcase with the sealed metal box containing Robbie and Justin's fingers inside and the hundred-dollar bill.

The cabbie placed the suitcase on the seat next to him and pulled out of line instantly, spewing out a spray of gray exhaust almost as smelly as its driver's cigar. It roared down the road.

Fred walked back to his pickup and drove back toward Everett down Highway 405 to I-5.

He turned off I-5 at the Mukilteo Exit.

In less than an hour, he was back at the RV Park.

#

Chapter 13

BOB ARNOTT

I was there when the cabbie made his dreadful delivery.

My presence was pure happenstance. Odd, the way coincidences seem to work sometimes. It wasn't even Jim who'd asked me to come over for reporting purposes, but Mark.

"Bob, I know you care a lot about Robbie and Justin. Dad told me he had filled you in on our situation. And I was just wondering if you could stop by for just a bit and sit and talk with us. I think it will help Joan get through this. She thinks the world of you. I know for sure it will help me."

My first thought was to say no. I had a lot of work to do, and the pain and fear that Mark and Joan were feeling would be distracting to my purpose. Besides, I was feeling my own dread and anxiety about Justin and Robbie. Surely, a raw infusion of the same from the parents would be hard to take.

After a pause to think, though, I answered, "Yes, of course."

I had to say yes for two reasons.

For one thing, I realized Mark was right. My presence could help by taking their minds off the kidnapping and hopefully turn to positive options. There was another self-serving reason for being there, and that was simple, it could assist me with my story if and when Jim called upon me.

For another, if the story dragged on, I'd need more content. Writing about the situation with the parents in a kidnapping would be perfect human-interest material. Like I thought, this may sound a bit self-serving, but in a way, I was part of the family.

So as I pulled my old Ford into their huge driveway and started the process of checking through the security agents the authorities had left there, the writer's observation equipment behind my eyes and ears kicked in.

The house that Mark had designed and built was a beautiful multileveled European influenced effort. His father's house was squarely Midwestern influenced. He'd used Frank Lloyd Wright styles only if they were efficient in building a great number of houses. In his heart of hearts, he was-old fashioned, so he sniffed a bit at what looked to him like odd angles and intersections.

It all looked good to me. I was far from a scholar about architecture, but I knew a few things and had an appreciation for design and so could carry on a conversation with Mark where his father could not. We could even talk about the Chinese concept of feng shui. Jim Malone thought feng shui was something with tofu and soy sauce in it.

Somehow, Mark had built the sprawling house without cutting down a lot of trees. The house nestled amid old oak, maples, cedars, and firs as though it had been there for a very long time. The shade was particularly comforting at this hot time of year. People not from Seattle don't realize that September is one of our better months. All in all, I guess I'd rather have been sipping iced tea with the family waiting for hamburgers to cook over charcoal. But now I was a journalist with a job to do, and so I braced myself to do just that even as deep down I hoped that my company would indeed be helpful.

I got through the security with no problem. Jim and Mark both had told the authorities I was their closest family friend. Nothing was mentioned about my profession, and for some reason, they accepted this with no questions asked. They probably thought that in times like this people needed close friends, and I was it.

Jim was inside the house, pacing and looking businesslike but grim. He seemed distracted with cell phone calls to his crew; and while he acknowledged my arrival, he didn't pay much attention to me there.

Mark smiled at me though.

"Bob! Bob! Thanks so much for coming. Come on into the library. Joan's there. We want to talk to you."

"Joan, she's in the library?" I said, surprised.

"Yeah, how about that? I know it's kind of our private place, but she's finding some comfort in the quiet, I think."

The library was the place Mark and I would go sometimes to get away from the rest of the household commotion. Mark had a terrific collection of architecture books, old and new; and often we'd pore over one, chatting about this and that.

Joan sat now in an Eames chair. She was peering out forlornly at a weeping willow by a kid's swing set in the backyard, probably envisioning Robbie and Justin playing there. In her hand, she gripped a highball glass, so I presumed she was drinking something alcoholic; but she didn't seem to be paying much attention to it. It seemed to be just something she was hanging onto.

The library smelled of the good cigars Mark occasionally smoked—and of the unmistakable scent of old musty books.

"Oh, Bob!" said Joan. "Thanks for coming!" Joan was in her late thirties now, but somehow her maturity seemed to make her more appealing. Unlike Deanna, who was the classic broad-shouldered, smiling Barbara Bush kind of dame who could host a cocktail party in the afternoon, and then pitch a softball game in the evening, Joan was the more diminutive, softer, and more feminine type of female. Slender and rounded, she looked good in anything. Today, in worn jeans and a faded red blouse and no makeup, her brunette tresses combed but a bit scattered, she looked beautiful but fragile and vulnerable.

I gave her a hug.

She was warm and giving, melting into me a bit.

Whenever I hugged Joan, it gave me a pang. It made me remember that I didn't have a woman like this to come home to in the evening.

A wave of rage swept over me at the thought of the men who would do something like this to this good family.

We broke apart and she said, "Bob, I'm sure you're reporting on this if and when it's needed will help get Justin and Robbie back."

"I'm just glad to be of any help at all if it comes to that," I said. "How are you holding up?"

"Okay. Okay, I suppose," she said. "I guess the Valium helped a bit at the time, and now I'm facing everything without using any."

"Just don't drink too much of that if you decide to take some more Valium, it doesn't mix you know," I said, pointing at the highball glass.

"Oh, I'm keeping alert. I mean, I have to, don't I? I have to stay awake and alert in case my boys need me. But this does help to take the edge off, and I'm only sipping one."

"A little too well, actually," I said. "I confess. I've been pretty blunt sometimes."

She laughed, and her eyes twinkled just for a moment—a wonderful sight to see. "There you go, you dear. You've cheered me up already."

"You want a drink, Bob?" Mark asked.

"Sure," I said, to be sociable. "But make it a weak one."

We were secluded from all the authorities and were able to talk privately. We talked a bit over the details. It was just nervous, comfort talk, reiterating things I already knew; but I didn't take a "Just the facts, ma'am" attitude because I knew that any talk at all was therapeutic for them as well as me.

I did, however, listen carefully in case anything dropped that I'd been previously unaware of might be mentioned. Mark helped himself to a drink, considerably stronger than the one he'd made me. It was when this drink was finished and another one started that I began to see exactly what was going on with Mark.

"I feel so damned helpless, my head is numb from thinking about the kids and praying for a small miracle," he said, gritting his teeth.

"Sounds like you're doing what you're supposed to do," I said, "What did Chief Hammond and the FBI tell you to do? And your dad as usual seems to have taken things over handily."

"My dad!" said Mark angrily. "My dad always takes things over. He thinks I'm an incompetent boob! Well, I'm not! I'll show the son of a bitch. They're my children, damn it!"

"Mark, Mark," said Joan. "Settle down! Your dad's doing a very good job! And you're doing plenty."

"I agree. And who cares who does what? We'll all be heroes if the boys get back safely. And being a hero isn't the point anyway."

"It isn't? Ask my dad about that!"

"Mark, Mark, I assure you. Your father is all about getting things done. He's about ideals and action, not about being a hero. Don't you know that?"

I hoped my words didn't sound hollow. In fact, I knew exactly how Mark felt because sometimes I felt them too. In a way, we both resented Jim Malone even as we admired him.

"I guess," said Mark. "All I know is I really want to hurt those bastards who've done this to Justin and Robbie and us; and I swear, if they hurt the boys . . . I'm going to kill them."

"Mark!" said Joan.

"That's not the first time I've said that. I told the exact same thing to Dad."

"Well, keep it in the family. I sure didn't hear it, Mark," I said.

I gently pried the drink from his fingers and set it to one side.

"And whatever you do, don't start talking that way around law enforcement. They take things at a literal, face value, and have got memories like constipated elephants!"

Mark shook his head and smiled a bit at the idea of elephants in need of Ex-Lax. He always enjoyed my way with words.

"Yeah, yeah, you're right as usual. Give me the drink back. I promise to be good. And this is my last one."

He only sipped at the drink, and we talked some more.

I was about to suggest maybe we should play a game of cards or a board game (we were all big on games and were passing the tradition on to Justin and Robbie). I thought it might ease the tension, but before I could express this idea, we heard a ruckus from downstairs.

"Something's happening! Someone is here!" said Joan in a startled voice.

Mark didn't say a thing. He just turned away, set his drink down, and hurried out the library door and down to the great room.

Joan and I followed.

Jim Malone was already there, along with others huddled around what appeared to be a medium size piece of luggage made of aluminum. The FBI was in the process of picking the lock to see what was inside.

The FBI agent doing the opening was wearing latex gloves just in case when they could dust for fingerprints he wouldn't compromise them. Apparently, it had already been tested. It wasn't a bomb.

"A taxi driver pulled up and gave these to the security people," explained Jim.

"Where is he?" asked Mark.

"Outside, still being questioned," said Jim. "We're sure he's not one of the kidnappers or even an associate. His story checked out. It looks like he was just hired to deliver that suitcase to us. That's all he knows. He wasn't even too sure on the identification other than the height. He said a guy with a beard or mustache gave him a hundred bucks to deliver a birthday present."

"Why would they send us a suitcase? What could it be?"

"Maybe you should go in the other room for now, Joan," said Jim. "Mark, you take her."

"I'm staying right here," said Joan resolutely.

"And I'm staying right here with her," Mark added.

I immediately put on my reporter's inner discipline and watched the proceedings.

The full details of the grisly contents of that luggage and their uncovering would become part of my newspaper story when and if that time ever arrives.

The suitcase lock gave way and inside was a small metal box sealed with scotch tape. When they finally unsealed the metal box and exposed its gruesome contents, the little fingers of Justin and Robbie, I cannot fully express the impact those dismembered fingers had on everyone. Not the least upon me.

I thought of Robbie and Justin then, and something inside of me turned into the red-hot contents of the sun.

Joan's scream brought me out of it.

"Oh my god," she shrieked. "Oh my god!" I grabbed her before she fainted and held her steady.

"How could they . . . ," said Mark. "I'll kill them! I swear, I'll kill the dirty bastards!"

Again, the rest of the scene is known. How sedatives were distributed and how Jim assured us he would see that no further harm was done to the kids if it was the last thing he ever did.

But in my heart of hearts, right then I knew something more was happening here beyond the story of my career.

#

CHAPTER 14

BOB ARNOTT

The thumbs.

Yes, it had been quite a revelation.

The revelation had drawn a few gasps from the gallery and had put a brief pause in the proceedings. But soon the court case of the *State v. James Malone* continued, and I sat back in chair with my notebook and jottings.

"Was there anything else unusual about the bodies?" Hammond was asked.

His answer was to the point, "None other than as I said before, they were missing their thumbs on their right hands."

I looked over to see how my friend was doing.

Jim Malone appeared to be lost in his thoughts. He sat very still, no expression on his newly lined face during this cross-examination. It was almost as if he wasn't even in the courtroom.

Then the severed thumbs had come up.

Jim immediately looked up at Hammond.

He was remembering.

I asked him later about this time of the trial, and he answered in detail.

He told me his thoughts were specific about the events that led up to that night in the RV. His mind did a complete recall of when he had decided that he had to begin his own seek-and-find operation.

He reviewed all of it for what seemed like the hundredth time.

For some reason the exact moment when he had requested his construction crew's active participation to intensify was eluding him.

Finally, he decided it was after the kidnappers made their second or third call; he wasn't positive, but he was sure it was one of those times. He remembered it was when the police and the FBI's investigation of the kidnapping appeared to be becoming seriously bogged down.

In Jim's judgment, due to the usual legal restrictions they were required to follow, plus the unusually large contingent of people they were trying to synchronize, caused them to move at a snail's pace.

It was well before the tragedies of the kids' fingers.

He remembered it vividly.

#

Deanna and Joan had returned from the vet and reported Bailey was going to remain at the doggie hospital and would be as good as new in a week or two.

The FBI had all the phone taps and recording devices in place. Everybody sat at Mark's house in the great room just waiting for the phone to ring. This was extremely stressful for all those involved, especially the Malone family.

Waiting for the kidnappers to call . . . waiting to hear the voices of Robbie and Justin . . . waiting to give the kidnappers one million dollars. It was between 10:30 and 11:00 p.m. when the phone rang. The first ring startled everybody out of their wits. It sounded louder than any ring they had ever heard.

As instructed, son Mark let it ring four times before he answered it. On the fourth ring, he answered.

"Hello," Mark had said.

"Listen closely. Have you got the money together?"

"We're trying; it's Labor Day weekend you know." Mark was really calm considering the situation.

"Don't fool with me, asshole," the kidnapper said. "I know you've got the connections, just get the money together. I don't care how tough it is, don't mess with me or you'll regret it. Just do it. And don't forget. Keep the cops out. Be ready. I'll call with instructions tomorrow. Don't do anything stupid if you want the kids alive!"

"Let me talk to them!" Mark's voice was a little too aggressive. It was noticeable he was losing it a little at this point. He held the phone to his ear, waiting for a reply from the kidnapper.

The line went dead.

Watkins, the FBI director, asked the phone operator, "If he was able to get a trace?"

"Too short," he replied. "Besides, we're sure it's on a cell phone again; and like I said before, they're more difficult to trace other than maybe to the registered owner and the cell tower link up. We're almost positive the phones they're using are probably stolen or in some anonymous name with a phony address. It'll take us some time to sort it all out."

"Don't we have equipment for tracing cell phones?" Watkins asked.

"LA is the nearest field office with that equipment. We called them, and they said they would fly it up right away. It was supposed to be here by now," replied the phone operator.

Jim had been watching and listening.

He could tell they were in trouble.

Jim knew for sure he'd have to take matters into his own hands.

#

CHAPTER 15

THE KIDNAPPERS

Lois and Dennis were sitting at the table playing cribbage when Fred opened the door.

Lois was feeling depressed for what she had just done to Robbie and Justin. Fortunately, they decided to kill some time playing cribbage while waiting for Fred to return. Although she sometimes wondered if Dennis could tie his own shoes (he always wore slip-ons); for some reason the stupid oaf knew how to play cribbage, and he was really adept at it. She thought he probably learned while he was in jail.

When Fred drove in and parked by the motor home, he was noisier than usual; and because of the commotion, Dennis jumped up and grabbed the gun he almost always had within arm's length.

Almost comically, he had a bottle of Bud in one hand and the gun in the other.

"Relax, Dennis, it's me," said Fred as he entered the motor home.

"Jesus, you're lucky as hell I didn't shoot first and ask questions later." Dennis said, trying to make a joke and not piss Fred off.

"Oh man!" boomed Fred. "You're wound up way too tight. Choke it down and put that gun away, it really bothers me!"

Lois was glad Fred finally said something about the gun to that dumb shit. He really was making her nervous. Especially now that he was drinking, what she thought was way too much. Turning to Fred, she asked, "Did you get the suitcase and the box delivered?"

"I gave it to a cabbie with a note and a hundred bucks."

"Dummy! He'll probably pocket the hundred, dump the box, and keep the suitcase. Anyway that's what I'd do." Dennis instantly wished he had kept his mouth shut. He hoped Fred would take his comment as a joke and not get pissed off.

"Not a chance." Fred beamed with self-confidence. He was too pleased with himself to react to Dennis's stupidity. Nonetheless, Lois couldn't help noticing that he was fidgeting a lot and fingering his fine damp wisp of a mustache as he always did when he was nervous. "I told him I had his number, and I would call where he was taking it in an hour to make sure it was delivered. Now, do you have everything done?" he asked Dennis.

"Yep," replied Dennis.

"License plates changed? Hoses and cords stored?"

"Yeah, yeah, we're good!" said Dennis, obviously annoyed his competence was being questioned.

Fred nodded. "Good. We can get moving up the road to that Indian casino near Marysville. We don't want to stay in one place very long; and if this goes smooth, we'll be out of there in at least a couple of days. Besides, they don't charge anything at those casinos, and the only thing they check is if you're parked right. And, Den, don't forget you're going to have to get that packing box ready down at the warehouse. We're going to need it later to put the kids in after we get the dough, and I don't want to have any delays"

"I already did it, fixed the door, and put a strong lock on it while you were doing the cab stuff. It was a snap. It's sitting in that boat warehouse place ready and waiting for the brats. Nothing to it," he said in a very braggadocio tone.

"Great, now let's get going. Lois, why don't you make sure the ropes on those brats are still secure. We also might need to hit a dumping station and get rid of that crap in the holding tank. That's if we find a convenient one."

#

Within an hour, they pulled out of the Mukilteo RV Park and headed north up I-5 toward Marysville and the Tulalip Indian Casino.

This time Dennis was driving the motor home. Fred was navigating, and Lois followed in the pickup.

"Drive through Everett out to I-5 and head north to Marysville. I'll call them on the phone while we're moving to make sure they got our little gift. Better yet, pull off at the next on-off ramp so I can get out and make a call and see if they got our little package," Fred directed Dennis.

Dennis did just that at the next exit and parked in a deserted service station driveway.

Fred picked a cell phone out of a box that contained several cell phones. He stepped out of the RV.

Lois pulled in behind them.

Fred dialed in Mark Malone's number.

Just like before.

Four rings and Mark answered.

"Malone residence."

Fred quickly said, "Just keep quiet and answer yes or no. Did you get our little gift?"

"You rotten, no-good bastard, I swear, you'll pay for this," cried Mark. "Let me talk to my children!"

"Shut up, asshole, and listen," Fred yelled back, cutting Mark off. "The brats are okay, but now you know we mean business; and if you do as I say, get the money together, you'll get them back soon with no more damage. Just be ready for our next call, and keep the cops out of this if you want them alive. Put the money in the suitcase we sent along with the metal box and our special gift. That's all there is to it . . . just be ready to deliver."

He then disconnected without letting Mark respond.

#

Turning to Jim, Mark said with serious concern in his voice, "Dad, what are we going to do? They're going to kill Robbie and Justin! I know it!" Jim responded immediately, "Mark, calm down. I'm positive they're still alive. Right, John?" He turned to Chief Hammond for some support.

"Your dad's correct, Mark. They want the money; and without the children alive, they know what would happen, no money," said Hammond. Then he turned to the FBI director Watkins.

"Did we get a fix?" Who in turn asked the same question to the phone operator.

The agent shook his head. "Too short again, and apparently they're using a different cell phone. The number was blocked out completely this time."

Director Watkins commented, "It looks like we don't have much choice. We're just going to have to wait for the money drop. Unfortunately, other than a man with a beard or mustache, about six feet tall, wearing a black raincoat, gave him a hundred bucks to make a delivery of a metal suitcase, the cabbie couldn't supply us with any other useful information. He couldn't even do a composite, and he had discarded the instructions so we didn't really get anything constructive from him. No fingerprints, nothing!"

Mark exploded, "If they were your kids I'll bet you would be doing something!"

Watkins responded quickly before things went too far. "Mark . . . Mark, keep cool, calm down. We must keep our composure. Everybody is doing everything conceivable under the circumstances. It's always a waiting game in kidnappings. We can't push too hard, or we could seriously endanger the children. And just like your dad said, I promise we'll get them back. We have everything organized so we can react in a minimal amount of time for anything occurring that we can't anticipate. Meanwhile, Mark, why don't you, Joan, and Deanna assist my staff in organizing the money and put it in the suitcase? It looks like they've almost completed writing down enough of the serial numbers so when they start spending the money, we'll be able to trace it back to the kidnappers. Regrettably, there's not enough time to list all the serial numbers, so we did a sequential listing.

#

After completing the call, Fred returned to the motor home.

As he got in and sat down in the passenger seat, he saw that Dennis still had that gun in his lap. Once again and more emphatically, he told him to put it away before it accidentally went off. Dennis could sense this time Fred really meant it, and so he got up and put the gun in a drawer by the sink.

Fred knew it was too late, but he was wishing he hadn't taken him on. Then again, Dennis was useful in some ways. But he knew he would have to keep an eye on this loose nut. Keep him away from the booze and the gun until they went their own direction; then he could care less what happened to him. He didn't have the same concern for Lois other than she seemed to be overreacting to the kids being left in the packing crate. She was way too soft, might bear watching her so she doesn't do anything stupid. "Okay, I put it away. Does that make you happy?" Dennis said sarcastically.

Fred nodded and said, "Keep it there." Then Dennis asked, hoping to change the subject, "Well, how did the call go?"

Fred didn't respond.

"I asked you how it went, the phone call," Dennis asked again. Fred hesitated before answering. He didn't want to tell Dennis about Mark's threat, so he lied, "Just like it was supposed to go, it'll make them get a move on. Come on let's get going to that Marysville casino."

#

The kidnappers made it to the Marysville casino in about forty minutes parked in the best location available and within an hour were set up.

Fred had decided they should stay out of the casino to avoid attracting attention. They remained in the motor home and now were sitting around the table. Dennis was drinking beer. Lois had been doing her crossword puzzles but stopped for a minute and walked back to see if the kids were okay. Fred was looking at maps and drawing lines on them for their escape routes.

When Lois returned from the back bedroom, Fred asked her, "How are the brats doing?"

"Both awake and okay," Lois said in a relieved tone. "I took their gags off and fed them a few bites of a sandwich and soup. They should become a little passive in a little while. Probably even go to sleep. I gave them each a mild tranquilizer in their soup. They'll be okay. But god I'll be glad when this is over."

"Don't get soft on me now, baby!" said Fred. "Only one more day; if there are no hitches, and there shouldn't be with my plan, then we'll get the money, leave the brats in that packing crate in that abandoned old boat warehouse by Scott, and we're down the road. It'll probably take a couple days or more for them to find the brats, and by that time we'll be long gone. We were really lucky to find that place by Scott Paper Company. Hardly anybody ever goes there. No security. It's just perfect."

"What if they don't find them soon enough and they die?" Lois asked in a concerned, almost motherly manner.

"Not to worry, babe, by then we'll be down the road and far away, maybe we'll even be in Mexico by that time. And besides, we'll leave them alive just like we promised to do. It wouldn't be like we really killed them. Right, Dennis?" Fred asked.

"Who gives a rat's ass . . . let's get the bucks and get going," said Dennis. "This is taking too damned long for me!"

#

CHAPTER 16

JIM MALONE

I sat in court thinking about everything that had transpired from Mark's first call to the moment of truth when I caught up with the kidnappers.

I was remembering the phone call with the instructions for the money drop and how the kidnappers had promised once we delivered the money they would return Robbie and Justin.

It was my feeling from the very beginning, deep down in my gut it wouldn't go down like the kidnappers promised.

It was just too simple.

I knew they would need time to escape; and if they had kept their word, well, let's just say from day one they planned to do everything just like it happened. They never intended to return Robbie and Justin until they had the money and time to escape. Jim in retrospect thought the FBI with all its expertise and experience should have factored all of these possibilities into their process. He thought their major miscalculation was thinking that the kidnappers were not very smart.

There was just no way to predict exactly how, when, or where things would happen. We were at their mercy. The kidnappers had all the control. We just had to wait for them to call. But that's not what I was doing.

I was never one to wait for crises to control me.

During the time the authorities were waiting for the kidnappers' calls, I was formulating my course of action. Deanna and I had moved to Mark's house so we could be there at all times. As instructed by the police, I appeared to be doing everything they requested, acting as normal as possible around my employees and keeping the company operating as if nothing was wrong.

What I was really doing was putting all the information together I was able to obtain by paying total attention to FBI Director Watkins and Chief

Hammond's findings. When they spoke to someone, I was purposely not far away from them.

I was almost always within earshot of both of them.

I would then jot everything important down when I was alone in my room.

From this information, it was becoming clear the FBI early deductions were correct. They concluded there were probably three kidnappers, two men and one woman. I thought to myself, *Good god, this was decided from the very beginning. Where's the progress?* They also deduced the kidnappers were located within a fifty-mile radius, and they were in two vehicles or more; but it was more probable only two. It wasn't much information, but I felt it might be invaluable if I had to take things into my own hands.

I had already formulated all basic options at my disposal. My instincts had always been acute. That's probably how I survived in Nam. I could almost always sense when the enemy was nearby and never wasted a moment in eliminating them before they eliminated me or my comrades.

My superiors knew this about me.

That's the reason I was frequently selected for the most sensitive and many times highly classified missions. I was so efficient in executing whatever was required even my comrades sometimes seemed to fear me. It was a quiet respect. And even though I was good at it, I truly hated it. I had always respected life too much.

Even the Vietcong knew of me and after the war referred to the silent American who had inflicted many casualties. And now, like then, I knew what I must do . . .

Search, find, and destroy so no one else would ever have their life torn apart by these scumbags.

And once my grandsons were home safe, it's exactly what I would do so those maggots could never again do their dirty work on another human being. In no way did I plan to kill them, but they would pay dearly, and they would know who did it to them. And now, here I am waiting, just waiting.

#

CHAPTER 17

THE KIDNAPPERS

Lois was at the motor home, cooking hot dogs and beans, when Fred returned with the money.

"Pretty soon there's no more of that crap for us, kiddo," boomed Dennis, making a face at the pungent odor of the Worcester sauce that Lois liked to lace this cheap concoction with.

Fred was ecstatic as he entered the motor home without knocking, his narrow face beaming with joy. "We did it . . . we fucking did it! We're rich! Didn't I tell you?" He tossed the suitcase on the table.

Fred then related all the events.

He had been outside the Hyatt, about one block away, well hidden from any eyes that may have accompanied Jim, but with a path of vision so he could still observe Jim when he arrived in front of the Hyatt.

From his vantage point, he was able to see Jim pull up, park, and watched as he tipped the doorman and dashed inside through the front entrance.

He described how he had been waiting in this same location all the time he was making his other calls, manipulating Jim from place to place. From this vantage point, he even observed the FBI and the other cops as they quickly moved into position around the Hyatt. As he was narrating the story to Lois and Dennis, he was thinking to himself how much smarter he was than all of them. He had a stupid smirk on his face that people possess when they are too self-satisfied.

Dumb cops and Malone, he thought to himself. *They're no match for fucking old Fred.*

He described how he waited for about ten minutes after Jim's departure. How he cleverly bided his time until he was sure all the cops had followed Jim. He was almost laughing out loud just thinking about how pissed they were going to be when they found out they were on a wild-goose chase to Hector's in Kirkland.

Then he described to Lois and Dennis how he simply walked down the street into the Hyatt through a side entrance away from the doorman, into the bathroom and walked out the same way with the suitcase in hand just like any other guest at the hotel, totally unnoticed.

"A million bucks, and it's all ours!"

Fred opened the suitcase, and Dennis just stood there with his mouth open and said, "Let's count it."

"Don't be dumb . . . it's all there . . . they wouldn't dare do anything stupid like that and risk losing the brats," said Fred, obviously slightly annoyed at Dennis.

"Let's get moving . . . we've got to get going tonight. Dennis, you get in the pickup and take the kids to that abandoned old boat warehouse down by Scott Paper Company. Lois, you get the kids and go with Dennis, both of you make double sure they can't get out of the crate. You did get everything set up there, didn't you, Den?"

"Yep, like I told you before, it's all ready . . . wooden packing crate with a swinging door, lock, and extra reinforcement so they can't kick it apart."

"You made sure no one saw you while you were getting this all done?" Fred asked. He was still apprehensive about Dennis paying attention to details.

"Just like you said, there was never anyone near there," replied Dennis. "All I need now is for Lois to grab the brats and we'll run down to the warehouse, dump them in the packing crate, and lock the thing up. Let's get going, Lowee. We're rich . . . we're rich," Dennis mumbled as he headed out the door to the pickup.

Fred said, "While you two are doing that, I'll get the motor home ready to roll so we can head down the road tonight . . . We're going over Stevens Pass, then up to Manson, and stay at the tribal casino for a day or two, then over to Two Rivers Casino and eventually down to Yakima, then in a day or two head South, free and rich. Kind of a roundabout way, but there should be lots of motor homes on this route, especially from Canada heading south; and a lot of them stop at these casinos, so we should go unnoticed. Like I told you, I planned it so we'll always be near all those Canadian travelers heading south for the winter; and with these British Columbia plates on our motor home and pickup, we'll blend in. Besides, I think the cops will think we're going South on I-5 toward Mexico. We'll take our time and relax. Even do a little fun gambling at those Indian casinos on our way; after all, we've earned a little R and R. Now get going we don't have time to waste."

Lois quickly went to the back bedroom and grabbed the kids each by one arm and said, "Come on, guys, were going to get some fresh air, and by tomorrow you'll be home."

The boys let her guide them out the door and into the pickup, and she and Dennis headed for the boat warehouse in Everett.

It was about a thirty—to forty-minute drive. Fred figured it would take them about two hours to get it all handled.

Plenty of time for him to stash the money in the closet, lock it up, and get the motor home ready to leave just as soon as Lois and Dennis returned from locking the two brats in the packing crate.

A piece of cake, he thought to himself. Then all of a sudden his subconscious mind took over, and he couldn't control his thinking process. It's almost as if he was actually there. He was six years old again, and his mother was there. It was so vivid, and he couldn't shake it. He hadn't had this occur for years. It usually only happened when he was taking meth or snorting coke. *Why now?* he thought to himself. *Please not now, please?* It didn't go away, and now it was dark. He knew instantly where he was—locked in the closet, and it would be hours before she opened the door to let him out. He could feel it—dark, cold, and frightening. His whole being started to quiver. Then, just as it had started, it left and he was back in the motor home waiting for Lois and Dennis to return from stashing the brats. He sat there somewhat dazed and shook his head. He thought he had killed all the memories of his youth long ago. *Why now?* He got up and went outside in hopes the fresh air would make this feeling would stay away.

#

CHAPTER 18

BOB ARNOTT

It was when the business with the gun came up that I realized this trial might go on for a while. Apparently, Judge Arnold had perceived the same possibility. He interrupted the proceedings and, due to the lateness of the day, adjourned the session until the next day.

That next morning promptly at 9:00 AM, Judge Arnold called the court to order and immediately addressed J. Edgar, "Does the defense counsel wish to continue his cross-examination of the witness?" asked the judge. He said this with great authority and ease, and yet I felt far from easy. The wood of the walls and ceiling seemed to be pressing claustrophobically now. The courtroom felt like a great big box with no airholes.

I just took a few deep breaths and endured . . . back to reporting. Attorney Ewing responded, "Yes, we do, Your Honor. We have a few more questions that seem important."

I leaned forward to catch the nuances of this part of the proceedings.

J. Edgar Ewing regarded the jury casually, and then turned slowly to face Chief Hammond. I could see he was making sure he was about halfway between Jim Malone and the jury. As long as I'd been watching Ewing walk the courts, I'd always noticed the skill with which he always positioned himself for the jury, the judge, the prosecutor, and the witnesses. He was like an accomplished actor treading the boards of a theater stage under the skilled guidance of a master director.

"Chief Hammond," he began, "were you able to ascertain the owner of the revolver admitted as exhibit A?"

"No, we have not. It's unregistered."

"You mean you don't have any idea where it came from or who might have owned it?"

"At this time that is correct; however, the FBI is still searching their files for more information."

Ewing pressed on, "Do you think it belonged to the kidnappers?"

Surprise! No objection from Shoemaker!

Hammond was able to answer without interruption. "We thought that was a possibility, but once again there was no proof."

J. Edgar pondered this answer for a moment and then continued, "I see. Have you been able to ascertain where the scalpel "Exhibit B" came from or who might have owned it?"

Hammond, "No, we have not, other than they were in the motor home when we found the bodies. They could have been obtained at any number of places." He purposely avoided suggesting the missing part of the trio might have supplied them. Shoemaker had advised him if possible to avoid any comments about Lois.

"Let's take a moment to review what you have told us," Ewing said, leaning against the rail casually. "According to your testimony, you were unable to discover anything in your extensive investigation that may indicate any culpability my client may have had in the so-called murder of these two kidnappers. So far during your testimony, you have not supplied one fact to connect my client, Mr. Jim Malone, to either the revolver or the scalpel. Isn't that correct?"

"Yes, sir, that's correct."

Ewing assumed a sarcastic tone, "Did you, perhaps, in your extensive investigation at the time of his arrest, run tests on my client, Mr. Jim Malone, to see if he had fired any firearms within a recent period after the murders?" He paused and shrugged his shoulders. "I mean if he had shot and killed the two kidnappers as the prosecution is attempting to prove, wouldn't he have had some powder residue on him?"

Shoemaker objected to Ewing's use of the word kidnappers in referring to the two murdered males. He indicated he thought the word *victims* would be more appropriate.

Judge Arnold sustained the objection, much to J. Edgar's surprise.

Ewing rephrased the question, referring to the kidnappers as individuals, not victims as Shoemaker requested.

Shoemaker seemed to accept this.

Hammond then responded to the question, "Yes, we did run the tests with the defendant's permission." He was careful to indicate Jim acquiesced willingly to these tests.

"And what did these tests prove?" asked Ewing,

Hammond knew since J. Edgar allowed these tests to take place without him interfering on any legal grounds he already knew the answer; and since Shoemaker hadn't objected, he responded, "They came back negative."

"I see," said Ewing. Almost as if he was somewhat surprised, he continued, "Let me also ask you whether in your continuing investigation whether or not you found any firearms in my client's possession."

Hammond answered, "No, we did not. He doesn't appear to own any guns of any kind. At least there are none registered to him, and we didn't find any when we searched his or his son's residences. That doesn't mean he didn't somehow have access to a firearm. Our powder tests were conducted two days after the bodies were discovered. That's enough time to have washed any residue off."

J. Edgar objected to the last part of the testimony and requested the judge to strike the last comment from Hammond's answer because Ewing felt it was irrelevant and prejudicial. Judge Arnold agreed and instructed the jury to disregard this comment and admonished the witness to respond in the proper manner.

I have to say from where I sat it did seem that Shoemaker enjoyed this part of Ewing's cross. He frequently would smile in a controlled way maybe to indicate his approval.

J. Edgar continued, forehead wrinkling thoughtfully, "I have only one or two more questions, Chief Hammond. When you ran tests on the scalpel, other than the DNA and blood types of the two deceased individuals, did you find any other blood samples on it?"

"Yes, we found two other blood types."

"And were you able to match these blood types with any individuals other than the prosecution's alleged victims or Mr. Malone's?"

Ewing used the word *victims* at this time but added *alleged*. I think he did this purposely to indicate subliminally to the jury that they shouldn't feel the deceased were truly not victims at all.

Only, alleged victims.

"Yes, we did," said Hammond.

"Objection, Your Honor!" The cry came from the prosecution. Shoemaker was anticipating what was coming next. "Other blood types on the scalpel are not relevant to this trial."

Ewing responded aggressively, "I beg to differ with my esteemed colleague. The other blood samples are very relevant, and the prosecution should know he can't just introduce half of the evidence. After all, it was my esteemed colleague who introduced the scalpel as evidence." J. Edgar added this last comment just to dig into Shoemaker's skin even farther. It worked.

"I concur," said Judge Arnold. "The prosecution's objection is overruled. The witness is instructed to answer the question."

Shoemaker returned to his seat and was not smiling. "I repeat," said Ewing, "were any other blood samples found on this scalpel?"

"Yes." Hammond looked uncomfortable with his answer.

"And did you do a DNA test in order to ascertain to whom these other blood samples belonged to?"

Hammond answered with another simple yes.

"And to whom did they belong?" Ewing asked.

Hammond's response was very short, "Mr. Malone's two grandsons Robbie and Justin Malone."

J. Edgar then asked, "Would you agree this indicates this was the same instrument used to cut Mr. Malone's grandchildren's fingers off?" Hammond answered somewhat evasively, "We thought that was a possibility, but we had no actual proof."

J. Edgar was satisfied he had accomplished all he could with this line of questioning and abandoned the subject, He continued, "Let me ask you this, Chief Hammond. At any time—and I mean from the moment Mr. Malone walked into your office to report the location of the two kidnappers to the moment you arrested him—at anytime, did you read him his Miranda rights?"

Chief Hammond squirmed a bit in the witness chair before he answered, "We did at the time of his actual arrest."

"You mean never prior to that time. Not even when Mr. Malone told you where you would find the two kidnappers?"

"That's correct."

"When did you actually arrest the defendant?"

Hammond then gave a detailed response, "We arrested him the same day in the afternoon. That was after we had found the bodies in the motor home in Yakima. We completed our investigation at the motor home and returned late in the afternoon. On our return from Yakima, we went immediately to Mr. Malone's home and placed him under arrest."

J. Edgar then asked, "Did you read him his rights at that time?"

Hammond answered, "Yes, I did personally." Ewing continued, "And what was his response when you read him his rights? Hammond answered, "He said he wished to speak to his attorney. So we ceased the interrogation immediately."

Ewing pondered this response for a few moments and then asked Hammond if they or the FBI had administered a polygraph test to the defendant. J. Edgar knew Jim had agreed to take the test with his approval, and he knew the results. Shoemaker rose immediately and objected. He also knew the results. Shoemaker voiced his objection to Judge Arnold. "The defense council knows a polygraph is inadmissible." Before Judge Arnold could respond, J. Edgar spoke, "Judge, the esteemed prosecutor doesn't need to remind me of the law, I'm very aware of the legality of polygraph tests. However, it was the prosecution's office who had requested my client take such a test. We agreed to comply in hopes that it would assist them in their investigation, and therefore, it would seem the results could be revealed to the jury even though they are not normally admissible. Is it possible the prosecutor is afraid to reveal the results of this polygraph test to the jury?" Shoemaker again objected to J. Edgar's last comments as being prejudicial and suggested that he should be censured for his action and the jury should be advised to disregard this entire portion of the trial. At this point, Judge Arnold called a halt to the proceedings and told both councils to be seated. J. Edgar and Shoemaker both complied and were seated. He took about two minutes before administering his ruling. The courtroom remained unusually quiet. Finally, he addressed the two councils and the court, "Polygraph tests and their results are not admissible in a legal sense and are administered only to give legal authorities guidance in their investigations, and therefore I cannot allow the results of this test to be presented. Furthermore, I want the jury to disregard Defense Council Ewing's remarks and caution him to take more care in his verbal comments while he's in my courtroom. J. Edgar was smiling inwardly. He felt the jury would assume Jim had passed the polygraph, and it could become a factor in their decision. Why else would Shoemaker object? Meanwhile, Shoemaker was seething, openly. He knew that once again J. Edgar had achieved his purpose. Judge Arnold then directed his attention to Ewing and told him to continue. J. Edgar was really brief this time. "I have no further questions. However, the defense counsel reserves the right to recall this witness at a later date."

My god, I thought then.

It was as though a breath of fresh air had blown through that close courtroom. J. Edgar still has it.

Jim's got a chance! I felt that J. Edgar was pretty successful in establishing for the jury that most of the prosecution's case was circumstantial.

Or maybe, it was my wishful thinking.

#

CHAPTER 19

THE KIDNAPPERS

It was around two o'clock in the morning when Lois and Dennis returned to the motor home in Marysville from their fateful task.

Rain had turned to a fine mist clouding the street lamps. The whole world smelled of damp. Lois felt as though she'd turned into one big shiver.

Or was it a shudder?

"It's about time you guys got back," demanded Fred, glaring aggressively. What the hell took you so damn long? I've been ready to roll for an hour!" He was pacing, twitching nervously. A cigarette was clutched in his hand.

"That goddamn Lois was pampering those brats. She even left them water, crackers, a flashlight, a pillow, and a sleeping bag that I had in the pickup, like they were going on a camping trip," Dennis replied, attempting to put the blame for taking so long on Lois.

"Butthead," Lois responded tartly. "Don't you have any decency at all, or are you just going to remain the big prick that you have been all your life?"

Dennis lunged for her. "Listen, you bitch, I've had just about enough of your fucking crap; I'm every bit as good as you and don't be giving me any of your shit or I'll knock the crap out of you."

Fred jumped in between them before any damage could be done. He still was feeling different and had not been able to eliminate that weird trip he took back to his childhood. The closet, it was still there.

"Okay, knock it off, you two. We've got to get on the road before the sun comes up. I've got everything ready here . . . all the cords and hoses put away." Fred turned to his big partner, twitching a bit with his own inner fear. "Dennis, you get in the pickup and follow Lois and me in the motor home. I'm heading out south on I-5 and then east at Everett on Highway 2 to Wenatchee. You follow, but don't stay too close; it'll be better if we don't look like a caravan. Here's a map with our route laid out in ink. If you happen to lose us, just follow what I put down. We're headed for Manson just north of Chelan; there's a big Indian casino there called Mill Bay. We'll gas up somewhere in Wenatchee; then I'll show you our direction again from there."

Dennis and Lois continued to glower menacingly at each other. He stank of a sour, disgusting sweat. *What a pig,* she was thinking.

"Let's get going . . . NOW!" Fred said as he gave Dennis a shove toward the door of the motor home.

"Okay, okay, I'm going; but you keep that bitch off my back or I'll put her on her back." The hulking guy left, slamming the door behind him and jumped in the pickup.

Fred turned to Lois. "You need to stop pissing him off . . . you know he's not the brightest bulb on the Christmas tree."

Lois didn't respond and simply plopped down in the passenger seat of the motor home, waiting for Fred to start moving.

She was still thinking about Justin and Robbie.

Her subconscious just wouldn't leave her alone. She hoped the sleeping bag would keep them warn enough and prayed there was enough water to keep them alive until they were rescued. *I wish there were new batteries in the flashlight,* she thought. She had told Robbie to keep cool and assured him that his dad and mom would find them soon. He seemed to understand what she was saying.

At least she hoped that was true, and she wasn't just imagining it.

She really regretted getting mixed up in this whole damned deal.

She sighed, realizing that it was too late to turn back now.

Besides, she had some ideas, ideas that had been lingering in the back of her mind all along.

Lois suspected it was just a matter of time before the story would break in the newspapers, and then it would be on radio and TV. This thought really frightened her.

At least I can then follow the story and maybe know how the little guys were doing if and when they're found, she was thinking silently to herself.

"Yeah, sure, let's get going," she finally managed to mutter.

Fred started the motor home. The big thing throbbed to life. Guided by Fred at the wheel, it surged forward.

They headed out of the parking lot to I-5 south and then turned on Highway 2 driving east to Wenatchee. It was close to 3:00 AM, Monday morning, Labor Day, when they turned on Highway 2 heading to Wenatchee over Stevens Pass.

"If we can get over the pass without any problems with the cops, we should have a big head start before they can even begin to look for us," Fred said, almost as though talking to himself.

Lois just sat there in the passenger's seat, thinking about Justin and Robbie—along with darker thoughts.

"Them calling in the cops turned out to be a blessing in disguise," continued Fred. "It gave us a legitimate reason not to deliver the goods. Telling them they would have to wait for a call until the next day gave us even more time to get down the road. Pretty slick . . . I'll bet those cops are still trying to figure out what hit them . . . A stroke of genius if I do say so myself. Don't fuck with Fred."

Fred was smiling; he liked that "Don't fuck with Fred" kind of musical and then realized he had been talking to himself as he glanced over at Lois. He could see she wasn't even listening and obviously didn't care how smart he thought he was. She seemed to be in another world. "What are you so deep in thought about?" he asked her.

"Nothing much," said Lois. "I just hope they get to the boys before anything bad happens to them."

"Let it go," Fred responded. "If the cops aren't smart enough to find them, then it's their fault, not ours. After all, I did tell the Malones to keep the cops out of it or else. They're the ones who broke the deal, not us. The way I see it, we kept our part of the bargain. Anyhow, what's done is done; and now, our big concern is to get out of this area and mix with the rest of the vacation travelers. So just get it all out of that beautiful fucking head of yours and think of the fun we're going to have on the million bucks back there in the suitcase."

"Yeah, sure," said Lois with some doubt in her voice. She was thinking of the entire situation. If there was any way to get out of this right now, even without the money, she would. But she knew it was too late for anything other than to stick it out. "How long are we going to stay at the casino in Manson or any of those other places you said we were heading for? And how are we going to cross into Mexico with a suitcase full of stolen money?"

"That I haven't totally figured out yet. We have time, and I'll get it handled. I've done pretty fucking good so far, haven't I?" Fred said this in somewhat of an angry way, hoping Lois would stop asking so many dumb questions, especially since he had no answers, at least not yet. His head was still throbbing from his trip back in time, and he had a migraine coming on. He was wishing he had some coke or even one greenie, but now was not the time to turn to drugs. He knew he had to keep his head clear.

Lois kind of got the message. She had seen him like this many times and knew, at times like this, it was best to leave him alone. So she just sat there silently continuing to think about the boys.

And her future, however, the only things her mind could conjure up were terrible.

#

Dennis followed them in the pickup.

Not too close, but regardless what fucking Fred said, I'm not about to let that money get more than a mile or two out of sight, he thought. "Hell, what I'd really like to do is to get my share and split!"

He knew he was better at running than Fred and definitely better than that dumb broad.

After all, he had been running from the law almost all his life. However, he knew for now he'd better just cool it. Even though he was a lot bigger than Fred, Fred was a bit of an unpredictable psycho at times, especially when he was snorting coke or messing with meth; and he had noticed when he and Lois returned from the warehouse he was a little strange.

"Just drive and stay close enough to see the taillights," he murmured to himself.

Deep thinking like this always gave him a headache, so he stopped thinking. *Just follow and listen to the radio.*

Rap music thumped out of his window into the night. They drove all night into the dark driving east and stopped only once for gas just on the other side of Wenatchee at a Shell minimart heading north on Highway 97. The turnoff to Chelan and Manson was just a few miles down the road.

All this time, while traveling, Lois was formulating a plan.

If the boys were not found in at least two or three days, she was determined to make sure nothing really bad happened to them, no matter what risks she had to take.

She knew if they weren't found in time they would probably die, and Fred or Dennis didn't give a rat's ass. She decided, right after she and Dennis locked them in that dungy old crate, she would do everything possible to prevent anything like that happening. She had to be prepared to act in no less than two days.

She also was acutely aware she had to be careful not to arouse any suspicion. If Fred or Dennis knew about her plan, she would be in big-time trouble, deep shit.

No way either one of them gave a damn about the fate of the kids.

Whatever happened though, she was not about to let them die in that box. A kid killer she was not. Not now, not ever. This was continuously going over and over in her head. She decided to wait a couple days before doing anything drastic. Maybe they'd be found before she had to do anything at all. There's no sense in taking unnecessary chances if there wasn't any need.

Lois had no way of really knowing how the boys were doing, so she just prayed silently that she had done enough to keep them alive for a few days, and they would be rescued in time.

The remorse she was feeling just thinking about the boys all alone in that dark packing crate was almost too much for her to bear.

She was thinking about how scared they must be and wondering what they might be doing at this very moment.

#

Bang!

The door had closed.

Darkness pervaded.

All that was left was the fear and the smell of their tears.

It took only a few minutes after Lois and Dennis closed the door to the packing crate before Robbie had turned on the flashlight.

A beam of light flickered in the eyes of a frightened little boy.

Justin said, "Robbie, I'm really scared. Are we going to die?"

"No. But my hand sure hurts."

"Yeah. Mine too. I think the end of my little finger is gone. Totally weird."

"I hope they give them back!"

Robbie was moving on his hands and knees around the packing crate. He pushed and kicked at the door to no avail.

After a lot of clattering from his kicking, he finally gave up and put his arm around his little brother.

"Don't worry, Justin . . . I know Dad and Grandpa will find us . . . they won't leave us here. We just have to keep quiet and wait until they get here. Like Grandpa always said, we have to be strong. We'll make this water last and eat the crackers until they find us."

"What'll we do if the light goes out?" Justin asked with a tremble in his voice.

Robbie answered and tried to make his voice sound confident, "We'll wait in the dark. It's probably a good idea to leave it off anyhow, except when we need to eat or drink some water. It'll make the batteries last longer. And if we have to go to the bathroom, we'll use that corner over there. Okay?"

Justin responded hesitantly as Robbie pointed the flashlight beam at a corner. "Okay, Robbie, but I'm really scared."

Robbie was scared too. He felt a shiver of ice buried deep in his back.

But he had to pretend he wasn't, for Justin's sake.

Then he had an idea, a way to calm his little brother.

"Let's just make believe we're out camping with Dad, Uncle Bob, and Grandpa; and it's just a long night before we get up to go fishing. I know they'll find us."

As nonchalantly as he could, as though he were out in the woods with the smell of pinecones all around and the whisper of the north wind through the upper branches of the trees, he spread out the sleeping bag.

"Okay, we're all set, so I'm gonna turn this thing off so we can save the battery."

He turned out the flashlight and put his arms around Justin so they could stay warm.

This became their routine for the duration of their captivity.

"Hey, Justin . . . we're not here . . . no, not at all."

"We're not?"

"Nope. Feel this thing. What is it?"

"It's a sleeping bag, silly."

"You bet. And we're out camping. That's right. We're camping, and Dad's gone off to go to the bathroom. He'll be back real soon."

So they told stories and sang songs like they always did when they went camping with their dad and grandpa.

It would be a long, dark, and lonely wait.

#

CHAPTER 20

JIM MALONE

The DA called witness after witness to verify a variety of evidence he was presenting. Qualified professionals like ballistic experts and medical experts. During this portion of the trial, I was recalling how my crew and I had operated in the search for Justin and Robbie.

I used only the part of my staff that had served in Nam with me.

There were eight of them, the size of a squad in the army. The leader was Ed Johnson.

Ed and I had been part of the same Special Forces group in Nam, and we served together until the last encounter that sent us both to a MASH hospital. I seldom ever let my mind dwell on that horrible ordeal, but sitting here in court I allowed many forgotten experiences to return.

The group also included their cohort and best friend, Leroy Dowdy.

Leroy was a huge Afro-American . . . six feet four . . . 240 . . . not an ounce of fat. He looked like that football player who'd become an actor—Jim Brown. Even though he was so massive, he still moved like a cat. He was the toughest person I had ever known in my entire life.

Both these men were not only tough . . . they were also smart.

They had learned how to build houses the way I wanted them built, and this team ran most of my construction crews.

The other six guys were part of that main construction crew and were every bit equal to Ed and Leroy. I called them my A team, which always amused them. Anyhow, one day after the kidnappers had made contact with Mark, I called a meeting with this group of veterans. At that meeting, I filled them in on the situation and explained how I might have to ask for their assistance if the police failed, or in my estimation ended up taking too long in finding Justin and Robbie. At all times I stressed if I requested their assistance, they should keep their participation in the operation secret from everybody else involved, including my son, Mark, unless I personally instructed or approved any other involvement by outsiders.

I confess. I was worried about Mark. He took after some of his mother's best qualities, and for that, I was grateful. But he was also hotheaded sometimes, the way I was before I had my Special Forces training. I was afraid he'd do something rash in this stressful situation, something we'd all regret later.

That's the main reason I basically just wanted him to stay home, comfort his wife, and stay out of the heat of this situation. A portion of his current personality was probably my fault, and I'd always regretted this particular interference in his growing years. When he was a kid, sometimes I'd catch the bigger kids intimidating him. And he didn't ever retaliate. I was furious at him.

"Don't ever let that happen, Mark! You're a Malone, dammit! Stand up for yourself!"

At this moment though, I didn't want him to stand up for anything except for calmness and patience. I just wanted to get my family through this, and I felt I was the only one who could or should become involved in these undercover operations.

I did keep in constant touch with Mark, so he didn't feel he was being left out, just as I kept in communication with my crew and especially Bob Arnott.

Whenever my crew or Bob became directly involved, I stressed at all times they must make sure no one other than me would be aware of their activities. And especially Hammond and Watkins were to be kept in the dark. My main purpose for insisting on such extreme confidentiality was to be the only known person involved, just in case I had to take drastic action.

Then, hopefully, only I would suffer the consequences for whatever happened.

I further explained to all of them, to predict everything they might conceivably encounter would be impossible, and some situations could necessitate the stretching of the law.

If this ever occurred, I wanted to reassure them again I would assume full responsibility for any such activities.

I said it was probable the authorities would not perceive their activities in the same way I did, so there was some legal risk on each individual's part. Because of this potential risk, I told them if any or all of them opted not to participate, I would understand. I assured them this decision would have no counter effect on present or future relationships. Their participation was strictly voluntary.

I gave them a few minutes to think about this when Ed spoke up, "Listen, Boss, I know I'm speaking for everybody here," Ed said. "We're with you all the way. We'll do everything possible to find these people and get Justin and Robbie back safe and sound. There's not much for us to go on, so we'd better get started now. As you said, it appears they're hiding somewhere in an area of around fifty miles from Seattle. Compared to Nam, this is a walk in the park. There are no swamps, nobody shooting at you from trees, brush, or caves. We know how to do the job. So why don't you go back with your family and the authorities and let us get to work? You know how we do it, and no one but you will feel our involvement."

"That's more than acceptable, Ed," I said. "Let's plan to meet every morning if possible in the office conference room at seven for coffee, and we can update each other on any progress. Plus, I can keep you informed on any thing I hear or see the FBI or the police discover that might assist you. As far as they're concerned, I'm meeting with you to keep my company functioning. If this meets with all you guys' approval, I'll get back to Mark's house and find out if there are any new developments. Before I leave though I want all of you to know there's no way I can ever express how I feel about your assistance in this. I knew I could count on each of you. Thanks."

Leroy then stood up and said, "Hey, you're the reason we all have jobs, wives, kids, and homes. We'll do anything you want. However, we need you to get the hell out of our way so we can get going."

"I'm gone. See you tomorrow at seven." I then walked out the door, and Ed took over. Ed took out the map I had left him and proceeded to prepare a search-and-find game plan. In his prior meeting with Jim, they concluded the police were going to concentrate their efforts on motels and houses north and south around Interstate 5. Therefore, they decided to concentrate on RV parks, campgrounds and similar type locations not only on Interstate 5 but also from Everett and Seattle to the top of Stevens and Snoqualmie Pass on highways 2 and I-90 going east. The area to search was huge and appeared to be an almost-impossible task for eight people. However, these are not average people. They're the best."

And as the events unrolled, I was proved correct.

#

CHAPTER 21

JIM MALONE/BOB ARNOTT

At this juncture in the investigation, the only information of any real value I was able to acquire from the FBI was they were positive at least three and not more than four people were involved.

Also, the FBI determined the kidnappers were operating with two vehicles, a full-size pickup and probably another larger vehicle that was unknown at the moment as to what kind.

Later, the FBI further concluded these individuals were more than likely operating out of a motel or a private residence. This conclusion came in very late, after the money drop.

According to the FBI, most of this was more speculation rather than fact. It was their contention the perpetrators were locals because they seemed to have an excellent knowledge of the area. That's why they concluded the kidnappers were operating from a house or a motel. I felt this was not a massive amount of information considering how many people were working on the case. That of course is if the FBI was telling me everything.

I returned to Mark's house and met privately with the family to appraise them on as much of my game plan as I thought they needed to know. The only purpose for even giving them this information was to instill a degree of confidence in their minds that something was being done. I hoped this would assist in relieving some of their emotional stress. Later I went back to the police headquarters to meet with Hammond and Watkins again to get a current update on their progress in locating my grandchildren or the kidnappers. This meeting took place in the conference room of the Bellevue police department. As I anticipated, this would prove to be a waste of time. Not to be negative, but their progress was not much further than my squad of recruits. It was difficult to comprehend this was the total amount of information their investigation had gathered. Because of this, I was beginning to question whether they were including me in on everything they had discovered. I hoped my paranoia was not affecting my judgment.

This meeting did confirm what Ed and I had surmised. They were concentrating their efforts on hotels and motels, north and south, along Interstate 5.

Watkins and Hammond had become firmly convinced that the kidnappers would be hightailing it south toward Mexico or north into Canada. Watkins indicated it was more likely they were headed to Mexico because of the more stringent extradition problems the Mexican government always posed. The FBI knew most criminals were aware of this extradition problem and frequently took advantage of it. Plus, with a million dollars, the kidnappers could buy a lot of secrecy and local protection. That was the major reason they decided to concentrate the majority of their efforts, staff, and time on highways heading in those directions, north and south on Interstate 5, and primarily south. Their people would be checking out places along these routes where they suspected the kidnappers could have been staying when they were executing the kidnapping or with any luck could still be hiding out.

I already concluded from our previous meetings this would be the direction of the FBI's investigation. Some sixth sense told me they were wrong, but I avoided telling them how I really felt, not that they even cared. Besides, it gave my squad the freedom to cover the other areas unimpeded and undetected.

Since the police were concentrating their efforts on motels, Ed's crew would focus on RV parks, campgrounds, and similar locations from Tacoma to Everett. We decided to cover the two main highways eastbound—Stevens Pass, Highway 2 and Snoqualmie Pass, Highway I-90. This should make our small crew more effective. We thought there had to be a lot less RV parks than motels and less traffic than on Interstate 5 where the FBI would be concentrating their efforts.

"Damn!" Ed told me later when he was filling me in on what he felt I needed to know about how he was coordinating this portion of the search-and-find operation. "Did I ever underestimate how many RV parks existed in those areas?"

After leaving this meeting, I called Bob Arnott and asked if he could meet me at noon on my boat.

Bob agreed.

He was already involved in this in a somewhat subliminal way by just hanging around Mark's house, supposedly only for his personal support as a close family friend. He didn't know it yet, but after the last meeting with Hammond and Watkins, I finally made the decision to utilize the media; and I needed his professional input as to when and how. Now he was going to have total access to almost everything along with the news story that would be under his complete control. I knew he had been patiently waiting for this moment. This was not only a great chance for an inside story, but something more.

Something much more was burning at the back of my mind.

I then called Ed's cell phone to see if his and Leroy's crews were organized and operating. Ed filled me in on what little progress they had made so far. We both knew it was way too early to have made any real progress. I told Ed everything the FBI had shared with me. It wasn't much and didn't contribute a thing to assist Ed and the guys. They did reconfirm where they were concentrating their search efforts, and this assured us that Ed's and my game plan, to concentrate on RV parks and similar locations from Tacoma to Everett and motels along the two main highways headed east, was correct. For the time being, this seemed to be the best approach and the most effective use of our small crew. Ed agreed this made a great deal of sense; and he, along with Leroy and the rest of the squad, would try to double their efforts. He said if there were no glitz, they might have made contact with the majority of the possible locations in these areas by no later than tomorrow night. I had a couple hours to kill before my meeting with Bob, so I decided to go on down early to the boat. This is my favorite private place for thought and reflection. I kept it moored at the Meydenbauer Yacht Club just minutes from my office or home.

I always think more clearly and completely relax when I was aboard. It hadn't changed. Today was no different. Once I stepped aboard and went into the stateroom, I immediately felt better. This was a forty-eight-foot 1948 tricabin Chris Craft, a true classic, not fast, but really comfortable. I had it restored to almost new condition several years ago and maintained it so it was always ready to go. They just don't make boats like this anymore, all mahogany and teak. It's funny I could never figure out why I felt different when I was here, but it always worked. Maybe it was the water lapping quietly on the sides of the hull or the slow roll of the boat as the water moved constantly as gentle breezes hit the craft. Kind of like the movement of a rocking chair or a crib. It felt so good I decided to call Bob and let him know I was already aboard just in case he wanted to come sooner.

"Sure, Jim," he said. "I'm almost ready to head that way. Let me wrap up a small project I'm working on and shut down my computer."

He didn't need directions because I had invited him on cruises into the San Juan Islands a number of times.

After calling Bob on his cell phone, I kicked off my shoes and then went up to the bow of the boat and sat down on the starboard side with my feet dangling over the side almost reaching the water.

It was one of those special days in Seattle.

Kind of like the song Perry Como sang in 1962 for the Seattle World's Fair, the Bluest Skies Are in Seattle.

As I sat there with my feet dangling over the starboard side of the boat, I reflected on the events that had brought my family, my greatest treasures, to this point in my life.

I told Bob later it was that instant when I made a personal vow no matter what, I would find my grandsons; and once they were safe, I would make the people responsible somehow pay for the pain and agony they had caused two of the most precious people in my life.

This world would be too small for them to hide from the wrath that was seething inside me. It wasn't vengeance I was looking for. I just wanted to make sure these people could never again do this to any other family.

I was just tired of the part of society that seemed to think we owed them something.

The part of society, who surfaced in the sixties to protest almost everything our government did, especially the Vietnam conflict. This was while I was fighting in Vietnam for their freedoms, and they continue to exist even now. To me, they evolved to become professional protestors. It was true they were almost totally correct about Vietnam, but to me there was more to being a citizen than just saying the government is wrong. Go to work, vote, and campaign or present an alternative plan. These things they never did . . . just protested, smoked dope, played their heavy metal music, and felt the government should support them.

As far as I was concerned, the kidnappers belonged to this part of our American society.

In other words, the part of society that thought they should get something for nothing. In my mind they expected—no, demanded unearned rewards. Maybe my thinking was incorrect, but that's how I felt.

I think it was on that day, aboard my boat, when I made a decision this was going to end.

Enough was enough. I'd had my fill of it.

I sat there thinking these thoughts for almost two hours until Bob arrived.

With all that was happening, I had forgotten how much I enjoyed sitting on my boat with the sun supplying all the warmth a body needed and the smell of seawater as it sloshed against the side of the hull creating a gentle rocking motion.

"Jim!" yelled Bob as he stepped onto the craft.

"I'm out on the bow. Come on aboard," I yelled back. Bob said, "Great, I'll meet you in the stateroom."

I saw Bob climb slowly aboard; and with much reluctance, I got to my feet, leaving all those thoughts behind. Bob and I had business to do, serious business. I walked back and down to the stateroom. As I descended the stairs, Bob was already aboard, and he extended his hand to me.

"Thanks for coming down to the boat. I just wanted to be away from everyone for a while. Sometimes it gets to be too much."

"Not to worry," Bob assured me. "Anywhere, anytime I'll be there. And believe me I totally understand, Robbie and Justin are like my own. I've been waiting to hear from you, so maybe I can finally be of some real help. I'm here at your disposal. Where do we start?" Obviously, Bob could sense the importance of this meeting.

I entered the stateroom, shook Bob's hand, and then dropped myself wearily into a nearby easy chair. I took a few minutes to gather my thoughts and hopefully present them to Bob in a way that he would find sensible. "I'm not sure how much you really can do, and I certainly don't mean to impose on our friendship, but I just don't know what else to do or to whom else to turn. There's no one I can trust like you. We discussed this subject before, and I asked you to keep silent until the situation called for a more aggressive approach. Thank you for keeping my confidence. I know you've been around the house during a lot of this, so there's not really a hell of a lot more to explain to you." I didn't wait for Bob's reaction I forged ahead. "Let me bring you up-to-date on where I think we are and an idea I have. I'll share my thoughts with you, and then you can tell me what you think. I'm referring specifically to what we had spoken about before. That if the FBI's methods seemed to be failing or at the very least be bogging down so time becomes a factor in finding Robbie and Justin. I'm of the opinion, factoring in the time element, this is exactly what has happened. Now it appears we need to look at our alternatives. Should we involve the press now or what other options do we have or maybe you have some other suggestions?"

I paused to give Bob some time to digest what I was referring to.

He took that moment to remove a small tape recorder and asked permission to record our conversation. He assured me that only he and I would ever hear what would be on the tape, and everything else that is communicated at this meeting would be protected by the constitution of our country.

I believed him, and he proceeded to turn the device on and set it on a small table between us.

I then filled him in on everything, including the evening of the money drop and how bad the end was. I described precisely the events and the people involved in the search for Robbie and Justin. I was careful to omit specific details about my crew, whose only objective was to find the location of Robbie and Justin. I shared with Bob my desire to keep their participation in the investigation private. No way was I allowing any of my team to be exposed to any legal responsibility. I firmly held with the notion that it was on my shoulders alone. "The same," I said, "also applies to you, Bob."

When I finished telling Bob the complete story, I sat back and looked him straight in the face.

"What do you think?" I said.

Bob sat there for a minute, reflecting on the scenario I had just laid out. He then turned his small recorder off and set it aside. "I don't think any more of this conversation should be recorded," he said firmly. It seemed to me like an eternity before he responded.

Then slowly and with well-chosen words, Bob said, "Jim, your idea of involving the press, I feel is the correct one. Anything we break in the press at this juncture should not in any way endanger the children any more than what danger already exists. From what you've told me about the kidnappers, they are probably long gone from the area. Hopefully, Robbie and Justin are still safe somewhere, and finding them is our main priority."

I noticed he avoided the word *alive*.

Bob continued, "I think if we break the story, and my advice is the sooner the better, we'll immediately have over two million people aware of the situation, and they would be on the alert for the kidnappers and the children."

And he added, "The State would also then be forced to issue an amber alert, about the children and the kidnappers, over all the radio, TV stations, and on the freeway alert signs." But he assured me, "He wouldn't do anything without my approval."

Then he asked, "Have you discussed this with Chief Hammond or Director Watkins?"

"No!" I responded quickly and emphatically.

"They'll do their thing, and you and I will do our thing. I've already done everything they've asked, including keeping the press out of it and delivering a million dollars to the kidnappers. This was their advice, and at the time, I agreed it was the correct decision. But now, it's time for me to get more directly involved in the finding of my two grandsons. I respect what they are doing, but there are just too many meetings for me." I paused, took a deep breath, and asked, "So where does that bring us? What do you think we should do, and how soon should we do it?"

Bob took a moment to ponder the question. Then he looked at me with concern and said, "Once we break the story, from that moment on, and even after Robbie and Justin are found, and the kidnappers are caught and brought to justice, there will not be a moment's peace or privacy in your family's lives. There will be TV reporters, broadcast remote trucks and helicopters outside your homes and office, twenty-four hours a day." He paused a moment to let this sink in and continued, "But I also know, deep down in my gut, now is the time. The sooner we break the story, the better chance we'll have in locating the kids. Time is short; and every day that goes by, there is a greater probability Robbie and Justin's situation will get worse. It's also conceivable the kidnappers will see the story; and they could panic, run, and, hopefully make mistakes that could lead to their capture and to rescuing Robbie and Justin. I'm also of the opinion, and I reiterate, I sincerely feel it would not increase the danger to the children. Hopefully I'm correct, but remember it's only my opinion, and there always remains a risk. Once again, though, and I can't emphasize this enough, once this story goes public your life will become a living hell. The press will hound you unmercifully; they'll have little regard for your privacy or the privacy of your family, friends, employees, and the involved authorities. You have no conception what the press is like when they cover stories of this magnitude. They'll be like sharks when they smell blood." Bob paused again and added, "It's your call, Jim."

I thought for a while. I knew now was not the time to make snap decisions, but it seemed obvious to me, time was of the essence.

As Bob said, once we broke the story, all hell would break loose.

I honestly felt there was only one conclusion. This could be the most important decision I would ever have to make, and I had better be right if I ever wanted to see Robbie and Justin again.

I got up and paced around the stateroom while Bob sat patiently waiting for my decision.

I didn't think long because I obviously had already thought this through and had come to the identical conclusion—break the story. "I don't think we have any alternative. As you said, Bob, time is of the essence to ensure the survival of Justin and Robbie. I think every time the clock ticks is one more minute Robbie and Justin remain in danger. Let's go with it. What do you need from me?"

Bob flashed a smile of relief.

"I've got it all here on my recorder, and with my notes, it shouldn't take long to write the story. Now let me make you aware one more time, so you know, the minute I call the editor of the paper there will be no turning back."

"Yes, I know," I said wearily. "Let's get out of here. We both have a lot to do, and I need to get with my family and fill them in on what they need to do in preparation for the story breaking and what they can expect from the press. Do you think I should call Hammond or Watkins and prepare them?"

"It's your call again. However, I don't think we should backdoor them. It's called CYA but be prepared, especially with the FBI, they are really paranoid when it comes to the press. They are going to go ballistic, pissed off beyond belief. If you do meet with them, give them my private home and cell phone number so if they want they can call me with any, and I mean any questions they may have. Once you tell them who I really am, they will immediately put two and two together and realize what I was doing when you first introduced me at Mark's house as a family friend."

Bob quickly tore a sheet out of his notebook and scribbled down his phone numbers. "Try to assure them we're only doing this to facilitate the recovery of Justin and Robbie. If everything goes according to our plan, tell them the story will probably be on the front page of tomorrow morning's first edition so they can be prepared. As a precautionary move, you may want to have the phone company change all your phones to unlisted numbers and make your office aware of the potential chaos headed their way. If you can arrange twenty-four-hour security, I would do it. If possible, when you call the phone company, if it's at all feasible, have them install a bank of an 800 number and phones for potential tipsters to call. You'll probably have to operate it twenty-four hours a day in order to make it effective. And another thought, do you want to offer a reward for the safe return of Justin and Robbie? If you do, I'll emphasize in my news story that it's only collectible with the safe return of Robbie and Justin. That should help you eliminate some of the nuts."

"Why didn't I think of that?" I said, "Certainly! How much do you think is enough?"

"A hundred thousand usually gets people's attention. Can you handle that?"

"Done!"

"I'll put it in my article. If you are able to get the 800 phone number installed today, be sure to call me immediately. I'll include it in the first story with the stress on the safe return of the kids in order to receive the reward money. Hopefully, it might assist in keeping the number of crank calls down. Okay, let's get going. I've got a lot of writing to do and people to meet with. Can you think of anything else before we split?"

"I hope we've covered about everything, let's get going." I stood up and clapped Bob on his back gratefully. "Good luck and thanks for being there for my family and me. Let's go get it done."

We both headed our own way—I to meet with the family and the police, Bob to call his editor to set up a meeting and, if it goes according to plan, start writing the story of his lifetime.

We were both aware how time was of the essence. Every second, every minute could mean life and death for Justin and Robbie.

Justin and Robbie.

Bob's excitement was surging inside him like some dark and depthless ocean. As he got into his car, he said a silent Hail Mary, praying they were doing the right thing.

Above all else, though, he was a professional news reporter.

The task ahead of him helped keep his feelings under control.

The task and the opportunity.

The reporter in him was reawakened like some sleeping giant.

He had a job to do. An important job!

#

I jumped in my SUV and put in a call to Chief Hammond on his private line.

"Hammond."

"John, Jim here. I need to have an emergency meeting with you and Director Watkins as soon as possible. Can you set it up?"

"Watkins is here in my office right now, Jim. We've been going over the case and coordinating the search. If you're available now, you can come to my office, and we'll both be able to meet with you."

"I'm about five minutes away," I finished, clicking off my cell phone without even saying good-bye and headed down the road.

I drove up Main Street to 116th and the city hall in Bellevue.

#

BOB ARNOTT

#

Meanwhile I called my editor, Albert Norton III, and requested a similar meeting.

Even though it was Labor Day weekend, I knew Mr. Norton would be in his office. I frankly wondered if the man really had a wife and a home.

The guy was the epitome of a workaholic. I stressed to him on the phone I had the story of the year, an exclusive, and a scoop over TV, radio, and all the other newspapers in the entire country. Nobody, I assured him, but his newspaper, the *Times*, would have the exclusive story until we broke with it.

This, I knew, would make him sit up and listen.

I was confident enough in our past relationship that he knew when I said I had a story and an exclusive, it was for real. When I stressed the magnitude of the story, he was doubly enticed. He instructed me to come to his office immediately.

I told him I was on my way as we spoke. I immediately headed for the Mercer Island Bridge from Bellevue and to the newspaper over on Boren Avenue in Seattle as fast as my old Ford would allow me to travel legally.

#

Jim pulled into the city hall parking lot and parked in the first spot he saw and dashed into the building. He knew exactly where Hammond's office was and caught the elevator to the third floor. He ignored the receptionist, walked straight by Hammond's secretary without a word to her, and into Hammond's office.

Director Watkins was standing to one side, studying a huge map with all kinds of dots, arrows, and different colored pins stuck in various locations. Chief Hammond was seated at his desk and appeared to be looking out his window at downtown Bellevue.

My unannounced entry startled them both. Hammond turned and, seeing me coming in, smiled cordially and said, "Have a seat, Jim."

Indicating a chair in front of his desk, I ignored the directive. "What is it you have that seems so important?" asked Hammond.

I finally sat down, and Watkins took the chair right next to him. I wasted no time and proceeded to tell them about my meeting with Bob Arnott and what was coming down.

Director Watkins rose out of his chair and loudly exclaimed his dismay at what Jim had told them. "Do you know what in the hell you've done? This may jeopardize our entire search, not to mention the total chaos it could cause, and it might make the kidnappers panic and cause them to do more harm to your grandchildren." He was standing only a few steps from me and directed those comments straight in my face . . . then turned to Hammond. "Didn't you tell him that he had to clear everything with you or me before he made a move like this?"

Before the chief could respond, Jim stood up to his full six feet two. He was a good half foot taller than the director. He pushed his face close to the director's to emphasize both his sincerity and his determination. "In no way do I intend to interfere with your investigation. My only concern is the safe return of my grandchildren. If I waited for you and your friggin' paperwork and bureaucratic mishmash, they could be dead. And you know I'm correct."

He then stood right in front of Watkins and stared through those steel blue eyes that would cause Watkins to turn away.

There was no doubt in Watkins's mind he was being confronted by a very angry man, a huge angry man; and quickly, gathering his wits about him, he asked, "What's this reporter's name and number? Let's see if we can put a cap on this before it hits the newspaper."

"You're too late!" I snapped. Then I wheeled and headed for the door without supplying the requested information. I stopped at the door, paused, and turned to face both the chief and the director and said, "I've got important things to take care of. I came here because I wanted to avoid blindsiding you both. So instead of sputtering, why don't you get to work and maybe, just maybe, you'll find the kids and bring them back safely before the story breaks tomorrow morning. The reporter is Bob Arnott, and here are two numbers where you can reach him. Bob said to call if you wanted to speak with him."

Before either Chief Hammond or Watkins could respond, I threw the numbers Bob had written down for me on the floor and walked out the door.

Instead of using the elevator, I descended down the stairs two at a time, out the front door, and jumped into my SUV. I was going to Mark's house to fill the family in on almost everything that had transpired, have them make all the phone arrangements, find twenty-four-hour security and phone-answering people, and organize an agenda for a meeting the next morning with Ed and my squad of veterans.

I had a lot to do and so little time to get it all done.

#

Back at the city hall, Hammond and Watkins just stood there for a minute after Jim departed, before speaking.

Watkins started first, "Do you know this reporter Bob Arnott?" For some reason he wasn't immediately recalling Bob had been the family friend hanging around the house.

Hammond said, "I know him very well, and you've met him. Think back a moment. He's the family friend." Watkins's response was swift, "Not the guy who's been hanging around the house? My god! Did you know he was a reporter?" Hammond responded, "I thought he was retired. He is their friend, a very old friend. I never gave it a second thought."

Watkins quickly asked, "Do you think you could stop him from printing the story or at least get him to sit on it for a few days?"

Hammond then answered, "I could try, but honestly, I don't think there's a chance in hell he would comply. After all, retired or not, he's a reporter and at onetime a damn good one. I'll bet he's meeting with his editor as we speak, and you know the press. They won't sit on it and take a chance someone else gets the story first. Think like them for a minute. What would you do?"

Watkins agreed and decided not to waste their time talking to Arnott or his editor. Instead, he said, "Let's both prepare for the onslaught we can anticipate coming tomorrow morning."

#

Meanwhile I had arrived at the newspaper building and was sitting in the editor's office, a superplush office with a wet bar, full bath, and a view of Puget Sound.

I proceeded to fill him briefly in on the story.

Al Norton listened attentively, tapping a pencil on the keyboard of his computer. A nervous habit. He had on tennis shorts and a hoody with a Stanford University emblem on it. I would have ragged on him about his disloyalty if this moment wasn't so important.

I knew once I told him the story, it would blow his socks off.

"Jim Malone, huh? Important local figure?" he asked. I didn't offer a response. *Tap-tap-tap* went the pencil. His tanned brow was knit below a widow's peak in his brown hair. Grey hair flecked his temples. He smelled of yuppie sweat, I'd caught him after a tennis match. He had just returned from the Seattle Tennis Club to shower in his office and as usual, work. I didn't even know he had a hobby other than dinner once in a while with his wife and obviously tennis.

The story flowed out.

Needless to say, Editor Al Norton III was ecstatic beyond words and instructed me to get to work immediately on the story. He directed me to stay right here in his office and use his computer to write the story. It was obvious he didn't want anyone to become aware of what was about to transpire. He immediately called downstairs and instructed his people in charge to hold the front page open on the next edition for a whopper lead story. He instructed them to move everything out of the way and be prepared for a blockbuster.

I sat down and began to write.

I could hardly contain my journalistic excitement.

I was almost beside myself.

This was a reporter's dream, a front-page byline. You could also bet the Associated Press would pick it up and all the syndicators.

My story would be in every major paper in the entire country.

It was my ticket out of the back forty where I'd been forced to graze for the last few years.

Even knowing all of this I did not lose my focus on what I hoped to achieve by writing the story.

The safe return of Robbie and Justin.

"How soon will you be done?" asked Norton.

"Soon, it's all in my head and here on my recorder," I said. "All I have to do is write it. I am waiting for a call from Jim Malone or his son on my cell phone with an 800 number for the public to call with tips on the whereabouts of the grandchildren. That's if the phone company will cooperate and get it hooked up. Oh yes, Jim agreed to offer a reward of a hundred thousand dollars for information leading to the safe return of his grandsons, Robbie and Justin. I hope you agree this should be prominently featured in the story."

The editor nodded his approval.

I turned back to the computer and continued to write.

What a story!

#

CHAPTER 22

JIM MALONE

After my angry and rapid departure from Hammond's office, I drove way too fast in getting to Mark's house. I parked right in front; and without a word to the security that still remained outside, I entered and, without delay, gathered everyone in the great room to prepare them for what was happening. I explained everything to my family, avoiding any explanation whatsoever about my squad's involvement.

Mark, Joan, and Deanna didn't question anything. After I completed filling in the details on what they must do in preparation for what was about to take place when Bob's story broke in tomorrow's paper, they immediately volunteered to take care of the phone arrangements.

They were confident they had enough friends who would willingly assist in manning the phones, especially once the story broke in the newspaper.

They began instantly calling everybody they thought they could count on, and would need in answering the phones, and invited them come to the house in the morning at 7:00 AM for an organizational meeting. The only explanation they supplied was a severe family crisis existed, and we were in urgent need of assistance. It was difficult not to offer more detail, but we needed to assemble as much manpower as we could in a short period.

Everyone they called knew neither Joan nor Deanna would ever make such an unusual request unless something serious was happening. In every instance, everyone, to the person, agreed to help in any way they could.

While my family was handling this part of the operation, I departed for my office to prepare my office staff for the onslaught that was coming. I did this without giving them too much explanation, other than an important news story in tomorrow morning's paper would explain everything to them.

I had also instructed Mark to call a twenty-four-hour security service to start before 6:00 AM tomorrow morning at his house and at our office. I told them to get it all handled regardless of the cost.

Mark totally agreed this would be needed in order to keep the general public and news services at bay and said he knew of an excellent security company he was positive he could hire on such short notice.

While all of this was going on, Ed and Leroy, the main part of the elite search-and-rescue squad, were covering RV parks and similar locations from Tacoma to Everett, while the rest of the team concentrated on Interstate 2 and I-90 heading east to the top of both passes, Stevens and Snoqualmie.

They couldn't believe how many existed.

Fortunately, there were fewer short-time or daily sites as opposed to more permanent ones, and it appeared to be more logical to concentrate on these type of facilities. So far, nothing had been discovered, but they had only covered about half of their list and were making what appeared to be progress. Ed and Leroy had developed a short list of questions they felt would not cause too much concern from the managers of the sites, but would give them and the squad members a clue whether any short-time suspicious people had rented space over the last few days. Unfortunately, their efforts had rewarded them zero information.

I was somewhat disappointed with our lack of progress, but we all knew this entire operation was a long shot at its best.

But at least something was happening, and thru the process of elimination, we knew where the kidnappers were not hiding.

#

CHAPTER 23

THE KIDNAPPERS

Only one day had passed since they had left the Everett area and pulled into the RV area at the Colville Indian Casino known as the Mill Bay Casino.

The check in was quick and easy. No fees to pay, nothing to sign, just find an unoccupied spot, park, and do all the hookups correctly.

That's exactly what Fred did and went ahead and set up the motor home. Before long, Dennis pulled alongside and parked. He apparently had taken a wrong turn down the road a ways and was almost forty-five minutes behind.

Just as Fred commented to Lois, he wondered what happened to him. Dennis opened the door and came in without knocking

Fred immediately chastised him, "For god's sake damn it knock before you come in."

Dennis snapped back, "Who the fuck else were you expecting?"

"How about the cops, you dumb shit!" Fred snarled.

"Fuck the cops, we're long gone," Dennis said, still acting like a smartass.

"Hey, don't be stupid." Fred was somewhat disgusted with Dennis anyhow, and his getting lost compounded his foul mood. "We have a long way to go before we're home free, about two thousand miles to the Mexican border. Besides, I haven't figured out yet how we're going to get across the border."

"Stop calling me stupid! Why don't we just drive across like everybody else?" Dennis said. Fred looked at him for a moment and finally gave up.

"Forget it for now. Let's go over to the casino and have breakfast at their Coyote Café; then maybe do some gambling, I need some fun for a change." He turned to Lois and snapped his fingers. "Come on, Lois, get off your butt and go with us."

"You guys go ahead, I'm going to take a shower and lay down for a little while. I'm totally bushed," Lois replied.

"Suit yourself. Come on, Den, let's you and me go pig out. I'm so hungry I could eat the asshole out of a skunk, and then maybe we'll play a little blackjack," said Fred.

Fred and Dennis walked out the door and headed for the café.

"Is she all right?" asked Dennis.

"I think so. She seems overly concerned about those two brats, but she'll get over it." He shook his head wearily. "What she needs is for me to give her a good banging. That'll quiet her down."

"Hey, when you get through why don't you give me a shot at her? I mean isn't that what buddies are for, sharing?"

"Maybe later, let her settle down a bit first. I agree that's what broads are for. Banging!" Fred laughed, finally smiling a bit after all the tension he was feeling. "Let's go in and chow down."

#

While they were gone, Lois showered.

After the refreshing water and soap and a touch of perfume, she changed into some comfortable sweats, took down the wood window coverings and put the curtains up in the back bedroom where they had been holding the kids, put the wood coverings in a nearby dumpster, and generally cleaned up the motor home.

Then she sat down.

Oh god, those two little guys.

Oh, how she wished and prayed they were going to be found before long.

She couldn't think of anything she could do immediately without getting into trouble, so she decided to try to put it out of her mind.

She thought, *If necessary, I'll execute the plan that I formulated during the trip over the mountains.*

But first give it a couple days, and do it only if the opportunity presented itself. She also came to the conclusion, getting away from these two buttheads was her only alternative for survival; and as soon as Fred gave them each their share, she was going to split.

She already had enough of Fred.

And Dennis!

Dennis was a jerk to top all jerks. She was aware with the way he looked at her he would like to get her in the sack. It was bad enough she still had to tolerate sex with Fred. But do it with Dennis, never in a million years.

It all sounded so great and simple at first. It was Fred who conceived the plot. He came up with it after she told him about her conversations with that rich lady, Deanna.

Now she knew it was too late to go back, but she really would if she could. There didn't seem to be any way out.

Better to try and put it out of her mind and figure how to get out of the situation she's in as soon as possible and, with a bit of luck, maybe even get out alive.

Just then she heard them coming back from breakfast.

Fred walked in first, followed by the asshole.

"You should've had breakfast with us. It was great. Right, Den?"

"Yeah," Dennis said, in high spirits. "Hey, let's take some dough like you said and do a little gambling. I've always wanted to rub elbows with the big rollers." He was chomping at the bit to get to the tables and win big money.

Fred agreed, "Good thinking. But don't introduce yourself to anyone. Remember if some one asks, we're Canadians from Rockford, British Columbia. And, like I told you both, it's a little town just over the border from Blaine, Washington in Canada. And if they ask where we're going, tell them we're heading for Texas to hook up with some friends for the winter."

Fred proceeded to unlock the closet door and took out the suitcase of money. He unlocked the suitcase as Dennis and Lois stood and watched. Dennis just stood there, frozen. His mouth was wide-open, greedily anticipating having more money in his hands than ever before in his life. He could hardly contain himself.

Fred counted out fifty twenties in three stacks and said, "A thousand for each of us. Now, Dennis, there's your budget for today, so don't go nuts. Probably tomorrow we'll head for that other Indian casino over toward Spokane. I've been there before. It's called Two Rivers, and it has a great big RV parking area with lots of Canadians. It's right on the Columbia River, really beautiful. We might even stay there for a couple days. Now, Den, go on over to the casino and keep a low profile. Lois and I have some business to attend to."

Lois looked up at the ceiling, dreading the thought of what business Fred had in mind. "Can I stay and watch?" Dennis asked.

What a sick bastard, Lois instantly thought. "Get on out of here and be cool over there. This won't take long," Fred said.

Dennis took his cue and closed the door behind him.

"Well, don't just stand there, come on over here."

Fred was already taking his pants off. "How about one of your great BJs to warm things up and then I'll get inside and make you happy."

Lois was hoping she could get him off with oral sex and then she would be done with him for today. Seldom had he ever really satisfied her. It was just sex to him.

With that in mind, she started caressing his cock, all six or so inches of it. Lois was very good at getting guys off. That's how she made money to get drugs before she got cured.

In fact, that was how she first met Fred; she'd been Fred's "sex provider" for over six years he'd been a client. Then a year ago, he convinced her to move in with him. By then, she had gone to drug rehab, stopped hooking, and was working part-time at Overlake Hospital Medical Center in Bellevue. Fred had just come back from making a drug run that netted him about a one hundred thousand. Or so he said. She was never able to tell what was true with him or whether it was just big talk. He had been in the Los Angeles area at the time. And only he knew why he came to the to Seattle area. He didn't really talk about it too much. Lois thought it was probably to avoid being killed by some drug people he had ripped off.

Anyhow, she was good at this sex stuff.

It took just a few minutes of work until Fred was breathing hard and moving his body with her mouth. Then he came.

Lois pulled back and continued to stroke him until his breathing became more normal. She took a warm washcloth and cleaned him off.

"God, you're good!" he said with a grin. "Want your turn?"

"Nah, go on and catch up with Dennis," she replied. "I'd feel better knowing you're watching him. He's pretty stupid, you know."

"Yeah, you're right." The grin somehow got bigger. "I had better get over and make sure he's all right. Knowing him, he probably already lost all his dough. You sure you don't want to come with me now?"

"I'll be over in a minute. Let me clean up and put on something more appropriate."

Fred pulled his jeans on, slipped into his loafers, grabbed his stack of bills, and barged out the door. He was like a kid in a candy store.

She was thinking again.

This was still Monday, Labor Day, they had been driving so much she was almost losing track what day it was.

If they haven't found the kids yet, that's two days. They've got to find them tomorrow or Wednesday at the absolute latest.

They couldn't last too long.

She decided to go over to the casino gift shop and see if they had a Seattle paper. But first she better hide most of her money. There wasn't any way she was going to piss it away at the casino like Fred and Dennis. She planned to kind of play the slots so they would think she was just like them and then they wouldn't rag on her.

Fred had put the suitcase of money back in the one closet with a lock on it.

So where could she hide her money.

She found a small cardboard box and hid it with the money inside under the sink way in the back. She knew neither Fred nor Dennis either one would ever peek under the sink.

She slipped into some tight but comfortable fitting jeans, put on a sweater, ran a brush through her hair after she had brushed her teeth, and headed for the casino with just a couple hundred bucks in her pocket.

She found a *Seattle Times* in the gift shop and sat down to leaf through it. Nothing!

At least nothing at all about the kidnapping.

Maybe there would be something tomorrow.

The casino was the usual clatter and clink of slot machines, the smell of carpet cleaner, floor wax, cigarette smoke, and the blank looks of card dealers.

She walked around the floor until she spied Fred and Dennis at a blackjack table with a stack of green chips in front of them. She couldn't tell if they were winning or losing, and she wasn't going near them to find out.

Finally, she headed for the slot machines to look for a nickel or penny slot machine. No way was she going to piss her money away at any casino. She planned to play it cool until she could find some way to get away from these two assholes.

And if things went right, she would take at least a quarter of million dollars with her. At the same time, she still couldn't get the kids out of her mind.

Lois played the slots for about an hour and went to tell Fred she was going for a walk and would meet them later for dinner.

They hardly paid any attention to her and turned back to the blackjack table to concentrate on losing their money.

Like they say in Vegas, she thought, *Welcome to town and good luck*. Sure there's a winner a minute . . . not to mention of a thousand losers a minute.

Oh well, she thought, *it's their money to lose*.

She headed for the entrance to take a walk down by the shore of Lake Chelan. It was a pretty good hike, past a golf course it smelled of new mown grass, across the road and into a park area with a boat dock and picnic tables.

The sun felt warm and nice on the back of her neck.

Pretty nice, she thought.

She strolled around the park looking at the groups of people, families, and a lot of couples just enjoying the water and the end of summer weather.

If only she could only be like them, playing in the sun, the water, picnicking with a real family, and not fear who might be looking for her.

She knew it wasn't to be, not now, not ever.

She had destroyed her life, and she knew it.

This family scene just made it more poignant.

Lois finally sat down on the grass just off the edge of the lake, daydreaming and enjoying the scent of nearby flowers. She was longing for a life like she was watching. She knew all too well this could never happen, especially not now.

If she survived this ordeal, she would be lucky. How easy it was to get involved in things, and how tough it was to get out of them. It seemed like it's what she had been doing all her life, getting in and out of trouble. One never seems to learn.

Her job at Overlake Hospital was about the only real occupation she had ever had in years.

She'd worked at a shoe store in a mall when she was in high school.

Then she found drugs when she was only sixteen.

For ten whole years, she lived for the next hit.

Fortunately, the last time she was busted for prostitution and possession, she went to rehab instead of jail.

It was the only option the judge gave her, and she'd grabbed it like a drowning person grabs a life preserver.

Everything at the time was going all right with her life. She liked the job at the hospital, the fellow workers, and the personal feeling that she wasn't a bad person anymore.

Then Fred found her again.

He was fun all over again, had a lot of money to burn, she was back into it once more, and then he came up with this new get-rich scheme. It sounded simple . . . get rich quick.

Once again, she had to admit she screwed up, and now her only option seemed to ride it out. Time would tell.

Only this time she knew jail was the only thing she could look forward to if they got caught, a long time in jail. And in her mind she knew eventually they would get caught. She could feel it; and her intuitions, even though she usually ignored them, were seldom wrong. So she concluded she had better enjoy what little freedom she had left.

Then the two children entered her thoughts again.

Their little images haunted her. The thought of them dying was almost intolerable.

God, how she prayed they would be found.

As she sat by the blue of Lake Chelan and the green of the grass, she started to feel a little more relaxed. She was thoroughly enjoying being outside. She saw some of the families starting their barbecues and couldn't recall ever doing it. It was really special just watching them enjoying their families and especially the children.

Nearby, some boater started his engine, and the noise startled her.

A blast of black exhaust spurted.

She came back to the real world and noticed she had been down here for a couple hours.

She'd better get back to the motor home.

Slowly and reluctantly, she got up from the bench she'd been sitting on and headed back to the motor home to see if the guys were back and maybe wanted to go to dinner.

Amazing how much time went by while she was down at the park!

Back at the motor home, she just sat in a chair with the door open to let the breeze flow in and tried to take a nap.

Every time she closed her eyes, though, the Malone kids would appear on the back of her eyelids. It was frightening; and no matter what she did, she couldn't shake it.

Fred and Dennis finally showed up about thirty minutes after she had been there.

As expected, they were extremely unhappy with their first day of gambling. But, like all bad gamblers, they weren't about to quit. They knew their luck was going to change.

They entered the motor home, and Fred immediately headed for the closet to get more money so they could go back to recover their losses.

What a dreamer.

This time he took out ten thousand for him and Dennis.

She was surprised when he handed her ten thousand, the most money she had ever in her life held in one hand.

At least Fred was dividing the money evenly.

He said they had already eaten and for her to go ahead and eat by herself. Then he and Dennis went out the door to continue playing blackjack and win their money back.

After they were gone, she stashed her ten thousand with the rest of her money and then decided to go over to the Coyote Café for dinner.

They had a prime rib special that night that turned out to be really good. She was thankful not to have to sit with those two assholes. Let them go ahead and lose their money.

She could care less.

#

Chapter 24

JIM MALONE

It was six thirty Tuesday morning. The sun was threatening to come up on the horizon. It looked like it was going to be a nice day.

I was driving to the office to meet with Ed and Leroy.

There was plenty on my mind.

On the way to the office, I had stopped at a Seven-Eleven and picked up a paper.

There it was.

Bob Arnott's story was on the front page just like he had predicted.

It covered almost half of the front page with huge headlines.

What a friend, I'd thought after I read the story. Let's hope it helps.

After I finished reading the complete story, I went back in the Seven-Eleven store and purchased a couple more papers in case the people I needed to see this morning hadn't picked up a paper. I got back into my SUV and drove on to the office.

I planned to get to the office early for the meeting before my crew arrived. However, when I walked in, I was surprised to find they were already there.

All eight members of my crew.

They had maps posted on the wall with pins and marks all over them, similar to what Watkins had on the wall in Hammond's office, and were busy designating everyone's responsibilities for today's search.

As I entered the room, they all directed their attention to me.

"Are we making any progress?" I asked in a concerned voice.

"We're over half done; and if finding out nothing, is good, then I guess we're making great progress," Ed responded a little dejectedly. "We've divided the area in half with the center starting from Seattle. Leroy has three going with him south along I-5 to Tacoma and east on I-90 to the top of Snoqualmie."

He stepped over and tapped the map.

"I have three with me, searching north on I-5 to Everett and east on Interstate 2 to the top of Stevens Pass. We thought we would get the north and south portions done first, and then we'll start east toward the passes. Who would believe that there are that many RV parks? We should have them all covered in these north-south areas by late today, and if any of us find anything concrete, we'll contact you immediately. Unless you have some suggestions, we'll continue until we've covered the entire area."

"It looks like you've got it all under control," I said and without hesitating, continued, "I want you all to sit down for a few minutes and let me fill you in on some new important developments. If you haven't read this morning's newspaper, you need to see what's on the front page. It should put another perspective on your efforts."

They had been concentrating so much on their search that none of them had even thought to pick up this morning's paper.

I had my copy with me.

I slapped it down on the table.

"I met yesterday with my friend, Bob Arnott, who as some of you know is not only a good family friend, but also used to be an investigative reporter for the *Times*," I said. "He broke the story this morning on the front page." I pointed at the paper and continued, "I'll leave this copy for you guys to read after I leave. After you read what's in it, if we get lucky, we may have thousands of people helping us. As I speak, Mark, Joan, and Deanna are coordinating an 800 number and a twenty-four-hour staff to man the calls that will hopefully be forth coming. Also, if you look outside, you'll see security being set up to keep the media and the public away."

I paused for a moment to let it all sink in and to heighten my announcement about the reward.

"When you read Bob's news story, you'll see I'm offering a hundred-thousand-dollar reward for Justin and Robbie's safe return. Now as I told you before, I want all of you to remain undercover and totally avoid any contact with the press. As far as they're concerned, you're just doing the work you are employed to do—build houses. If you are ever contacted, let me know immediately; and in all cases, tell them you know nothing, and they need to talk directly with me. That should be the end of your communication with the press. But beware, always have your guard up at all times, and take extra care because they are very competent; and it's their job to grind until they get a story. Bob told me they don't let up until they get something they can use, and they'll do almost anything to get a scoop. So let me stress again, be extra careful."

I turned to my right-hand man.

"Ed, why don't you check with me twice a day on my cell phone for anything that may have been called in on the 800 lines we have set up, and at the same time you can update me on any progress you may be making? The family will keep me informed at all times if anything important comes in we need to further investigate."

I took a deep breath and cast my gaze over them all, one by one.

"Now, unless you have something else, I'll get out of your way and let you continue. Any questions before I leave?"

There were no questions for me.

I thanked them again from the bottom of my heart for their loyalty and their help.

#

I left my office to head for Mark's house to see how Operation Save Our Kids was progressing.

The security people were already in place at the office location, and so I turned around and went back to ask Ed to fill the office staff in on the security and explain the newspaper story to the office personnel so they wouldn't be too shocked at all the activity.

I also told Ed to tell them the phones were being changed to keep calls coming in from the outside to a minimum.

This all took about another thirty minutes before I was finally able to drive to Mark's house.

As usual, the traffic at this time of day was atrocious. It took me over forty minutes to get there. Probably the same as always, but since I was in a hurry, it seemed much more congested.

But the day after Labor Day everybody was returning to work, so I was sure it was not just a typical day.

There's nothing I could do about it.

So I just tried to keep cool and be careful. An accident at this time would be terrible, and I knew it, so I took extra care.

I finally pulled into Mark's driveway.

Fortunately, the press hadn't showed up yet, so access at the entrance was easy. For this I was thankful. I wasn't ready to face news people yet. In fact, Bob was the only one of their number I really cared to deal with at all.

The security people Mark hired had already set up barriers to prevent unwanted outsiders from entering the premises. Guys in official-looking uniforms were positioned in front of these barriers in order to prevent unauthorized access. They stopped me at the entrance where they had the metal barriers set up, checked my ID and license plate before letting me proceed. Apparently, before letting me pass, they called the main house on a two-way radio, informing them who was trying to get access.

This pleased me immensely. After getting clearance, I continued down Mark's driveway and couldn't believe what was there.

There must have been a dozen cars parked all over the front yard.

It looked like someone was having a party, but I knew better.

I found the most convenient place to park and started to go inside but was stopped immediately by more security people. They were stationed at the front door and allowed me to enter after rechecking my ID.

Apparently, they were the ones, who the front gate had called for access approval.

Everyone was gathered in the Great Room.

They had brought in extra chairs and tables, so there was a place for all those involved to sit.

Mark had filled all the people in about the news story, even though a few of them had already read it in the morning paper.

The story was the main topic they were discussing before Mark started the meeting. They were aware now why they had been recruited to assist with answering the phones. Mark was in the process of completely indoctrinating them on everything that had transpired, including telling them about the portion of the story concerning the reward and the 800 number.

As I entered the room, he was in the process of passing out sheets of paper with full instructions on how to handle calls. There were places to fill in any important information callers may supply. At any time when a phone answerer received any information of importance, they would verify the caller's name, address, and phone number and would be asked if we could call them back.

If the answer was yes, they would then deliver this to Mark, Deanna, or Joan would make the follow-up call. They would proceed to do a more assertive phone interview in order to ascertain the veracity of the caller; then this information would be evaluated, and a decision would be made whether it warranted following the lead or if we needed to notify the authorities and let them do the follow up.

With a hundred thousand dollars on the line, we expected more nuts than real callers, but we were trying to cover all our bases. I listened to Mark's presentation as he handed out the instruction sheets. I was more than impressed by all the paperwork he, Joan, and Deanna had prepared for this meeting. I had spent the night at our house so they handled it all alone. They must have stayed up most of the night. Obviously, they had it all under control. At his finish, he asked for me to speak and maybe add some more information.

I filled them with a few more details about the story and mentioned my gratitude to the writer, Bob Arnott. They all sat there somewhat stunned by being so close to such an overwhelming tragedy. I paused to ask Mark if the phones were all ready. He confirmed the phone company had cooperated fully in changing all the phones to unlisted numbers and succeeded in getting the 800 number connected. He did say the phone company offered some resistance because of the holiday and the lack of needed personnel to do the job, so he had to implore Chief Hammond to call the powers that be at the phone company in order to get their full cooperation.

I asked him how Chief Hammond treated him during this call.

Mark said he was really cordial and did not hesitate to assist. I knew I could count on his support, more than Watkins, even if they had not agreed with me for getting Bob Arnott and the newspaper involved.

Deanna confirmed she had called Bob Arnott and gave him the 800 numbers that he wanted to include in his story. Since I had already read the story, I was aware of most everything they were telling me, but I chose not to interrupt. As I concluded a brief review of what we hoped to achieve with the 800 calls, I then added a few words about how wonderful it was to have friends like them and thanked them from the entire family for their participation.

After completing this meeting and feeling confident Mark had everything here pretty well under control, I decided to leave and go back to my house to try and bring my thoughts together. Everything in the last few hours moved so quickly I wasn't positive that even I knew what was happening.

I asked Deanna if she wanted to go with me, but she chose to stay with Mark and Joan.

So I went on by myself.

There was a lot to think about . . .

And there was something I had to deal with inside myself. What I was really going to do if the situation caused me to take a course of action that would involve only the kidnappers and me?

#

CHAPTER 25

BOB ARNOTT

The trial seemed to be moving at supersonic speed. My hand ached from all my note jotting.

The DA and his staff were confident they had prepared a prima facie case whose objective, regardless of the fact a great preponderance of the evidence was circumstantial, was to produce a guilty verdict.

At the same time as the trial was in progress, the FBI was continuing their search for the third member of the kidnapping trio. They released an APB out to all law officials from coast-to-coast to be on the lookout for her. When they conducted their search of the motor home, they found some notes with a name on them.

Lois Griffin.

They ran a background search through all the files available, and a Lois Griffin showed up.

This Lois Griffin had a record of minor offenses in California for prostitution and drug possession. She hadn't done any hard time, but was still on parole from her drug conviction. The last connection her parole officer had with her was when she was working at Overlake Hospital in Bellevue but had failed to report for her last three appointments.

After compiling all this information, they felt there was no doubt she was the third member of the kidnapping trio. It was the FBI's decision, during this investigation, to keep the enormity of their efforts to find her as quiet as possible. They figured if they were able to catch her and the press became aware they had her in custody, it would turn into a public press nightmare and maybe make her ineffective as a witness for the prosecution.

The DA's office emphasized if the law enforcement authorities were successful in apprehending this Lois Griffin before the trial was concluded, they could hopefully persuade her to testify for the prosecution. Shoemaker thought her testimony could contribute a large amount in bringing the state's case to an ultimate conclusion, leaving the jury with no alternative other than to find Jim guilty of these two deaths. In the prosecution's mind, there was still time to capture her and, with any luck, get her somehow to cooperate.

District Attorney Shoemaker reemphasized to Watkins and the FBI that he felt Lois Griffin would be extremely useful even if they had to use her testimony in the rebuttal phase of the trial after the defense concluded the stating of its case. This gave Watkins a little more elbow room in which to operate in his quest to locate her.

The trial was taking an excessive amount of time because Shoemaker had witness after witness from the various casinos testify about the "victim's" activities during the days they had spent gambling at their establishments. He was able to call several casino employees who were able to identify Jim as the person who had been asking questions about three friends he was supposed to meet.

Most of them, however, as far as I could detect, didn't really offer any crucial, damaging evidence. Most of it was fluff, and Shoemaker's attempt in establishing Jim as a killer in pursuit of his victims seemed to be ineffective.

During their testimony, several of them after they looked at pictures of the two kidnappers, did verify the two men Jim was being accused of killing were in the casinos, accompanied by a female. Like I said, some identified Jim and confirmed he had been in the same casinos inquiring about three people he referred to as some friends he was supposed to meet up with. The latter part most certainly didn't help Jim because it did establish he was pursuing the kidnappers. However, it was Ewing's sentiment when he did his cross-examination of each of these witnesses he could create a more empathetic attitude by the jurors toward Jim than they would have for the kidnappers.

As the trial progressed, even though Jim had assured him he had not killed the two kidnappers, J. Edgar felt the DA was presenting a pretty convincing circumstantial case. Therefore, he had to not only create reasonable doubt in the jury's mind, but to also hope they would agree what Jim was accused of doing was not totally illegal; they might even construe it as self-defense if they concluded Jim had in fact killed the two kidnappers.

It seemed obvious to me Ewing wanted to firmly plant in the jury's minds that the "crime" the prosecution was trying Jim for was exactly what they, too, as private citizens, would have done had they been faced with the same situation.

He thought all of this could go a long way in influencing the jury to return a verdict of "not guilty."

Ewing knew it was a long shot.

But it appeared to be one of the only ways out for Jim.

And he only had to convince one out of twelve.

The prosecutor even called the people who had volunteered their help in answering the phones at Mark and Joan's house to testify. Plus, he'd subpoenaed Jim's office staff, including Ed and Leroy.

Shoemaker was attempting to illustrate to the jury how intense Jim's determination was to find the kidnappers. And to me, Reporter Bob Arnott, he appeared to be doing an effective job.

In all instances in J. Edgar's judgment, without exception, these testimonies contributed nothing that would aid the prosecution in proving Jim had killed the so-called victims. At least it's what he kept telling Jim, who in return communicated this to me when we had an opportunity to talk.

When Ed and Leroy testified, they were both treated as hostile witnesses; and true to their word without fully committing perjury, they denied any direct knowledge linking Jim with the murders. Much to the DA Shoemaker's chagrin, he was unable to make them admit to anything other than being in Jim's employ and sharing his concern along with assisting in a minor way, just as the general public had done, in finding the Malone grandchildren.

In fact, that's exactly what Jim had asked the squad to do, and so there were no real opportunities to have Shoemaker suggest they were perjuring themselves.

J. Edgar was certain the jury would agree Jim was within his rights in doing everything conceivable in trying to capture the kidnappers in hopes of locating the whereabouts of his grandchildren. At the very least, it's what he perceived they would think. He was confident he could convince the jury this is every citizen's right. The biggest problem facing him was Jim had continued to pursue the kidnappers after he had rescued Robbie and Justin. No matter how hard he tried, J. Edgar couldn't disagree with this fact. He knew this was a monumental problem. And he had not yet come up with a legal method to overcome it. But he was not done yet.

Then the prosecution called me, Bob Arnott. When I was first subpoenaed, I told J. Edgar I was going to fall back on the Constitution's freedom of the press and refuse to testify. But J. Edgar, after reviewing my notes and what had transpired verbally between Jim and I, concluded there was really nothing the prosecution could discover that would be damaging in court. And he felt if I refused, the jury could misconstrue it and think we were trying to hide or cover up something.

So with J. Edgar's and Jim's approval, I testified. About all Shoemaker extracted from me was, Jim had met with me privately to ask for advice in relationship to what I thought could happen if he told the media what was going down. He attempted when I was on the stand to have me admit I made a deal with Jim to write a favorable story in return for an exclusive. This I adamantly denied under oath. I did acknowledge that after we discussed the situation and Jim decided to release the story, I had agreed I would do everything within my power possible to get it in the newspaper. I also explained to the court that I was a professional newspaper reporter, and it was my job to write stories and especially stories such as the magnitude this particular one would have. As I said on the stand, in other words, I willingly volunteered to lend my professional assistance to utilize the press to help locate his grandchildren and bring them home, safe and sound. And I told the court I was more than willing to do this not only as a personal friend, but as a qualified newspaper reporter. And I added I would do this for any citizen who might be faced with the same dilemma.

And, once again in reality, that is all I had really done.

The prosecutor had subpoenaed all the notes I had in my possession and entered them as evidence in his attempt to show I was not being truthful or had committed perjury. I resisted his efforts at first for a brief period of time on the grounds this was confidential material protected by the Constitution of the United States. Besides, the tape was erased way before Jim was arrested.

Defense Counsel Ewing, after reviewing all my notes completely, felt they contained almost nothing, which would contribute anything extra to the prosecution's case against Jim. And most of my information would also verify that Jim had for the most part only requested me to assist him via the press. And as the prosecutor was trying to contend, I definitely did not commit perjury. Therefore, J. Edgar let all of it to be entered by the prosecution as evidence without raising a single objection. That is until Shoemaker asked me his final question.

When Shoemaker asked me whether I thought Jim had killed the two individuals, J. Edgar objected on the grounds that my opinion was inadmissible and totally irrelevant.

Judge Arnold sustained the objection, much to my relief. I had no idea how I would have answered the question if I were to be totally honest. Thank you, J. Edgar.

During his cross-examination of the prosecution's witnesses, especially me, Ewing was very successful in achieving his objective, namely, to get the witnesses to say something that would cause the jury to be more sympathetic toward Jim. Many times the DA, Shoemaker, frequently interrupted the trial proceedings with his objections; but it was Ewing's sensation, every time he did this, it only made what he was attempting to achieve more poignant. He knew, as the DA also was aware of, you can't totally erase what a jury hears once it is spoken, even if an objection is sustained.

When an idea has been implanted in the jury's minds, it remains right there, and all the objections cannot eliminate them from their subconscious.

Jim let Ewing do what he had hired him to do, defend him, in the most effective way possible.

I knew Jim was cognizant of how bad the case appeared, and there were times during the trial I'm sure he thought if he were on the jury he, too, would find it difficult to bring back a not-guilty verdict.

After four days of testimony, the prosecution rested its case. J. Edgar kept his opinions mostly to himself, but he did express to Jim he felt the prosecution had not presented any unexpected revelations, and most of their case was circumstantial. He did say Jim's continued pursuit of the kidnappers remained a major obstacle and one he wasn't positive he could overcome.

Now it was J. Edgar Ewing's turn. Judge Arnold granted Ewing's request, over the strenuous objections of the prosecutor, since it was late Thursday, he would appreciate a delay in the proceedings until the following Monday. The judge did him one better, due to another conflict, he allowed a delay until the next Tuesday.

What Ewing really wanted was the jury not to be sequestered during the delay; and if they weren't, he felt they would have time to develop thoughts, Ewing believed, would be favorable to Jim. He also assumed, even though the jury was not allowed to view TV, listen to the radio or read newspapers they would in some way be tainted by the press or the public, who had become very favorable to Jim's side of the case.

In fact as is their nature to try to involve the public in the event, the press was running public polls about the trial, and over 90 percent were in favor of an acquittal for Jim.

The public agreed, put in the same set of circumstances. They would have done the same thing.

Now, Ewing knew these polls and everything he was doing in court would not guarantee a favorable decision for Jim by the jury; but it almost seemed to be, considering the evidence mounted by the prosecution even if most of it was circumstantial, his only hope for acquittal.

Once again, over the prosecution's strenuous objections, the judge chose not to sequester the jury. Judge Arnold reiterated his order, he had previously stated at the time the jury was sworn in, they were not to discuss the case with anyone and to ignore the press totally. He specifically told them, once again, reading newspapers or listening to TV/radio news or talk programs was strictly forbidden.

After he completed giving these instructions to the jury, Judge Arnold terminated the day's session.

It was Defense Counsel Ewing's sentiment that this was a major blow to the prosecution.

Before he departed, he told Jim that he would like to meet privately with him, probably late on Monday, to review how he intended to handle the defense. Regrettably, Jim had to remain incarcerated in the King County Jail facilities due to his earlier refusal to request bail. This coupled with the prosecution's assertion, due to the seriousness of the crime, he should be remanded. Therefore, it had been the judge's only option.

Naturally, Ewing was somewhat dismayed when Jim, at their very first meeting, said he wanted to forego posting bail and would not even allow J. Edgar to have a bail hearing. Because of this decision by Jim at the very beginning, the judge had no alternative other than ordering him to continue being held in custody. Jim had no real problem with this and accepted the decision without any outward display of emotion. In a way, as stupid as it may have sounded to J. Edgar and the average citizen, he inwardly felt this jail time was owed for some of the things he had done.

He was immediately returned to his cell.

For some reason nobody understood, even J. Edgar didn't know why, after Jim had spent several days incarcerated with other prisoners, they moved him to a private cell.

To Jim this was great because he didn't want to talk to anyone about the trial or the charges the state had brought against him, especially to other inmates. He truly appreciated the privacy. It was lonely, but he was given some time to see Deanna at least once a day.

During these short visits, she always kept a positive attitude, similar to Jim's, even though in the back of their minds they both knew there was no guarantee Jim would be exonerated.

Deanna told him all the positive things happening with the press and the public polls. This did help in raising Jim's spirits a little.

Jim had three more lonely days before the trial was scheduled to resume. Three days to think about all the events that had led him to his grandchildren and his encounter with the kidnappers.

He knew what he had done was wrong in a legal sense, but he had no regrets, regardless what verdict the jury returned.

Just to know these two scumbags could never repeat their crime on anybody else, ever, gave him much satisfaction.

If he had to sacrifice himself for the general good of society, then so be it. At least he kept telling himself this was true. And there was another problem lingering in his mind. A dark, foreboding problem and he couldn't deal with it or even come up with a possible solution. He knew he couldn't discuss it with anyone, especially his attorney or Bob Arnott, so he buried it deep into his subconscious. By doing this, he didn't have to keep turning it over time after time, and maybe if he ignored the thought, it would disappear. He knew it wouldn't, but it seemed to be his only alternative, at least for now.

When he was alone in his cell, Jim told me later he spent a lot of time thinking about Lois and wondering how she was doing.

Could she avoid being captured?

#

CHAPTER 26

THE KIDNAPPERS

When the story finally broke, the kidnappers had fled further from the Seattle area to a casino called Two Rivers just off the Columbia River a few miles northwest of Spokane, Washington.

And that was all right with Lois because sitting in one place too long gave her too much time alone, and all she thought about was Robbie and Justin. It was consuming her entire being. This coupled with dealing with her cohorts, caused her a tremendous amount of anxiety twenty-four hours a day. Robbie and Justin never deserted her.

They had spent only one day at the Mill Bay Casino before splitting Tuesday morning for the Spokane tribe's Two Rivers Casino.

They were still at the Two Rivers Casino on Wednesday after the story broke in the newspapers, and soon all the other media was on the story. It was shortly after eight in the morning, and both Dennis and Fred were still in the sack resting from a hard night of losing their money.

Lois had slept in the front room on the couch and was up early.

After her third cup of coffee, she went over to the gift shop and picked up the latest edition of the Seattle paper.

There it was on the front page. It was one of those things you know is going to happen, and then when it does, you still can't believe your eyes. Lois sat down in the coffee shop to read the entire article.

All the details about the kidnapping, the ransom, the Malone family, an appeal for the safe return of Robbie and Justin, the reward offer, and what really jumped out at Lois was the 800 phone number the public could call with information. It was in extralarge print with details set off in a box by itself, but still on the front page.

She instantly thought about calling this number herself, but ended up rejecting the idea, thinking it would be too dangerous. She read the entire story twice before heading back to the motor home to wake Fred and Dennis so they could read it too.

"Come on, buttheads," she yelled as she hurriedly entered the motor home. "Get up and read how much trouble we're in now. It's on the front page of the newspaper!"

That was the first time she had ever talked assertively to them. Well, maybe not that asshole Dennis, but he didn't really count.

She did get their attention because as soon as she mentioned a news story, they almost simultaneously jumped out of bed and came into the living room area in their underwear.

Fred snatched the paper out of Lois's hand and sat down to read the article. He started reading out loud so Dennis wouldn't have to bother.

Dennis's reaction was typically stupid.

"Wow, we're celebrities!" he exclaimed.

"Just be thankful they don't know our names or have descriptions," Fred replied, not even glancing up.

Lois interjected, "According to the story, they do know there are three or four of us, and one of us is a woman. I wonder how they know there's a woman."

Fred continued to read aloud. Dennis just sat there with a stupid look on his face—mouth open and chin hanging loose—it illustrated how basically ignorant he really was.

He had no real conception of the gravity of the article. Fred finished reading the story and laid it aside. Looking at both of them, he said with some concern in his voice, "I think we'd better head southward this afternoon or no later than tomorrow morning."

"We're worth a hundred thousand bucks!" Dennis blurted out.

"That's a hundred thousand for the kids' safe return, not us, stupid!" Fred corrected him.

"Plus the million we have," Dennis said.

While they were discussing the article, Lois was thinking about the kids again.

She knew right then what she was going to do when the opportunity presented itself.

She wasn't quite sure how, but she knew somehow she had to talk to Jim Malone or the reporter whose name was in the news story, Bob what's his name, and let them know where they could find the kids.

She fully understood this thought was hers alone. And she needed to be ultracautious because, first, she didn't want to be captured by the police; and second, if Fred or Dennis even suspected what she was planning, they would probably kill her.

She would have to bide her time until a perfect opportunity presented itself and soon. She figured that the kids would be okay for at least one or two more days, and maybe because of the news story, they would be found. At least she prayed this was true.

"Let's do this," Fred suggested. "We do a little bit more gambling this morning and then this afternoon we head on down the road. We could be near Yakima before dark and stay at the tribal casino near Wapato for a day or two. We'll let this thing chill off before we head south. By what I read, it appears they don't know about the motor home, so if we're lucky, they'll be looking in all the wrong places. And I'll wager they are searching for us on I-5 heading south to Mexico or up into Canada. It's exactly what I wanted them to think, and why I went this way. Plus, remember we're Canadians, and they'll be looking for Americans."

"Are you sure?" Lois asked.

"Haven't I been right so far? Haven't I beaten them every time?" This was more of a braggadocio statement rather than a question.

Dennis nodded yes.

Lois realized he had no comprehension what was even going on.

She didn't say anything for a minute then asked, "How long are, you guys, going to be gambling?"

"How about until two o'clock?" Fred said, looking more at Dennis than Lois. "Since you don't seem to be gambling too much, you can get everything ready to roll while Dennis and I win back some of our money."

"That's fine with me," Lois said, thinking maybe this was the opportunity she had been hoping for. Then as an afterthought she added somewhat sarcastically, "Just don't lose any of mine."

Dennis jumped in, "And you get none of our winnings either! Come on, Fred, let's get dressed, grab some dough, and let's get with it. I'm ready to win."

You wouldn't know what winning was if it bit you in the ass, Lois thought to herself.

But she kept quiet.

However, her mind was working and thought maybe this was the opportunity she was waiting for. If she could somehow get rid of them for a few hours, she could put her game plan in action without arousing any suspicions from either of them.

She wasn't sure how long she would need, but assumed at least one or two hours would be sufficient time to make the right connection. First, she had to find a phone number that would reach only Malone or that reporter or her plan wouldn't work. She thought again it's best to avoid the 800 numbers that appeared in the newspaper. That would be her last resort if nothing else worked.

The plan she had in mind was to find a phone number and use one of those cell phones Fred had kept stashed in the back bedroom closet. That's if she could find one that was still charged up. Fred had been so excited when he got the ransom money he completely forgot about dumping the phones.

She only hoped at least one of them would still work.

While she was deep in her thoughts, Fred and Dennis dressed. They grabbed another ten thousand apiece, gave Lois a matching stack of bills, and headed out the door.

"Be ready to roll by two o'clock. And get all the hookups put away," Fred yelled over his shoulder as they went out the door.

Lois looked at her watch and thought this should give her plenty of time to accomplish what she felt she must do, for her own peace of mind.

As soon as she was sure they were gone, she put her ten thousand dollars in the box under the sink and went into the back bedroom where Fred had kept all the phones in a box in the bedroom closet. She dumped them all out on the bed and sorted through them until she found two cell phones that indicated they were still charged up.

Then she started searching through Fred's stuff looking for phone numbers she hoped would connect her directly to Jim Malone.

It took about thirty minutes before she found a note in the box where the cell phones were kept with the 425 area code on it.

There were actually three numbers on it with the 425 area code.

Looking upward, she prayed that at least one of them would work since this might be her only opportunity to put her plan in action.

She decided to make her first call after eleven this morning, and if she didn't make a connection right away, she could continue trying until around one o'clock. If this failed, she didn't know what she would do. Just keep praying it worked.

Now, she had better hurry and get the motor home ready to roll before those jerks lose all their money and came back to get some more.

Lois couldn't believe how time was flying by.

Before she knew it, eleven o'clock was almost here, she had the motor home clean, hoses and cords put away, and ready to roll. It was time to find a secluded place to make a call out of sight from Fred and Dennis so they couldn't see her on the phone if they happened to run out of money and came back to get some more. She decided to take the pickup and drive somewhere down the road completely out of their sight. If they did come back and found her gone in the pickup, she knew she would have to come up with some lie about why she went for a ride.

Cross that bridge when you come to it, she thought.

She got the keys to the pickup and drove down the road, keeping her eye on one of the cell phones to check out the signal strength.

She was kind of heading in the general direction of Spokane when she saw a sign indicating to turn right to Seven Bays Resort.

If her luck held out, there undoubtedly would be a good cell phone signal near a resort. The sign indicated it was just a couple miles down the road, so she turned right to head for Seven Bays.

In a couple of minutes, she saw some houses; and just down the road, there was kind of a turnout. She slowed down to make sure no one was following or nearby, then pulled over into the turnout and stopped, turned off the engine, and sat for a minute to get her mind right.

For some reason she was shaking all over and could hardly catch her breath; it was warm in the pickup, so she rolled down both windows and let the breeze cool her off before she proceeded.

Talk about fear!

Then, taking out the piece of paper she found with the phone numbers on it, she picked up one of the cell phones.

Great!

There was a strong signal.

She stared at the numbers on the piece of paper for a long while, took a deep breath, paused for just a minute, and dialed the first one. It rang only a couple of times before a recording came on and answered, "The number you've dialed has been disconnected." God was she scared.

What was she going to do?

After this first failure, she was afraid all the numbers were probably the same, disconnected.

"Calm yourself down," she silently whispered as if someone was there to hear her.

What if she failed to connect?

What then?

She waited a few more minutes and picked up the other cell phone, looked at the next number, hesitated, and finally dialed it. It rang and rang. About ten times before a voice came on with a questioning, "Hello?"

When the voice came on the phone, she almost jumped out of her skin and barely uttered, "Who is this?"

A man on the other end replied this was a pay phone in Lake Hills. He said since the phone was ringing and he was the only person nearby, he answered it. Lois quickly replied that she must have the wrong number and immediately disconnected.

Two down and only one more to go.

What then, what was she going to do?

This was almost too much for her to handle.

Then she thought of the positive side of things. At least someone answered her last call. If everything else failed, she could call the pay phone number back and tell whoever answers what to do. She could give the person answering Malone's 800 number, the kids would be saved; and whoever answered the Lake Hills phone would probably collect the hundred-thousand-dollar reward.

Not a bad option, it could work, she thought to herself.

This seemed to have a calming effect, she had stopped shaking a little, and her breathing was becoming more normal.

It was almost twelve-thirty by now. Time was running out; she knew it wasn't long before she would have to beat it back to the motor home before Fred and Dennis returned from their gambling session.

Her second fear resurfaced.

"What if they ran out of money and got back early and were waiting for her. They would be pissed." She knew it was too late now to worry about that happening. If it did, she would be ready with some story. She knew it would be difficult to concoct a story they would believe why she took a ride in the pickup, but she would come up with something. She'd better hurry. There would be no more time. The remaining number would be her last effort to save the little guys. Like the other numbers she had dialed, she had no idea whose number she was calling. Finally, after a long hesitation, she took a deep breath and dialed. A million things were going through her mind as the phone rang.

Once.

Twice.

Five times the phone rang before it was answered.

"Jim Malone, can I help you?"

She was so startled to hear his voice she almost dropped her phone.

"May I help you?" the deep resonant voice asked again.

Lois didn't know it, but this was the phone Fred had left at the Bellevue Inn to call Jim at the Hyatt and at Hector's during the money drop. Fortunately, it had nothing to do with all their private numbers they had changed or cancelled.

For some unknown reason, Jim had inadvertently kept this from the police, and maybe subconsciously he had been thinking there might be an outside chance it might be useful at a later date.

Finally, Lois got her composure back long enough to utter, "Look in the old boat warehouse down by Scott Paper in Everett."

She immediately disconnected.

It was like an elephant had been lifted off her shoulders.

She could breathe again.

Her only hope now was he believed her and would do the right thing. *Don't wait, Mr. Malone. Do it soon. Immediately!*

Glancing at her watch, she saw she didn't have much time left before Fred and Dennis were due to return to the motor home from gambling; she had better get going and be ready to hit the road.

Lois started the pickup and, with the windows open, drove back to the casino. The fresh air blowing through the open windows was just what the doctor ordered, almost a godsend. She was soaking wet from perspiration after the phone ordeal. By the time, she pulled alongside the motor home she had totally cooled down, and her shaking had stopped. She parked, sat motionless for just a brief moment, and let all the events flow through her mind. It had been a long time since she had felt a sensation this good. She thought maybe doing something right for a change was not such a bad thing. She got out of the pickup and went inside the motor home.

Thank god the two idiots were still in the casino.

She put the keys back where she had found them and went into the bathroom to freshen up before the assholes returned. She then finished getting the motor home ready to go. Glancing at her watch again, she was surprised to see it was almost two o'clock.

That's cutting it close.

Just about then Fred and Dennis walked in.

Lois knew it would happen; they were bitching about losing all of the money they had taken with them.

"But we've still got plenty left, and we're not done yet. Let's get going to Yakima. Maybe that casino is a little looser, and we can get some of their money. Hey, did you go somewhere in the pickup?" Fred asked Lois. She didn't respond, but he got her attention.

"I noticed the windows are rolled down, and I remember they were up when we left."

He caught her completely off guard. Then thinking as fast as her mind would allow when caught in a pickle, Lois quickly said, "I thought it'd be a good idea to let it cool off inside before we hit the road."

"See, Dennis, she does like you," Fred said.

If you only knew, thought Lois to herself.

"Everything's ready," she said quickly. And before Fred could inquire further about the pickup, she continued, "If we go now, maybe we can get there before dark." She didn't want Fred to ask any more questions.

Dennis went out the door and got in the pickup. Fred started the motor home and drove out the parking lot heading south. He had already mapped out the route the night before and told Dennis not to get lost this time. Down the road, they were finally headed for Yakima.

With a burden lifted, at least slightly, from one of the passengers' soul.

#

Chapter 27

THE REVELATION

It was early evening on Monday.

Jim Malone had just returned to his cell after his brief meeting with his attorney and was sitting on his bunk bed trying to piece together all the events that had transpired up to now during the trial. He felt deep inside Ewing was doing his job very effectively.

How the jury was reacting was another question. They appeared to him, as he watched the facial reactions as each witness testified to be more receptive to the defense side. However, he realized it could be only wishful thinking.

But as Ewing said, don't ever get too complacent, juries are easy to read in the courtroom; but when they're by themselves in the jury room, away from the spotlight, they can do a total about-face.

As he said, it doesn't take much to reverse their judgments.

Jim decided, what was actually happening was out of his control, and it's what Ewing was being paid to do.

What he was really thinking about was the phone call he had received about the whereabouts of his missing grandchildren. He had never shared with anyone, especially not the authorities, how or from whom he had received the tip. He told the authorities he had a revelation. He said that a vision somehow miraculously had come to him. Nobody was really buying it, but then again he had found Robbie and Justin.

He even told the family, including his squad and Bob Arnott, the same story, a consistent, necessary, white prevarication.

He had decided it was important to keep the call and the caller's identity to himself.

There was no way anybody believed this story.

Unbeknownst to Jim, the police even reviewed all Jim's phone records from that day; but obviously, nothing showed up as to him having received any strange outside calls. And they had totally forgotten about the cell phone the kidnappers had left him during the money drop. Fortunately, for some unknown reason, Jim had kept it. He remembered perhaps somewhere in his subconscious mind he had sensed it might somehow be useful. The sixth sense that almost all people possess but seldom recognize. It had saved Jim's and several of his comrades' lives many times in Vietnam.

The police had no alternative at the time, but to accept what Jim had told them.

At least they would accept it for now, but knew it was not the truth; and they continued their investigation in an attempt to find the real answer. Anyhow, when Jim received the call, he knew immediately the person on the other end of the line was the female kidnapper. He knew it was her even before she uttered those few words of hope.

The conversation was so brief. Jim had to repeat it several times in his own head before it totally registered what the caller had actually said. His first clear thought was, *This is too easy, so don't get too excited until after you prove it's right or wrong. Surly,* he thought, *no one except one of the kidnappers would have this number, and the caller had to be the female part of the trio.*

Regardless, he knew even if it turned out to be a wild-goose chase, he had to follow it up; this was life and death, and every minute and every second would count. The only person he would call was Ed Johnson, just in case he needed a backup. He told Ed to meet him in his office parking lot as fast as he could. He added this was urgent, high priority.

As usual, Ed didn't question anything Jim said. He said he would be there in fifteen minutes.

It was about how long Jim calculated it would take him to arrive there too. He didn't call anyone else because he didn't want to get the family's hopes up; he definitely didn't want the press there, not even Bob Arnott, and he certainly did not want the police to be involved. If a problem developed, he was confident he and Ed could handle any situation that might arise.

While he was waiting for Ed, he double-checked his trunk to make sure his first aid kit was there, just in case. It was, along with some bottled water he kept for emergencies. Within minutes, Ed pulled into the parking lot. Ed got out of his car and jumped into Jim's.

He was already moving before Ed's door was closed. "What's up, Boss?" Ed asked with a concerned look on his face.

Jim had already decided to keep the phone call to himself, so he told Ed the concocted revelation theory he had decided to use. He knew those close to him were aware of how his mind worked and would not question anything he said.

"This morning I had a revelation, a vision, on where Robbie and Justin might be. It just wouldn't leave my mind. It was so vivid I thought we should check it out. Everything was there, the kids, the location, everything."

"Oh," said Ed noncommittally.

As he steered onto the ramp to take them onto 405 headed north to Everett, Jim filled Ed in on what few details of his vision he thought Ed needed to know. He disliked telling Ed this little prevarication, but he thought it was best for now.

Ed had been with Jim before in Nam when he more than once had kept them safe because he somehow could feel or sense danger.

Almost always, he had been correct.

Therefore, Ed accepted what Jim told him without any hesitation whatsoever. Jim knew exactly how to get to Scott Paper Company and calculated they could be there within forty to fifty minutes at the most. Fortunately, it was just after 1:00 PM, so the traffic on 405 wasn't too congested.

The only problem, Jim perceived, would be in locating the abandoned boat warehouse the caller said to look for. He did think there might not be too many located in this area, so if they were lucky, finding it could be a minimal problem. *Keep thinking positive*, he silently told himself.

Heading west on 405, neither one spoke.

They sat in total silence, just the sound of road noise as they drove toward Interstate five and then proceeded north to Everett.

Both were obviously afraid to get their hopes too high.

Actually, Ed didn't really know what to think other than keeping positive thoughts about what Jim had said was correct. It just seemed too easy to be true, so they drove in silence and kept their inner thoughts to themselves.

After about twenty minutes, 405 merged with I-5 headed north. Another twenty-five minutes, they turned off I-5 and were only five minutes from Scott Paper down by the bay on Puget Sound.

"There's Scott Paper, now let's see if we can find a boat warehouse. Keep your eyes alert," Jim said. "Let's start at the far south end on the frontage road and drive all the way down north until we spot anything resembling a boat warehouse."

Ed was keeping his eyes on every building they approached. So far, they hadn't seen anything that even looked like a boat warehouse.

They were about three fourths from the end of the frontage road when Ed shouted "Jim," said Ed in an excited voice. "There! About two blocks at the end of this street on the right! That looks like what we're looking for!"

"I see it! That could be the one! Looks abandoned. Nobody around. No fence. Let's try it."

Jim parked almost at the front entrance, and both got out simultaneously and headed for the door. It took just a minute for Ed to get the door open.

Jim could feel the adrenaline pumping. Hopefully, the kids would be there, alive and well.

As they stepped inside, a ray of sunlight, almost like an omen, highlighted a large packing crate at the very end. It appeared to have been altered with a makeshift door on one end, and it looked like a new lock had been recently installed.

They both knew this had to be it and were praying they weren't too late.

Jim yelled as loud as he could, "Robbie, Justin, it's Grandpa. Can you hear me?"

Not a sound.

The boys inside were afraid to respond and moved closer together in fear the kidnappers had returned. Jim glanced at Ed with a look of total devastation.

He yelled again, only louder this time.

"Robbie! Justin! It's Grandpa!"

No response! Only Silence! Frightening silence! Jim's heart was pounding so hard he thought he was going to explode maybe they were too late. God forbid. Ed wasn't much different.

Then all of a sudden, there was a sound.

It sounded like kicking on the inside wall.

Inside the box, both boys finally realized it was Grandpa's voice and started kicking the door. Ed and Jim's faces lit up, they could hardly contain their emotions, and their anticipation of what they had heard was overwhelming.

"It's them, I know it's them! Hold on, guys, we'll get you out!" Jim shouted.

Meanwhile, Ed found a piece of angle iron he could use as a pry bar on the lock; and in what seemed like eons, when actually it was only a minute or two, it popped off and they immediately reached inside and gathered both boys in their arms.

They didn't look very good, and the odor in the box was wretched, but they were alive. When they got outside, Jim said, "Let's head for Providence Hospital here in Everett. It's much closer, right up the hill." He pointed to a large building sitting up on a hill to the south and about three-quarters of a mile away.

Jim jumped in the backseat with both boys, and Ed drove.

He had both arms around the boys, clutching them close to his body. The boys were silent, just desperately holding on to their grandpa.

The hospital was about ten minutes from Scott Paper. Ed drove as fast as he could safely go. He had his emergency lights blinking and horn honking at intersections as he maneuvered through them, right up to the hospital emergency entrance. He opened the back door, and they both rushed inside, each clutching one of the boys in their arms.

A nurse met them just as they stepped through the door, and Jim explained who he was. It was all he had to say. She knew right away who the boys were from all the publicity and reacted instantly with an emergency stat call.

Jim and Ed had never seen so many people rush to the aid of someone, like they did that day at the hospital. Two doctors appeared almost instantly, four nurses, and others who wanted to lend assistance, just in case they were needed. They took the boys from Ed and Jim, placed them on gurneys, and whisked them away to examination rooms. Jim followed.

It all happened so fast the boys didn't have a chance to react; and after what they had just been through, this was a piece of cake. Besides, everyone seemed to only be concerned with how they were feeling and their safety. And besides, Grandpa was here, and he assured them they would be safe and explained as they were being wheeled to the examination room the doctors had to check them out to make sure they wouldn't get sick.

Once the doctors took full control. Jim returned to where Ed was waiting and asked him to call Mark, Joan, and Deanna and tell them the good news and where they were.

"Tell them to hold off coming down. Explain I'll call them back in about thirty minutes. Assure them the boys are alive, and they have more doctors and nurses with them than presidents." He was barking orders so fast Ed could barely understand it all.

Then Jim returned to the exam rooms where the boys were.

Ed did as instructed. Mark answered the phone. Ed proceeded to give him the good news. Mark could hardly believe his ears, never in his life had he had such a feeling of elation as he did at that moment. Ed had to repeat the news. Finally, Mark settled down so Ed could fill in a few details and give him the instructions from Jim to wait at home until he called back.

As expected, Mark's first reaction was they were coming to the hospital right now. Finally, after much persuasion, he agreed to wait for Jim's call. Ed hung up and waited for Jim to return from the emergency room.

Ed promised in about thirty minutes his dad would call. Actually, Jim came back out to the waiting area within twenty minutes and called the family. The doctors had told him, other than severe dehydration and some minor infection in their finger wounds, other than that, they were going to be just fine. He said they were both sedated at this time and had IVs in their arms in order to counteract the dehydration.

Jim told them the doctor said he didn't think they should be moved for a day or two until they were more stabilized, and he wanted to keep them under observation until all the blood tests were completed. Jim told Mark he had agreed with the doctors' recommendations.

Then Deanna came on the line and said Mark, Joan, and she were coming down right now and added Mark and Joan wanted to spend the night with the boys, if the hospital could accommodate them. The doctors later agreed this was an excellent idea, and arrangements for accommodations were made immediately.

Mark came back on the line and said he had something new to tell Jim; he indicated it was something really important, and he would prefer to tell him in person rather than on the phone so there would be no opportunity of anybody overhearing it.

Jim could sense the sound of Mark's voice was somewhat ominous and agreed he should hold it until they all came to the hospital. They then terminated the call, and Jim returned to where the boys were.

The boys would actually stay two nights at Providence and then were cleared to go home to recuperate. Four days in the box had certainly taken its toll on their little bodies. They both had lost weight and were in need of much liquid; but fortunately, all the tests came back negative, and there was no sign of infection other than the minor one in their little fingers where the ends had been severed.

On the second day, Robbie was talking continuously. He didn't always make sense, but he was talking. He did describe how Bailey had attacked the kidnappers and how nice the woman had been to him and Justin. Justin on the other hand, showed signs of serious trauma; he spoke very little, and all he seemed to want was to be held by his mother.

The psychiatrist they had called in to evaluate the boys told the family this was natural, and he assured them normalcy should return in time. He said what they really needed was a lot of TLC. The entire staff at that hospital did more than could ever be expected. They even allowed the police to have security at the hospital entrance and in front of the boys' room.

This was done not only for their protection, but to keep the press from causing any interruption during their recovery. Finally, once Jim was confident everyone was okay, he called me, Bob Arnott.

He told me the boys were found, safe and sound. He filled me in on the hospital where they were being treated and confirmed, according to the doctors, the boys were responding to treatment.

I inquired how he was able to locate them, and Jim told me the vision story. I could detect a break in his voice as he was telling me this rather miraculous story, and I knew he wanted me to accept it at face value and not to question it any further.

I didn't, and besides, I said this version would be even more appealing to the public even if it was beyond belief. I told Jim the public preferred to believe in miracles, and they would completely eat this version up.

Another scoop for Bob Arnott!

I was aware, even though radio and TV news would break the story before the newspaper came out, I would still have another front-page story. Besides, I knew no one would have my inside information, like the vision story and Jim's direct input. As Jim was sitting in his cell reflecting on all the events that had led him to his grandchildren, he also recalled the information Mark told him privately when they all arrived at the hospital. After seeing the boys, Mark and he went outside so they could have privacy.

Ed had already departed in Jim's SUV and was meeting with the search squad to bring them up-to-date on what had transpired and end their part of the quest. He also had told Jim he would take care of the security teams at the house and office, but Jim said he wanted to keep them for a few more days while things settled and to keep the press at bay. Jim and Mark were out on the steps in front of the hospital when Mark told Jim what happened at the house just before Ed called with the news about Robbie and Justin. He said this morning Deanna was covering the phones for incoming calls. He said just before noon, she answered a call from a man at a twenty-four-hour Shell station located just north of Wenatchee on Highway 97.

The man said he recalled a man and woman filling up with gas in a motor home early Labor Day morning. He said, he remembered them after he read the newspaper story about the kidnapping a day or two later and felt because the time of day they were there filling up was a little unusual, and he became even more suspicious when a pickup with another person showed up. He said they obviously knew each other because they had an extended conversation and had been looking at a map together on the hood of the pickup.

"Who else knows about this?" asked Jim.

"I didn't tell anyone else not even Joan. Only me, mom, and now you know about it. Mom told me right after she got off the phone, and I told her I thought we should keep it to ourselves until we talked to you," Mark said.

"Good thinking. Did she get his name and number?" Jim asked.

"She did, and I've got it right here." He handed his dad a piece of paper with the information.

Jim looked at it, put it in his pocket, and then quickly said, "I want you to forget about this. Forget you ever saw it and that you ever gave it to me. If your mom asks you about it, tell her you checked it out and it was nothing. Now that we have the boys back safe and sound, she probably won't even remember telling you."

Mark then asked, "What are you going to do with it, Dad?"

Jim said, "Nothing, right now; but once we know the boys are okay, I'll check it out, remember, forget you ever gave it to me. Now let's get back in and see the boys."

Mark knew by the tone of his dad's voice he was never to broach this subject again, so they both went back into the hospital to be with the boys.

Anyhow, those were his thoughts as he sat in his cell waiting for the trial to continue. His last thought, before he lay down for the night, was about Lois.

Even though she was a kidnapper Jim felt he would always be in her debt. It was the main reason Jim had allowed her to escape when he finally caught up with them in Yakima.

But that's another story.

For now, that's all he wanted to think about in recalling these past events. He certainly had no continuing hatred for Lois.

But as for the other two kidnappers . . .

#

CHAPTER 28

THE KIDNAPPERS

Dry and yellow.

It was about four in the afternoon when the kidnappers reached Interstate 90.

The hills were dry and yellow, with the sky blue and practically cloudless above.

Fred had decided to take the back roads to Wapato since the Indian casino was closer to Wapato than Yakima.

They were cruising along being careful not to exceed the speed limit the ever-vigilant Washington State Patrol was the last thing Fred wanted. They were just cruising along, listening to some radio station playing country music. Lois had selected the station. Country music was what Fred liked. It made things more pleasant for her when he was happy.

Yes, dry and yellow Eastern Washington in the late summer and early fall, except for the orchards and alfalfa fields.

As the miles rolled, it was all she had to look at, yellow and dry hills from the summer heat.

However, the stretch of road they motored on now ran parallel to the Columbia River. On both sides were several apple, pear, peach, and cherry orchards, still green from the constant irrigation systems pumping water from the Mighty Columbia River to the orchards. The apple trees were loaded with its fall reward, and the bounty had just begun to turn red. On the edge of the orchards, the migrant workers were arranging large boxes in preparation for the fall harvest.

Almost picking time, thought Lois.

The green of the orchards against the yellow and brown backdrop of the hills that surrounded the area created a motif only the great masters can paint.

Lois was actually feeling much better, thinking the boys now had a chance. That's if Jim had believed her and did the right thing. All of a sudden, the music was interrupted for an important, breaking news story. Lois was startled out of her brief moment of serenity. She immediately reached over and turned the volume up just as an announcer came on with an important news flash.

"The Malone boys—Robbie and Justin Malone—kidnapped last Saturday have been found and first reports are they are alive."

"What the hell," cried Fred! "Lois, turn that damned thing up!"

Lois reached over and adjusted the dial even higher.

The reporter went on to say, "At the present time, there was no information as to their condition and how they were found, but to stay tuned and when the authorities released more information, the station would have it on the air immediately."

Lois turned to look at Fred to see his reaction. She could tell from the look on Fred's face he was shocked. Fortunately, he had to keep his eyes on the road so he couldn't detect the relief on her face.

Thank god Jim Malone listened to me! Lois silently thought to herself.

"How in the hell could they find them this fast?" Fred shouted.

Then he did the unexpected.

He took his eyes off the road and glared suspiciously at Lois.

"You'd better not have done anything to tip them off!"

She had already prepared herself for this. "What, you think I'm crazy? I don't want to go to prison either."

Fred then added, "You'd better not be bullshitting me, or." He stopped at that point. He knew she was aware what the or meant. Then she offered a well-prepared explanation.

"I would have bet that once the newspapers broke the story, someone would find them. I'll bet hundreds maybe thousands were looking to get the hundred-thousand reward money."

Fred turned back to focus on his driving, then said, "Yeah, you're probably right. It's unbelievable what people will do for money." His remark was humorously sarcastic. He even sort of chuckled as he was saying it.

Lois sat back in her seat, relieved because Fred seemed to have bought her theory. Then she added, "Maybe they'll stop looking for us since they found the boys."

"There's not a fat chance in hell of that happening. Now all they have to do is concentrate on finding us. Remember, we still have one million dollars of their money. We'll wait a couple days in the Yakima area and see what develops. I wonder if Dennis has his radio on. Maybe I'd better pull over at the next wide spot and tell him what's going down, just in case he doesn't know."

Within just a few miles, he found just such a place and eased the motor home to a stop. There wasn't a great deal of traffic on this road; and within a few minutes, Dennis pulled in behind and got out just as Fred was walking back to the pickup.

He was right.

Dennis was listening to RAP music on one of his CDs, and the volume was cranked up so high it was earsplitting even from where Fred was standing.

Figures, thought Lois as she watched Fred approach the pickup.

He had it cranked up so loud even Lois could hear the noise inside the motor home. Dennis got out of the pickup and was lighting a cigarette as Fred walked back to where he had parked.

Dennis took a big drag; and as he blew his pollutant out, he asked Fred, "What's up? What'd we stop for?"

Fred filled him in on the news story that had just come over the radio. Dennis was too stupid to understand the gravity of this announcement and how it might affect their escape plans.

Fred knew it was a waste of time to even try and explain it to him, so he said they should both get back in their vehicles and continue toward Yakima. He told Dennis he would keep listening to the radio; and after he got more information, they would discuss their options when they arrived at the casino in Yakima. He then returned and got in the motor home, and Dennis went to the pickup.

"What'd he say?" Lois asked.

"Nothing, he's really too stupid to figure anything out, you know," Fred said. "Let's just drive and keep listening to the radio for more info. Why don't you try to find one of those all news stations? They'll probably talk this thing to death, but they should have more information than this country station."

Lois was glad it was his idea because that's what she had wanted to do all along. It wasn't hard to find one. Fortunately, she found a Yakima AM talk-news station, KIT, so they could listen to it all the way to the casino. Just like Fred said, it was the featured subject, and they were already talking it into the ground. A little more information was being released, and then the local talk show host began taking calls from listeners, getting their reaction to the news story.

The announcer asked each caller for his or her opinions concerning how the kidnappers should be dealt with, when and if they were apprehended. Almost every caller thought the police would eventually find and hopefully kill all of the kidnappers.

Most of the callers seemed to feel this idea would save the court time and explained verbally how the police should do it. After all many of the callers said, it's what the kidnappers deserved. This didn't appear to bother Fred one iota.

But it frightened Lois.

However, just knowing those two little guys had been found, gave her a tremendous degree of relief.

The only thing remaining was for her to be patient until Fred gave her the rest of her share of the million dollars. If worse came to worse, she now had stashed over twenty thousand bucks in her box under the sink, enough to escape from these buttheads if need be.

She also assumed Fred would give her more money when he and Dennis continued gambling once they reached the casino near Yakima. It took them about two more hours before they pulled the motor home into the Yakima tribe's casino RV parking area.

There were quite a few other motor homes and trailers already parked in the RV area. Fred pulled into a spot on the far end where he had plenty of room for Dennis to park the pickup alongside and still leave a few extra feet between them and the other vehicles. They were at the very end, and to the right of their parking spot there were several trees and shrubs with a picnic table and a fire pit.

Dennis arrived within minutes and helped Fred set up the motor home. He was obviously anxious to get in the casino and win money so this didn't take them too long. Lois almost laughed out loud as she watched them scramble to get all the electrical cords and hoses hooked up so they could get in the casino and continue winning.

Winning, yeah sure they would! Lois thought to herself.

However, she was also anxious because she knew or at least she hoped Fred would give her a matching amount.

For some reason, no one said a word about the news story, and the radio station had not released much new information.

To Fred and Dennis it was like nothing had happened.

They both came in after getting the motor home set up, and Fred took out the money suitcase, counted out three stacks of bills, handed her and Dennis one each, grabbed his stack, and he and Dennis went out the door and were almost running for the front entrance to the casino.

They didn't say a word to Lois, just grabbed their stack of money, and ran out the door for their opportunity to win big bucks.

Talk about a gambling habit. It was almost like they had been in a desert and here was an oasis.

Lois quickly counted her stack.

Much to her surprise, Fred had given her twenty thousand dollars. She smiled to herself because that meant they would soon be poorer by twenty thousand later tonight, and she would get some more later when they returned to get some more, and she knew this would happen. She stashed this with the rest of her money in the box under the sink.

After freshening up, she wandered over to the casino to give the appearance she was as stupid as her two partners.

She walked around until she spotted them both at a blackjack table it had a sign that said, Minimum $25, Maximum $1,000.

At that rate, it shouldn't take more than a couple hours before they needed to go back to the money stash in the motor home and get some more. It was only six thirty now, so by eight, she would go back to the motor home and wait for the inevitable to happen.

To kill time she played a nickel slot with some of the money she kept for appearance's sake, and then she got a bite to eat. Actually, the food at the casinos was very good and quite reasonably priced.

After eating, she returned to the motor home.

It turned out she was correct.

Both of the guys came back broke in less than two hours for more money exactly as Lois had calculated. Fred went directly to the money closet, took out the suitcase, and counted out another twenty thousand apiece.

At least he was being fair.

While Fred was counting out the money, they both were cussing about how rotten their luck was and how they both knew it was about to change.

Suckers, Lois thought to herself.

Fred and Dennis grabbed their money and were out the door in minuets heading for the casino.

To continue their winning streak, Lois sarcastically thought.

She quickly stashed her new pile of bills in her box hidden under the sink. *Twenty thousand more, wow,* she thought to herself. *Just a little bit more and I'm down the road as far away as I can get from these Two Pricks.*

\#

CHAPTER 29

THE DEFENSE

Tuesday morning arrived faster than Jim anticipated.

At first time dragged by because of the solitary confinement and then at what seemed to Jim like supersonic speed, it was 6:00 AM Tuesday morning.

Jim was already up when the guards came to let him shower, get dressed in a suit and tie, and prepare himself for the trial that was scheduled to start at nine o'clock. Per his request, they brought him a light breakfast—orange juice, two eggs fried too hard, one piece of burnt toast, and a cup of awful black coffee with no cream. As bad as it was, he was able to choke it down; and surprisingly, he kept it down.

Just before eight, they came back to get him so he could meet with his attorney, J. Edgar Ewing, prior to the trial proceedings.

They led him into the client-attorney waiting room where Ewing was already sitting at a desk with a raft of papers in front of him. After the guards removed his handcuffs and leg shackles, Ewing came around the desk to shake Jim's hand.

"Are you okay?" he asked.

Jim smiled and lied, "It really is not all that bad, boring. The guards seem to care about my comfort and the foods a lot better than we had in Nam."

J. Edgar motioned for him to take a chair at the table, and after Jim was seated, he took the only other chair available directly across the desk from Jim. "Let me prepare you for some of the details on how I'm going to present the defense. I'll be brief because time is short, we only have about an hour before we start," Ewing said.

"I'm in your hands," responded Jim.

Ewing proceeded, immediately explaining how he was going to present the defense. He started with a list of people he planned to call to testify.

In almost every instance, the list included people who J. Edgar felt would verify Jim had never, ever indicated to any of them, he had any plans to kill the two kidnappers. These people would also testify that in their opinion, Jim was incapable of ever committing such an act of violence regardless of his prior service to his country, and that the picture of a predator that the prosecution had tried to establish was totally erroneous.

The exception to these character type witnesses would be the few professionals Ewing would call to testify that Jim's actions were a normal psychiatric reaction to a situation created by the kidnappers. As J. Edgar explained, these witnesses would assist in establishing Jim did what any sane person would do, if placed in a similar situation. In other words, the mental stress that the family, including Jim, had endured from the time Robbie and Justin had been abducted and how the physical abuse the boys had undergone by the kidnappers affected not only Jim's judgment but that of the entire family. He explained to Jim that he was sure the DA would mount objections to many of these witnesses on the grounds of relevancy.

"As I said before, you can't erase all of what the jury hears after the fact, even though Judge Arnold will instruct them to forget they heard it," Ewing continued explaining his defense procedure.

He planned to lead off by recalling Chief Hammond. He said it was his feeling that Hammond was more sensitive to Jim than Director Watkins even though he had testified previously for the prosecution. He said there might be a chance he could get Hammond to admit or make a slip that in reality they had no actual proof Jim had killed the two kidnappers.

He also felt he might be able to glean something new from Hammond. Something he may have held back when he was testifying for the prosecution. Then he said, after he called on all the others he had subpoenaed to testify on Jim's behalf and after Shoemaker completed his cross-examinations, he wanted to close or rather rest his case after Jim testified.

Jim then asked, "Are you positive you want me to testify?" Ewing looked at him intensely and then said, "Only if you're in agreement. But let me tell you this before you say yes or no. It's my experience that in trials similar to this one, if the person charged does not testify on their own behalf, it creates more doubt in the jury's minds as to one's guilt. If you agree with my recommendation, I promise to keep your testimony very brief. All I'm basically planning to ask is a few preliminary questions and then I'll ask you if you killed those two people. Your answer will obviously be, no. Let me remind you again. When you answer, I want you to be sure to look directly at the jury with your answer. Do not smile. Try to look like you're remorseful for their deaths, but above all else, don't look guilty or pleased that they are no longer alive."

Jim had no idea how that look should be and didn't ask.

"Then unless something unexpected occurs, I'll announce that the defense rests," J. Edgar continued. "What Shoemaker asks you on cross-examination will be more difficult to totally predict; however he is, legally, only allowed to cross-examine on the matters I ask you previously. I'm positive Judge Arnold won't allow him to go too far afield, and if he does, I will object. That reminds me, and this is very important. So don't forget it for one moment. When Shoemaker asks you any question and I mean any question, I want you to hesitate just a moment in case I want to raise an objection. Give me time to make that decision. And do not, under any circumstances, lose your composure; do not show anger in any form, answer his questions honestly, and be as brief as possible. Let me stress another important point. Do not think for one instance you can take Shoemaker on. Remember at all times, you'll be playing in his ballpark, and he's every bit as good as I am. Do not ever underestimate him. He's good and he's smart, and winning is his only goal, and this trial could make his career."

"Am I making myself clear?" J. Edgar asked with added emphasis.

Jim hesitated, glanced away from J. Edgar for a moment, and then he answered somewhat reluctantly, "Yes, very clear."

"Good," said Ewing. He glanced at his wristwatch. "It's time. Let's go face the lions!" His comment wasn't intended to be humorous, just real.

He motioned Jim to the door that would take them down the hall and into the courtroom.

As they walked into the courtroom, accompanied by guards, they observed the prosecution team was already seated at their table; the gallery was full of reporters, spectators, and Jim's family, except for Robbie and Justin.

When Jim's eyes connected with those of his wife, Deanna's, he smiled, nodded his head to indicate he was doing okay, and tried to display an air of confidence.

However, as I'd noticed many times before, he avoided looking at Mark. I had an idea why.

Mark had not always been there, but was today. In actuality, he was following Jim's instructions—"Keep the company functioning."

Deanna smiled, and he returned the smile and nodded again. If there was any discord among the family, they certainly were good at disguising it. The jury could not have any other impression than this family stands together firmly behind the contention of Jim's innocence.

Jim and Ewing were seated at the defense table waiting for Judge Arnold and the jury. The judge entered momentarily followed shortly by the jury, escorted by the court clerk. Everybody was seated in the formal manner a trial demands and then Judge Arnold asked if the defense was prepared to present its case. Ewing responded affirmatively.

Judge Arnold then said, "The defense may call its first witness."

Ewing rose slowly, looked at the jury, then the prosecutor; and as he was turning toward Judge Arnold, announced, "The defense recalls Chief of Police John Hammond."

Hammond was seated on the aisle in the front row directly behind the prosecutor.

This came as no surprise to the prosecution since Ewing had included him on his witness list. Then when he was testifying for the prosecution, Ewing had reserved the right to recall him at a later time. Chief Hammond walked toward the witness stand where Judge Arnold reminded him, he was still under oath and did not need to be sworn in again. He then sat down in the witness docket and waited for Ewing to begin.

Ewing rose slowly and walked around in front of the defense table. He greeted Hammond cordially, thanked him for his services as chief of police of Bellevue, and said he only had a few important questions in order to clarify his earlier testimony.

J. Edgar had no idea if this was true or not. He did know much of what he intended to ask Hammond was just fluff for the jury, but he hoped it would relax Chief Hammond. In reality, he was on a fishing expedition to see if Hammond had held anything back and maybe persuade him to express the fact he was a personal acquaintance of Jim's and acknowledge he felt Jim was an extremely responsible citizen incapable of murder.

He than began with some superfluous, somewhat redundant questions. How long had he been in law enforcement? Did he know the defendant? Was he aware of Jim's philanthropic activities? All were designed hopefully to make the chief noncombative and say things reflecting on the defendant's good character. For some reason, Shoemaker during this process had not raised a single objection.

When J. Edgar got the feeling this was accomplishing very little and it was probably boring the jury, he then began to probe more deeply with more penetrating questions. Once again, they were somewhat redundant from Hammond's prior testimony.

Questions like during their investigation had they found any connection to Jim and the weapon used to kill the kidnappers? Were they able or had they even tried to locate any witnesses who could actually put Jim at the crime scene when the murders took place?

All these questions were asked in hopes of illustrating to the jury the prosecution only had a case based on conjecture, not facts.

Ewing rephrased the question about what Jim had said to Hammond on the day he went to his office to report the whereabouts of the two kidnappers.

He also asked if Jim had ever made reference to them being anything other than being alive.

Hammond reiterated the actual scenario once more.

Shoemaker started to object again but decided he wanted this to come to a close before the chief caused him any serious damage. Ewing finally was satisfied he had accomplished all he could from questioning Chief Hammond. He felt the chief's testimony reaffirmed to the jury the police had no real proof that Jim had killed the two kidnappers, only circumstantial evidence. Ewing had the chief confirm, one more time after Jim had apprehended the two kidnappers, that he told the chief where the kidnappers were located and indicated he had left them alive, bound, and gagged waiting for the authorities to arrest them.

J. Edgar then concluded with a courteous thank you.

"Does the prosecution have any questions of this witness?" Judge Arnold asked, looking directly at Shoemaker.

"Just one," responded Shoemaker as he rose out of his chair and walked slowly toward the witness. He stopped, turned toward the jury, looked back at Jim, the defendant, and then asked, "Chief Hammond, do you think the defendant, Jim Malone, killed those two people, the victims?"

Ewing immediately objected, before Hammond could say anything, on the grounds the chief's personal opinion could not be legally introduced and it had no relevance whatsoever with the case.

Shoemaker argued, as he had before, because of the chief's position and experience his opinion should be admissible.

Judge Arnold agreed with Ewing and sustained his objection, and instructed the jury to disregard the question and indicated Shoemaker could continue. Shoemaker then asked Hammond to reiterate the time when Jim had informed the authorities as to the location of the kidnapper's bodies.

Once again, Ewing objected on the grounds that the chief had in prior testimony said Jim had only told him and the other law enforcement authorities where they would find the live kidnappers, not the bodies. He added that the prosecution is not only trying to lead the witness, but to also get him to alter previous testimony and prejudice the jury."

Ewing sat down to wait for the judge's response.

Judge Arnold didn't hesitate to give his opinion. "The court agrees with the defense counsel. The objection is sustained. The jury is to disregard the prosecutor's reference to bodies. Would the prosecutor like to rephrase the question?"

Shoemaker's response was quick, "I withdraw the question, and I have no further questions of this witness."

Having completed his cross of Chief Hammond, Shoemaker returned to the prosecutor's table and sat down. He was satisfied he had accomplished reasserting or rather implanting in the jury's subconscious that Hammond would have confirmed he thought Jim had murdered the two victims.

Judge Arnold then excused Hammond with the court's appreciation.

After Hammond testified, Ewing took command again, and he stayed in charge for the next two days.

Much to the chagrin of Shoemaker, Ewing called a variety of people to testify about Jim's exemplary character and his philanthropic involvement in the community.

Shoemaker knew, as did J. Edgar, the majority of these witnesses had nothing in reality to contribute in connection with the case; and therefore, in most instances, Shoemaker either objected to their testimony as to their relevancy or declined whatsoever any cross-examination.

While this was proceeding, Jim went into his own world.

He was remembering the events that led him to the kidnappers.

#

CHAPTER 30

JIM MALONE

When I was positive my grandchildren and family were secure, I called a meeting with Ed, Leroy, and the rest of my search crew. After the children had been rescued, they redirected their mission and were concentrating on locating the kidnappers.

At this meeting, I told the entire crew I wanted them to abandon their efforts in tracking down the kidnappers and to return to work.

As surprising as this was to them, especially to Ed and Leroy, they accepted my decision without question. I also emphasized they were to forget totally their involvement in the search for the children and the kidnappers.

I thanked them for their efforts from the bottom of my heart and then excused myself. I knew now what I must do, and there was not a second to waste. I called a meeting with the family and told them I would be out of town for a few days and not to worry.

I assured them I would keep in contact with Bob Arnott and Mark to see how Justin and Robbie were recovering. I instructed Mark to get to work on the current housing projects we had in progress and to take care of the family while I was away. I told him, Ed, Leroy, and the rest of our workers were waiting for his direction. When we were alone, Mark tried to inquire where I was going; and after it became obvious I was not going to share anything with him, he agreed to do as I directed. Mark knew there was no sense in butting heads with the Old Man, and it was a total waste of time for him to continue questioning me. Besides, he had some thoughts of his own and did not plan to share these with anyone either, especially not with me.

After this meeting on Thursday morning after Labor Day, I threw some clothes and stuff into my suitcase that I felt would be needed in this quest and immediately headed for Wenatchee over Stevens Pass on Highway 2. My first intention was to follow up on the phone call Mark told me about at the hospital.

This sounded like a real lead and could assist me in picking up the kidnappers' trail.

I knew what my plan entailed once they were in captivity, and they weren't going to like it.

What I must do.

I took the same route I presumed the kidnappers had taken. Highway 2 through Monroe and up over Stevens Pass to Leavenworth into Wenatchee and then north on Highway 97 toward Canada.

Normally this would be a pleasurable trip. Passing through the Cascade Mountains just as summer was coming to an end and fall was beginning was usually a beautiful ride.

The hills were covered in a scarlet carpet as the vine maple leaves turned color for fall. There was already a smattering of snow on the very top of the mountains when I reached the summit of Stevens Pass. This usually means we would probably have an early winter.

The skiers will be happy.

I continued driving down the eastside of Stevens Pass and into Leavenworth, a unique little town promoted by their chamber of commerce as the Alpine Village of the Northwest. It was bustling with tourists who congregate here annually for the fall leaf festival.

I drove slowly around the town, especially the RV areas, just to check for any suspicious-looking vehicles or people. This was a safety reaction just in case the kidnappers were stupid enough to hang around under the cover of so many tourists. I had no real idea what I was looking for other than two men and a woman, so I did a pretty quick tour of the Leavenworth area and then headed on down the road.

I didn't think my prey would be the type to enjoy the Alpine atmosphere. Continuing on down Highway 2 into Cashmere and Wenatchee, the scenery became even more beautiful. Wenatchee is the Apple Capital of the World, and the apple trees dripped with Red Delicious, Green Granny Smith and other varieties of apples and pears.

Just before entering downtown Wenatchee, I turned and headed north on Highway 97 as instructed by the phone call Deanna received. The caller said he had a minimart Shell service station located just about ten miles north on 97 out of Wenatchee. I had driven just few miles when I saw a Shell sign on the right. I was a little low on gas anyhow, so I pulled up next to the pumps. After sliding my credit card in the slot, I started the pump and walked into the store while the tank was being filled. There was only one person working the store, a man behind the counter. And there were no other customers in the store at that moment, a perfect opportunity to inquire if he was the person who made the call on our 800 line with information about the kidnapped Malone children.

The man I was talking to confirmed he had made the call.

I introduced myself politely, thanked him for the call, and explained now that my grandchildren were safe I was just doing a little follow-up in hopes of assisting the police in getting a line on the kidnappers. To make the attendant even more comfortable, I showed him some ID without having it requested. After seeing the ID, the attendant was more than eager to help and told me everything he could remember.

It was really more information than I had hoped for. He gave me a complete description of the motor home, the pickup, and the three occupants. This was more information than the FBI compounded in over a week of investigation. It sounded like these may be the people I was searching for. The service station attendant wouldn't venture a guess where they were heading, but he did feel they were continuing north on Highway 97. He confirmed there were a man and a woman in the motor home and only a single man in the pickup. The man apologized for not being able to supply more information. I expressed my sincere appreciation for his cooperation and said it was considerably more than I had before.

It wasn't much, but at least now I knew what kind of vehicles to look for and exactly how many people I was pursuing with a vague idea what they looked like. I implied to him the authorities would prefer if he, the attendant, would mind keeping this information to himself for now. I asked him if I could reimburse him for any expenses he might have incurred, like the phone call or any other expenses. The attendant seemed to understand my request and confirmed he would keep everything confidential and said no to my offer of payment. He added he had kids of his own and was just trying to help. He did express how the kidnappers should be punished. We were in total agreement.

He wished me luck even though he had no idea what my goal really was other than gathering information or maybe catching up with the people in question. He did presume I was working in conjunction with the police and so he had no adverse reaction to any of my questions. I hopefully left him with that impression. There was no way I wanted the police or the press to have this information, at least not yet. I got back in my SUV and continued north on Highway 97 with a great deal of information I was certain would assist me in my quest.

I pulled over down the road a ways and took a map out of the glove box. I studied it to see if I could figure out where the kidnappers might be going.

There seemed to be two options—to Canada through Oroville or up to Chelan.

Since the attendant had mentioned he noticed they had Canadian plates on both vehicles, I deduced it would probably be difficult for them to cross into

Canada without corresponding documentation that matched the registration of the vehicles, the license plates, and their own, personal identification.

For some reason I didn't think there was any possibility the kidnappers were really Canadians, and therefore they were probably using stolen plates from some other Canadian vehicles.

After digesting this information, I decided there was a very good chance Chelan would be their destination. After contemplating this thought more deeply and factoring in the money they possessed, I was almost certain they really were going to Manson and more specifically, the Colville Tribal Mill Bay Casino. I was trying to think like them, and I concluded that's exactly what I would do if I had money burning a hole in my pocket and was as stupid as these three people had to be.

I knew I was on their trail. I could almost smell my prey.

I would not fail.

The town of Chelan was about an hour or less from where I was and maybe thirty minutes more to Manson where the casino was located. I calculated I should be there by about two or three in the afternoon at the very latest. I hit the road through Chelan and along the shore of Lake Chelan to Manson.

Just about exactly like I figured I arrived at the Mill Bay Casino just after 2:00 PM.

The Mill Bay Casino was a fairly large casino, considering the remoteness of Manson and was located just off Lake Chelan near a golf course with a huge parking area, including a restricted area for RVs and campers.

After driving around the RV parking areas and not seeing any vehicles resembling the Shell attendant's description, I parked my SUV and entered the casino. As I strolled around the casino, I began casually inquiring if any of the casino employees had noticed two men and a woman in the last few days who were gambling fairly heavy. This made almost everyone laugh, and they reminded me this was a casino, and it's what people do at casinos. Stupid question, stupid answer, it gave me a reason to think how dumb my questions must have sounded.

Realizing my first approach was pretty naïve, I tried a new line. I told them I was looking for three friends of mine from Canada, and I was supposed to meet up with them a couple days ago, but I got delayed until now because of business. The reaction and answers were much better with this approach. However, no one could confirm one way or another seeing anyone that fit the vague descriptions I supplied. To be honest, I wasn't sure I was right about their appearances. My descriptions were pretty general. All I really had to go on was how the Shell attendant had described them to me, and his descriptions weren't too precise. Most of them said everybody kind of looks pretty much the same, and there were a lot of people who gambled aggressively.

Finally, after talking to several casino employees, one blackjack dealer said she had a couple guys last Monday or Tuesday who she thought had lost a lot of money. She said they had told her they were Canadians and were headed for Texas to spend the winter, but she had not noticed them in the company of a woman. After questioning her further, I concluded there was a strong possibility these could be my prey.

However, apparently, they had departed after just a day or two of gambling, and the dealer didn't have a clue where they might be headed. I then returned to my SUV and took out my map again to see if I could figure out my next move.

I had asked the dealer I interviewed if there were any other casinos located near here. She told me Okanogan had one, and it was only about fifty miles away, another one in Coulee Dam and a pretty big one called Two Rivers not too far north and east of Coulee Dam. Looking at the map and plotting my course, I decided to try Okanogan next. I took off for Okanogan and, within an hour, walked into the Okanogan Casino.

After driving around the parking lot, it was just like Manson except a lot smaller. I didn't see any motor homes with a pickup that even came close to matching the description the Shell guy supplied, and when I walked inside the casino, I instantly knew they probably hadn't stopped here anyhow since it only had slot machines and bingo.

Just to be positive I was on the right track, I then inquired again where there might be another casino nearby that had blackjack and crap tables. The person at the front desk presumed I was a gambler looking for action, so she was more than happy to help me. She recommended another casino called Two Rivers. The same as the Mill Bay dealer referred to.

She went into great detail telling me it was located on the shores of Lake Roosevelt and the Spokane River. Lake Roosevelt was formed when the Grand Coulee Dam was built during FDR's presidency in the middle thirties. It was part of the Columbia River, and the dealer told me the Two Rivers Casino had a fantastic marina and a large parking area for RVs. She then showed me on a map what was the shortest route for me to drive there. I took out my map when I got back in the SUV to double-check her directions. I decided to check this one out, and if they weren't there, I would head south to Yakima where there was another big Indian Casino because it was becoming obvious to me these people were enjoying having money to spend. My money.

I thought that south would really be my best bet but rather than going there first and since I was already just a few miles away from the Two Rivers Casino, I decided it would be more than logical to check it out.

So there I was on the road again. Out of Omak over a pass called Desautel Pass . . . then through an all-Indian town by the name of Nespelem . . . and down the hill into Coulee Dam. It was getting late by the time I drove into Coulee Dam on my way to Two Rivers Casino. When I was checking my map, I saw there were actually four towns located here by the Great Grand Coulee Dam.

The first one was Elmer City, and it wasn't a city, looked like about four hundred population if that many.

Then next was Coulee Dam.

Bigger and nicer, with tree-lined sidewalks, a smattering of stores; and just outside of town I had seen a sign advertising a casino in Coulee Dam.

Once again, I thought it wouldn't hurt at least to check it out while I was here. It was getting late, and I had been driving for hours. The sun was just going down, so I decided this would be a good place to stay for the evening. Before checking out the casino, I went ahead and registered at the motel right next to the big dam, the Columbia River Inn; it was located facing the Great Grand Coulee Dam. I got settled in my room and drove back across the bridge that crossed the Columbia River below the dam to check out the casino.

This didn't take long because all they had was slot machines just like the Okanogan Casino and no RV parking area. I suspected these high rollers weren't going to waste their time playing slots, and besides, where would they park a motor home? I did a quick walk through, and just as I suspected, nothing.

I got a bite to eat at the nearest restaurant, the Melody Inn.

After I finished eating and was walking to my SUV, the famous Laser Light Show started on the face of the dam. I had heard of it, but had never seen it since I hadn't been in this part of Eastern Washington for many years.

It was fairly early, and I wasn't really too tired, so I sat down on a bench and watched the presentation.

It was really quite good, depicting the history of the various Indian tribes in the area, the migration of people from the east, and the construction of the dam during the Franklin Roosevelt era and how the power generated by the dam contributed to winning World War II and then later how its water was the reason millions of acres in the Columbia Basin around Moses Lake was turned from sage brush and desert into fantastic farmland.

The desert turned green with potatoes, wheat, alfalfa, corn, and sugar beets. Not particularly good for coyotes and jackrabbits, but that's progress.

The Laser Light Show was actually a treat for me. It succeeded in taking me on a journey, away from this very stressful quest, a nice reprieve from all the driving.

Just as soon as the Laser Light Show was completed, I went to bed so I could get an early start the next morning. I must have been more tired than I realized because I had slept like the proverbial log.

The light show probably contributed to helping me relax. As usual, I woke up at 5:00 AM, quickly showered, dressed, and grabbed a roll and coffee at the front desk when I checked out.

Checking the map, I thought I could be at Two Rivers by eight or nine this morning. Driving away from the motel, I proceed up a hill to the top of the dam and immediately entered one of the other of the four towns, Grand Coulee, and adjacent to it was the fourth town, Electric City.

The entire area, I surmised, was a total government project. Why else would they have four towns right next to one another with less than six thousand people combined in all of them?

Stupid, but that was government for you.

Just about twenty miles outside Grand Coulee, the road merged with Highway 2 going east toward Spokane; and then another twenty miles on Highway 2, I turned off to another road going north and followed the signs to Two Rivers Casino. I pulled into the Two Rivers Casino's parking lot within two hours driving time, and like the girl at Manson said, it was big.

There must have been fifty or more motor homes, fifth wheelers, and pickups with campers in the huge parking area. I slowly drove around and much to my disappointment did not see anything that fit the description I had been given by the guy at the Shell station. If they didn't have Canadian plates on, I didn't bother even slowing down. After canvassing the parking lot, I came up empty again, so I parked and went into the casino.

Because it was so early, it wasn't overly crowded. I wandered around, trying to appear like a normal gambler, all the while I was casually checking out everyone at the various table games, trying not to be too obvious. Every now and then I would stop and put a few bucks in a slot machine and continue moving around. I was also watching to see if I could corral an employee who maybe could supply me with information. This early, there were only two blackjack tables in operation, so I decided to play a little and see if I could casually inquire from the dealers if they might recall seeing three of my friends I was supposed to meet here at the casino a day or two ago. After using this ploy in Manson, I had decided it was my best approach, and it seemed to make it easier for the dealers to talk to me. They were rotating dealers about every thirty minutes. I must have played for almost two hours before I had a dealer that seemed to recall a couple players fitting such a description.

Once again, the dealer had not particularly noticed a woman, but the dealer did remember two guys that gambled heavy and fit the profiles I gave her. She told me the same story I had heard in Manson. They said they were Canadians heading for Texas to spend the winter with some friends.

After hearing the same story from the dealer in Manson, it made me more positive that I was on the right trail. She said she hadn't seen them for at least a day or two, but then again she wasn't dealing twenty-four hours a day. She then offered to ask some of the other casino people, but I told her not to bother.

I was convinced these were the people I was pursuing, but it appeared they had already left the casino. I missed them again, but maybe I was closing in. For appearance's sake, I played another twenty minutes before I departed and walked out to my rig to plan my next course of action. For some reason I had a deep sensation I was getting close to finding them.

It was just a matter of time. I was closing in.

I could feel it in my bones, just like I could when I was in Nam.

Yakima, that's where they were headed next—south. I knew there was another casino there. Deanna and I had even been in it gambling a couple of times when we went over to Yakima Downs for the horse races and to visit the many wineries and vineyards in that part of Washington. Some of the world's best vineyards and finest wineries are located around Yakima and the Tri-Cities. But I wasn't here for pleasure. I had something more important on my mind. I was confident I was on the right track. I took out my map and plotted the most direct course I should take to get there in the shortest time possible. Looking at my watch, I calculated it would take about three to four hours. It was almost noon now. So the estimated arrival time should be around three or four this afternoon.

For some reason as I pulled out of the Two Rivers parking lot, I started humming Willie Nelson's theme song "On the Road Again." I hadn't thought of that song for years, but it was certainly appropriate at least at this moment in time.

Strange.

Finally, the silence was getting to me, and I turned the radio on and punched the scan button until it stopped on a station that was featuring Bill O'Reilly, my favorite radio talk show person. Listening to Bill O'Reilly would make the time driving more pleasant and keep me from dwelling on the encounter I soon would be facing. At least I hoped to be facing such an encounter.

That afternoon the subject O'Reilly was talking about was Jessica's Law, and the states and judges who were light on putting away child molesters. Obviously, due partially to what my family had just been through I was in total agreement with O'Reilly. I knew, especially after this recent ordeal with my grandchildren and the people I was pursuing, O'Reilly was correct, the states' and judges' light on child molesters should be chastised, impeached, or voted out of office. And the state of Washington was one of those states soft on child molesters and rapist.

Three hours of driving time flew by.

On the route I had mapped out, the traffic was light, and I was able to exceed the speed limit just slightly. I didn't know it, but this was the same route the kidnappers had taken. Not too fast so I could avoid being stopped by the Washington State Patrol. I didn't want anyone to know my location, especially the state patrol. It was just past three when I drove over the bridge crossing the

Columbia River, just a few more miles, a little more time. Now was not the time to hurry. I knew I had to be cautious, no mistakes. I silently was saying to myself.

I decided to pull over for just a minute, stretch my legs, and check the map again. A quick call to my friend Bob Arnott on his cell phone and give him a little heads-up, but not too much. After Bob and I finished talking, I thought he was a little strange sounding. Plus he hadn't said a word about Mark. Strange, I couldn't quite put my finger on it, but the conversation was stilted or something. I shrugged it off as nothing, probably my imagination, and resumed driving. I was getting closer, just a few more miles.

And there it was. The Yakima Tribal Casino located just east of Yakima near a town called Wapato. I would be there in the parking lot in about ten more minutes.

I knew it was ultraimportant, especially at this time, to get total control of all my emotions.

Don't let them suspect I'm getting close. That's if they were there. I knew they had never really seen me close-up, and so they shouldn't be able to recognize me until I was ready.

Surprise was the name of the game.

I remembered that surprise was a major element for achievement when serving in the Special Forces. During my stint in the Special Forces, I'd been trained to handle situations similar to what I was now embarking to undertake.

Who would have thought I would ever again be called on to use those talents? This was the first time I could remember being thankful for having developed those skills. I had just turned on to the freeway that went from Tri-Cities to Yakima, and a few more miles down the road, I saw the casino.

The Yakima Indian Tribe had improved it since Deanna and I had been over. It was much bigger. Now it was a pretty good size casino.

I pulled into the parking area and saw over to the east end of the casino there was an area designated for motor homes and similar modes of transportation. I crawled along at five miles an hour around the RV parking area, a normal speed for a tourist. But I wasn't the typical tourist. I was only interested in locating a specific motor home and a pickup. And there they were, at the very end, near some trees and bushes. At least it matched everything the Shell guy had told me.

Perfect!

A beige Ram pickup parked alongside a blue-and-white motor home with Canadian plates, just like the guy at the Shell station had described.

There appeared to be no one around, which was a good thing. I certainly didn't want them to feel my presence. I came too far to blow it now.

I went on by and parked on the other side of the casino where daily and local gamblers parked, got out, locked up, and decided to go in and do a little light gambling while I searched for the kidnappers.

The place was pretty big, much larger than I remembered. The design was similar to a tribal longhouse. It was more or less in a hexagon shape with all kinds of Indian paraphernalia and tribal pictures on all the walls.

And to add to my dilemma, there was an overabundance of people playing the slot machines and the table games.

Luckily, I found a slot near the blackjack area where I thought my prey would be gambling. I tried to appear to be concentrating on what the slot machine was doing and, at the same time, peruse the black jack players.

I inserted a hundred-dollar voucher I had exchanged at the moneychanger's thing and then noticed that it was a dollar machine. A hundred bucks, I thought, wouldn't last too long unless I got lucky and won a few times.

Fortunately, I did hit some winners; so while the machine was racking up my winnings, I would glance at the blackjack tables, trying to locate the kidnappers without being detected.

There must have been ten or fifteen tables in operation, so it would probably take a little time to spot the kidnappers, if they were there.

To my relief, it took less time than I anticipated to spot what I thought could be the two male kidnappers. There they were, at the $100-minimum-limit blackjack table, high rollers, betting my money. I casually observed them from my slot machine location and was somewhat surprised to see them so aggressively gambling away their ill-gotten gains and appear not to be worried they were being pursued not only by me, but also by the police. I shrugged off the thought because if they were stupid enough to kidnap my grandchildren, then they were certainly stupid enough to be here gambling their ill-gotten gains like there was no tomorrow. Besides, I knew in their minds it was easy money.

And, I knew for them, there would be no tomorrow.

I didn't see their coconspirator, the woman; and until I could locate her, I knew I had better be ultracautious.

Even though I thought she was the person responsible for saving Robbie and Justin, she was still a kidnapper; and eventually if my plan works, I would have to deal with her.

I knew what I had planned for the two males.

I wasn't too sure yet what I would do with her. I did have some thoughts, but we would have to wait until later to see if any of them applied to her.

These ideas were floating around in my head, but nothing concrete.

That decision could wait.

And just then a woman approached one of the kidnappers.

It was her! I was positive.

From her appearance, she looked like she'd been ridden hard a few times and put away wet; but I still thought, even from that distance, there was a human being inside that body.

Maybe my judgment was biased because of her phone call. I was positive she was the one who made that phone call that led Ed and me to Robbie and Justin. Who else could it have been? Enough for now, there were things I had to do in order to be prepared for what I planned as a welcome home party later tonight.

As I was about to leave to prepare for tonight, the male kidnapper she had been talking to stood up and said something that seemed to bother the other card players at the blackjack table. I was too far away to hear, but she instantly turned her back to him and rapidly headed for the casino entrance. The male kidnapper sat back down and placed another bet, as if nothing had transpired.

What a jerk.

I closed down my slot machine by pushing the cashing out button and, without even bothering to look at my ticket, stuffed it in my pocket. I followed the female out the door, being careful to be far enough back so she wouldn't notice me.

I got outside just in time to watch as she walked in the direction of the motor home. This more than confirmed my assessment; these were the kidnappers, and it was their motor home.

I paused just long enough to watch her go through the side door. Then I returned to my SUV and drove off to find a hardware store to purchase the things I would need for this evening's party.

My list included duct tape, rope, nylon packing tape, and three small cloth bags, just big enough to cover a persons head.

Not too many fun things for a party.

I drove into Yakima and found a Home Depot where it would be possible to purchase everything needed. After completing my shopping, I found a motel just a half mile from the casino back toward Yakima. It was my plan to shower and rest until it got dark.

Not long to wait.

I knew with what I had planned, and it was not going to be a pleasant evening for anyone, including me. I finished showering, laid out the dark clothes I had brought with me so I would be completely prepared for later this evening.

I was finally able to lie down on top of the bed and shut my eyes in hopes of relaxing for a short period of time before it was time to move into action.

#

Lois was terribly upset when she returned to the motor home.

She had tried to suggest to Fred that maybe he and Dennis should slow down on their gambling, take a break, have some dinner, and try their luck later. Boy did that piss him off.

Oh well, at least she had tried.

She hoped maybe they would get out of here tomorrow and head south just like Fred promised.

If they didn't get going pretty soon, she was going to take the pickup and go it alone with the money Fred had given her so far.

Besides, she seriously suspected they would need more money as the evening progressed. She already had close to a hundred thousand in her little box. She couldn't believe it. That means in three days they each lost as much or maybe even more. She smiled to herself, and then another thought came to mind. *How long will it be before they've lost all their money?*

And then who has money left?

Right, only her money, and she knew what they would do then.

The thought brought her to conclude no matter what, tomorrow she was splitting before they lost all their money and started gambling with her share of the ransom.

Now that she had made that decision, she decided to go for a long walk and kill some time before dark.

She walked quite a ways before she looked at her watch, and she saw it was just after eight o'clock, getting dark, so she decided she had better get back and see if her cohorts were there. As she was walking back, she spotted Fred and Dennis coming out of the motor home.

It was just like she had assumed, they would need more gambling money.

"Aren't you guys tired of losing your money yet?" she asked.

Fred backhanded her.

"Keep your fucking mouth shut, bitch. We'll do what we want, when we want to, and no dumb-fucking broad is going to tell us anything. You get it?"

Lois didn't say anything more.

She just glared at Fred and rubbed her cheek where he had smacked her. Her lip was split a little. He smacked her pretty good.

"Now get your pretty little ass in there and shut up," he continued. "I left your fucking share in the bathroom sink, so you'd better grab it before Dennis decides he wants it. And by the way, be ready for BJs for both of us when we come back. Now get your ass in there and shut up."

Then without waiting for her to respond, with their wad of money in hand, he and Dennis trotted off to the casino. Boy was he pissed. The losing was getting to him, and she could foresee what was coming next, and it wasn't going to be fun.

Lois went on into the motor home's bathroom to wipe off a trickle of blood where Fred had backhanded her.

While she was doing this, she mumbled to herself.

"That's it, no more. And if that asshole thinks I'm going down on either one of them, he's got another thought coming. I'm packing right now, and I'm out of here." Even though there wasn't anyone around to hear what she said, it made her feel better. Then she saw the money in the sink and proceeded to count out fifty thousand.

Wow!

Great, now she had over one hundred thousand. It made the smack by Fred a little more tolerable.

She then counted it again.

She was right, this time Fred had left her fifty thousand dollars. And she knew she was right about what they would do if they ran out of money. No, she rethought, not if, but when. She decided now was the time to leave before it was too late to get away from them.

Give Fred credit, she was thinking, *at least he was fair.* She retrieved her box of money from under the sink and went to the back bedroom to get her suitcase out and pack.

There wasn't much to pack, and besides, with all this money she could buy all new stuff. She was thinking it would take them a little time to lose their fifty thousand, but she wanted to be well down the road before they came back.

#

What Lois Griffin didn't know (nor did Fred or Dennis) was I had already left my motel and was just off to the side, hidden behind some shrubs, waiting for them and observed this entire altercation.

When Fred and Dennis came back to get more money, I held my position in the shadows. I didn't know where Lois was at the time, so I remained hidden. The two men were leaving the motor home, I assumed to continue gambling, when she came back from her walk. I watched her get backhanded and heard their conversation. They were obviously very uptight about losing money and demonstrated it by backhanding the woman. I knew I couldn't do anything to help her at the time of the altercation, and it wasn't dark enough yet to put my plan in action. So I remained out of sight behind the shrubs, but I still had enough clear vision to see the approach to the motor home and observe anyone entering or leaving. I would wait just a few more minutes to let the two men go back to the casino and get busy with their gambling.

Once I was sure the two men returned to the casino and after the woman entered the motor home, I came out of my hiding spot.

I decided to wait just a couple more minutes while she settled down before I would confront her. The situation appeared ideal for what I was planning. There was absolutely no activity in the area around the other motor homes or RVs. Everybody must be in the casino gambling because there was not a soul around, nobody.

That's a good omen, I thought to myself.

I had the bag with me that contained my purchases earlier at the Home Depot.

Finally, I walked around to the side entrance of the motor home and quietly tried the doorknob.

Great, not locked.

I silently opened the door and cautiously crept inside. I could hear the woman moving around in the back bedroom, talking to herself; and with the stealth of a cougar, I came up behind her.

Before she could say a word, I grabbed her and clamped my right hand over her mouth.

I spoke quickly, but quietly, "Don't struggle, and you won't get hurt!"

She was no match for me anyway and did exactly like I asked.

I then told her who I was.

However, Lois instantly figured that out the minute I grabbed her.

She nodded yes and thought, *Who else would be here?*

"I'm going to tie you up and put a gag in your mouth," Jim said tersely. "Don't struggle, and like I said, I promise you won't get hurt. When I ask you a question, I want you to nod your head yes or no. Do you understand?"

Lois nodded yes.

For some reason, she didn't feel frightened of this man. Maybe, just maybe, she would later, but not now.

I proceeded to put a washcloth in her mouth and then used the nylon tape to bind her hands, feet, arms, and legs. After completing this, I sat her down on the edge of the bed to ask her some questions.

"You're the one who called about how to find my grandchildren, aren't you?"

Lois nodded yes.

"You don't know when your buddies will return, do you?"

Lois shook her head no.

"Okay, then we'll wait together."

I noticed the bruise and cut on her lip.

"Do you like getting slapped around like that?"

Lois didn't respond at first, and all of a sudden it dawned on her; she realized I had seen the entire scene with Fred and Dennis. Then she shook her head.

"Well, try to get comfortable while we wait for your partners."

I laid her back on the bed and sat down in the dark to wait for the two kidnappers.

I suspected they'd be back for more money. With those idiots, it was just a matter of time. All I needed was patience.

And I was patient when I had to be.

#

CHAPTER 31

JIM MALONE

"The defense calls Jim Malone to the stand." J. Edgar Ewing's voice jolted Jim back to reality.

He hadn't realized how long he had been thinking about all the events that had transpired in his pursuit of the kidnappers.

Ewing's parade of defense witnesses had moved at breakneck speed partially because the prosecution had chosen not to cross-examine most of them. Therefore, they were never on the witness stand for more than five or ten minutes while J. Edgar did his thing.

It was apparent Shoemaker felt there was no need for any cross-examination of the majority of J. Edgar's so-called witnesses.

Most of those called to testify contributed nothing toward proving Jim wasn't guilty of what he was charged. Shoemaker apparently decided that all of this only assisted in illustrating that good citizens also can and do commit murder.

So here they were at the moment in the trial when Jim would be called to testify.

His counsel, J. Edgar Ewing, had already prepared him for this crucial part of the trial.

Jim knew what the questions would be and how he was supposed to answer them. J. Edgar had been extremely precise in his preparation of Jim's testimony. And he stressed Jim was not to waver one iota from these instructions. He emphasized how Jim responded to the questions even his voice tone and facial expressions could be the difference in how the jury would perceive his guilt or innocence.

He added what he didn't know what Shoemaker would ask him when it was his turn to cross-examine, and other than taking his time to respond to Shoemaker with objections, he could not fully prepare Jim for everything. He once again told

Jim to remember that he was no contest for Shoemaker and don't even consider taking him on in his arena.

Time had run out.

It was Jim's turn to explain what really transpired—on the stand, under oath, sworn in to tell the truth.

The truth from the horse's mouth, so to speak.

At least that's what the gallery, especially the media was anticipating and hoping would transpire.

They wanted to hear Jim's description of how he was able to rescue his grandchildren, track down the kidnappers, and how he disposed of them.

They wanted to hear every gory, bloody detail.

Unfortunately, they were to be sadly disappointed. That was not J. Edgar's game plan.

J. Edgar was completely prepared.

He was cognizant of the fact; this may well be the most important portion of the trial. It could be a make-it or break-it time.

And now, he was ready to begin. Just seconds elapsed after J. Edgar had informed the court he was calling Jim Malone, the defendant, to testify in his own behalf.

The court's clerk ordered Jim to come forward to be sworn in and begin his testimony.

Slowly, and hopefully exuding a degree of humble confidence, Jim approached the witness stand.

The clerk swore him in, and Jim took his seat in the docket, ready to begin his testimony. His facial expression was almost totally void of any emotion.

J. Edgar Ewing walked about halfway to Jim and stood directly in Shoemaker's vision path so neither he nor Jim could see one another. At the same time, he made sure Jim and the jury could make eye contact. It was Ewing's feeling the only thing that would save Jim was the jury and their perception that the prosecution's circumstantial evidence was not sufficient enough for them to convict him. It was Ewing's honest conviction Jim had told him the truth. He was innocent of the murder charges. At the same time, it was also his honest assessment Shoemaker had presented a comparatively strong circumstantial case against him.

He began with some basic questions like name, address, occupation. All designed to put Jim and the jury at ease.

J. Edgar then asked Jim about the variety of medals he received during his service to the country in Vietnam.

Jim had always been uncomfortable with being honored for doing what was required of him during his tour in Vietnam. His answers as they had been in rehearsal were brief, and he displayed total humility when referring to them.

Then J. Edgar asked, "Did you remove the thumbs of two people the law enforcement agencies were pursuing for the kidnapping of your grandchildren?"

There was a stirring among the spectators when this question was asked. This is what they wanted to hear. It's why they stood in line overnight.

This was what they wanted—blood and guts.

Jim had confessed this portion of the escapade to counsel, and Ewing explained he was going to ask this question before Shoemaker had an opportunity to pursue it during his cross-examination. He told Jim he wanted him to answer it honestly, get it out in the open, and demonstrate to the jury he had nothing to hide.

The part of the operation Jim had neglected to tell Ewing was Lois had assisted him in the operation on the thumbs.

It was his judgment that he and he alone should be held responsible.

Jim waited for a moment after J. Edgar asked about the thumbs and then slowly, softly replied, "He had done this act."

Ewing then asked, "Why?"

Jim then responded, "Because these kidnappers had cut the little fingers off his two grandchildren, and he guessed he felt they should feel the same pain they had inflicted to his grandchildren."

In their rehearsal, J. Edgar had instructed him to avoid using such words like *retaliation* or *revenge*. He explained words like *revenge* and *retaliation* had a connotation closer to murder.

Good, Jim responded as instructed, thought J. Edgar silently.

He then asked, "Do you regret having done this?"

Jim's answer was simple, and unfortunately, it came out louder than he had intended. "No!"

It even sounded kind of aggressive, much to J. Edgar's chagrin. But he realized it was too late again to back up and change the answer to a softer no.

So his only choice was to move quickly on to the next question before the jury could think too much about how aggressive Jim had answered.

During their earlier private meeting prior to the resumption of the trial, Ewing had asked him directly if he had killed the two kidnappers.

Jim emphatically told J. Edgar, "I absolutely did not kill them."

On this point, he was unshakable; and regardless of what Ewing personally thought at the time, he had accepted Jim's statement as fact. He did tell Jim he felt that Shoemaker had presented an extremely solid circumstantial case against him, and he felt it was going to be very difficult to convince the jury of his innocence, but he would give it his best. He was aware he had mentioned this to Jim several times. He purposely did this to keep Jim on his toes and not become complacent. Ewing paused just briefly before his next question.

He then turned to face Jim and asked, "Did you kill these two people?"

Jim looked directly at the jury, per his attorney's instructions, and answered with as much conviction on his face as he could muster and much softer than his last answer, but loud enough so the jury would have no doubt about his response.

"Absolutely not."

Ewing then turned to Shoemaker and said, "Your witness."

He then returned to his seat.

"Does the prosecution wish to cross-examine this witness?" Judge Arnold asked Shoemaker.

"We certainly do, Your Honor," Shoemaker responded.

He rose from his chair and did the same thing Ewing had done but, in reverse, placed himself directly in the way of Ewing and Jim's path of vision. Eye contact between them became impossible.

He then looked at Jim and asked, "Weren't you in the Special Forces in Vietnam?"

J. Edgar didn't have time to object before his client responded.

Jim quickly answered, "Yes, I served in Nam."

J. Edgar thought to himself, *Jim, slow down, like I told you to do. Give me time to raise an objection.*

Shoemaker then, without a second delay, asked his next question in hopes he already had Jim in control because of how rapidly he had responded to his last question without giving his attorney an opportunity to mount an objection.

"Did you kill anybody there?" Jim hesitated and remembering J. Edgar's instructions for him to wait to see if he was going to raise an objection.

He did.

J. Edgar stood up rapidly and objected on the grounds that Jim's past was not on trial here and his service in the military, and especially the question the prosecution just asked was totally irrelevant.

Much to Ewing's surprise, the judge sustained his objection, and Shoemaker for some unknown reason decided to abandon this subject.

J. Edgar concluded maybe Judge Arnold's ruling was a show of respect for a true war hero. Whatever reason the judge had for his ruling, J. Edgar was quietly appreciative.

Shoemaker then asked, "Let's see, you admit you chopped off the two men's thumbs, is that correct?"

Before Jim could answer, Ewing immediately objected to the use of the word *chopped*.

The judge sustained the objection and instructed the jury to disregard the word and for the DA to rephrase the question. Shoemaker then restated the question replacing *chopped* off with *cut off*.

Jim answered simply, "Yes."

"And you expect the jury to believe you cut their thumbs off, then walked away without killing them, isn't that what you want the jury to believe?"

Shoemaker turned toward the jury and kind of smiled, waiting for Ewing's anticipated response.

It came immediately.

"Objection, Your Honor," Ewing said as he rose to his feet, "is the prosecutor asking a question or making a statement regardless it's improper and totally irrelevant?

"The objection is overruled." Judge Arnold ruled against the objection, for some unknown reason to Ewing and then said, "The witness will answer the prosecutor's question."

Jim took a moment before he responded and then answered, "That's all that happened."

"You didn't kill them?" Shoemaker asked again.

Before Jim could respond, Ewing said, "Objection, Your honor, the defendant has already been asked the question and answered it."

"The objection is sustained. Move on with your examination of this witness," Judge Arnold instructed Shoemaker in somewhat of a stern manner. J. Edgar thought the judge might have regretted his previous decision.

It made Ewing a little more comfortable with the judge.

"Let me ask you this, Mr. Malone, why did you cut off their thumbs?"

Jim cringed inwardly when Shoemaker asked the question and waited for an objection from Ewing.

When none came, he slowly, and with some anger in his voice, answered, "As I said before, that's what they did to my grandchildren!"

"Cut off their thumbs?" asked Shoemaker.

"They cut off my grandchildren's little fingers," Jim said in a very emphatic manner with his head turned to face the jury.

"You mean an 'eye for an eye' revenge?" asked Shoemaker.

"You could say that!" Jim responded somewhat angrily.

And once again, J. Edgar silently cringed when Jim responded so rapidly he didn't have time to raise an objection, and regretfully there was an obvious tone of anger in Jim's voice. That coupled with Jim sort of agreeing maybe it was for revenge caused J. Edgar to cringe inwardly.

He silently thought to himself, *Slow down, Jim, slow down, think before you answer, don't let Shoemaker control you, remember I told you he was very good.*

J. Edgar hoped Jim would remember and take his advice, noting this was the second time Jim had let Shoemaker control him.

Then Shoemaker turned to the jury and asked again, "And you didn't kill them for this?"

"Objection," declared Ewing in a very loud voice as he rose to his feet really quick before Jim could say a word and stared at Judge Arnold!

Before the judge could respond, Shoemaker said, "I withdraw the question." Then he paused for a couple minutes as he walked back to his table, picked up a legal pad, and turned back toward Jim and again asked, "Did you want to kill them for what they did to your grandchildren?"

"Objection, I strenuously object to this line of questioning by the prosecution, it's totally out of order and definitely irrelevant!" Ewing shouted again, almost a soon as Shoemaker had ask the question.

Ewing continued, "The prosecutor's question is absolutely hypothetical, and any response from the defendant is completely irrelevant to this trial."

Judge Arnold once again sustained the objection and instructed Shoemaker to move ahead with his cross-examination of the witness.

J. Edgar was seething inside. He thought Shoemaker had succeeded, the damage had been done, and there was no way to retrieve it. Then Shoemaker turned to Judge Arnold and said, much to Ewing's surprise, "The prosecution has no further questions of the defendant."

Shoemaker returned to his seat.

Judge Arnold excused Jim, and he immediately returned to his seat next to his attorney, J. Edgar Ewing, who gave him a comforting pat on the knee after he was seated.

Judge Arnold then asked the defense counsel if he had any more witnesses he wanted to call.

Ewing responded somewhat reluctantly that the defense rested its case.

He silently felt Shoemaker had been somewhat successful in his cross, and there was now only a fifty-fifty chance he had been successful in persuading the jury that they should find Jim innocent.

Not the odds he had hoped to achieve.

He was more than concerned about Jim's aggressive answers during Shoemaker's cross. He was afraid Jim's rapid and aggressive responses could be damaging and influence the jury's impression of him.

But, it still seemed to him, there remained a degree of hope the jury would empathize with the situation and agree Jim had done the right thing when he cut off their thumbs.

He even thought there was a chance that the jury would even conclude the kidnappers should have been killed, and Jim had every right to do it. Like he always said, you never know what juries will really do once they're alone pondering their decision of guilt or innocence.

Judge Arnold then directed his next question to Shoemaker, "Does the prosecution wish to offer any rebuttal?"

Rising, Shoemaker said in a very loud voice, "We do, Your Honor. We wish to offer a new witness in rebuttal."

Shoemaker's announcement came as a complete surprise to J. Edgar. There had not been any other names on the prosecution's witness list. What or who does Shoemaker have up his sleeve for him to wait until now to spring it on the court.

"Does this witness have a name?" asked Judge Arnold.

"Yes!" Shoemaker said. "The prosecution plans to call Lois Griffin to testify!"

After hearing Shoemaker make this announcement, total bedlam broke out in the courtroom as reporters ran for the door so they could get this new revelation instantly on the news.

Ewing loudly objected to this turn of events; it was as if Shoemaker had poked a dagger in his back. Shoemaker wasn't smiling, but he was enjoying watching J. Edgar squirm.

After Judge Arnold restored a degree of decorum to the courtroom, he excused the jury for thirty minutes and emphatically told both attorneys he wanted to meet with them in his chambers.

"NOW!" he said with much authority and in an extremely loud tone of voice.

He immediately rose out of his chair above the courtroom and headed for his chambers, closely followed by J. Edgar Ewing and the prosecutor, Robert Shoemaker. Jim just sat there at the defense table somewhat dumbfounded. He didn't seem to comprehend fully what was transpiring.

"How had they found her?" He was turning this over in his mind.

As Ewing and Shoemaker entered the judge's chambers, he instructed them, in a somewhat curt tone of voice, to be seated.

Before Ewing could say anything, Judge Arnold asked Shoemaker for an explanation why this witness had not appeared on the prosecution's witness list prior to this announcement and added it had better be good.

Shoemaker was quick to explain the FBI and, more specifically, FBI Director Watkins had apprehended this person only a few days ago in California where she had been hiding out. And to protect her from possible harm and away from the press, they had kept the capture under wraps.

He further explained that it had taken this long to meet with her legal counsel, get her extradition from California approved, and confirm she would testify.

Ewing still voiced his objection.

He knew what the prosecution also had been doing while she was hidden away, prepping her on her testimony, and probably working out a deal of some kind for her appearance in court for the prosecution.

The judge reminded Ewing that because of how this was handled by the prosecutor, if his client were found guilty, he would more than likely have a better case with the appeals court rather than here.

Then, turning to Shoemaker, he said in a more personal tone, "Bob, as much as I regret to, and only because of strictly legal reasons, I'm going to allow the testimony of this witness to proceed. However, trust me, if you do anything out of line legally, I'll stop you instantly and instruct the jury to ignore this woman's entire testimony. It's even conceivable that a mistrial could be declared. Do I make myself clear?"

"Perfectly clear, Your Honor," said Shoemaker.

"How soon will this person be available to testify?" he then added. "If at all possible I would like the trial to continue in an expeditious manner. Do you understand, Mr. Shoemaker?"

Judge Arnold directed the question and statement straight at Shoemaker in a disgusting tone of voice and paused for Shoemaker's response.

"She arrived last night, accompanied by legal counsel, FBI Director Watkins and a federal attorney. She's prepared to testify tomorrow if you so order."

J. Edgar thought to himself, *I'll bet she's ready to testify.*

"Then that's what we'll do," said Judge Arnold.

Then he turned to Ewing and continued, "John, I apologize personally, but you've been in my court before, and you know I'm legally always fair. You do have a right to meet with the witness prior to her testifying if you choose to."

Ewing responded, "If it's acceptable to you and the court, I would like to confer with my client prior to making that decision. With your approval, Judge, I would prefer to make the choice in the morning prior to the opening of court."

"I don't think your request is out of line, and so it is granted," said Judge Arnold. "Be aware, both of you, if Mr. Ewing decides to meet with the witness in the morning and this meeting lasts for any extended period of time, there's a possibility that it could cause at the very least a one day delay or more in the proceedings. Before you object to Mr. Ewing's request in any way, Mr. Shoemaker, remember you created this situation, and you should feel fortunate I'm even letting her testify. Do I make myself clear?"

Both attorneys said they understood.

Judge Arnold continued, "Be ready to go tomorrow. I think we should meet at 8:00 AM for Mr. Ewing's answer concerning the witness; and if he chooses not to meet with her, then we'll continue the trial at 9:00 AM. Or if he decides to meet with the witness, we'll proceed with the trial at the conclusion of Mr. Ewing's interview. I'll make the final decision when this is completed."

He then directed his next comment directly to Shoemaker rather than Ewing. "Have your witness here at the courthouse ready and available at eight in the morning for a possible meeting with Mr. Ewing. And once again I want to impress on you, if the defense counsel feels a delay in the proceedings becomes necessary, I will grant it, so don't even think about mounting an objection. Now, you're both excused until tomorrow morning. I'll notify the jury we are going to recess the court for the remainder of today, and we will continue tomorrow morning promptly at 9:00 AM. Thank you both, and we'll see you at eight o'clock in the morning. I'm sure the two of you have a lot to prepare, so get out of here."

They immediately left Judge Arnold's chambers without speaking another word to each other.

Shoemaker was obviously feeling euphoric.

Ewing was very concerned. He knew it was urgent to meet with Jim right away and see if Jim could tell him anything concerning what Lois might say on the stand.

J. Edgar would need to know everything Jim could remember in his encounter or with his dealings with Lois Griffin the night of the event in Yakima.

Perhaps something else important might have occurred prior to that night, and his client had just neglected telling him. He knew this thought of course was naive and was only wishful thinking.

His experience told him Shoemaker must have something of great value to the prosecution's case or he wouldn't allow her to testify.

And he certainly wouldn't have made any deals with her unless she had something to offer, if in fact that was what he had done in return for her appearing in court as a prosecution witness. He had to convince Jim no matter what it was he may have held back or why he had not been totally factual when it came to discussing this Lois person, he must do so now.

Without the truth, there was no way he could prepare for his cross-examination of this witness or even decide whether he needed to meet with her privately, prior to testifying.

On J. Edgar's return to the courtroom, the clerk told him a deputy had taken Jim to a waiting room and directed him to where it was located. He went there; and as he entered the room, after excusing the deputy, he turned to face Jim head-on. "Are we in deep shit now or what?" He stared directly at Jim with a look on his face that Jim had never seen before. Obviously, he was excessively angry.

Jim didn't respond. He just sat there waiting for what was coming.

He'd already had time to think about what could Lois know other than the part about assisting in cutting off the thumbs, and he hadn't told his attorney she had participated in doing the operation. He didn't think it was important; and besides, if she did help, what does that have to do with who killed the two kidnappers? He was about to find out!

No matter how he tried, he couldn't think of anything else. He knew he had to tell Ewing this portion of the story.

And he knew Ewing would be pissed off, to put it mildly.

He thought about everything, and there was nothing else.

Or nothing else he was willing to share, even with his attorney.

There was something, but he would never bring it up. As hard as he thought about it, he could not figure out who killed these two people. He had some thoughts, but they would remain only with him.

It was why he was so firm in his testimony, so resolute.

After taking a few minutes to let his stare and anger sink in, Ewing then asked in a fairly loud and harsh voice, "Okay, what's the story, and I mean the real story? What does Shoemaker know that I don't? And don't lie to me. I know this Griffin person knows something, and Shoemaker has it, and you'd better be able to tell me what it is or we're going to be up to our butts in crap. So what is it?" He had said this very strongly and stood there in front of Jim, arms crossed across his chest, waiting for his answer.

Slowly, Jim stood up and then started to talk as he paced the room, "All I can think of that I haven't told you is this." He then told Ewing the complete story of the night when he found the kidnappers at the Yakima Casino.

He tried to make sure he left nothing out from the moment he saw their rigs in the parking area, observed them in the casino gambling, how he had hidden in the bushes by their motor home waiting for them to return, his capturing of Lois first, tying her up, and then how he captured the two men. How he had subdued them by using a sleeper hold on each of them when they returned that night to the motor home. He described in detail how he then had bound and gagged them.

And more important to J. Edgar, he told him about her involvement in the removal of the thumbs, and that the reason he hadn't told him this part was simply because she was the one who had called him directly on the cell phone he had in his possession about the location of the kids. He explained that this was the cell phone the kidnappers had left him the night of the money drop, and for some reason he had retained it.

He emphasized that if he had not kept it, the phone tip from Lois that led him to where Robbie and Justin were hidden would probably not have happened, and they would be dead. He also added he had tossed it into the Puget Sound some time after he had rescued the boys and could not really find or tell J. Edgar where it was dumped.

He said for all those reasons he chose to keep her name out of the thumb incident and any other involvement. Jim added he thought he owed her at least that much, along with letting her escape and allowing her to keep three hundred and forty thousand of the ransom money as a reward for the safe return of the kids. He further explained she left the motor home before he did, and he thought she had headed south toward Bend, Oregon, on Highway 97.

He continued to explain to J. Edgar, after she left, he made sure the two maggots were not in danger of bleeding to death after losing their thumbs and were tied securely so they couldn't escape before the authorities found them after he notified them where they were located.

He said he then left for Bellevue over Snoqualmie Pass and stressed they were both alive when he had shut the door and departed for home. Once he got to Bellevue, he went to his house to shower and change clothes before he reported to Captain Hammond and informed him where the kidnappers could be found.

After finishing this final part, he turned and was looking out the window with his back to Ewing.

"That's it. All of it?" Ewing asked.

Jim slowly turned back to face Ewing and took just a few moments to respond.

"That's honestly all I can think of that might connect. Are we in trouble?"

"Big-time trouble, but if you're telling me the truth, maybe, just maybe there's room for hope. Not much though, it's pretty grim, but I think there is some room. A lot will depend on what this Griffin woman has to say."

Ewing thought for a moment. And much to Jim's relief, J. Edgar's face had returned to normal.

He continued keeping his slate gray eyes fixed on Jim. He wanted to make Jim as uncomfortable as possible, and it appeared he was being successful.

"Okay, here's the situation we're in. Shoemaker and the Feds have a witness we didn't anticipate. Other than the thumb incident, the phone call, the money, and your vision story, we don't have the foggiest what she is going to say. Unfortunately the prosecution does, advantage for the prosecution. However, if she adds anything other than what you have told me. It should be a lie, as long as you haven't lied to me." He moved a little closer to Jim to make sure he got his message, paused, and then continued. "And if we trap her in a lie, I can probably impeach her entire testimony. Sometimes, as you have already found out, when a person takes the stand, things unexpected can happen, even when you're prepared."

Ewing scratched his gray distinguished temple.

"Now let's continue our review. What do we have? A defendant, meaning you, who lied on the witness stand or at the very least, omitted some valuable information during his testimony. I might get the jury to understand why you did it. Then when I get an opportunity to examine the witness either prior to her testifying or when she is on the stand, maybe she'll confirm everything you've told me. Advantage still the prosecution. Now, I still think I can turn this thumb story around so the jury will, in their minds, if they were in the same situation as you, think they would do the identical thing. Maybe, just maybe, advantage us. It's a long shot, but we don't have much wiggle room. What else can you think of?"

Jim shook his head and made no comment.

"What does she look like?"

"Kind of beat up for her age, but attractive," Jim said. J. Edgar scratched his chin as if he was thinking about this and said, "Trust me, the prosecution will make her look like a schoolteacher, and she'll be impeccably rehearsed in how she is going to testify, along with what and what not to say, just like I did with you. We can bet on that.

"The way I see it, Jim, is we shouldn't speculate on what we don't know, it could only cause confusion, and right now we seem to be at their mercy. They have the upper hand now, but it's only temporary. We're going to have to wait until we hear her testimony in the morning or find out what she might say if I decide to meet with her prior to the trial resuming at 9:00 AM. From what you have told me, if you haven't left anything out, I can't see any reason for my meeting with her prior to the trial continuing. I think it's better to let her worry about what we know and what we will ask when she's under oath. Who knows what she may have not revealed, even to Shoemaker. I'm sure he may have the same concerns. Now, one last time, once again, are you positive you have now told me everything? I can't stress enough what problems, surprises can cause in a trial."

Jim took a few minute just to recount everything in his mind and finally said, "That's everything I can think of. Honestly!"

Ewing said in a much softer tone of voice, "Okay, I have no alternative except to believe you, so you had better be right. Now I'm going to leave and go back to my office and try to sort this all out. You think about things some more; and if you remember anything, I mean anything at all, you'll have to tell me at eight before the trial starts in the morning. That's when I have to give Judge Arnold my answer on whether I decided to meet with Ms. Griffin before she testifies at nine. If there's nothing more, let's get out of here. I've got a lot of work to do."

He opened the door, and the deputy came in to take Jim back to his jail cell.

Jim went quietly. He walked very slow, obviously thinking.

He'd done it. He'd managed to keep the big dark truth to himself.

What happened to him really didn't matter because Jim Malone knew he hadn't killed Fred and Dennis. *But he thought he knew who had.*

#

CHAPTER 32

LOIS

While Jim and J. Edgar were meeting, Shoemaker left the courthouse and went directly to the hotel where they had stashed the state's star witness, Lois Griffin. The day had gone a bit blustery and grim. Rain threatened. Shoemaker hardly noticed.

A federal attorney was waiting for him with a fresh haircut and a blank face. He smelled of Old Spice and professionalism. They were going to meet with Lois and review her testimony for the next day.

This was the same federal attorney she and her California attorney met with in Long Beach after the FBI captured her, and the state of Washington expressed their desire to extradite her and have her testify at Jim Malone's trial.

Before she agreed to testify and let them extradite her from California, her attorney in California and another attorney from the state of Washington negotiated with them for a deal in return for her testimony.

They were more than successful.

The Feds and the state of Washington granted her sweeping immunity against prosecution on either the kidnapping, extortion of money, the cutting off the thumbs, or any other involvement with the murders. What a deal!

That's how much Shoemaker and Watkins wanted to win this case. Watkins, to save face with his bosses; and Shoemaker, to further his political career by convicting Jim of first-degree murder and showing the public no matter who you are or how much money you have, you cannot break the law. After all, he's not O. J.

At the hotel, the police had two guards at her door, one local and one federal. Director Watkins didn't want any outside access to his captive and insisted on maximum security. Shoemaker and the U.S. attorney both entered the room after politely knocking. Lois invited them to come in.

Lois was seated near the window where she had a view of Elliott Bay. She was staring out the window and thoroughly enjoying the panoramic view before her. There were ferryboats going and coming, big freighters entering or leaving port, and sailboats with their sails in full bloom, a typical day in Elliott Bay.

"Nice view," said Shoemaker as he entered the room.

"Just about the best I've ever seen," said Lois as she turned to face them.

The U.S. attorney had met her in California during the extradition negotiations and had accompanied her with a U.S. Marshal and Watkins on a private jet to Seattle. Shoemaker met with her the previous evening on her arrival from California, so introductions were unnecessary.

"Ms. Griffin, or can I call you Lois?" "Lois is okay," she said. She was wearing a beige blouse and fashionably worn jeans below a freshly pressed jacket. Her makeup was sharp, but muted. Her attorney had advised her to keep it modest.

"We're going to tape this conversation if you have no objections," said Shoemaker and added, "If you like, you can have your attorney present."

Lois said she didn't object, and it wasn't necessary to call her attorney since he had assured her all the agreements were ironclad and totally documented.

Shoemaker then proceeded with the interview.

"Let me review what you have told us; and if anything sounds wrong, stop me, and we'll make the needed corrections."

"Okay," replied Lois meekly.

"According to you, Jim Malone found you and your two companions at the Yakima Tribal Casino parking lot in your motor home. As you said last night and also told FBI Director Watkins in California, he seized you first from behind, bound and gagged you, and kept you in the back bedroom while he waited for your partners to return. You said the first one, Fred Halsey, came back alone to get some more gambling money. And when he entered the motor home, Jim Malone rendered him unconscious and then bound, gagged, and blindfolded him. Then according to your story, about thirty minutes later your other partner, Dennis Rice, came to see what was taking so long for him to get some more gambling money; and Malone repeated his performance on him. Is this correct?"

Lois thought for a minute.

"Yes," she said but added, "I was in the back bedroom, so I didn't actually see how he knocked either of them out or how he tied them up. I just know when he brought me out to the front room, they were tied up, gagged, and had cloth bags over their heads."

Shoemaker coughed nervously; he then leafed over another page of his legal pad. "You said Malone explained to you he needed your help in cutting off their thumbs. And fearing for your life, you agreed. Is that correct?"

"That's right," she said, then added, "He told me what he was going to do and wanted me to help. It was obvious he was going to do this with or without me. I didn't really think I had an option, so I agreed. While he was untying me, he warned me not to even think about trying to escape or I would be next. I believed him."

"Therefore under duress, you got the scalpel and other things you needed for the operation. Then as I understand it, you and Jim Malone surgically cut off both of your partner's thumbs without any anesthetic or anything. Just cut off their thumbs while they were conscious. Is that what you said?"

Lois then added, "That's correct, except he removed their blindfolds so they would have to watch. But they didn't."

"Didn't what?" asked Shoemaker. Lois answered, "They didn't watch. Fred was first, and he passed out before we even started the surgery, colder than a mackerel; and Dennis fainted just watching what was happening to Fred. They didn't fully come to until after I had them bandaged up and cleaned up the mess."

She started shaking noticeably while she told this part.

"Calm down, Ms. Griffin," said Shoemaker, trying to appear somewhat empathetic to her. "I know this is difficult, but we'll be through shortly. Would you like a glass of water or something?" Lois declined and indicated she was okay. He gave her a moment to regain her composure and then he continued, "Then as I understand it, Mr. Malone told you to take the money as your reward for phoning him about the location of his grandchildren and kind of for helping him to get his revenge by cutting off your partners' thumbs for what they had done to his grandchildren. Is this correct?"

Lois nodded her head.

Shoemaker continued, "He then told you to get in the pickup and go get good and lost. Correct?"

Lois responded, "Exactly, except he didn't say anything about revenge."

Shoemaker thought to himself, we are really cooking now. He could hardly contain his enthusiasm and ignored her last comment about the word *revenge*.

He was feeling more confident by the minute. Her testimony was going to prove the accused, Jim Malone, not only lied on the stand but had purposely omitted much of his crime. That along with his vision story on how he located the whereabouts of his grandchildren, all of this combined should show the jury he is prone to lie when it's to his advantage. Shoemaker continued, "Let's presume it was obvious this was part of the deal. Then you said he insisted you were to take three hundred and forty thousand dollars in return for your phone call to him about where to find his grandchildren; then you put the three hundred and forty grand in your suitcase, and you departed in the pickup for California. Is that right?"

Lois corrected him with a tone of irritation toward Shoemaker for obviously twisting her words, "No, what I said is I left in the pickup, drove to Bend, Oregon, ditched the pickup in the parking lot at the bus depot with the keys in it. I had hoped someone would steal it. And then I boarded the first bus out to California. That's how the FBI said they found me. The police apparently stopped the guy who stole the pickup for speeding, and when he couldn't produce registration that matched him or the Canadian plates, they arrested him for possession of a stolen vehicle. He confessed to the police where the pickup was when he stole it and then somehow they contacted the FBI, and they tracked me to the Long Beach area. At least, that's what those FBI guys told me is how they were able to find me. I guess I wasn't very smart."

"That's not important. But this is. In reality, you did not actually see Malone kill your partners. But they were still alive when you left. Is that correct?"

"Yes, that's right. At the time I walked out the door to get in the pickup, they were awake and alive. They didn't look very good though." She put the stress on, at the time and added, "They were all tied up and missing their thumbs."

"Where did the gun come from?" asked Shoemaker.

Lois explained, "It was right on the countertop by the sink when I left. It's the one Dennis was always playing with. I don't know much about guns, but I know it was loaded because Fred was always warning Dennis to be careful before it accidentally went off."

"Okay, that'll work," said Shoemaker to himself, smiling. He continued, "Then what happened?"

"I don't know. I was just thankful to get out of there."

Then Shoemaker got up, turned the tape recorder off, he asked the U.S. attorney if he had any further questions for Lois, and he said he had none.

"Okay, Lois. Treat yourself to nice dinner tonight on the government, try to get some sleep, and be ready to go by seven in the morning. Be sure to wear the blue suit and blouse we bought you. Were the shoes the right size?"

Lois said she had already tried them on, and they were okay, a little snug, but okay.

"Oh, your hair looks fine now, Lois," said Shoemaker and then added, "Do try and keep it presentable. Oh yes, I forgot to add, the judge granted Malone's attorney permission to meet with you at eight in the morning prior to you testifying. That's only if he chooses to, it's his option. We won't know his decision until eight in the morning. But if you do meet with him, all you have to do is tell him everything you told us. Don't try to alter anything, and don't lie to him. His name is J. Edgar Ewing; he has a grandfather appearance, but don't misjudge him. He's an excellent attorney, more like a silver fox. Just be ready to tell the same story tomorrow you just told us when I put you on the stand tomorrow and also to Malone's attorney, J. Edgar Ewing, if he meets with you at eight before the trial begins. Remember, we'll be here at the hotel to get you promptly at seven in the morning. Be dressed and ready. Do you have any questions?"

Lois said she thought she understood everything.

"The guards will be at your door twenty-four hours a day if you need anything and also to prevent anyone from bothering you."

Shoemaker and the U.S. attorney left feeling confident they couldn't lose tomorrow.

Shoemaker could hardly wait.

This trial was consuming him, and finally he felt he was going to achieve his goal—to have the opportunity to defeat the great J. Edgar Ewing and convict Jim Malone! It was almost too much to handle, even for him. Two Washington State Bastions of the Right, fallen. Defeated! He sincerely relished trials like this one. In his liberal mind, they gave him an opportunity to take down another Fat Cat. Plus, having J. Edgar Ewing as an opponent, it was a twofer. What more could you ask for?

After winning this case, his career would be gold.

Pure gold!

#

After they departed, Lois looked at the menu in the room and ordered room service.

They said it would take about an hour.

Just for a steak, fries, and salad?

Oh well, that was fine with her, it would give her time to shower and put on her pj's. She knew it was going to be a long night, so she figured she might as well get comfortable.

Her timing was perfect. She had just finished her shower and was dressed when the server knocked on the door; then accompanied by one of the guards stationed outside her door, he wheeled in her dinner. The server was overly curious who he was catering to and was about to say something to Lois before the guard said he should leave and handed him a tip.

She was making out so much better with this than she ever thought possible. This whole deal was better than dumb ole Fred's plan. She was smiling to herself when she thought of dumb ole Fred. Boy, would he be pissed if he could see her now?

#

CHAPTER 33

A VERY LONG NIGHT

Jim was sitting on the edge of his bunk bed in his cell, thinking about Lois.

He was searching his mind, trying to figure out what Lois could possibly say in her testimonial that could affect the trial.

No matter how hard he concentrated, he still couldn't think of anything else, other than what he had already told J. Edgar. Not a single thing, other than the part about the cutting off the thumbs and giving her the money and telling her to get lost.

According to his attorney, because he had omitted confessing this information when he testified, it could be quite damaging.

But J. Edgar said he thought he could overcome the problem without too much difficulty unless there was something else. That night, Jim hardly slept at all just thinking about what he had left out of his story.

There was so much—his crew's involvement, his taking Bob Arnott into his confidence almost from the very beginning, and more important avoiding any mention to J. Edgar about who he felt may have really killed the two kidnappers.

He just prayed it all remained hidden, especially the thought he had in his mind, who really killed the two kidnappers.

#

J. Edgar Ewing had now returned to his office and was sitting at his desk reviewing everything that transpired earlier at the trial and especially afterward at the meeting with his client.

He lit a pipe and puffed on it absently, watching the smoke from the aromatic Virginia tobacco twirl toward the ceiling.

Except for the Lois surprise, everything was progressing just as anticipated.

After thinking long and hard, he came up with no new solutions.

He finally concluded he would have to wait for her testimony and then utilizes all the skills he possessed to overcome or at the very least impeach whatever it was she revealed. That is unless tomorrow morning his client had any new revelations. God forbid!

If Jim has no more surprises and had been totally truthful, he saw no necessity for meeting with Lois prior to her testifying.

He did respect the DA's abilities and knew, or at least thought he knew, Shoemaker wouldn't put her on the stand unless he was confident she had something extremely valuable to contribute to proving Jim's guilt.

And also he was positive Lois wouldn't be testifying at all unless she received something in return, probably a sentence reduction for her part in the crime or immunity of some kind. He thought maybe he should reconsider meeting with her and, at the very least, get the specifics about what her deal was with the prosecution.

But then again, why bother?

He knew there was a deal, and he decided it might be better for him to have her admit what it was, when she was on the stand, in front of the jury. Why let her rehearse the story with him? Let him sweat it out of her on the stand in front of the jury, the judge, and the spectators. Nobody gets a free ride.

He was confident Shoemaker wouldn't broach this subject during his questioning of the witness and by him having her admit what deal she had received for her testimony, should have some influence on the jury. He hoped it would cause them to question almost anything she would have said when she was on the stand and questioned by Shoemaker.

Her credibility should come into question, especially after J. Edgar questioned her about her past—namely, her drug use and involvement in prostitution and breaking her parole.

Then when he pointed out to the jury, her complicity in the kidnapping, abuse to the grandchildren by cutting off their little fingers, and her participation in the removal of her coconspirators' thumbs, all of this combined with whatever her deal was, could nullify or at the very least neutralize her testimony.

Once again, he would have to wait until she testified when she was on the stand sworn to tell the truth, and the prosecution was in control.

And then, it would be his turn to glean this information from her lips during his cross-examination. He was an expert in making witnesses sweat, and he would make Lois sweat more than Shoemaker could ever have prepared her for. It would be impossible for her to anticipate what she was about to encounter.

With that last thought in mind, he put everything he would need in his huge briefcase and went home to get a good night's sleep.

He would need it.

#

CHAPTER 34

FOREBODING FRIDAY

Few of the trial participants really slept that night, except for Shoemaker and Ewing.

After all, trials were their meat and potatoes. They were used to this kind of stress.

And Shoemaker was more at ease than anyone because he knew what was coming down. At least he thought he did.

He was extremely confident Lois's testimony would illustrate to the jury, Jim was the last person with the victims when they were still alive.

Plus, he would also establish the weapon used in the murder was at Jim's disposal, and he knew how to use it due to his Special Forces training. It would prove he had lied under oath about how the kidnappers' thumbs were removed, plus he omitted the part about giving Lois bribe money for her assistance in his revenge and then telling her to get lost. The jury should conclude only guilty people lie or do cover-ups. Add these to the lie he told about how he was able to find and rescue his grandchildren. A vision my ass. Another lie!

Shoemaker felt with all of this, even if it was still somewhat circumstantial, it should be enough to convince the jury without any doubt whatsoever, Jim Malone was guilty of these murders.

What was their alternative?

In Shoemaker's thinking, there was absolutely no other option, ABSOLUTELY NONE. He could hardly wait, but he did get a good night's sleep.

\#

Then once again, seemingly at cosmic speed, it was eight o'clock, Friday morning.

The guards had brought Jim to the attorney-client room where Ewing was still preparing for the pending proceedings.

Jim entered, and the guards removed his shackles and left him alone with his attorney.

"Did you get some sleep?" asked J. Edgar Ewing.

Jim answered with a simple, "Not much."

There was only an hour before the trial would continue.

With time so short, Ewing immediately moved ahead in his conversation with Jim concerning what Lois's testimony might reveal.

"Were you able to think of anything we may have overlooked in relationship to your or her involvement?"

Jim confirmed he couldn't come up with anything additional.

Then Jim asked Ewing what he thought.

Ewing took a long time to respond.

He perused his legal pad, looked out the window, and finally turned to face Jim and began to recap, "We know she has to admit her participation in the removal of the thumbs. Shoemaker will make a big thing of this in order to illustrate to the jury that you lied, under oath. He'll even try to convenience the jury you committed perjury during your testimony about this portion of the so-called crime. When I do my cross, I'll bring out that she was the person who cut off Justin and Robbie's fingers. This should assist in making her look a little less acceptable to the jury."

He took a deep breath and shook his gray head.

"Hopefully, when I cross-examine her, I can make them believe you did it in order to protect Lois from prosecution in return for phoning you the whereabouts of Robbie and Justin, an appropriate reward. Since you and I both know that's the truth, the jury should also see it the same way. It should make you look like the good guy. He'll undoubtedly attempt to bring your phony vision story to the foreground as another indication you are prone to lie when it's convenient. I don't foresee this as a major problem. Make us uncomfortable, yes. Is it a problem? I don't think so. Then he'll ask about you telling her to take the money and to get lost. I feel he'll attempt to make this appear to have been bribery on your part in order to secure her silence. Shoemaker will try to make this seem to the jury to be a logical conclusion. But once again I should be able to counteract this after we get her to reconfirm she was the person who called with the tip where the grandchildren were hidden and convince the jury this was sincerely part of your appreciation for the safe return of Robbie and Justin. I'm presuming this subject will be a component of her testimony when Shoemaker examines her. If he doesn't, I will bring it out during my cross.

"Then if I were Shoemaker, I would direct the jury's attention to the availability of the murder weapon. In redirect, I'll somehow reestablish in prior testimony by Chief Hammond, there were absolutely no prints on it and their tests further proved that you had not recently fired any gun and you do not posses any weapons whatsoever. I'll also point out to the jury this weapon was also available to other people. Hopefully, the jury will agree none of this proves you used the weapon, and the prosecution is again asking them to accept this circumstantial evidence as proof, lots of room for reasonable doubt.

"What we do have going for us is the fact the kidnappers were alive when Lois left the motor home. This means she won't be able to testify factually she saw you kill them. She can only speculate; and if Shoemaker attempts this, I'll object, and it won't be factored into the jury's thinking. I hope. And remember, you already testified they were also alive when you left; and when you saw Chief Hammond, you specifically told him where the live kidnappers could be found, not where the bodies of the kidnappers could be found. I think during the jury's deliberation, this will contribute significantly to the reasonable doubt we are attempting to create. Other than that, unless there's something we are missing. Shoemaker will conclude Griffin's testimony for the prosecution. Certainly there's more to it than this, but in its simplest form, I think that is about all they have."

Without waiting for Jim to respond, Ewing continued, "Then it's our turn. So you'll be aware, here is what I plan to do. First, I'll ask about her background. We know she was a hooker at some time in her life, used drugs, been arrested, broke her parole, and anything else I can think of to instill in the minds of the jury that she was and still is a terrible person, prone to lie, say anything to save her own skin, and to do anything for money. The prosecution will probably object to most of this, and the judge will probably sustain many of these objections. But like I said before, once the jury hears something, it always remains in their subconscious minds. Then, and this is the important portion of my cross-examination. I'll ask her what she received from the prosecution and the Feds for her testifying against you. I know they made some kind of arrangement. I'm positive they gave her either reduced time in prison or immunity of some kind to absolve her of any guilt in the murder, responsibility for the thumb removal, extortion of money, maybe even some kind of immunity for her participation in the kidnapping and cutting off the fingers of your grandchildren."

"Just a minute," Jim interrupted J. Edgar's deluge of words causing him to at least pause for a moment, "what exactly does this all mean?"

Ewing paused and took a deep breath then let it out with the answer.

"If she received immunity, no matter what happens with the jury's decision on the prosecution's charges, she either walks away free or does minimum time in a nice prison for her part in the crime. It all depends on what kind of a deal the Feds and Shoemaker made with her. Then when she tells us what it is exactly, I mean what specifically she received for her testimony, then I'll make it look like she would tell the jury anything the prosecutor wanted her to say in return for this immunity."

Almost as though on cue, after Ewing spoke those words, the deputies came in and said it was time to escort them to the courtroom.

It was time.

They had consumed the full hour Judge Arnold granted the night before.

Ewing had sent a note to Judge Arnold earlier, informing the judge he decided not to meet with Ms. Griffin prior to the start of the day's proceedings.

J. Edgar knew the judge would like this because there would not be any delay in the trial.

Judges intensely disliked delays.

#

While Ewing was meeting with Jim, Shoemaker and the U.S. attorney had already picked up Lois at the hotel and had ensconced her in another waiting room just down the hall from where Jim and Ewing were having their meeting. They briefly reviewed her anticipated testimony; and after assuring themselves it would go as designed, they then went into the courtroom, leaving Lois behind with a deputy, until spectators including the huge abundance of reporters had all been admitted and seated. J. Edgar and Jim were already sitting at the defense table.

The jury was in place, and Judge Arnold called the court to order. A deathly, somewhat foreboding silence covered the courtroom in almost-vulgar anticipation with what was getting ready to unfurl.

Judge Arnold opened, "Is the prosecutor ready to call its witness?"

Shoemaker responded affirmatively. "Yes, Your Honor, the prosecution calls Lois Griffin to the stand."

"Would Lois Griffin please come forward?" said the court clerk in a very loud, clear voice.

A guard opened the courtroom door. Lois entered the courtroom very slowly.

She walked right in front of me, Bob Arnott. And as I stared directly at her, she did not show any signs of recognition. I didn't expect any.

I stopped taking notes.

J. Edgar was correct when he told Jim the prosecution would make her looked like a normal citizen in her new blue suit and her hair brushed in a conservative style.

The epitome of an average citizen.

All in all, the way the prosecution had her dress, she could have been a member of the jury, not a key witness.

#

The clerk immediately swore her in.

Then Judge Arnold directed her to be seated in the witness docket.

Lois complied, sat down, and placed her hands in her lap.

She was obviously already feeling the pressure and appeared to be very apprehensive about what was going to happen next. In her mind, she was thinking this isn't at all similar to what Shoemaker had said it would be.

All these people, Shoemaker had neglected to prepare her for the feeling it created.

It was overwhelming.

Silently she said a short prayer to help her cope and be able to get all the way through the anticipated ordeal she knew was coming. She took a deep breath and let it out slowly.

She knew she had to tell the truth. She secretly hoped that her testimony would not accomplish what Shoemaker had indicated, help him convict Jim. But what was her alternative, prison?

Not much of an option.

She avoided any eye contact with Jim or his attorney, focusing only on Shoemaker and the defense table.

She accomplished this with ease, exactly how Shoemaker had instructed her to perform in their morning meeting.

Rising slowly, Shoemaker, with an air of extreme confidence, approached halfway to Lois and took a position between her and the defense table so there would be no chance of eye contact by her with Jim or Ewing.

The jury of course had a complete view of Lois.

He began, "Please state your full name for the record."

Lois complied.

"Lois L. Griffin."

"Ms. Griffin," Shoemaker continued, "would you tell the court where you were on the eighth of September of this year?"

Lois, as previously rehearsed, answered that she was in a motor home parked at the Yakima Tribal Casino.

"And that evening, did a person unknown to you at the time enter the motor home?"

Lois answered again affirmatively.

Shoemaker continued, "Is that person in the courtroom today?"

"Yes," Lois answered.

Shoemaker, "For identification purposes and for the benefit of the jury and the court, could you indicate who that individual is?"

Shoemaker then stepped to the side so Lois could have a full view of Jim and the defense counsel.

Lois responded as instructed, "That's him sitting right there at the table." She pointed directly at Jim.

Shoemaker then immediately stepped back to position himself again between Jim and the witness. Jim had not even made eye contact with her when she identified him.

Shoemaker continued, "Let the record show the witness has identified James Malone, the defendant, as the person who entered her motor home on the evening of September 8 this year. Now, Ms. Griffin, could you tell the jury in your words what events transpired the night the defendant entered your motor home!"

Lois then began telling her story how Jim had come up behind her while she was packing, how he had tied and gagged; how Jim also subdued the other two people when they entered the motor home; and how he had bound, gagged, and blindfolded them using cloth bags placed over their heads. J. Edgar started to object on the last part of the statement since he knew Lois was in the back bedroom and could not have observed what Jim was doing to her partners, but he let it slide, thinking he could correct this portion of her testimony in his cross and maybe add another nail to her credibility or rather lack of credibility.

Lois paused at this point and remained silent for a moment.

She was thinking maybe this was the place where it would be time to tell the part about the cutting off the thumbs of the victims.

Shoemaker asked her to continue with what occurred next. With obvious emotion and a great deal of trepidation, she then told the jury how Jim had untied her after she agreed to assist him in cutting off her partners' thumbs and promised not to cause any trouble.

With urging from Shoemaker, she further explained to the jury that she agreed to this mainly due to the threat Jim made if she did anything other than as he instructed.

She then narrated the story of how they, she and Jim, had cut off the thumbs of the two victims.

She described how they had passed out even before the operation even stated.

When Shoemaker asked if there was much blood, Lois said yes and explained it was difficult to stop the bleeding.

She described everything in detail that she could recall of the evening.

Ewing was listening to every word she said. He kept his eyes on the jury to see if he could gauge their reaction to the story Lois was telling.

He purposely avoided raising too many objections because he knew the only way he could overcome her testimony would be when he had his opportunity to cross-examine her. He wanted her to complete her accounting of the evening as rapidly as possible.

He kept writing things down on his legal pad when Lois mentioned something he speculated would be useful when his turn arrived. Then Shoemaker asked Lois to relate what happened next.

Lois continued telling the jury Jim told her to take the money as a reward for the call she made about where they had hid his grandchildren, and then he instructed her to get in the pickup and disappear. Shoemaker attempted in turning this testimony around to use the term *bribe money* in place of reward money.

J. Edgar objected on the grounds the witness had already testified it was reward money, not bribery.

Judge Arnold sustained the objection and admonished Shoemaker.

Then at Shoemaker's urging, she explained she drove to Bend, Oregon, left the pickup with the keys in it in the parking lot and caught the first bus available to Los Angeles, and more specifically, to the Long Beach area where she had an old friend from her street days, who would let her stay there and never question why she was hiding.

That's where she said the FBI had apprehended her.

Once they located the pickup, they then had tracked her from Bend to the Los Angeles area and then with the assistance of the LAPD and the California State Patrol were able to review all Lois's prior arrest records that occurred while she was in their jurisdiction. All of this information had been supplied to J. Edgar the night before.

Apparently, when they were checking these files, they also pulled up all the names of people arrested on the same dates in the same precincts. Sure enough there was one name that kept reoccurring; this person was not only hauled in several times at the same time as Lois, but was also charged with prostitution and drug possession almost every time Lois was charged.

Once they were able to gather all this information, the rest was fairly simple. Where else would she go?

Even though her friend was now going straight, she still let Lois stay at her Long Beach apartment for old time's sake. The FBI then quietly and, with a cloak of confidentiality, arrested her at the friend's residence in the Long Beach apartment complex.

Her friend wasn't too difficult to locate because she had to report to her probation officer regularly, and he was able to supply her current address to the FBI. They could have charged Lois's friend with harboring a fugitive and for breaking her parole but decided her silence was more worthwhile.

Lois admitted, during her testimony, she wasn't very good at running. Ewing sensed this was almost the end of her testimony.

Thank god, he thought to himself. Enough damage had been done, especially the part about the cutting off the thumbs. The portion about the money hadn't helped either.

Ewing felt Shoemaker was successful in illustrating to the jury that Jim had not told the truth about cutting off the thumbs.

And he also had omitted telling about Lois's involvement in the surgery and the part about offering her the money, in Shoemaker's words—bribe money for her silence. Ewing thought all of this could be very damaging. He must succeed in reversing if not all of it, at least impeaching some of it and get the jury to empathize with Jim and not the kidnappers or the witness, Lois Griffin.

He knew this would challenge every legal courtroom skill he possessed. J. Edgar was deep in thought when Shoemaker then asked Lois what would be his final question.

"Ms. Griffin, do you think Jim Malone killed these two people?" asked the district attorney.

The question immediately registered with Ewing.

He stood up and said in a very loud and clear voice said, "The defense objects; the witnesses' opinions are not admissible and certainly not relevant!"

As Judge Arnold was sustaining the objection, Shoemaker withdrew the question and announced he had no further questions of this witness. He thanked her for her willingness to undergo this very trying ordeal.

Shoemaker then walked cockily to his chair, a smug smile on his face.

He was positive Lois's testimony would pound the final nail in Jim's coffin. He assumed, after this testimony, the jury, no matter what they personally felt about the crime or Jim, would not have any option other than delivering a "Guilty as Charged," a first-degree murder verdict.

Even if much of the prosecution's evidence was circumstantial, he knew he had presented a case based on proof of Jim's guilt beyond any possible reasonable doubt.

Now, he thought to himself confidently, *let's see what the great J. Edgar Ewing can do.*

He knew Ewing was good.

He'd seen him in action.

But he hoped not that good.

We'll see, he thought. *I've done what I can*

And in his mind, he was sure no one could done a better presentation.

\#

211

CHAPTER 35

J. EDGAR EWING, ATTORNEY AT LAW

J. Edgar Ewing picked up his legal pad and moved to the same position he had during prior questioning of prosecution witnesses, between the prosecutor and the witness, in order to prevent any eye contact.

Once in position, he began his cross-examination of Lois Griffin.

The courtroom became deathly quiet as he asked his first question, "Ms. Griffin, let me ask you a couple questions about yourself."

He purposely paused for a minute with his back to her to cause Lois a little discomfort from the very beginning of his cross-examination and then turned slowly to look directly at her and asked in a somewhat casual manner.

"Have you ever been a prostitute, a hooker?" Shoemaker immediately objected, and Judge Arnold sustained his objection.

Ewing knew this would happen as it would in the next few questions he would ask about her previous lifestyle. It was his intention of doing every thing legally possible in discounting Lois as a creditable witness in the eyes of the jury.

He proceeded, "Have you ever used drugs?"

Same objection.

Same ruling by Judge Arnold.

Ewing continued with similar character assassination questions, including her arrest record, and Shoemaker continued with his objections.

Judge Arnold sustained most of them before he had finally had enough. He was totally aware of what Ewing was attempting to accomplish, but it was time to put a stop to it and move to more relevant questions.

He then admonished Ewing and instructed him to abandon this line of questioning.

Ewing presumed this would occur, but he also perceived he had accomplished his objective. And that was to have the jury recognize that Lois was not a particularly good citizen and in her lifetime had done a lot of bad things—criminal things.

J. Edgar then changed direction with his cross-examination and asked, "Ms. Griffin, prior to your coming here to testify today, did the district attorney and the federal attorney offer you anything for your testimony?"

Before she could respond, Shoemaker rose and aggressively objected that this was totally irrelevant. J. Edgar immediately responded that he felt it was *very* relevant. Much to Shoemaker's chagrin, Judge Arnold agreed with J. Edgar and overruled the objection and then directed Ms. Griffin to answer the question.

"According to my California and Washington attorneys, I was given sweeping immunity for everything," Lois responded in a confident tone of voice. J. Edgar appreciated her confident attitude when answering his question. Shoemaker swallowed hard.

Ewing was somewhat taken aback the prosecution had gone this far in granting her immunity in return for her rapid extradition to Washington State from California and for her testimony against Jim.

To him this was almost unprecedented.

Total immunity! He almost couldn't believe it.

Wow, what a deal! But that's what she said she had received for her testimony, and she wouldn't lie about something this important to her.

He now knew to what degree the prosecution would go to find Jim guilty. He turned to look directly at Shoemaker, then at the jury and with a slight, subtle shrug of his shoulders, turned his attention back to focus on Lois.

He then, with an incredulous tone to his voice, asked her to repeat the offer. He wanted to be sure the jury would have no doubt why she was testifying. He was still amazed at what they had granted, so it wasn't difficult to ask the question in a tone showing a degree of shock and disbelief.

"You mean you have immunity from being prosecuted for any of your involvement in the kidnapping, abuse to the children by cutting off their fingers, extortion, cutting off the thumbs, murder, and perjury? Is that correct, Ms. Griffin?"

Before she could answer, Shoemaker objected, stating the prosecution had not given her immunity for perjury, and he resented the implication from the defense council.

Judge Arnold agreed and instructed the clerk to strike the word *perjury* from the official record and also told the jury to disregard that portion of the defense attorney's question.

He then directed Ewing to restructure the question.

J. Edgar really appreciated being able to restate all of this previous question with the exception of the perjury portion. But he knew the jury had already heard it, and it was implanted in their subconscious minds.

He complied as directed, but this time he was facing the jury.

He asked the same question being careful to omit the word *perjury*. After asking the question, he turned to face Lois in anticipation of her answer.

Lois then said, "That's what my attorney in California and again here in Washington told me."

"That's a pretty good deal considering your involvement in these crimes. The prosecutor must really want to win this case in order to let a criminal go totally free."

Shoemaker loudly objected to Ewing's last statement as being reckless, irrelevant, totally out of line; and besides, it wasn't a question at all, it was the defense attorney's statement and that is truly inadmissible.

Judge Arnold concurred, sustained the objection, and instructed the jury to disregard the defense attorney's last statement in its entirety.

He then admonished J. Edgar and instructed him to either ask the witness questions appropriate to the proceedings or conclude his examination.

"Okay, Ms. Griffin," Ewing continued as if nothing had transpired to interrupt his questioning of the witness, "let's see if you can answer these questions. In your previous testimony, you said you left the motor home per Mr. Malone's approval after removing the thumbs from your fellow kidnappers' hands. Is that correct?"

Lois said that it was.

Checking his notes, he then asked, "Who did most of the cutting when the thumbs were removed?"

Shoemaker objected, and before Judge Arnold could rule on the question, J. Edgar said he withdrew the question.

Judge Arnold sustained the objection anyhow.

J. Edgar paused for moment and next asked Lois if during the kidnapping was she the kidnapper that cut off Mr. Malone's grandchildren's little fingers. Before she could respond, Shoemaker objected to relevancy, and Judge Arnold sustained his objection and instructed J. Edgar to move on to other more pertinent areas. J. Edgar accepted the ruling and was thankful he had at least let the jury hear him mention the children's fingers and allude to the fact that Lois probably performed the operation. He continued, "You also said in your previous testimony, when Mr. Malone entered the motor home you were in the back bedroom, is that what you said?" Lois confirmed he was right.

"What were you doing at that time?"

Lois answered she was packing.

This answer peeked J. Edgar's curiosity, and he followed by asking Lois a simple question. "Were you packing clothes or money?"

"Both, but only my share, my share of the money." She was careful to emphasize, only her share.

"You mean your share of the ransom money paid by the defendant, Mr. Malone, for the safe return of his grandchildren?"

"That's right."

"In other words, you were planning to leave your partners and make your own escape prior to these other events you described and even before Mr. Malone offered you the money?"

"That's right," Lois muttered.

"I didn't hear your answer," said Ewing, "Would you repeat it so the jury can hear your response?"

She answered again more clearly this time.

Then Ewing asked, "Why?"

"Why, what?" said Lois, obviously flustered. "I don't know what you mean."

Now this was good!

It was becoming obvious to Ewing that he was starting to get to her.

He continued to probe somewhat sarcastically.

"Why were you leaving or rather why were you leaving without telling your partners good-bye?"

Lois was somewhat trite when she answered, "Just because."

Ewing thought for a minute, he was somewhat surprised that Shoemaker hadn't objected to this line of questioning.

Then all of a sudden during this pause, he had an even greater sensation that he was getting somewhere.

He wasn't sure where, but he could feel that there was something here the witness was hiding, and unfortunately at the moment he was failing to grasp what it was. He decided to stay with this line of questioning, but he knew he needed to dig much deeper to discover what Lois wasn't saying, what she must be hiding. There was something here, and if he was going to bring it to light, he would need to continue to probe more.

He ignored her "just because" answer and continued probing even deeper, "Didn't you think your partners would be mad when they found you had left with your share of the ransom money and took the pickup?"

Lois answered yes.

"Then can you tell the court specifically why were you leaving?"

Shoemaker objected on the grounds of relevance, and after J. Edgar appealed to Judge Arnold this was an extremely hostile witness and since her testimony could affect the trial enormously, he felt the court should allow him some flexibility.

Judge Arnold agreed and said he would allow the question. Shoemaker's face revealed he didn't appreciate Judge Arnold's ruling.

Ewing then repeated the question. He waited for her to answer.

He could sense his probing was working.

Lois was thinking for too long a time.

There was something here, something she was avoiding! What was she hiding?

He could feel it in his bones.

"Please answer the question, Ms. Griffin. Or do you want me to repeat the question?" he directed, somewhat curtly.

Lois hesitated, she was obviously angered by the question, but she finally answered. "They were mean to me."

"How mean?" Ewing asked.

Lois responded, "They slapped me around a lot and made me do things I didn't really want to do." Now he had her going. He knew that now he had brought her to areas she hadn't rehearsed with Shoemaker.

She was now stranded in his ballpark. He felt that now even Shoemaker couldn't save her.

Ewing then inquired, "What kind of things?" Lois blurted out two words, "Sex things!"

J. Edgar chose not to ask for sex details. That sort of thing was best left to the jury's imagination where it would become much more sordid.

"Was there any other reason?"

Lois answered quickly and offered more detail than J. Edgar could have hoped for, "They were losing all their money gambling, and I knew it was a matter of time before they would want some of mine."

Shoemaker at this point finally rose to object on grounds that the defense had gone too far afield on this obvious fishing expedition. He asked the court to have defense council get back to questions more pertinent to the trial and stop wasting the court's time.

Judge Arnold then questioned J. Edgar as to what the reason might be for this line of questioning. J. Edgar assured the judge he would tie it all together soon; and since Mr. Malone was being tried for murder and much of the prosecution's case seemed to depend on this secret witness's testimony, he felt the court could continue to indulge him with a little leeway.

Once again, Judge Arnold's ruling surprised him.

The judge agreed with Ewing and overruled the prosecutor's objection. However, he warned J. Edgar to use extreme care in his examination of this witness and to move forward.

Regaining his thoughts and returning to face the witness, J. Edgar was positive he was making real progress in getting to the bottom of what the witness was not telling.

What is she hiding?

"Let us skip from here to when you and Mr. Malone were alone in the trailer."

"Was he, mean to you?"

"Not really, he tied me up, but he wasn't mean, he didn't hurt me."

Good, thought Ewing.

"Did you ever tell Mr. Malone where the gun, the murder weapon, was?"

"I didn't have to tell him, Dennis had been playing with it and left it right there in plain view on the counter by the kitchen sink. I'm sure he saw it." J. Edgar didn't want to dwell too long on the gun subject. His only goal for asking the question was for her to acknowledge she knew where the gun was located.

Then Ewing switched directions. "Let's move to the period after you and Mr. Malone removed the thumbs from your partners." He said *you* a little louder than Mr. Malone and paused long enough for the jury to be aware she had assisted in the thumb removal. He then continued, "You said Mr. Malone told you to take the money as a reward for letting him know the location of his grandchildren, is that correct?"

"Yes."

"Then you testified he instructed you to get in the pickup and get lost, is that correct?"

"Yes, not in those words, but he told me to leave and indicated I should get lost."

"Were your partners still alive when you left the motor home?"

Lois answered, "Yes."

J. Edgar asked again, "You're quite positive they were still alive when you departed?"

"I said they were alive, didn't I?" she returned, a bit angrily.

Ewing asked the same question again somewhat more aggressively.

Lois then answered with even more irritation in her voice and much louder, "I told you they were alive!" Shoemaker objected on the grounds that the defendant had answered the question three times, and the defense council should refrain from badgering the witness. He said it was unnecessary for her to keep answering the same question.

Judge Arnold agreed and sustained the objection.

He instructed Ewing to move on.

Ewing then turned his attention back to Lois and asked, "Are you aware Mr. Malone has already testified, under oath, when he left the motor home your partners were alive and he drove directly to Bellevue, Washington, to inform the authorities where they could locate two of the individuals who had kidnapped his grandchildren?"

"No, I didn't know that." Once again, her voice was hard and angry.

Ewing was getting that feeling only great trial lawyers get—that he was on to something.

But he was aware he still had a long way to go, and he hoped Judge Arnold would continue to indulge him.

It was his feeling that the score was still seven to nothing, in favor of Shoemaker and the prosecution.

However, the game wasn't over.

The final whistle hadn't been blown.

He took a moment and walked to the defense table to review his notes and decide where he wanted to go from here.

Then turning slowly around to face Lois, in reality, he was trying to gain some time to think, so he ask Lois if she wanted a break or a glass of water.

She said she was okay.

Then he walked to the defense table again and poured himself a glass of water, took a sip very slowly, and then set the glass down on the defense table.

He turned back to face Lois. "That's what Mr. Malone did, he told the authorities where to find your coconspirators, and at the time he indicated to the Bellevue police they were alive. At least it would seem logical that he wouldn't kill them and then tell the police where they were, especially if they were dead. Don't you think that's logical, Ms. Griffin?"

Surprise! No objection from the prosecution. Lois then answered, "I don't know."

Ewing then decided to change course a little and maybe surprise the witness even more.

"Do you think Mr. Malone killed them?" he quickly asked.

Shoemaker shot to his feet.

"I object!" He knew that Lois was somewhat sensitive to the defendant and didn't want Ewing to have an opportunity to have his prized witness even suggest that she wasn't sure whether Jim had killed them or not.

Shoemaker objected on the grounds that the opinion of the witness was not relevant and added that he thought the judge should suggest the defense counsel should hurry up and complete his fishing expedition.

Judge Arnold sustained the objection and suggested the defense council should move to areas more directly related to the case.

Ewing ignored Shoemaker's interruption even though he had hoped the objection would take place. He smiled inwardly, thinking that he was now getting a little control over Shoemaker too. He really had not wanted Lois to answer the last question, but he was sure he may have made the jury curious how she would have answered it if Judge Arnold had permitted her to answer. However, he could tell that some of his questions were beginning to bother the witness extremely. That's exactly what he was striving to achieve. Now, he thought to himself. Let's change gears and go to the heart of a hunch he had come up with during Lois's agitated reactions to many of his questions and also to some Shoemaker asked previously.

He knew it was a long shot, but if his hunch or better yet the theory he was developing proved valid, he could end this trial today without sending it to the jury. He knew Shoemaker would object to his last question and take the opportunity to participate in the proceedings.

All Shoemaker had been doing was sitting on his butt and listening to almost nothing, this was much appreciated by J. Edgar.

And, except for a few important questions he had asked Lois, he knew it was boring.

J. Edgar only hoped he wasn't taking too much time with the boring portion, or the jury might let it influence their judgment. He certainly didn't want to allow that to happen; therefore, he had better get moving or he would talk himself right out of a victory.

Victory for him certainly, but what was even more important, victory for his client, Jim Malone. That was his job. What he gets paid to do.

It was time to take the big plunge!

He only hoped the water wasn't too deep or too shallow. He didn't want to do either one, drown or to hit the bottom.

"Okay, here goes," he silently whispered to himself as he turned his attention to Lois.

Before he continued, he walked back to his table and glanced at another legal pad as if he was reviewing something of value. He then put the one he had been carrying down on the table and picked up the other one.

Shoemaker had seen J. Edgar use this ploy in court before and thought nothing of it.

"Sorry for the delay, Ms. Griffin." J. Edgar now had the new legal pad in hand and would, on occasion, look at it like there was something important written on it. He continued, "Let's start from the time you left the motor home at the Yakima Casino. You said you drove to Bend, Oregon, and left the pickup in the parking lot at the bus station with the keys in it, hoping someone would steal it. You then caught the first available bus out to the Los Angles area, is that correct?"

Lois answered again in that annoyed voice, "Yes, that's what happened."

J. Edgar appreciated this anger and asked, "How long did it take you to drive from the casino in Yakima, Washington, to Bend, Oregon?"

Lois responded, still obviously angry, "I don't remember."

J. Edgar continued to probe, "Okay, you don't recall how long it took you to drive to Bend, Oregon. Maybe you'll remember what time you caught the bus to California or what time you left the motor home on the night in question?"

Lois answered with a nervous, irritated voice, "I caught the bus at around 6:00 AM, I think. And I'm not sure when I left the motor home. Around ten or eleven, I didn't actually look at the time."

J. Edgar answered for her, "According to the FBIs investigation, your bus departed from Bend to Los Angeles at precisely 6:45 AM. Does that refresh your memory?"

Lois now appeared even more agitated and snapped back, "Six, sixty forty-five, what difference does that make?"

J. Edgar liked this response and answered for her again. "Quite a bit, Ms. Griffin, it should have taken you no more than four to five hours to drive from the casino to Bend, Oregon. If you left the motor home between 10:00 PM and eleven, you would have arrived in Bend, Oregon, no later than around 5:00 AM."

Lois glared at Ewing, and he could see a hateful, twisted expression beginning to develop on her face. Good, he wanted her to lose her composure.

"What did you do for at least one hour and a half to maybe two hours before catching your bus?" He continued pressing.

Lois responded again even more irritated, "What difference does it make? I went to the john, I got a cup of coffee, and I caught the bus, just like I said."

Ewing let her squirm for a little while.

Not too long.

He didn't want her to have too much time to think. He thought he had her on the run, and her composure was slipping drastically.

Shoemaker just sat there, and it was obvious he didn't have a clue what J. Edgar was attempting to accomplish with this line of questioning. Jim was sitting up straight in his chair, intensely watching the proceedings. J. Edgar had not shared this portion with him, and he was supercurious what his attorney was doing.

He had no idea what Ewing was attempting to achieve with this line of questioning, but it seemed to be developing into something. He was totally fascinated by what was transpiring. J. Edgar knew, or hoped he knew, Shoemaker would never anticipate or be prepared for what was coming next. It was a calculated risk he felt he must take, and he hoped he could get it all accomplished before Shoemaker realized what was happening.

Ewing knew it was time to see if his hunch had any validity. What he did know was when he finished, it would have some major effect on Lois, the jury, and especially the prosecutor, Shoemaker. The big plunge was about to happen, he was poised at the end of the diving board and was ready. Welcome to the big leagues, Mr. Prosecutor, I'm about to hit a home run, over the fence and out of the park, I think.

At least that's what he anticipated would happen.

Ewing continued, "There is a difference, a big difference, Ms. Griffin, an hour and thirty minutes to possibly two hours difference. Let us, together, see if we can reconstruct what really happened and see if we can fill in that hour and a half or two hours at the most that you don't seem to be able to recall."

Shoemaker noted a change in Ewing's voice. Something was happening.

He thought to himself, *Where is that Clever Old Fox going now?*

Sitting up straighter in his chair, he decided he'd better be prepared to react. He could sense something dramatic was going on, and he didn't have a clue as to what it was. He'd better be prepared. He had been up against J. Edgar Ewing before and had lost every time.

Not this time, he said to himself.

His thoughts were interrupted by Ewing's voice.

The tone was definitely different.

It was so different that he had an inner sensation that Ewing was making his move, but where, Shoemaker had no idea; but he would be prepared to launch an objection. He was ready for anything. At least he thought he was ready.

He watched as J. Edgar Ewing was utilizing his entire courtroom splendor, and to say the least, he was magnificent.

This was his game, and he was at the top of it. J. Edgar then began his promised recreation of events that involved the witness's trip from Yakima, Washington, to Bend, Oregon, on September 8, 2005. Ewing began in a slow but a very deliberate, dramatic fashion.

"How does this sound to you, Ms. Griffin? You left the motor home, located east of Yakima at the tribal casino at around 10:30 PM at the very latest. You drove toward Bend, Oregon, on Highway 97. You had $340,000 with you. More money than you had ever dreamed of having. Plus, since Mr. Malone gave it to you as a reward, for the tip that led to the safe return of his grandchildren, you were almost home free. No guilt. No worries. You were home free."

"Wrong!" J. Edgar put extra emphasis on the word.

"After driving for say thirty minutes or less, you had time to think. What did you think about? You thought about old Fred and Dennis, all tied up back in the motor home. What if Jim Malone didn't carry out the plan you presumed he had, after he instructed you to leave? You thought he would kill your partners. Then you had a second revelation, what if he didn't? Then what? You thought about what your partners would do to you for taking the money and cutting off their thumbs if they got loose; or even if they got caught and went to jail, you knew they would somehow come after you, and they would have their vengeance. They would kill you or damage you in some way. That's what you thought about, wasn't it?"

No response from Lois, she just sat there in the witness box, mute.

Astonishing Ewing thought to himself, but he hadn't wanted a response.

Plus, no objection yet from Shoemaker! And he definitely didn't want that to occur at least not yet.

He wasted not a second and continued, "When you left Mr. Malone you presumed he was going to eliminate your partners himself, and the reason he told you to leave is he didn't want any witnesses.

"But what if he didn't kill them?"

"You had to know. You had to be absolutely positive they could not hurt you. So you turned around and returned to the motor home to see if they were dead. But when you got there, they weren't dead. They were still bound and gagged just like Mr. Malone had reported to the authorities. What did you then do?"

Lois just sat there. She didn't have a clue how to respond and was hoping Shoemaker would somehow rescue her. Shoemaker sat there too, somewhat confused and definitely enthralled by what J. Edgar was doing. And the members of the jury were sitting straight up and obviously were trying to comprehend fully this interesting twist that J. Edgar was putting on the trial. J. Edgar Ewing knew this was the moment for which he had been building to.

The moment he thought could either save or destroy Jim had finally arrived.

He was ready and hoped he could get it in before Shoemaker objected. He was aware he must hurry before Shoemaker gathered his thoughts and raised an objection.

Without any reaction from Shoemaker, Judge Arnold was letting J. Edgar continue. With his back turned away from Lois, facing the jury, he then slowly turned to face Lois without waiting for her answer to the prior question. He sprung his real question on her.

"You then took the gun and shot them yourself, didn't you?"

Shoemaker was dumbfounded. He definitely had not anticipated this.

J. Edgar was doing it to him, again and he was letting him.

The courtroom had come alive, Judge Arnold was pounding his gavel for order, Shoemaker was finally objecting to this turn of events.

He asked the judge to strike the entire last portion of J. Edgar's so-called cross-examination. Finally, order was restored. Judge Arnold responded to Shoemaker's objection by sustaining it. Ewing just stood there, enjoying every precious minute of the mêlée he had created. Once order was fully restored, Judge Arnold told Ms. Griffin she did not have to respond to any of Mr. Ewing's scenario and especially the last question.

He also instructed the jury to disregard totally the last question and the scenario J. Edgar had created, in its entirety.

Then he asked Ewing if he had any more question of relevancy of this witness, and if not, he should sit down.

J. Edgar Ewing said calmly that he had a few more questions.

Judge Arnold told him to proceed, but if he pursued the course that had created the previous problem, he would terminate his cross—examination and find Mr. Ewing in contempt of court.

Ewing apologized to the court, Shoemaker sat down, knowing he had screwed up, and he let it happen. The trial continued. Ewing knew he didn't need much more time. He had already planted enough reasonable doubt in the jury's minds. At least he hoped he had. Plus, he himself believed what he had presented was close to what actually happened. He was going to continue to see if he could get Lois to admit he was right. He continued his cross with some easy questions that Lois responded to with much resentment in her voice.

Ewing liked this.

He was the consummate warrior.

This was his battlefield.

Finally, he asked her, as he had previously done, if she thought Mr. Malone had killed her partners.

As J. Edgar anticipated, Shoemaker swiftly objected, and Judge Arnold sustained the objection and admonished him again. Jim just sat there totally enthralled with J. Edgar's performance. Plus, he was relieved to think; what if this story was true, his feeling as to whom he thought had committed the murders was not what happened at all? The real story was J. Edgar's. What a relief.

Then J. Edgar Ewing asked his final question.

He asked her in a very loud manner so the jury would be sure to hear the question once again, "Did you kill Dennis and Fred?"

Shoemaker rose to his feet and all but shouted he objected again.

Judge Arnold sustained the objection, and, as promised, terminated J. Edgar's examination of this witness and found him in contempt and assured J. Edgar that a considerable fine would be levied, and that he might even call him before the bar's ethics committee.

He once again directed Lois and the jury to disregard the question.

And with that, Ewing politely apologized to the court and said he had no further questions of this witness.

He sat down next to Jim, exhausted.

This is what he gets paid big bucks to do, and today he was the best. He loved these moments in the courtroom. Judge Arnold said if the prosecutor had no further witnesses for rebuttal, then both the prosecution and the defense would be called on to make their final summations to the jury tomorrow morning. That was after Shoemaker responded that he did not have any questions for redirect. The judge excused the jury, announced adjournment, and retired to his chambers.

Jim sat there with Ewing for several minutes, neither spoke, finally Jim broke the ice.

"What do you think?" he asked.

Ewing responded with a very soothing tone to his voice, "I think there's room for optimism. I only wish she had confessed. They've already given her total immunity. Besides, I think she did it just about the way it laid out, or in a way very similar."

Jim did not respond.

J. Edgar was wound up like a top.

You could feel his optimism, and he continued to talk.

His voice was steady and confident.

"Let's just hope the jury buys it."

He had interjected some doubt. He didn't want Jim to get the impression that he was out of the woods. He was aware that there were still lots of unanswered questions.

Like he always said and now reiterated to Jim, "Never predict what a jury will do once they start deliberating away from the court proceedings. However, like I told you, trials are always very unpredictable, and this one is as tough as they ever get. Say a couple Hail Mary's tonight, and we'll give it our best shot in the summation tomorrow. Then it'll be a waiting game while the jury deliberates. Personally, at this point, I like our chances; but you never know until they, meaning the jury, returns with a verdict. But let me assure you, if it turns out bad, we do have lots of room for appeals. Now, I'd better get going and prepare for tomorrow. You try to rest, and don't waste your time worrying, it doesn't help."

Jim thought to himself, *Sure, not to worry. Let's be real, he would be consumed with apprehension until it was all over.*

The deputy was already standing there to return Jim to his cell.

#

Shoemaker and the federal attorney returned Lois to her hotel room.

They accompanied her all the way to her room and explained she had to remain at the hotel until the trial was over. This meant she would live here until their summations were completed and the jury returned with a verdict.

Shoemaker told her he had no idea how long this would take, and besides, neither he nor the defense had delivered their summations. He said that would be tomorrow and then Judge Arnold would explain to the jury their obligation, other options if there are any, and instruct them to retire to the deliberation room.

Shoemaker added it could be days or just a few hours.

In his mind he wanted to ask her about the scenario Ewing had created. He wanted to know if there was any possibility of it being true, and then again, he knew better than to ask. Who knows she might tell him it's true. And this he didn't want to know. He knew if he asked and she confirmed it was true it would be his obligation to bring this to the court's attention; and with her sweeping immunity, it would be over.

Besides, he believed it was one of J. Edgar Ewing's court fantasies, and neither he nor the jury were about to buy the story. His case had been based on legal facts and real circumstantial evidence, not fantasy like J. Edgar's, and therefore he felt he would win.

At the same time, he did feel J. Edgar's creative fantasy was or could be very damaging to his case even though Judge Arnold had instructed the jury to eliminate totally this part of the trial from the record.

Sure they will!

He and the U.S. attorney left the hotel room, Shoemaker had to prepare his summation, and he knew it had better be good.

After they left, Lois looked out the window at the bay, deep in thought. She was thinking about what had transpired.

But mostly she was thinking about the three hundred and forty thousand dollars.

Would she be able to keep it?

Nobody, but her, seemed to care about the money. Her attorney said he thought she would be able to keep it since Malone said it was a reward for her phone call.

But after what that smart-ass attorney just did, she was becoming a little apprehensive about the money. This was way too much to think about, this and that thing that happened during her testimony.

Damn, that smart-ass attorney.

With that last thought, she picked up the phone and ordered room service.

#

CHAPTER 36

BOB ARNOTT

The day finally arrived; the day for the two attorneys, Shoemaker and J. Edgar, to present their summations to the jury. Their final battle scene, and everyone in the courtroom was expecting it to be something really special.

You better believe I was there, notebook in hand, with extra pens in my pocket. And now that I'm called Mr. Arnott by the guards at the entrance to the courtroom and by the court clerk, I'm able to get a prime location in the press area. This really irritates some of the other lesser recognized media people. On the front page of this morning's paper was my story with my byline; it was about everything that had transpired yesterday with much embellishment. I even included J. Edgar's scenario on how the kidnappers might have been killed. If Shoemaker read the story, I'll bet he's still fuming. I felt my creation would really make the public feel better toward Jim and assist in closure if the jury finds him not guilty. Besides, it was good reading. Nice story, J. Edgar. Thank you very much. Who knows, maybe you got it almost right.

It was 9:00 AM. The courtroom was packed, the jury members were seated, and the prosecution team was ready.

Shoemaker appeared nervous and looked like he had not slept well.

He probably hadn't! Then again who did?

J. Edgar Ewing was more than ready. I knew he had always relished this portion of trials; he could perform without fear of interruption by anyone, and he always sleeps well.

Jim just sat there, looking like a hero, as usual. Major relief was written all over his face. The worried look he had on his face throughout the trial had all but disappeared. J. Edgar had removed a huge weight from his shoulders. He felt all he had to worry about now was the jury and the final verdict.

Judge Arnold had just rapped his gavel to call the court to order.

He directed his comments to the attorneys, asking if they were ready to begin their summations.

Both responded in the affirmative.

The prosecution would go first, and Judge Arnold instructed Shoemaker it was time to present his summation to the jury.

Shoemaker rose and walked toward the jury with his legal pad in hand and began. He was dressed neatly as usual in his dark blue suit, matching tie, and starched white shirt. But somehow today, he seemed to have a slightly frayed appearance. The back of his hair was even slightly mussed. His appearance didn't spew the maximum confidence he had displayed when the trial first began or at the conclusion of his examination of Lois.

He rose slowly from behind the prosecutor's table and approached the jury. He began, "First let me thank each of you from the state of Washington for the patience you have displayed during these proceedings. It has been a long process from the day we started this trial to arrive at this moment, the final day, before you will be instructed by Judge Arnold to begin your deliberation deciding whether the defendant, Jim Malone, is guilty of first-degree murder.

"My reason to be here is the same as yours, to sort out the facts and arrive at the truth. That's exactly what the state has done, presented a trial based on facts. We have shown the defendant tracked down the victims with vengeance in his heart and mind. We proved he mutilated the victims before they died. The state established with facts, he was at the scene of the crime, had access to the weapon that was used in murdering two people, and we have presented facts to show the defendant did commit all these acts with premeditation and malice.

"The state has presented a case of truth, not fantasy. We presented proof the defendant pursued the victims, tracked them down and, in fact, did kill them. It's not germane to the case and your decision, whether or not these two were good or bad people, the only thing important is the laws of the state of Washington are written to prevent anyone and I mean anyone from taking the law into their own hands. And the state calls upon you to assist in upholding the law. I have full confidence, as law biding citizens of this great state, that's what you will do, uphold the laws of the state of Washington. Once you review the facts in this trial, I'm positive your only option will be to find the defendant, James Malone, guilty of first-degree murder.

"Once again, I thank every one of you for your service to the state; I know you will do what is right."

After making his final statement, Shoemaker returned to the prosecutor's table and sat down in somewhat of a rigid way, stiff, and sitting up very straight.

He had kept his summation brief on purpose and had avoided any direct reference to Ewing's alternative creation as to how the crime was committed, other than using the word *fantasy*. After all, Judge Arnold had already instructed them to disregard it totally and emphasized they were not to consider any of this in their coming deliberation. Shoemaker certainly didn't want them to hear it again, especially not from his lips.

During Shoemaker's performance, J. Edgar was making some additional notes and a few alterations for his summation. He looked up just as Judge Arnold was asking if the defense council was ready for his summation.

"Yes, I am, Your Honor," Ewing said.

He picked up his legal pad and approached the jury. His appearance and demeanor was exactly the same as it had been throughout the entire trial—competent and professional.

"As Mr. Shoemaker said, he and I both thank you for the time taken out of your lives, away from your families and jobs, to come here and sit for days while we search for the truth.

"That's what trials are all about. Finding the truth, establishing what really happened. The prosecutor said his case was based on facts.

"Not true! Almost all of the prosecution's case is based on circumstantial evidence and innuendos, not truth and certainly not facts." He paused for added impact.

"Here is a fact. Jim Malone did pursue and find the individuals who had kidnapped and mutilated his grandchildren. That is truth. It is true in retribution. He administered, as he admitted, punishment to the two kidnappers similar to what they had done to his grandchildren.

"But notice, he cut off their thumbs. Why? So they could never commit the same kind of crime they'd committed, ever again. They could never again, kidnap and hurt any more children. Yes, it's true. He tracked them down when the authorities failed. His reason for doing this was like we all desire, so they could never again kidnap any children, ever!

"Now I want you to ponder this, why would Jim Malone bother to make that distinction between little fingers and thumbs if he intended to kill the kidnappers? He knew without thumbs they would never be able to handle weapons. They would be alive, but never a threat to society.

Another fact, Jim Malone told the authorities where they could find the two kidnappers, live kidnappers. These are the only real facts the prosecution presented. Once you begin putting the pieces together, I'm sure you, the jury, will find that this case has a tremendous amount of reasonable doubt.

"Let us now stop and remember all the testimony you have endured, especially that of the prosecution's star witness. This person received total immunity from the prosecution for her part in the kidnapping and mutilation of Mr. Malone's grandchildren. Plus, she received immunity from the prosecution for any involvement she had in the removal of the two kidnappers' thumbs or murders of her two coconspirators. She also received immunity for extortion in relationship to the ransom money, and I repeat, for cutting off Jim Malone's grandchildren's fingers. No matter what she did or said during her testimony, she was home free, and she knew it. All she had to do for the prosecution was to point her finger at Jim Malone and the prosecutor would let her walk away, free as a bird." J. Edgar paused again to let this last statement permeate the mind of each juror.

"That's how bad the prosecution wants you to find the defendant guilty.

"We may never know what really happened, we all have our suspicions as to who actually killed these kidnappers, but we don't really know, reasonable doubt.

REASONABLE DOUBT!

"And with reasonable doubt, there is no alternative other than for you, twelve responsible citizens of the state of Washington, to do, other than return a verdict of not guilty. Let Jim Malone return to his family and allow him to watch his grandchildren grow into young adults. I thank you once again for your service to our community."

J. Edgar Ewing immediately returned and sat down next to Jim and gave him a comforting pat on the knee.

Much to the chagrin of those present in the gallery, like the prosecutor, J. Edgar had kept his summation brief; and during it had taken the opportunity to remind them subliminally, there were other alternatives as to who actually committed the murders.

He felt somewhat confident the jury would find in Jim's favor but was very careful not to appear overly confident. He knew he had presented a case and summation to the jury that logically offered them reasonable doubt and other alternatives. This sentiment would not be conveyed to his client because no one can ever predict outcomes, 100 percent, when it comes to what a jury of our peers will do when they are all alone in the deliberation room. It only takes one rebel to mess things up. It was now Judge Arnold's time to address the jury. He completed this obligation explaining the charges, possible alternatives, and what their responsibilities were as representatives of the state of Washington. He excused them, and they proceeded to retire to the deliberation room.

The courtroom emptied.

Jim was returned to his cell after a brief conversation with Ewing. J. Edgar and Shoemaker returned to their offices to wait for the jury's decision. Like all good reporters, I went off to file my story and then grab some lunch.

The wait would be excruciating for everybody.

Time.

It was nine o'clock Friday morning, the final day, when all of this had started, first with the summation proceedings and then Judge Arnold's responsibilities, instructing the jury as to their duties and options. It was amazing, it was all completed by eleven that morning.

It had gone fast.

The jury retired for their deliberations just before lunch. The only thing anybody knew for sure was lunch was going to be served to the jury in the deliberation room. Wait. Wait for the verdict. Nobody had more to lose than Jim, and his wait would be more excruciating than anyone's. He was the only person whose life hung in the balance, in the hands of twelve people.

Wait.

That was the only option.

Then at three in the afternoon, much to the surprise of everyone, the clerk notified all the concerned parties . . . the DA Robert Shoemaker, J. Edgar Ewing, Jim Malone, and the press that the jury had concluded their deliberation and notified Judge Arnold they had arrived at a verdict.

The judge requested that the prosecutor and the defense return at four o'clock to the courtroom so the jury could render their decision.

THEIR LIFE, DEATH, OR FREEDOM DECISION!

Both attorneys were astonished at how rapidly the jury had brought their deliberation to its culmination.

Frightening!

The trial had taken days, the jury's deliberation only a few hours.

Like Ewing had told Jim, "You never can predict juries!"

He met with Jim prior to returning to the courtroom and unfortunately still could not or would not offer a prediction on what he thought the verdict would be.

The prosecutor, Shoemaker, had a similar feeling.

Finally, they were all present in their proper places. Jim's family, everyone concerned was present, except the grandchildren, all were seated in anticipation of the return of the jury and the verdict.

The press, me included, was certainly present in anticipation of a front-page story along with the ghoulish spectators that had been fortunate enough to get a seat in the gallery. They were all assembled waiting to hear the verdict.

The star witness, Lois L. Griffin, was in her hotel room watching and listening to a television news reporter, who was broadcasting live outside the courtroom, tell his viewers the jury had completed their deliberation and was due in a matter of minutes to render a verdict.

Judge Arnold had just issued instructions for the clerk to bring the jury in and let them be seated.

They were filing in slowly.

Jim, Ewing, and Shoemaker were studying the faces of each juror as they took their seats in the jury box.

All of them, Shoemaker, J. Edgar, and especially Jim were focusing on the jury, attempting to get some indication on the coming verdict.

Nothing was detectible.

Not a single juror looked directly at Jim, Ewing, or Shoemaker. After the jury was seated, Judge Arnold asked if they had agreed on a verdict; the jury foreman confirmed they had. Satisfied with this, Judge Arnold then addressed the court and took a moment to express the need for all those present to resist any overt reaction in the courtroom when the jury reads its verdict. He seriously doubted that this warning would achieve its purpose, but it might help.

Judge Arnold then turned to the jury and formally asked the foreman again if the jury had agreed on a verdict.

The foreman again acknowledged with an answer, yes they had. Judge Arnold instructed the foreman to please give it to the court clerk. The foreman complied as instructed and handed the verdict to the clerk, who then presented it to Judge Arnold. Judge Arnold took an abnormal amount of time reading the verdict; and without any display of emotion, he handed it back to the clerk, who returned it to the jury foreman.

Judge Arnold then asked the foreman if the entire jury concurred with the verdict.

The foreman said, "Yes they do, Your Honor."

Judge Arnold then instructed the foreman to read the verdict.

The foreman rose and in a strong, clear voice, said, "We the jury in the case of the state of Washington against Jim Malone find the defendant, NOT GUILTY!"

Total chaos broke out.

Reporters were trying to get out of the courtroom to use their cell phones, TV cameramen and newspaper photographers were taking pictures, Jim's family rushed to throw their arms around him, a lot of happy people except for the DA, Robert Shoemaker and his assistants.

Finally, after about ten minutes of this chaos, the judge returned the court to a degree of tolerable decorum.

Judge Arnold then proceeded to thank the jury for their services, excused them, and turned to Jim Malone and said, "The jury of your peers has found you Not Guilty of all the charges filed against you by the state of Washington; therefore, you are free to go. This court stands adjourned."

Judge Arnold instantly stood and disappeared to his chambers. Jim and J. Edgar Ewing excused themselves from the ensuing mêlée so they could have a moment alone. They were led to a private room just off to the side.

Jim walked over to the window to look outside. He could see Elliott Bay from there. Sun sparkled on its surface, seagulls gliding above the blue. He could almost smell the breeze that danced over the surface, below the clouds.

Ewing walked over behind Jim and said, "Looks good, doesn't it?"

Jim turned and said, "The greatest. Thank you! That was a hell of job you did in there. Bob Arnott was correct, you are the best."

"That's what I get paid to do," Ewing drawled. He put a hand on Jim's shoulder. "Besides, you were innocent. Now get going, your family is waiting. I made prior arrangements for you and them to leave from the parking garage just in case we won, and I'm sure they are already down there, waiting to take you home to Robbie and Justin. The deputy will escort you, so you can avoid all those reporters and TV cameras, enjoy the weekend. Give me a call on Monday. We'll arrange a final meeting, and I'll tell you the really bad news. See you then."

He gave Jim the smile of all smiles. Jim knew what it meant—his fee. J. Edgar waited for the deputy to escort Jim out and then left to face the press.

This was about the only time he enjoyed talking to the press, and he especially disliked television reporters. He usually referred to them as the worst thing that had ever happened to our judicial system.

#

Meanwhile, Shoemaker had already met with the press and expressed his dismay at the verdict, but he did say the people had spoken and he would respect that.

He avoided or refused to answer any questions relating to Lois Griffin, her immunity, or that concocted scenario J. Edgar Ewing had sprung on the jury.

He quickly left the premises, totally avoiding any further comments to the press, and was now entering the hotel where his star witness was residing.

He was going to tell her the news.

He had no idea whether she would think it was good or bad. At this point he was tired of it all—Lois Griffin, Jim Malone, the press, and especially J. Edgar Ewing. After conferring with the two security guards, he knocked, announced who was knocking and Lois opened the door to let him enter.

Before he could say anything, she said, "I know. It was on TV, not guilty. I'm sorry."

Shoemaker thought her voice didn't seem to be sincere, and certainly no tone of regret was detectible.

He addressed her in a formal manner, "It was just a trial, and there will be others. You're free to go, as we promised. I would appreciate it if you would totally avoid talking to the press and leave town as soon as possible for wherever you're going, you owe me that."

She said with a little sparkle to her voice, "Don't worry. I definitely do not need to talk to any reporters. But what happens to the money I have?"

Shoemaker sighed, he was obviously really tired of this entire trial, but he did answer, "That's between you and Jim Malone. He did say he gave it to you as a reward. So it's probably yours." He paused and softened his voice, "If you want, I can have my secretary help you make reservations for whatever transportation you need and wherever you need to go."

Lois said for him not to bother; now that she had some money, she could handle it by herself. She added if it was okay with him, she would leave in the morning.

He said he had no objections, he hesitated, bad choice of words, thanked her for her testimony, and added that he would keep a guard at her door if she wanted until she left the hotel in the morning. She said it wasn't necessary, and that she had already been enough of a problem. Shoemaker didn't argue. He turned to leave, hesitated again, then quickly turned back to face Lois.

"Let me ask you one final question." Shoemaker stood up to his full height, reaching for every shred of dignity he had left.

"You owe me at least that."

She looked at him in a curios, questioning way and then responded in a soft voice, "Very well, what's the question?"

"Was there any truth to the story Ewing told in court?"

Lois raised her eyebrows slightly. She had not anticipated this question.

She went to her purse, pulled out a pack of Virginia Slims.

Lit one.

Breathed out a stream of smoke.

She walked over and looked out the window at the view of Elliott Bay for just a minute, then turned back to face Shoemaker and with a kind of wry smile on her face.

She said very quietly, "Justice Was Served!"

She then turned back to look at the view of Elliott Bay.

Robert Shoemaker, prosecuting attorney, coughed from the smoke. It was a nonsmoking room, but he didn't turn her in, he'd had enough of Lois Griffin.

He shook his head.

Without another word, he left the room.

#

BOB ARNOTT

I knocked on the door of the hotel room.

Lois Griffin opened the door.

"Hello, Bob," she said.

She'd called me an hour before to tell me at her request that the guards had been dismissed. I could come see her total being was composed.

"So, Bob Arnott," she said. "Scotch?"

"Sure."

She poured me one, Chivas Regal nonetheless.

"Smoke?" I pulled out my pack of Luckies. Showed them to her. She took one. I lit both of us up.

She told me what Shoemaker had said to her.

"Don't you have to write your story?" she said.

"Story's already filed," I said. "I'm truly appreciative of all your information."

"You'll talk the Malones into letting me keep the money without any hang-ups?"

"I'm sure there's no problem. That was the deal."

Her eyes flashed. "They'd better! And you know why!"

I smiled. "I do."

"Well, I'll keep you informed of my whereabouts, Mr. Great Reporter. You might want to do a follow-up story."

"Great," I said. I downed the drink and walked to the door but turned back toward her with one more thought.

"And, Lois."

"Yes?"

"Isn't justice grand?"

"Go to hell," she said.

I did. I went back to my newspaper to begin my new reign.

EPILOGUE

Justice is served.

A while after the verdict of "Not Guilty" was delivered, justice was served a delicious turkey dinner with all the trimmings. It wasn't Thanksgiving, but it did seem appropriate.

I washed it down with a nice bottle of Chablis, watching Robbie and Justin gobbling up their chocolate cake, which Joan had baked herself.

Thanks to the miracles of modern psychology—and a warm and loving family—the boys were recovering nicely. True they were both missing the ends of their pinkies and had nightmares regularly. But if anything, the experience of the kidnapping and sharing that crate had increased their brotherly bond, and among their peers they had become celebrities. It did my heart such good to see them healthy and happy as they went off after gobbling down their chocolate cake to play a board game.

After dinner, Mark and I went back to his library for coffee and cognac and cigars.

After Mark got a snifter down, he poured himself another, using it to salute me.

"I gotta hand it to you, Bob. Who was the guy who said there are no second acts in American life? You certainly have proved them wrong. Book contracts, guest spots. And who did I hear is talking to you about your own show?"

"That would be Fox News, Mark." I shook my head. "But I'd happily give it all back to take those days out of Robbie and Justin's life."

"Out of all our lives." He shivered. "Well, something good came out of it."

"And your dad's a hero."

"Dad's always been a hero. He's getting all kinds of chances to stand up for what he believes in." He took another sip of cognac. "I just wished he believed in me."

"He'll come around," I said. "It'll just take a little time, that's all, Mark."

"It all makes sense now, but before I didn't really get it. The Old Man was acting the way he did during the trial because he thought I'd killed those jerks!"

"Lois Griffin killed them," I said. "We all know that. And like she told Shoemaker—justice was served. She told me she had to get rid of them forever during our last meeting after the trial. Good riddance to a bad lot."

"But if it hadn't been for you . . . ," Mark said.

Amid the swirls of smoke and the fumes of alcohol, my mind cast back.

#

The summer night was heavy with dark and drizzle in the RV park. Fresh tarmac had been mixed and poured recently in the parking lot. Its smell, twined with the mulch of wood chips, hovered amid the damp. I felt excited but frightened. All of what had happened before was people and horror and frustration. Now here, in Eastern Washington, was the possibility of action.

Here I was in the middle of my story.

All the time Jim had kept in touch with me. He'd filled me in with all the details of his discoveries and his progress. He'd told me all these things because he trusted me and because he needed a control. If he was killed in these actions, he felt I could do something with the press, with the media.

So I knew where he was going, and I followed him, unbeknownst to him.

This was my story, after all. This story was going to liberate me from my wilderness years.

There I was, in the middle of it all.

From the shadows, I'd watched.

I'd heard the muffled screams of Fred and Dennis as their thumbs had been cut off. I'd seen Jim leave the RV park.

When Lois left, I stopped her and spoke to her, but let her leave—with my number. I'd demanded hers if and when she got one.

She did and called later. Then Mark had arrived, wild-eyed. I had called him a few hours earlier and let him in on the location, but unfortunately, he didn't heed my advice to keep cool and stay away. He was the one who'd found the gun, waiting, in the RV. He didn't pick it up, though, because I stopped him. He'd seen the unconscious kidnappers and meant to kill them.

I talked him out of it.

I talked Mark into going home, promising I'd not mention a thing about all this to anyone. Later, I assured him that I'd talked to Lois. It was her who'd come back to kill Dennis and Fred, and for damned good reasons.

Mark left me alone with that gun, and half a story, and the kidnappers who had hurt Justin and Robbie so very badly.

Hurt my guys.

#

"Yes," I said to Mark after that dinner. "If it hadn't been for me ..."

He shuddered and put his head in his hands. "Thanks so much. Thank you."

"You can thank me, Mark, by putting all this behind you. You can thank me by not talking about all this to anyone else."

"Do you think that my father still thinks I might have shot them?"

"No. I told him that I knew for certain that Lois Griffin did it. He doesn't know I was even there at the casino RV park ... and you should not tell him, ever. Let's leave well enough alone, eh? All's well that ends well, eh?"

He nodded.

We never spoke of it again.

#

This is a story of life, death, and rain.

This is a story of a kidnapping.

This is the story of a trial.

This is the story of grandchildren, Jim's precious grandchildren.

Me?

Call me Narrator.

#

INDEX

A

Allen, Paul 13
Apple Cup 12
Arnold (judge) 45, 46, 56, 58, 60, 62, 63,
      64, 65, 98, 99, 100, 101, 102, 141,
      142, 165, 166, 168, 187, 188, 189,
      192, 195, 207, 208, 210, 211, 212,
      213, 214, 215, 216, 217, 218, 222,
      223, 224, 225, 227, 230, 231
   addressing the jury 229
   meeting the two attorneys 190, 191
Arnott, Bob 11, 49, 66, 70, 80, 81, 82,
      85, 107, 110, 121, 124, 133, 134,
      135, 137, 140, 143, 145, 152, 156,
      170, 178, 201, 207, 231
   meeting with Lois Griffin 233
   Mr. Great Reporter 234
   talking with Jim 113, 114, 115, 116,
      117, 118, 119
   thoughts on the kidnapping 52, 53, 55
   Times 11, 16, 120, 134
Arnott, Robert. *See* Arnott, Bob
Associated Press 16

B

Bailey (dog) 9, 21, 25, 29, 30, 31, 33, 34,
      36, 86, 156

Bellevue Inn 67, 149
Bellevue Square 14
   Armani 14
   Fredrick and Nelson 14
   J. C. Penney's 14
   Macy's 14
   Nordstrom 14
   Sears 14
   Tiffany 14
   Victoria Secret 14
Brinkley, David 40

C

Cascade Mountains 14, 171
CNBC 16
CNN 16
Collier, Don 35
Columbia River 64, 128, 144, 159, 174,
      175, 178
Colville Tribal Casino. *See* Mill Bay
      Casino
Coulee Dam 174

D

Desautel Pass 174
Dowdy, Leroy 109, 111, 114, 125, 133,
      140, 170

E

Eastside 12, 13, 14, 20
  comprised of 14
Elliott Bay 197, 231, 233
Ewing, J. Edgar 17, 45, 46, 47, 51, 139,
    141, 143, 151, 164, 165, 166, 167,
    168, 169, 193, 194, 195, 199, 200,
    204, 205, 208, 230, 231, 232, 233
  briefing with Jim Malone prior to Lois
    Griffin's testimony 205, 206
  during Lois Griffin's testimony 210, 211
  hearing Jim Malone speak of the entire
    story 194
  his cross-examination of John
    Hammond 61, 62, 63, 64, 66, 98,
    99, 100, 101, 102
  his cross-examination of Lois Griffin
    212, 213, 214, 215, 216, 217, 218,
    219, 220, 221, 222, 223, 224
  John Hammond's testimony 57, 58,
    59, 60
  listening to Lois Griffin's testimony 209
  meeting with the judge 190, 191, 192
  questioning Jim Malone 184, 185, 186
  reading the verdict 231
  Robert Watkins's testimony 57
  Shoemaker's cross-examination on Jim
    Malone 187, 188, 189
  summation 228

F

Fox News 16, 235
Freeman, Kemper 14

G

Gates, Bill
  Microsoft 13
Griffin, Lois 9, 51, 63, 72, 73, 130, 138,
    139, 160, 162, 163, 180, 181, 182,
    183, 186, 190, 192, 193, 196, 202,
    203, 204, 205, 206, 207, 230, 232,
    233, 236, 237
  calling Jim Malone 147, 148, 149

  cutting the kids' pinkies 74, 75, 76, 77,
    88, 89, 91, 95, 103
  Ewing's cross-examination 212, 213,
    214, 215, 216, 217, 218, 219, 220,
    222, 223
  formulating a plan 106
  headed to the boathouse 96
  Lowee 53
  meeting Bob Arnott 233, 234
  on Shoemaker's last question 233
  reading the newspaper 145
  Seven Bays Resort 148
  star witness 196
  taking a walk 130
  talk with Deanna Malone 55
  testifies in court 197, 198, 199, 207,
    208, 209, 210, 211

H

Halsey, Fred 9, 53, 54, 55, 72, 73, 74, 77,
    78, 88, 89, 91, 95, 96, 103, 104,
    105, 106, 126, 127, 128, 129, 130,
    131, 132, 144, 145, 147, 149, 150,
    159, 160, 161, 162, 180, 181, 182,
    195, 197, 198, 199, 221, 236
  after the package was delivered to the
    Malones 89
  childhood memory 97
  Jimi Hendrix fan 72
  physical characteristics 52
  talking to the cabbie 78, 79
Hammond, John 22, 24, 25, 29, 31, 34,
    36, 48, 56, 66, 67, 68, 69, 70, 85,
    90, 94, 112, 113, 117, 118, 119,
    120, 121, 122, 124, 133, 137, 165,
    167, 168, 194, 206
  testifies in court 56, 57, 58, 59, 60, 61,
    62, 63, 64, 66, 98, 99, 100, 101,
    167
Hector's Restaurant 68, 70, 95, 149
Home Depot 180
Huntley, Chet 40

J

Johnson, Ed 51, 109, 111, 113, 114, 121, 125, 133, 135, 140, 170, 180
finding the kids 152, 153, 154, 155, 157
Johnson, Lyndon 19

K

Kennedy, John 18
KIT (radio station) 161

L

Lake Chelan 130, 131, 173
Lake Roosevelt 174
Lake Washington 12, 13, 14
Laser Light Show 175
Leavenworth
Alpine Village of the Northwest 171
Little Lord Fauntleroy 75
London Fog 12

M

Malone and Son Inc. (Malone Construction) 20
Malone, Deanna 23, 24, 31, 34, 43, 69, 82, 91, 93, 124, 127, 134, 136, 137, 143, 155, 156, 171, 177
meeting Jim Malone 18
phone call from a Shell attendant 157
Malone, James. *See* Malone, Jim
Malone, Jim 11, 15, 16, 18, 26, 80, 81, 83, 85, 90, 95, 139, 140, 141, 142, 143, 151, 152, 160, 164, 165, 166, 167, 168, 192, 193, 194, 195, 196, 197, 198, 200, 201, 202, 204, 205, 209, 210, 211, 213, 218, 220, 221, 223, 224, 226, 227, 228, 229, 230, 231, 232, 236
calling Chief of Police John Hammond 22
childhood 12, 13, 14, 18, 19
executing the plan to run after the kidnappers 170, 171, 172, 173, 174, 175, 176, 177, 178, 179, 180, 181, 182, 183
final briefing with Ewing before Lois Griffin's testimony 205, 206, 207
finding his grandchildren 152, 153, 154, 155, 156
John Hammond's testimony 57, 58, 61, 65, 70, 98, 99, 101, 102
Lois Griffin's call 149
Meydenbauer Yacht Club 114
reading the verdict 231
receiving the package 84
seeing John Hammond and Robert Watkins 120, 121, 122
Shoemaker's cross-examination on him 187, 188, 189, 190
talking with Bob 116, 117, 118, 119
telling Ewing the entire story 193
testifies in court 184, 185, 186
the day of his grandchildren's kidnapping 11
thoughts on Lois Griffin 143
Malone, Joan 20, 39, 40, 41, 43, 44, 69, 70, 80, 81, 82, 86, 124, 134, 136, 155, 235
receiving the package 83, 84
the day of her sons' kidnapping 21, 22, 24, 25, 33, 34, 35
Malone, Justin 9, 20, 21, 22, 25, 37, 39, 40, 46, 50, 66, 69, 71, 80, 81, 82, 83, 84, 86, 88, 90, 93, 101, 104, 109, 110, 115, 116, 117, 118, 134, 140, 144, 153, 157, 160, 165, 166, 170, 179, 193, 232, 235, 236
cutting the finger 74, 75, 76, 77, 79
fiding of 154
Harry Potter 39
Providence hospital 156
while in the packing crate 107
Malone, Mark 11, 14, 20, 37, 38, 39, 40, 43, 44, 69, 80, 81, 82, 83, 90, 93, 109, 110, 124, 125, 134, 135, 136, 137, 155, 156, 157, 166, 170, 178, 235, 236
answering the kidnappers' call 43, 67, 86, 90

architect 20
arriving at the kidnappers' motor home 236
getting instructions from the kidnappers 66
receiving the package 83, 84
seeing the boys 157
the day of his sons' kidnapping 21, 22, 23, 24, 25, 29, 31, 32, 33, 34, 35
Malone, Matthew 18
Malone, Robbie 9, 20, 21, 22, 25, 37, 39, 40, 46, 48, 50, 66, 69, 70, 80, 81, 82, 83, 84, 86, 88, 93, 101, 104, 109, 110, 116, 117, 118, 134, 140, 144, 153, 160, 165, 166, 170, 179, 193, 232, 236
apple of Jim's eye 39
cutting the finger 74, 75, 76, 77, 79
finding of 154
Providence hospital 156
Superball 40
while in the packing crate 107
Mercer Island Bridge 120
Mighty Columbia River. See Columbia River
Mill Bay Casino 63, 126, 144, 173
Moses Lake 175

N

Nelson, Willie
"On the Road Again" 177
Nespelem 174
New York Times 27, 72
Norton, Al
Seattle Tennis Club 123

O

O'Reilly, Bill
Jessica's Law 177
Okanogan Casino 174, 175
"On the Road Again" (Nelson)e 177
Operation Save Our Kids 135

P

Pacific Coast Conference (Pac Ten) 12
Puget Sound 11, 36, 122, 153, 193
Pyle, Howard 39

R

Rice, Dennis 9, 54, 55, 72, 73, 74, 75, 77, 78, 88, 89, 91, 92, 95, 96, 97, 103, 106, 107, 126, 127, 128, 129, 130, 132, 144, 145, 146, 149, 150, 160, 161, 162, 180, 181, 183, 195, 197, 198, 217, 221, 236
antithesis 52
Black Sabbath 72
cutting the kids' pinkies 76
headed to the boathouse 96
his thoughts on the money 106
quarreling Lois 103
Robin Hood 39
Roosevelt, Franklin 19, 175
RV 52, 53, 54, 57, 78, 79, 89, 111, 113, 114, 125, 126, 128, 134, 162, 171, 173, 175, 178, 236, 237

S

San Juan Islands 40, 114
Scott Paper Company 54, 153
Shoemaker, Robert 46, 51, 62, 63, 64, 65, 99, 100, 101, 139, 140, 141, 165, 167, 168, 169, 184, 185, 187, 194, 195, 196, 202, 203, 204, 205, 206, 212, 213, 214, 215, 216, 217, 218, 219, 220, 221, 222, 223, 224, 225, 226, 230, 234
announcing Lois Griffin as witness 190, 192
final meeting with Lois Griffin 233
his cross-examination on Jim Malone 187, 188, 189
in the hotel with Lois Griffin 196, 197, 198, 199
meeting the press 232

meeting with the judge 190, 191, 192
questioning John Hammond 56
questioning Lois Griffin 207, 208, 209,
 211
reading the verdict 231
summation 227
Smith and Wesson 60
Special Forces 19, 48, 49, 51, 65, 109,
 110, 178, 187, 204
Spokane River 174
Spokane Tribal Casino.*See* Two Rivers
 Casino

T

"The Ransom of Red Chief" 75
Truman, Harry 19
Two Rivers Casino 64, 96, 144, 174, 175,
 176

U

Uncle Bob. *See* Arnott, Bob; *See*
 Arnott, Bob
University of Washington
 Huskies 12
USA Today 16

W

Wal-Mart 72
Washington Post 27
Washington State University
 Cougars 12
Watkins, Jack 25, 28, 30, 31, 32, 33, 34,
 35, 36, 43, 57, 62, 66, 67, 86, 90,
 93, 110, 113, 120, 121, 122, 133,
 165, 190, 196, 197
Boston Legal 29
Sherlock Holmes movies 34
testifies in court 47, 48, 51
Yale 47
Wenatchee
 Apple Capital of the World 171
 Green Granny Smith 171
 Red Delicious 171
World War II 18, 19, 175
Wright, Frank Lloyd 81

Y

Yakima Indian Casino 57